"*F*orgive me, angel."

"Forgive you?" she asked, her voice a shaky whisper.

"For making light of what must have been a first for you."

"I never knew. . . ."

"Knew what? That lovemaking could be so wildly pleasurable? That you could feel such sweet fire?"

"Yes . . ."

Damien smiled. "There is far more to passion than what you just experienced, if you will allow yourself to discover it. I would very much like to teach you, sweeting." He bent his head, letting his hot breath caress her cheek. "I want to be the one to show you the mysteries of pleasure, Vanessa. The one to reveal all the sweet secrets between a man and a woman. . . ."

The Seduction

Nicole Jordan

IVY BOOKS • NEW YORK

This book contains an excerpt from the forthcoming paperback edition of *The Passion* by Nicole Jordan. This excerpt has been set for this edition only and may not reflect the final content of the forthcoming edition.

An Ivy Book
Published by The Ballantine Publishing Group
Copyright © 2000 by Anne Bushyhead
Excerpt from *The Passion* by Nicole Jordan copyright © 2000 by Anne Bushyhead

Ivy Books and colophon are trademarks of Random House, Inc.

www.randomhouse.com/BB/

Library of Congress Catalog Card Number: 99-90517

ISBN 0-449-00484-8

Manufactured in the United States of America

First Edition: May 2000

10   9   8   7   6   5   4   3   2   1

To the best friends a woman could have:
Ann White, Gin Ellis, and Sandra Chastain.
You've hung with me through
thick and thin, and I thank you.

Prologue

London, March 1810

The silken bonds bit into his wrists with exquisite pressure, heightening the sense of pleasure. A willing captive, Damien Sinclair lay defenseless, his bare arms fastened to the bedposts with scarves of scarlet silk.

He could see his reflection in the gilt-framed mirror overhead: his naked, muscled body juxtaposed against the snowy sheets; the full, hard length of his arousal jutting from the curling ebony hair of his groin.

His tormentor, the lovely Elise Swann, stood over him, clad in only the sheerest of muslin negligees, if one didn't count the emerald bracelet he'd presented her as the opening gambit of their game of seduction. The green stones adorning her wrist glittered in the flickering dance of candle flame, while the rouged nipples of her lush breasts peeked daringly through the delicate fabric, with a lasciviousness calculated to stir the passions of the most jaded connoisseur.

London's premiere actress, dubbed the Silver Swann because of her silver-blond hair, was staging a magnificent performance. They both understood this was an audition for the post of his mistress. The enchanting Swann meant to persuade him to take her into keeping.

"Now that you hold me in your power," Damien commented, his tone a teasing murmur, "I trust you intend to have your wicked way with me?"

"Indeed, I do, my lord. I rather like having you at my mercy," she said in the low, musical voice that could hold theatrical audiences enthralled.

"I am all attention, sweeting."

From atop the bedside table, she picked up a riding crop and raked his chest lightly with the tip. Damien raised a curious eyebrow, wondering if the actress mistakenly assumed she must resort to singular methods to arouse a man of his jaded lusts.

In his youth he had led a life of pleasure and license. Yet despite his scandalous reputation, despite the fact that he still sought out novel experiences upon occasion, he hadn't reached the point where he needed perversions to gratify his physical whims. His sexual appetites were strong and immediate, especially with a beautiful woman.

And the Silver Swann was quite beautiful. Apparently she was perceptive as well, for she hesitated when she met his inquiring gaze.

"I suppose," she observed thoughtfully, "there is no need to exercise force to stimulate you further. You are aroused enough as it is. You are enormous."

In the bantering spirit of their game, he returned a charming grin. "Does my size dismay you?"

Her red lips curved upward as she gave a laugh. "On the contrary, my lord."

With a nod of his head, he indicated the whip. "I've always considered pain overrated as an aphrodisiac. Surely you can be more inventive, pet."

"Perhaps I can."

She let the crop fall to the carpet and put a finger to her luscious lower lip, musing aloud. "Let me think. A man whose lovemaking prowess is legend . . . A devilish rogue who is said to make women weep for joy. How can such a magnificent lover be entertained?"

Slowly she unfastened the clasp of the bracelet at her wrist. With a sly smile, she draped the links over his jutting arousal and gently refastened the clasp. His blatantly rigid erection swelled further.

The hard stones felt cool against his heated flesh. Damien shuddered at the sensation, while smiling in acknowledgment of her resourcefulness.

"Is this inventive enough for you, my wicked Lord Sin?"

He chuckled, a low, rich sound of pleasure. "I commend your imagination."

"I gather that you admire boldness in a lover?"

"Boldness does have its merits."

"Then let me demonstrate to you how bold I can be."

With cool deliberation she curved her fingers around the pulsing crest of his manhood, stroking him slowly.

"I have seldom seen," she said in a throaty timbre as she bent over him, "so fine a stallion."

Damien closed his eyes with a pleasured sigh and gave himself up to the Swann's skillful ministrations. With lips and tongue and teeth she attended his throbbing cock, utilizing a tantalizing expertise, until he was teetering on the brink of spending himself.

"You . . . are testing my stamina, sweeting," he said, his voice a low rasp.

"Is that not the point, my lord?" She gave him a coquettish smile.

"Yes, but I would have you join me. It would be unforgivably selfish of me to claim all the enjoyment. Come and sit on me," he invited.

She stepped back, intent on teasing him. "You are in no position to make demands, I believe."

"No?" With his arms still tied above his head, Damien twisted suddenly and stretched his leg out, hooking his calf around her curving thigh. Catching her by surprise, he drew Elise down on top of him.

"Well . . . if you insist." With evident eagerness, Elise stretched her full, voluptuous length on top of him, her lush breasts nuzzling his face.

When he caught a peaked nipple through the delicate muslin, she drew a sharp breath. Controlling his own carnal urges, he took a turn arousing her, suckling and nibbling and softly biting the fullness of her flesh.

Moaning audibly now, she shifted her hips to straddle his loins and rub herself feverishly against him. Damien winced as the forgotten emeralds dug into his groin. He let out a breathless laugh. "The bracelet, sweet. If you don't wish to unman me, you will kindly remove your jewelry from my person."

She eased herself upright, her heavy-lidded eyes glazed with passion as she fumbled for the offending bracelet. When she had tossed it heedlessly on the floor, she gazed down at him. "My lord . . . please . . ."

"Please what?" He smiled tauntingly. "I believe you are the one in control just now. I am merely your helpless prisoner."

She lifted herself up again, positioning her lush cleft above his rigid shaft. He could feel the triangle of auburn curls between her thighs soaked in her own juices.

"Yes, sweet, ride me."

Without further urging, she mounted him, impaling herself on his erection with a blissful sigh. Damien let his head fall back, savoring the feel of her. She was sleek and wet and pulsing around him. Deliberately then, he raised his hips and thrust deeper into her slick, hot passage, eliciting a whimper of pleasure from her.

He had to repeat his powerful upward thrust before she grasped the cue and took over riding him in a sensuous rhythm that quickly increased to a frenzied pace. Damien matched her movements, devoting himself to her pleasure, until the luscious, hot-blooded woman above him was frantic with need. She was writhing . . . on fire . . . bucking and grinding against him with an animal savagery. With a gasping incoherent cry, she found ecstasy in a breathless, trembling orgasm.

Even when she collapsed upon him with a sob, Damien prolonged the moment, allowing the pulsing convulsions to recede before losing himself in the dark grip of passion. Arching his back against the explosive need, he let his own savage lust claim control.

He regained his senses to find Elise still sprawled upon him, her breath making delicate ripples on his sweat-cooled skin, the silken scarves biting uncomfortably into his wrists.

"Pet, would you oblige me?"

Weakly she reached up to untie the knots, then fell back among the pillows, her eyes heavy with languorous contentment.

"They said," she murmured in tones of wonder, "you were a man of legendary passions. 'Wicked and wonderful' was the phrase I heard used. I can now attest that the rumors didn't exaggerate. Yet I never expected you to be so . . . considerate a lover."

His smooth response came almost at once—the sort of praise she would wish to hear. "Your own reputation does not do you justice either, Elise. You are every man's fantasy."

"So, you found my . . . services satisfactory, my lord?"

Sexually satisfied yet not entirely replete—which seemed to occur often of late—Damien prevaricated with a murmur that could be taken as agreement. There was really nothing lacking in her performance. Rather—he'd begun to believe—it was something in himself.

The sumptuous Swann should have been the perfect mistress. As famed for her performance in the boudoir as on the stage, she was sensual and hot-blooded enough to excite his passion. All London found her fascinating, even to the point of dueling for her favors. If she was unable to satisfy the restlessness that had been brewing in him recently, well then, perhaps he was expecting too much.

Damien opened his eyes to find her studying him intently. Doubtless she was calculating the remuneration he could be expected to furnish her—house, carriage, servants, jewels.

"I understand," she began carefully, "that you are unencumbered by a mistress at present."

"How could you have failed to hear of it?" he replied dryly, referring to the scandal inspired by the end of his last liaison.

"Indeed. It was the talk of the town for days."

"Any reports were likely embellished."

"Perhaps so. The wicked Baron Sinclair does tend to be prime fodder for the gossipmongers. But still, there must be some truth to the matter."

"What precisely did you hear?"

"That when you gave Lady Varley her congé, she threatened to fling herself into the Thames. And you offered to drive her to the docks in your curricle yourself so that she might accomplish the feat."

Damien grimaced in remembrance. "I merely offered to drive her home. She was distraught."

"I imagine you find such scenes a bore," the Swann remarked. "As do I. I well know how tedious it can be, being the object of such unwelcome attention. You cannot enjoy having noble ladies swooning over you, declaring their undying love."

"The lady was not in love, I promise you. She merely fancied herself so."

"Still, you are said to have broken scores of female hearts, my wicked lord."

He gave a noncommittal murmur.

In a sensual gesture, Elise reached up to smooth back a disheveled lock of raven hair that had fallen across his forehead. "There is a moral to the tale, I suppose. Never give your heart to a rake."

Damien smiled his usual charming smile, but it did not reach his eyes. "A wise philosophy, sweeting. But I subscribe to an even simpler conviction. Never give your heart at all."

" 'Tis just as well, then, that I consider love merely a business proposition."

She was shrewdly trying to reassure him, he knew. Promising that she wouldn't create a scene or make unwelcome demands when they inevitably parted—which was fortunate.

He had no desire for any sort of permanent arrangement. His dalliances lasted a few months, rarely more, and he made it a practice never to keep any mistress longer

than a Season. He knew from experience how destructive
lengthy affairs could be. And he had no intention of emulating his late father by becoming obsessed with a beautiful temptress. Not even one as alluring as the Silver
Swann.

Before he could respond to her pledge of restraint, however, he heard swift footsteps on the landing outside the
bedchamber.

The tentative rap on the door held a distinct reluctance.

"Beg pardon, ma'am," a nervous female voice called
out, "but there's a gen'lemun to see 'is lordship."

Her lovely face stiff with sudden anger, Elise leapt from
the bed and crossed to the door. Drawing it open a crack,
she hissed in a harsh whisper, "I've told you never to inter-
rupt me when I am entertaining!"

"But 'e said it was the utmost urgency. Said to tell 'is
lordship 'is name was Mr. 'askell."

Damien caught the name of his secretary and frowned.
Wondering what the urgent matter could be, he swung his
legs over the side of the bed and reached for his satin evening breeches. While the graceful Swann railed like a fish-
wife at the poor servant girl, he gathered the rest of his
clothing and went to the door.

"You say Mr. Haskell is here?" he demanded of the
servant.

"Aye, milor'." The quaking maid bobbed a curtsy, even
as she cast a fearful glance at her mistress. "I've put 'im
below, in the green parlor, milor'."

Damien turned abruptly for the stairs. Behind him, the
actress snatched up a wrapper and followed.

He found the parlor without difficulty and entered to
discover his secretary pacing the floor. George Haskell
was a tall, pleasant-looking man with even features, non-

descript brown hair, and gold-rimmed spectacles. Normally possessed of a lively sense of humor, he appeared at the moment as grim as his employer had ever seen him.

"What goes, George? The matter must be very important to bring you here."

The secretary glanced at the actress, who was lingering in the parlor doorway. "I've come on a matter of some urgency, my lord. If I might have a word in private?"

Finding the attention on herself, Elise flushed prettily. "Of course, I shall leave you alone." Obligingly, she backed out and shut the door.

"What is it?" Damien demanded impatiently.

"I fear I have grave news. Your sister has suffered an accident."

Damien felt his heart clench. "Olivia?"

It was a reflexive question. He had only one sister, a girl some fifteen years his junior, who lived quietly at his country estate of Rosewood, the family seat of the Barons Sinclair. "What manner of accident?"

"I do not have all the particulars—the message your bailiff sent was written in apparent haste. But it seems Miss Sinclair fell down a flight of stairs. When she regained consciousness, she had lost all feeling in her lower limbs. The doctor was called, and while he could find no broken bones, he believes her spine to be damaged. The possibility exists that she may be permanently crippled."

Damien stared, shock rendering him mute.

"I fear that is not all," George added quietly.

"There's more?" he said hoarsely.

"From the note, I gather the injury occurred during a—"

"A what, man? Tell me!"

"You will not care for this, my lord, but . . . it was an aborted elopement."

"A *what*?" Damien shook his head. He could not credit that his shy, sheltered sister would attempt an elopement. Or that the strict governess he'd hired to look after Olivia would permit it. "That is impossible. There must be some mistake."

"Perhaps so," George said dubiously.

"Who was the man?"

"The man?"

"Her seducer. Whom did she think to wed?"

"The missive makes mention of Lord Rutherford, but it isn't clear if he is the culprit."

Damien knew of a Viscount Rutherford, a rather wild young man who had just come into the title.

"Here," his secretary said, "you will wish to read Bellows's letter for yourself."

Damien took the proffered sheet of vellum and hastily perused the nearly illegible scribble in his bailiff's hand. The tragic mishap had occurred in Alcester at the Four Lions, a busy coaching inn near the Sinclair family seat of Rosewood. The note described the extent of Olivia's suspected injuries and went on to suggest how the accident came about. Bellows wrote:

> *It pains me to deliver such disastrous tidings, but I gather your sister planned an elopement. At the last moment, however, the gentleman in question reneged. Miss Olivia fled in dismay, which precipitated her fall. Lord Rutherford summoned the doctor immediately, but the damage was done—to her person and, I fear, to her reputation as well.*
>
> *I hope to hush up the sorry tale for as long as possible, but I know it cannot be forever. I beg you, my lord,*

send me your instructions and advise me how best to deal with this dire situation.

Your humble servant, Sidney Bellows.

Raggedly Damien ran a hand through his raven hair. He'd been the subject of more scandals than he could count, but he had kept his younger sister sheltered in the country, with the most decorous of governesses in charge of her upbringing. Now it seemed Olivia had created her own scandal. Worse, she had been gravely injured . . . perhaps crippled for life. . . .

A fierce anger ripped through Damien, lodging in his chest. The letter did not specifically name her seducer, but whoever had harmed Olivia would feel his wrath. He would put a bullet through the bastard or, better yet, throttle the life out of him with his bare hands.

"I took the liberty," his secretary murmured, "of having your traveling carriage readied. I assumed you would wish to go home at once."

"Yes . . ." Damien said distractedly, still numb with shock.

Rousing himself to action, he finished dressing in seconds. His cravat was left on the floor as he shrugged into his coat. Then, flinging his greatcoat over his shoulders, he made for the door.

Elise stopped him as he came out, delaying him by placing a graceful hand on his sleeve. "Surely you are not leaving, my lord?"

"Forgive me, but I must."

"But we have not concluded our . . ."

Arrangements was what she meant to say.

Damien clenched his jaw impatiently, while his reply

was completely devoid of its usual charm. "I have urgent business to attend to."

She smiled apologetically. "I am gravely disappointed. Your visit has been so brief."

"I will return when I can." He sketched a brief bow and withdrew his arm from her grasp.

The beautiful charmer forgotten, he followed his secretary out into the chill night, fury and fear for his sister roiling inside him, along with a fierce craving for vengeance.

Chapter One

London, May 1810

Despite the lateness of the hour, the private gaming hell boasted a sizable crowd. Liquor flowed freely, the guests quaffing great quantities of claret and champagne along with a delicious late supper. Yet beneath the laughter and conversation, a serious undercurrent coursed through the gamesters and dandies and nobles playing deep at macao and hazard and faro.

From a discreet distance across the card room, Vanessa Wyndham watched her nemesis at the faro table. Even with her stomach tied in knots, she tried to study him with dispassion.

Lord Sin. The appellation seemed exceptionally appropriate. She could see no signs of dissolution on the ruthlessly handsome face, yet there was a wicked knowledge in those penetrating gray eyes that compelled attention.

Vanessa shook herself, aware she was guilty of staring. Yet Lord Sinclair was a captivating man, with his raven hair and chiseled, harshly beautiful features. His physical form matched his arresting, dark masculinity—tall, lithe, muscular, graceful. His exquisitely tailored black coat seemed to have been poured over his elegant shoulders.

She had come to London expressly to seek him out. To prevent him from destroying her family out of revenge.

Apparently she was not the only one whose interest was roused by the Baron Sinclair. Behind her, a whispered conversation between two ladies caught her ear.

"I see Damien is wreaking havoc at the gaming tables as usual."

"I cannot comprehend why," the second voice complained petulantly. "He's rich as a nabob. He has no need to add to his fortune."

The first woman laughed. "Come now, you are simply piqued because he has chosen to ignore you all evening. Confess, darling, if the irresistible Lord Sin were to beckon, you would swoon at his feet."

Unwillingly Vanessa's gaze strayed back to the notorious nobleman, as it had all evening. She could well understand why women found him fascinating. That combination of polished elegance and raw virility commanded notice, while his abundance of wicked charm presented an alluring danger to the female sex.

Vanessa shivered, despite the myriad candles blazing in crystal chandeliers that lent a welcome warmth to her bare shoulders. She'd worn the empire-waist gown of emerald satin even though it was three seasons out of date, hoping the low neckline might appeal to a rakehell of the baron's stamp.

He was known as Lord Sin among the beau monde. Since the early days of her disastrous marriage, Vanessa had been aware of the infamous aristocrat. Although they'd never been formally introduced, they had once traveled in similar circles of society. Damien Sinclair was renowned for his scandalous conquests in the glittering ballrooms and bedrooms of Europe. It was said he took wickedness to new heights.

How could such a man be prevailed upon? How could she even summon the courage?

She'd had her fill of rakes. Her late husband had given her a disdain for profligates and libertines. Every feminine instinct warned her to keep her distance from the wicked Lord Sinclair. Yet she was desperate enough to approach him—this evening, if she could manage it.

"Will you call the turn, my lord?" the female dealer asked the baron.

A sudden hush settled over the card room.

Vanessa was familiar enough with the game of faro to know that to "call the turn" was to bet on the order in which the last three cards would be dealt from the box. The house held the bank, and the odds on the wager were five to one.

Lord Sinclair's arresting features wore a casual, even slightly bored, expression as he predicted the order of the deal—deuce, six, queen—as if there were not a fortune at stake.

Vanessa held her breath along with the rest of the crowd as the dealer turned the cards over one by one. . . . Deuce of spades. Six of clubs. Queen of hearts.

Lord Sinclair had just won *twenty thousand pounds*.

The tall gentleman standing beside him laughed richly and gave the baron a friendly slap on the back. "Stap me, Damien, I vow you have the devil's own luck. I don't suppose you would care to divulge your secret?"

A smile claimed the beautifully carved mouth. "No secret, Clune. My rule is always to bet on a lady. In this instance, the queen."

Just then Lord Sinclair's gaze lifted. To Vanessa's shock,

he looked across the room, directly at her. His eyes were the striking color of silver smoke—and just as heated. She felt the sizzle all the way down to her satin slippers.

Dismayed to discover herself trembling, Vanessa turned away and took a sip of wine to bolster her frayed nerves.

"Damn Aubrey . . ." she murmured under her breath. Her scapegrace brother had put her in an untenable position, gambling away their family home to that man. But she was determined to get it back.

She spent the next hour wandering the card room and keeping a wary eye on Lord Sinclair, debating whether to find someone to afford her an introduction, or to contrive some other means to speak to him. It would not do to appear too desperate. Nor would she care to evoke gossip by accosting him in front of an audience. It was rash enough to have come to a gaming hell alone, using her brother's membership subscription to gain entrance. Despite the half-mask she wore to conceal her identity, there were several of her late husband's cronies here tonight who would recognize her if she created a stir.

In the end she decided it better to make any meeting look like a chance encounter and then ask for a private word with him. She did not relish the role of supplicant, but there was nothing left but to throw herself on his mercy and hope that he had a shred of human decency left in his dissolute soul.

The hour was nearly three in the morning when her opportunity came. Lord Sinclair had collected his winnings and was preparing to depart the card room.

Suppressing a display of haste, Vanessa managed to reach the doorway before him and paused long enough to drop her lace handkerchief on the carpet. It was an obvious ploy to gain his attention, but she hoped he would be flattered enough to overlook her artifice.

Like a gentleman, he bent to retrieve the handkerchief and offered her a graceful bow. "I believe this is yours, madam?"

As he politely presented the article to her, his long fingers brushed hers, whether by accident or design she wasn't certain. More startling than the warmth of his touch, though, was his glance. Penetrating her mask, his gaze connected with hers and held her captive.

For a moment, Vanessa stood frozen, staring up at him. The half-smile on his sensual lips held a measure of his famed charm, yet his face was alert, the gray eyes filled with a keen intelligence. It would never do to underestimate such a man, Vanessa warned herself.

She forced a smile of her own and murmured her appreciation as she accepted the glove. "How careless of me," she replied, withdrawing her hand.

His look held a hint of doubt, but he let the lie pass without challenge. "I regret that I haven't the pleasure of your acquaintance."

"I am Vanessa Wyndham."

He eyed her expectantly, as if her name didn't strike any chords.

"I believe you knew my late husband, Sir Roger Wyndham."

"Ah, yes. We were members of the same clubs."

Roger had been killed in a duel over an opera dancer, but if Lord Sinclair knew of the scandal, he was too gallant— or too indifferent—to bring it up.

"So how may I serve you, Lady Wyndham?" When she remained mute, he added gently, "You obviously wish something from me." His gaze was quizzical, probing, though his smile held a self-deprecating charm. "Forgive me, but I cannot fail to notice when a beautiful woman scrutinizes me all evening."

Vanessa flushed at his forthrightness. Only a bold rogue would remark on a lady's interest. "Truthfully . . ."

"Yes, let us be truthful by all means." The lazy drawl held a hint of cynicism.

"Truthfully, I hoped I might speak to you on a matter of some urgency, my lord."

"Consider me at your service." He gestured toward the door. "Shall I escort you to your carriage?"

"If you would be so kind."

She moved through the door ahead of him, and he fell into step beside her.

"I confess my curiosity is aroused," he admitted as they moved down the hall toward the sweeping stairway. "Your examination of me all evening suggested interest, perhaps calculation, yet it was not flirtatious or coy or in the least amorous."

"I fear I never mastered the art of coyness," Vanessa replied rather tightly, annoyed that he'd managed to put her on the defensive so easily.

"Would you care, then, to tell me what engenders such seriousness?"

"Aubrey Trent, Lord Rutherford," she said quietly, "is my brother."

He came to an abrupt stop. The eyes he turned to her were suddenly a deep, storm-gray. There was no mistaking his anger.

His expression was potentially lethal, yet she held her ground. "If you please, I wish to discuss your wager with Aubrey."

"Have you come to pay his debt?"

"Not . . . precisely."

"Then what, *precisely*?"

Vanessa took a deep breath. Two nights ago, Lord Sinclair had challenged her brother at piquet. Aubrey had played recklessly and far too deep—and wound up losing his entire inheritance, including the Rutherford estates and the London town house, leaving nothing for his dependents to live on.

She herself was not especially daunted at the prospect of spending the rest of her life in genteel poverty; she'd endured worse. But she had her mother and sisters to consider. It was one thing to live with creditors nipping at your heels. It was quite another to be literally thrown out on the streets to starve.

"I've come on behalf of my family. I was hoping . . . you might consider, at least partially . . . forgiving Aubrey's debt of honor."

Sinclair stared at her. "Surely you jest."

"No," she said quietly. "I am entirely in earnest. He has two younger sisters to care for, you see. And a mother who is ailing."

"I fail to understand how your family circumstances concern me, Lady Wyndham."

"They don't, I suppose. Except that in claiming the Rutherford estates, you will take away their only means of support."

"That is indeed unfortunate." His tone conveyed no remorse.

Disheartened, Vanessa made another attempt to plead her case. "My lord, my brother is no gamester. He had no right to gamble away our family home."

"Then he ought not to have done so."

"As I understand it, you left him little choice. Surely you don't deny deliberately challenging him to cards?"

"I don't deny it. He may count himself fortunate I didn't follow my first impulse and put a bullet through him."

Vanessa felt the color drain from her face. Sinclair was known to be a crack shot and an expert swordsman. He had fought two duels that she was aware of, and doubtless more that she wasn't.

"I wonder that you didn't," she murmured.

His jaw hardened. "A duel would only have compounded the scandal to my sister."

"I'm not aware of every particular," Vanessa said in a low voice, "but I do know of your sister's injury."

"Then you know she was crippled, perhaps for life."

"Yes. I'm dreadfully sorry."

"Are you?" The terse question was cynical, even savage.

"Yes, as is my brother. Aubrey deeply regrets his actions toward your sister. They were cruel, unforgivable. The behavior of a spoiled, thoughtless youth." When Lord Sinclair made no reply, Vanessa gave him a beseeching look. "I well know how selfish my brother can be. He's young and a trifle wild. Surely a man of your reputation can understand that. Rumor has it that you've indulged in your fair share of wildness."

"My character is not at issue here."

"No, but . . . I entreat you to reconsider. My brother is a mere boy."

"Obviously. A man would not send his sister to beg in his place."

She started to protest that Aubrey had not sent her, but that wasn't quite true. Certainly he hadn't objected when she declared her intent to seek out Lord Sin.

Vanessa placed an imploring hand on the nobleman's

sleeve. "My lord, have you no mercy? No compassion at all?"

A muscle flexed in his jaw. "Your brother is not deserving of compassion. He destroyed something precious of mine. And I intend to destroy him in turn."

The declaration was cold, ruthless, implacable.

He glanced dismissively down at the slender hand that detained him. "My carriage awaits, Lady Wyndham. It is not my practice to keep my horses standing."

Deliberately he stepped back. Then he turned away, leaving Vanessa to stare after his retreating back in dismay and despair.

Vanessa fiercely fought back tears as she entered the London town house that had been in her family for four generations. She had seldom cried during the unsavory period of her life when she was wed to a notorious libertine, or in the two difficult years following Sir Roger Wyndham's death—and she would not cry now.

A hollowness in her heart, she climbed the stairs to the drawing room. Her brother had opened the London house for the Season, even though he could ill afford it.

Aubrey was waiting for her in the drawing room, anxiously pacing the carpet. For a moment Vanessa watched him, wondering how the loving boy she remembered from childhood had turned out so wild. But she knew the answer. The favorite and only son, he had been raised in unchecked license by parents who coddled and indulged him. The lack of discipline would doubtless prove his ruin.

"Well?" Aubrey asked the instant he spied her. "Did you see him?"

Aubrey was tall like herself and possessed similar coloring. His tawny, light brown hair was almost a shade of amber, while his dark eyes were luminous and could sparkle with laughter. Just now they held only anxiety.

"I contrived a meeting with Lord Sinclair, yes," Vanessa replied, coming into the room. "He refused to speak to me once he discovered my connection to you."

"Then I am lost," Aubrey said hoarsely.

She wanted to dispute him. She wanted to console him, to wrap her arms around her brother and make his troubles vanish. But he was right. Indeed, they were *all* lost. She sat down heavily on the blue brocade settee.

Aubrey flung himself into the wing chair beside her and buried his face in his hands. After a long moment, he asked quietly, "He refused even to negotiate?"

"We didn't reach the point of discussing negotiations. He wanted nothing to do with me."

"Damn and blast him . . ."

Not for the first time, Vanessa felt a surge of anger at her brother's childish effort to shift the blame. "You can hardly expect Lord Sinclair to return the estates you gambled away so recklessly, simply because a stranger asked it of him."

"He means to ruin me."

"Can you blame him? His sister suffered a debilitating injury . . . at your hands, I might add. She may never walk again. Or have you so conveniently forgotten that small particular?"

"I haven't forgotten!" Aubrey's hands clenched in his hair. "Don't you think I regret every moment of my foolish conduct?"

"What could possibly have possessed you to be so cruel to a young girl?"

"I don't know." When he raised his head, his dark eyes held grief and remorse. "It started merely as a lark, a wager.

A means to earn a substantial sum from my gaming friends. With my pockets to let, I needed the funds. And perhaps we were a trifle . . ."

"Were what?"

"Bored."

"Hunting in the country didn't provide you enough pleasure? Cockfights and boxing matches weren't sufficient entertainment?" Vanessa's tone held a hard edge of ridicule. "So you had to ruin a young girl's life. Destroy her reputation and make her a bedridden cripple."

Aubrey's grimace displayed agony. "I never intended it to go that far, you must believe me."

"Then what *did* you intend?"

He took a deep breath. "I told you, to win a wager, simply that. When we met Miss Sinclair at an assembly . . . I suppose we'd all had too much claret before arriving. At first the discussion centered on how to get her away from her dragon of a chaperon, but somehow the goal turned more serious. I ended up wagering I could make her fall in love with me. Wooing her proved . . . far easier than I expected." He hung his head. "Olivia had led such a sheltered life, she was eager for . . . affection."

"So after some weeks of clandestine meetings, you lured Miss Sinclair to a posting inn with the promise of an elopement. You never intended an honorable marriage at all?"

"It would not have mattered how honorable my intentions. I could never have afforded to wed her, even had I wished to. She's an heiress, but she won't come into her fortune for three more years. Sinclair would cut her off without a penny if she wed without his permission."

To his credit, Aubrey's expression held shame. Vanessa sighed. She well knew how he chafed at his financial state.

But there was little point in bemoaning his lack of wealth, for it was a family failing.

Their father had been a poor manager with no head for business. Hoping his eldest daughter could repair the family fortunes by making a grand match, he'd convinced Vanessa to wed a young baronet who had squandered his vast inheritance and been killed in a senseless duel within the year. Upon her father's death in a riding accident shortly afterward, Vanessa had willingly escaped London and returned home to live with her family.

She'd spent the two years since managing the household and attempting to persuade her ailing mother and two younger sisters to live within their humble means. Aubrey, however, was the chief problem, demanding funds to support his pleasures and depleting his remaining income on gaming and wenching.

But if they were deep in dun territory before, their situation was now dire.

"Perhaps Charlotte could make a match," Aubrey suggested in a low voice.

"No! That is out of the question," Vanessa said fiercely. Charlotte was only fifteen and Fanny thirteen. As long as she had a breath left in her body, her sisters would not be sold into marriage for wealth and position, as she had been.

"Then what do you propose?"

She rubbed her temples wearily. "Perhaps we can simply decline to vacate the premises. Lord Sinclair might find it distasteful having to call in the bailiffs."

Aubrey shook his head. "My obligation to Lord Sin is a debt of honor. It must be paid, even if we all starve as a consequence."

She stared at him as her anger rose again. "You've lost

our home, our sole means of income, and all you can think about is your precious gentleman's honor?"

"If I cannot pay, I might as well put a bullet to my head."

"Aubrey, don't speak that way!" she exclaimed sharply.

He seemed not to hear. "Perhaps I deserve a bullet. When she fell—" He squeezed his eyes shut. "—I thought I had killed her."

His expression was tortured, distraught, and it frightened Vanessa. "Aubrey, I beg you—"

Abruptly relenting, she rose and went to kneel before him, despite her expensive gown. She took his hands in her own, finding them chilled. "We cannot change the past. We can only strive to be better in the future."

After a long moment, he nodded. "Pray calm your fears, sweet sister. I don't have the courage to end my life at my own hand. I haven't your strength."

Her heart aching for him, she attempted to divert the direction of his dark thoughts. "What do the doctors say about Miss Sinclair's condition?"

He drew a shuddering breath. "I don't know. I was not allowed near her. I wish . . . I wish I could somehow make amends. That was my intent when I called on Lord Sinclair this week, the instant he returned to town. When he invited me to attend his club, I thought he might have forgiven me. . . . What a fool I was."

Aubrey forced a twisted smile. "I suppose I am fortunate he chose that means of revenge rather than challenging me to a duel. I deserve his wrath, I know. Had someone treated my own sisters so appallingly, I would have wished to kill him."

Vanessa felt herself soften. Her brother was not a bad man, simply weak. And she loved him dearly. He was a scapegrace, true. But he had supported her through her difficult marriage; he had made her laugh at a time in her life when she found little cause for joy. And he seemed truly sorry for his abominable actions toward Lord Sinclair's sister.

"We will think of something, Aubrey, I promise you. I won't allow our mother and sisters to be thrown out on the street to starve."

The pleading hope in his eyes was heartrending to see. "What can be done?"

"I don't know, but I haven't yet given up trying to persuade Lord Sinclair to see reason."

"He wants vengeance."

"I know." She shivered, remembering the storm-gray eyes that had seemed to penetrate her very soul. His compelling image rose in her mind's eye: elegant, virile, dangerous. The wicked Lord Sin was a man to be reckoned with.

"He is a heartless devil," she murmured, "but I shan't accept defeat just yet."

Chapter Two

With trepidation Vanessa stepped down from the hired hackney carriage to stand before the magnificent Sinclair residence in fashionable Mayfair. Shivering, she tugged the hood of her pelisse around her face, less for protection against the gray morning drizzle than to conceal her identity. A lady did not call at the home of a gentleman, especially one of Lord Sin's infamous reputation.

Yet she was driven by desperation. Summoning all her willpower, Vanessa climbed the marble steps to the imposing front door. When a stately majordomo answered, she presented her card. Not even by a twitch of an eyebrow did the elderly servant display surprise at her presence.

"I will inquire if his lordship is in, my lady," he intoned. "Would you wish to wait in the blue salon?"

She accepted the offer. Entering the salon, she drew back her hood but remained standing, barely noticing the elegance of her surroundings that bespoke wealth and taste. The gates of Hades would hold more appeal just now.

She despised licentious noblemen. And Damien Sinclair, Lord Sin, was a profligate of the first order. He was known to be a leader of the notorious Hellfire League, a fraternity of depravity for wealthy lords, patterned after the club of a similar name made infamous a half-century before.

Still, she would have to quell her distaste if she cherished any hope of saving the Rutherford estates.

In only a few moments, a young gentleman appeared in the salon. He bowed politely while surveying her curiously through his spectacles.

"Lady Wyndham? I am his lordship's secretary, George Haskell. He asked me to inquire how I may be of service."

"Is Lord Sinclair not at home?" she asked, unsurprised to be fobbed off on an employee.

"He is preparing to go out. I would be happy to assist you if I may."

"I'm afraid that is not likely. I've come on a matter of some urgency, which only his lordship may deal with." Her tremulous smile was apologetic but determined. "Will you tell him that I shall wait for him to come down?"

Mr. Haskell bowed and withdrew. He was back shortly, wearing a troubled frown.

"His lordship bade me inform you, my lady, that he will grant you a short interview . . . upstairs. If you will please follow me?"

She expected to be shown to a drawing room, but when they had climbed the wide staircase, the secretary led her down a wide hallway to a private chamber. With another bow, Haskell left her, shaking his head in evident disapproval.

The room was large, Vanessa saw as she entered, and was tastefully decorated in crimson and gold and rich mahogany furnishings. In the center of the vast chamber stood a huge bed, whose covers were still in a tangle.

Vanessa felt her heartbeat quicken. This was Lord Sin's bedchamber.

"Do come in," a lazy, sardonic voice drawled from the opposite side of the room.

Vanessa took a single step and stopped short. The wicked nobleman was shirtless, dressed only in breeches and boots. The expanse of bare skin was stunning. With wide shoulders, a broad chest corded with lean muscle, a hard flat stomach, and narrow hips, he had the physique of a Greek god, his muscularity suggesting his devotion to athletic sport. Add to that the fact that he was treacherously handsome, and her pulse went wild.

She had forgotten the dismaying impact this man had on her.

He offered her an apologetic smile as he drew on a loose cambric shirt. "Forgive me for receiving a lady in such a state of undress, but you did insist."

Indeed she had. Even so, his receiving her here was a blatant attempt to intimidate her, she realized. If it was known she had visited his bedchamber—a den of iniquity, without doubt—she would be thoroughly compromised. Still, she was in no position to challange him. To have any hope of persuading him, she would have to swallow both her dismay and her nervousness.

"I can manage," he said to the manservant attending him. He took the flowing stock and dismissed the valet, who bowed and obediently withdrew.

Alone with the premiere rakehell of London, Vanessa made a futile attempt to quiet her rioting pulse.

"You don't mind if I continue dressing?" Sinclair moved to stand before the cheval glass, where he began tying his cravat with consummate skill. "I am pressed for time. I don't wish to be late for an appointment with my tailor. My secretary would like me to take my place in the House of Lords, which requires my being suitably attired."

His dry tone suggested cynical amusement, but Vanessa could not believe he was overly concerned about his style of dress.

He was a bold rogue, with a natural sense of arrogance bred into him, but he was no fop. And he had no need to rely on his tailor to present a favorable appearance. Men feared and respected him, while his looks and charm alone had seduced legions of females. Vanessa could not deny that her every feminine instinct came alive in his presence. Those stunning gray eyes of his, fringed with thick lashes, could only be called beautiful.

Swallowing with effort, she found her voice. "Thank you for agreeing to speak to me," she began on a conciliatory note.

That swift masculine smile flashed in the mirror. "I had no choice but to yield gracefully, my lady. You are quite persistent . . . determined enough to camp on my doorstep, I suspect."

"Necessity compels me to be. But I wish only ten minutes of your so valuable time."

"You may have ten minutes, but I warn you, ten hours would not be adequate to change my mind regarding your brother. Pray be seated."

Vanessa glanced at the wing chairs before the hearth, and the chaise lounge beneath the far window. "Thank you, but I prefer to stand."

He inclined his head to signify his indifference and made a delicate loop of the cravat. "Does your brother know you are here?"

"No, and I have no intention of telling him. He would be scandalized to know I even called upon you, let alone that you received me in your bedchamber."

"Notorious despoiler of feminine virtue that I am?" Sinclair asked ironically. "I do hate to disillusion you, but I don't lie in wait for helpless females to ravish." His eyes met hers in the cheval glass. "Although in your case, I confess I might be tempted."

She took a deep breath. "You were correct, my lord. I did come here to discuss my brother's debt of honor."

"How clever of me to have guessed."

"Perhaps," Vanessa continued, striving for a reasonable tone, "you don't comprehend the hardship that fulfilling the debt would place on his family."

He gave a sigh of resignation. "I gather you mean to tell me."

"My mother and sisters will be destitute, with no place to live."

"Your brother can always apply to the cent-per-centers to redeem his vowels."

"No moneylender would advance such a sum without the Rutherford estates as collateral. Even were he able to pay his debt of honor to you, once in the clutches of the moneylenders, the result would be the same. Aubrey would lose his estates and be thrown into debtor's prison and his family driven from their home."

"I still fail to see how that concerns me."

Vanessa fought down an angry reply. It would do no good to antagonize Lord Sinclair. "You have every right to wish revenge on my brother, but must you make his family suffer as well?"

"That is an unfortunate consequence of his actions."

"Not only of *his* actions. You are a practiced gamester, my lord. You lured him into deep play, you admitted as much last night."

"Indeed, I had every intention of ruining him."

"Fleecing green boys should be outlawed," Vanessa murmured bitterly.

"So should destroying the lives of innocent young girls," he retorted. When she simply stared at him, he added with impatience, "Did you come here to play the disapproving paragon, Lady Wyndham?"

"No, I came here to persuade you to see reason."

He ignored her comment.

"Aubrey has threatened to shoot himself if he cannot find a way out of this difficulty."

"I confess that would not break my heart."

"It would mine."

His eyes searched hers, as if to judge her sincerity. Then he shook his head, while his jaw hardened. "Your brother must pay a price for his reckless cruelty. But I will grant you one concession. If and when he is man enough to come to me himself, I shall discuss terms of payment."

Her heart lifted a measure at his offer, but it was not enough. "What good are terms when he cannot manage to pay his tailor's bill, let alone a wager the size of the one he owes you?"

"You are singularly interested in his financial affairs, are you not?"

"I have good reason to be. I manage the Rutherford estates for Aubrey, since he has little head for accounts."

He raised an eyebrow. "And you have?"

"Enough to recognize when he is in dire straits. And I must say he is not wholly to blame for his dwindling resources. The chief difficulty has always been persuading our family to economize. I fear we are spendthrifts." When she received no reply, she pressed on. "Is there no way you would consider reducing the debt?"

"What do you have to offer in exchange, my lady?"

She bit her lip, and Damien felt his gaze drawn to her lush mouth. It required a herculean effort to harden his heart against her pleadings. Lady Wyndham was a celebrated beauty, and he had always been partial to beautiful women. Those dark eyes of hers were luminous enough to drown in, while her hair was a lustrous sherry color, shimmering with the gold and russets of autumn.

But she was calculating enough to have wed for title and property, and during her marriage she had run with a wild set. She could be cut from the same cloth as her wastrel brother and her late husband. Sir Roger was known to have squandered his inheritance while blazing a trail of scandal and debauchery, before meeting an untimely end. If rumor could be believed, his friends had been more than eager to console his grieving widow. Vanessa Wyndham did not seem as superficial and fatuous as other ladies of the ton, Damien admitted, yet she could be playing a role for his benefit.

While her striking eyes were wary, there was awareness in her gaze, a sexual awareness that told him clearly she felt the attraction between them.

"I fear I have little to offer you. My husband's death left me in rather straitened circumstances," she acknowledged quietly. "Our home was so heavily mortgaged that there was nothing left when it went to pay his debts."

"You had best seek a rich husband then."

He saw her grimace of distaste. "Even were I inclined to wed again—which I am not—there isn't time for me to find a husband."

"You do have a dilemma, it seems. But a beautiful woman like yourself can always take a lover. Or perhaps you already have one?" His tone was leading, curious.

Vanessa set her teeth. "I have no lover, Lord Sinclair."

"Yet you are not above using your feminine charms to gain your ends. I expect the revealing gown you wore last evening was for my benefit?"

Vanessa flushed, but she held fast to her temper.

His gray eyes raked her from head to toe. "It should not be difficult for you to find yourself a protector. You have abundant charms with which to bargain. Use that lovely body of yours to advantage."

"I am not a lightskirt, my lord." She said it through clenched teeth, so fiercely that he had to believe her sincere.

Her indignation gave Damien pause. He was accustomed to women throwing themselves at his feet. To her credit, the lovely Vanessa had not tried to ply him with tears or devious tales. She wasn't attempting to wheedle a favor from him. She was simply pleading honestly with him to let them keep their home.

He had to confess he admired her forthrightness, as well as her courage. He even admired her determined defense of her brother, however misguided it might be.

But it was unwise to allow himself to soften toward her. Vanessa Wyndham was clever, with spirit enough to be intriguing, and beautiful enough even for a man with his jaded, discriminating tastes. Under ordinary circumstances, he might enjoy pitting wits with her, perhaps even engaging in a game of seduction. But these were far from ordinary circumstances. Her brother had shattered his innocent sister's life and would have to pay.

"Have you never done anything that you regret?" she was saying. "Aubrey was raised with no concept of responsibility. Our father was a poor role model for him."

"An edifying tale."

"My lord, my brother is merely a boy."

His gray eyes hardened. "And my sister is merely a girl, whose life Rutherford callously ruined."

"I am not excusing his behavior," Vanessa managed more civilly. "But I should think you would wish to devote your energies to aiding your sister rather than seeking vengeance."

"I have been devoting my energies toward that end."

"Indeed? Did you not leave her alone in the country while you returned to London to your life of leisure?"

It was Damien's turn to set his jaw. "I fail to see how it concerns you, Lady Wyndham, but I am in town to seek a companion for her, if you must know. My chief reason for coming was to investigate employment agencies and interview prospective candidates."

And to visit your tailor. It was all Vanessa could do to hide her disdain. The mighty baron evidently didn't wish to be bothered with his invalid sister, not if he planned to shirk his responsibility and palm the girl off on an employee. "Is that not rather coldhearted, to fob her off on a stranger?"

"Is it not rather unwise to antagonize me, Lady Wyndham?" he replied in a silken voice edged with steel.

Vanessa hesitated as she surveyed the storm gathering in his eyes. She had angered him, which was indeed foolish. Lord Sinclair was a dangerous man because of his implacable will. When he moved toward her slowly, it was all she could do to stand her ground. She was too aware of his body, the size and strength of it, of his raw masculinity.

He stopped before her, gazing at her hard. The heat and intensity in his eyes were unnerving. Then his tone dropped to a low murmur. "You are here alone, in a notorious rake's bedchamber. I could have my wicked way with you, and no one would gainsay me."

It was a threat, but somehow he made it sound like a sensual promise. Even more unnerving was the way his scrutiny shifted to her bosom. She could feel his gaze like a tangible caress, could feel her breasts tighten as if he had actually touched her.

She stood frozen when his hand rose to her throat. Her breath caught as his elegant finger trailed a featherlight path downward to the vulnerable hollow. "Do I fluster you, Lady Wyndham?" he taunted softly.

"No . . . of course not."

"So why is your breathing so shallow, your lovely skin so delicately flushed?"

It was true she was suddenly breathless and overly warm. But if he thought to intimidate her, he would learn that he had met his match.

Vanessa lifted her chin defiantly, returning his gaze. "I had hoped to appeal to your better nature, my lord, but I see you haven't one."

Lord Sin smiled coolly. "My nature is quite charming under most circumstances."

"I have seen little evidence of it."

"But then you scarcely know me."

For a moment he stood looking down at her. But then he shook his head, as if recalling where he was. "As much as I enjoy sparring with you, I have an appointment to keep."

Vanessa gave a sigh of frustration. He was right. This was getting nowhere. With a heavy heart, she made one last attempt at persuading him.

"You asked, my lord, what I could offer you in exchange for returning my brother's estates. Well, I am willing to offer my services—"

Ah, he thought, irrationally disappointed in her. *Now we come to the point of negotiations*. "You begin to interest me vastly."

"—as companion to your sister," Vanessa continued.

He frowned at her. "Companion?"

"You said you were seeking one for Miss Sinclair."

"Give me a single reason why I should entrust my sister's welfare to you."

"Because I could be of help to her. By all reports, she is faring poorly. I understand she cannot leave her bed and has become a recluse."

"Your point?"

"Dealing with ladies in poor health is not a new circumstance for me. My mother is a semi-invalid and often confined to her bed, so I have some experience. And I could lend your sister the consequence of rank. I still retain my husband's title, and I am the daughter of a viscount. No governess-companion could offer as much."

Damien studied her, trying to judge if this was a ploy. She seemed entirely sincere, yet he wondered how far she would go to sacrifice for her family. He nodded slowly, deciding to test her resolve.

"You have courage, I'll give you that. But I wonder to what lengths you are prepared to go."

"I will do whatever I must to spare my family."

"Is that so?" He smiled thinly. "Well, you are in luck, sweeting. You find me in an indulgent mood. But I have in mind a more intimate arrangement than the one you envision. I shall make a bargain with you. I will offer you the position of companion—but not to my sister. To me."

"I . . . don't understand."

"Then I shall put it more plainly. I will cancel your brother's debt if you become my mistress."

From her shocked look, she was clearly taken aback. "It

would not be forever. Merely till we tire of each other. Say . . . for the summer?"

She stared at him. "I cannot believe a man of your reputation would lack for paramours."

He gave a casual shrug. "You find me between paramours at the moment. The position is yours, if you want it."

What she wanted was to slap his face for his insulting proposal. He could not be serious . . . could he? "You are offensive, sir."

He simply looked at her and smiled a slow, cynical smile. "Come now, sweeting. Your pretense of outrage is a bit overplayed. You're a woman of the world. You can't profess to be shocked."

He closed the distance between them and raised his hand to her breast. When he brushed the nipple with the back of his knuckles, she felt the sensual impact clear through the fabric of her pelisse and gown. The boldness of the gesture alarmed her as much as the fiery sensation it engendered.

Drawing a sharp breath, Vanessa took a step backward to a safer distance.

Graciously Lord Sin smiled in triumph, the slight curve of his lips radiating male charm. She could well understand why his conquests were legion. He had captivated countless women with that wicked, sensual smile.

"So you decline my offer?" he murmured, obviously presuming he had won.

"I did not say that!" she returned sharply.

"Then what do you say?"

"I . . . I will consider it."

"Well, consider swiftly, my sweet. But I give you fair warning. If you bargain with me, you bargain with the devil."

Chapter Three

Their gazes locked and warred.

"Is the price too high, my lovely?" Damien inquired lazily.

Vanessa swallowed at the question. What he was suggesting would ruin her. But would ruination be too high a price to save her family?

"What . . . would I be required to do as your mistress?" she asked, stalling for time.

He cocked an eyebrow. "You cannot guess?"

"I suppose you would expect us to share . . . carnal relations."

"That is the usual custom, yes." His mouth curved in dry amusement. "But I daresay you would not find your duties too onerous. I would visit your bed whenever I wished, naturally, and you must learn to please me."

"You will likely be disappointed in me. I have no talent in that direction."

"I won't know until I have you beneath me."

Her breath caught at his bold speaking, yet his continued attempts to intimidate only angered her. "I have no experience as a mistress, only a wife. My only . . . intimacy with a man has been with my husband. And I found that side of marriage . . . extremely unpleasant. Indeed, I cannot comprehend why your gender finds lust so agreeable."

Her tone at the end was scornful, cutting, yet Damien couldn't tell if she was angry at him, her late husband, or males in general.

"But then by all reports, your husband was a boor. And by your own admission, you have never had the benefit of a proper lover. At the risk of seeming immodest, I am skilled enough to teach you whatever you need to know. I believe I can safely predict you will enjoy your education."

Her chin rose regally. "How can you possibly divine what I might or might not enjoy? You know nothing about me."

"But I know women, cherie. And I understand pleasures of the flesh. You cannot be so different from the vast majority of your sex. One night in my arms and I'll have you trembling for me."

"You were correct, my lord. You *are* a devil. An arrogant one."

He smiled. "My crimes are legion."

When she remained silent, Damien studied her curiously, wondering if her scornful haughtiness was an act. If she was feigning reluctance in order to excite his interest, her ploy was working. He couldn't remember the last time he had been so aroused by the mere presence of a woman.

And why else would she hesitate to snap up his extremely generous offer? No mistress, however magnificent, was worth a hundred thousand pounds, and he was giving her a chance both to redeem that enormous sum and to save her worthless brother. She would be a fool to refuse.

He doubted Vanessa Wyndham was a fool. Obviously accustomed to scandal, she must be experienced and sophisticated and worldly enough to use her body to gain her ends, as were so many of the grasping, shallow beauties of his acquaintance.

It was possible, he supposed, that she truly was cold and unfeeling, incapable of real passion. Then again, it could be pride or fear driving her. Was that guarded, vulnerable look in her dark eyes genuine?

"Do you fear me, Lady Wyndham?" he asked quite seriously.

"Considering the tales told about you, it would be remarkably imprudent of me not to fear you—a man for whom no rule is sacred and from whom no woman is safe."

"You have no reason to be afraid."

"Said the wolf to the lamb."

He smiled at her sharp tongue. It was strangely refreshing to find a spirited beauty who wasn't afraid of earning his dismissal by speaking her mind.

Casually Damien walked over to a rosewood side table, where he searched in a drawer. Withdrawing a deck of cards, he held it up.

"I beg to differ, my lady. I am no wolf. But I am a gamester, as you said. So I propose to give you a sporting chance. We each draw a card; high card wins. Even odds. If you are the victor, I forgive your brother's debt entirely. Lose and you serve as my mistress for the summer."

She stared, her dark eyes wide and uncertain. Damien fancied he could see himself in their lustrous depths, even across the room.

"Your answer, my lady?"

Vanessa shut her eyes as she struggled with the impossible dilemma. It was an outrageous bargain, trading her honor in a desperate bid to gain his aid. She had sold herself once, in marriage, and had vowed never to do so again.

Yet would giving her body to this man be any more repugnant than her marriage had been? Many women would leap at the chance to share Damien Sinclair's bed. He possessed a legendary reputation for lovemaking. Women found him undeniably desirable—and she was no different, God help her.

And he was offering her an even chance to triumph. She might actually win. But if she lost? She would be ruined.

His proposal was dishonorable, even cruel. But her passion was his price for mercy. And to shield her family from his wrath, she would bargain with the devil.

"You give me little choice," she replied in a low, toneless voice.

To his credit, he showed no amusement. "You may do the honors. Shuffle the deck and draw first."

She moved reluctantly toward him and accepted the deck. She had played whist and piquet often enough to be proficient at shuffling, but her hands were so unsteady, the task took a moment.

"Choose your card, sweeting," Lord Sin prompted.

Spreading the deck on the table, she drew a single card and turned it right side up. A jack of hearts. Hope rose in her breast. It was possible a jack would outrank his draw. Vanessa held her breath, feeling her heart thud.

Lord Sinclair selected his card then, turning it over with long, elegant fingers.

Vanessa stared down at the king of spades, unable to hide her despair. She had lost.

"There is still time," he murmured, "for you to change your mind."

Curiously he was giving her a final chance to withdraw. Numbly, she shook her head. She would honor their agreement.

"Then we have a bargain?"

She drew a measured breath, striving for control. She was no coward. And her family would be saved. She had to be content with that.

Indeed, their salvation was far more than she had dared hope for when she had come to plead with Lord Sin. "Yes, I accept."

She was startled when he raised his hand slowly to touch her cheek. It was all she could do not to flinch.

"Vanessa." He said her name softly, his tone almost a caress.

When she looked up, their gazes locked for a heartbeat.

"Would you honor me with a kiss to seal our agreement?"

Her gaze dropped to his lips. He had a beautiful mouth, she thought incongruously. She felt her pulse quicken dangerously.

She stood frozen as he bent slightly to bring his mouth into delicate contact with hers. It was the slightest brushing of flesh against flesh, barely that, and yet she felt the sensation like a burning brand. Abruptly she shivered.

When he lifted his head, she could see satisfaction in his smoke-silvered eyes.

"Was that so difficult?"

"I suppose not," she admitted bleakly.

With a casual finger, he flicked the high collar of her pelisse. "You must be warm, sweeting, wearing so many layers. You do not need this, do you?" His voice was husky, a low caress.

She regarded him in confusion, unable to understand the question.

"Will you take off your pelisse for me?"

"W-why?"

"Because I wish to see you."

She felt alarm begin to rise within her, an alarm he must have sensed.

His eyes captured hers and held them. "I make you a promise, Vanessa. I won't take you unwillingly. I give you my word."

Vanessa did not know if she could believe him, if she could trust the promises of a notorious rake, but it really made little difference. He had paid for the privilege of undressing her if he wished.

With trembling fingers she unfastened the buttons of her pelisse. When she hesitated, he drew the garment from her shoulders and laid it casually across the table.

"I confess disappointment," he murmured as he scrutinized her plain day dress of brown merino wool. "I much prefer the gown you wore last evening. This does not do your lush figure justice, although it brings out the rich color of your eyes.

"Come, sit with me a moment." He took her hand in his and led her to the chaise lounge.

She willed herself not to resist as he drew her down beside him, with the cool assurance of a man who inevitably got his way. Sitting rigidly, Vanessa held her breath, feeling her heart race with trepidation. Did he mean to seduce her here and now?

His face was disquietingly close to hers. She found herself staring at his mouth, that incredibly sensuous, beautifully carved mouth.

Damien saw where her gaze rested and his loins stirred. Yet he made no move to touch her.

He wanted her, he freely admitted. Too much to risk a precipitous action. He was glad he had won the draw, and not because of the vast sum at stake. He was wealthy enough that he would not miss even so large a fortune. But now he would have the opportunity to explore the hidden depths of this spirited, intriguing woman.

His well-honed male instinct told him she was not being coy. She was afraid . . . and very, very vulnerable. Someone had hurt her—badly, he suspected. It would take every ounce of control he possessed to go slowly with her, to wait until she responded to him freely, but the treasure he would uncover at the end would be well worth the effort.

He couldn't allow her to leave just yet, not before he began his campaign to vanquish her fear of him and to win her trust. Once out of his presence, she would only torment herself with dark imaginings, build him up in her mind till he was an evil monster.

No, first he wanted her to sample a taste of the pleasure he could give her, so she could begin to see he wasn't really so fearsome.

The sweet scent of her rose up to tease his nostrils, but with iron-willed control, he forced his desire to remain in check.

"Will you look at me, sweeting?"

When she acceded reluctantly, he went on, keeping his tone disarming. "You think me a libertine, I know, but am I such an ogre?"

"I . . . don't know you well enough to make such a judgment."

He smiled. "True. And like you, I have never faced this particular circumstance before. We shall just have to improvise."

Vanessa couldn't look away; there was something warm and tender in his eyes that allayed her panic.

"I should like to kiss you again, Vanessa. Will you deny me a kiss?"

She felt her heart beating a wild pulse in her throat. "Are you giving me a choice, my lord?"

"Indeed. The choice will always be yours."

She searched his face, looking for signs of deception, finding none. He had promised he wouldn't take her against her will. Perhaps he truly meant it.

When she made no reply, he raised his hand again to her cheek. "You have such lovely silken skin."

His thumb stroked her jaw, his touch lingering and provocative. She wanted to move, to flee his disturbing nearness, yet she was held captive by the intensity of his gaze, by the raw, powerful sexuality emanating from him.

His knuckles brushed over her moist, parted lips. A frisson of fiery sensation sparked from his fingers to her skin.

"Your answer, sweet Vanessa?" He tilted her face up to his. "Will you kiss me?"

His voice stroked her senses like velvet, weakening her defenses. The need to protect herself from this man was strong. And yet . . . she didn't want him to stop touching her.

"Yes . . ." she murmured, her voice a whisper of sound.

It was enough. His palm cradled her face gently, with infinite tenderness. Vanessa watched, spellbound, as his ebony lashes lowered to shadow his sensual eyes. His breath fanned warm against her lips, before his mouth settled on hers with the slow, sure pressure of experience.

A heated rush of feeling assaulted her. His kiss was a languid, intimate knowing of her mouth, one that stole her breath away. When she made no protest, his tongue penetrated her lips in a sensual invasion. The taste of him was arresting. Her hands rose to press lightly against his chest, yet she didn't really want to push away. She could feel the hardness of his corded muscles beneath her fingers, the heat of his powerful torso, smell the arousing scent of him, warm and faintly musky.

His tongue played in a leisurely, erotic dance while he continued his tender assault with his fingers. Vaguely Vanessa realized he was caressing her again, stroking with hushed delicacy the column of her throat, her bare collarbone, her shoulder. . . .

Some moments later his long fingers curved over the square neckline of her gown. She tensed when he drew down the bodice to reveal the full, rounded contours of her breasts above her chemise and corset. As if from a great distance, she heard him whisper.

"Don't be afraid, angel. . . ."

The insinuating murmur of his husky voice quieted her alarm.

Slowly he bent his head, his lips following the path his fingers had taken, his soft caresses holding her entranced. A tremor shook her as he tugged on the edge of her chemise. She felt the soft brush of his breath on the ripe swells . . . and suddenly went rigid. He meant to kiss her bare breasts!

Her breath fled, not so much from his shocking intentions as from the primitive sensations he aroused in her. A whimper escaped her lips when he freed her bosom. She couldn't prevent the shameful tingling of her breasts, the brazen heat that coiled inside her, and yet . . . The appalling realization struck her that she wanted him to kiss her there.

She flinched when he grazed the aching tip of her nipple with his tongue, but not with pain; the responsive arousal that pulsed between her thighs startled her and made her tremble. With expert skill he drew the soft, swollen flesh between his lips, capturing the pouting crest. Vanessa shuddered at the blatant carnality of it.

He went on arousing her, teasing the furled bud with his velvet-rough tongue, sucking gently with his warm mouth. Stunned, she arched toward him, wanting the searing pleasure he ignited in her.

A soft moan escaped her at his tantalizing devil's sorcery. At the sound, he left off tasting her nipple and took her mouth again, his kiss turning suddenly hot and hungry. The unexpected fierceness of it dredged a raw whimper from deep in her throat.

Involuntarily her hands rose to press against his shoulders. Then, suddenly, the spell between them shattered. Lord Sin abruptly seemed to recollect himself and inexplicably broke off his kiss.

Brusquely, he pressed his forehead against hers and gave a ragged laugh, as if straining for willpower. A wave of disappointment crushed Vanessa. She hadn't wanted his embrace to end—nor had he, it seemed.

He drew a measured breath, but his husky voice held a raw edge when he spoke. "Forgive me. I momentarily forgot myself."

His beautiful, chiseled face came into soft focus. Vanessa stared at him, torn between dismay and desire. Never had she had such a primal reaction to a mere kiss.

"I think you vastly underestimate your charms, sweeting. If you can inflame me without trying, I have no doubt you will make an apt pupil."

Vanessa felt a surge of shame at the unnerving, inexplicable response he'd drawn from her. Only a wanton would desire such a man.

It was impossible to recover her dazed senses abruptly, but she made an effort to collect herself. She couldn't look at Lord Sinclair as she fumbled with her disheveled bodice, or when he gently pushed her hands aside and solicitously aided her in covering her bare breasts.

Vanessa accepted his assistance grudgingly. She should be grateful he had ended his embrace before it went too far, for she'd been helpless to resist. She would have let him have his way with her, given him whatever he demanded.

He must have sensed her discomfort, however, for he rose from the chaise and moved an easy distance away.

"Perhaps we should discuss the particulars of our arrangement," he said casually. "I hope to leave for the country within the week, just as soon as I can employ a companion for my sister. I should like you to accompany me."

With effort, Vanessa dragged her attention back to the matter between them. She had agreed to be Lord Sinclair's mistress.

"Where do you plan for me to live?" she asked in a low voice, although loath to contemplate such an irrevocable step.

"I can set you up in a house not an inconvenient distance from my estate." When she hesitated, his mouth curved cynically. "I shall, of course, provide a carriage and horses for you and assume any other expenses."

He thought she was bargaining for greater remuneration, Vanessa realized. "Having a carriage was not my concern, my lord."

"No?"

"I was thinking of appearances. If you furnish me a house and carriage, the world will know I am your mistress."

"I imagine so," he murmured guardedly. "That is the usual way of things. But if you have a better suggestion, I am willing to listen."

"It is not only my reputation I must consider, but my sisters' as well. They will only suffer, perhaps irreparably, because of my . . . relationship with you."

When he glanced at her, the gray eyes had lost warmth. "You wish to renege on our bargain already, angel? If so, it is still not too late to change your mind. You have only to walk out that door."

"I have no intention of reneging, my lord. But I should like to repeat my original offer. I am willing to serve as companion to your sister. It will provide an excuse, however thin, for my presence in your district. And I believe I could truly be of help to her."

Damien frowned, but he repressed his first inclination to dismiss her offer out of hand. He'd been urgently searching for a companion for Olivia, it was true. But he hoped to hush the scandal of her aborted elopement as much as possible. With that end in mind, he'd planned on hiring the strictest, most respectable governess he could find, one with an unimpeachable reputation. Yet a more worldly woman might be more sympathetic and accepting of Olivia's circumstances. And Vanessa Wyndham was already privy to the sordid details.

"I'm not sure you comprehend the difficulties you would face," he said skeptically. "Olivia is completely bedridden. She suffers from despondency as well as paralysis. To act as her companion would require the patience of a saint."

"I understand, my lord, and I assure you, I've learned to cultivate patience over the years. As I said, I have experience caring for my invalid mother as well as my sisters. And," she added quietly, "while it might prove little consolation to you, I should like to try to make amends for my brother's vile actions."

Damien walked over to the window, where he stood staring down at the elegant thoroughfare that ran in front of his London mansion. His sister was the one truly good thing in his jaded world. Yet he had failed her, leaving her upbringing to the tender mercies of servants. He intended to try to make up for the years of neglect. And he would do anything—*anything*—to help her recover from her paralyzing accident.

Perhaps the lovely Lady Wyndham was right. Perhaps she might actually be able to help Olivia. And if she managed to salvage her reputation in the process, all the better. He couldn't blame her for wishing to protect her sisters. If he were honest with himself, her willingness to shield her family, even at the cost of great personal sacrifice, was a prime reason he was drawn to her.

"I suppose," he said slowly, "that we could put it to the test. You could stay at Rosewood as companion to Olivia for a trial period, a week or two, perhaps. We can always change the arrangement if we find it doesn't serve."

Vanessa let out the breath she hadn't realized she was holding. If she could conceal a shameful liaison with Lord Sin behind the decorous guise of companion, she might at least retain a shred of reputation.

"Naturally," he added after a moment's thought, "it would be best to conceal the fact that you're Rutherford's sister. Olivia most definitely doesn't need to be reminded of him."

"Of course. But I doubt she knows of my relationship to him. Aubrey says they never discussed his family in any detail, and my married name is different from his. Some of your neighbors, however, might make the connection and tell her."

"They wouldn't have the opportunity," Sinclair responded. "Olivia is bedridden and refuses to receive anyone."

"Perhaps then you could simply say that as a widow of limited means, I'm required to seek a position."

She saw Sinclair glance at the ormolu clock on the mantel. "That reminds me . . . I'm late for an appointment with the employment agency. They have several candidates for me to interview. I was about to set out when you arrived."

She eyed him with a frown. "I thought you said you had an appointment with your tailor."

"I prevaricated, I admit."

"Do you do that frequently?"

He flashed a wry smile that was edged with effortless male charm. "I didn't wish to tarnish your staunch opinion of me as a libertine."

Unwilling to let herself be charmed any further by this man, Vanessa realized it was time to take her leave. "Pray don't let me keep you any longer then," she said, rising to her feet.

"I will ring for a servant to show you out," he offered.

"I can manage to show myself out, my lord."

"Under the circumstances, I think we may safely dispense with the titles, don't you? My name is Damien."

"Very well . . . Damien."

"I like the sound of that on your lips."

At his provocative tone, she sent him a sharp glance. He was deliberately reminding her of their recent intimacy.

Vanessa gave herself a fierce mental shake, not wanting to remember the taste of his kiss or the sensation of his hot mouth on her breasts. Such lascivious behavior was so unlike her. She'd never been aroused by her husband, not once in their endless year of marriage. Carnal relations had been a duty, an extremely unpleasant one. And she felt sure she would find it just as unpleasant to surrender to a dissolute rake like Lord Sin, no matter how skilled he was at lovemaking and charming the fair sex.

Her thoughts were thus preoccupied as she moved to fetch her pelisse, so that when he came up behind her, she flinched.

"Easy, sweeting," he murmured in a tone he might use to soothe a frightened mare.

With great reluctance, she accepted his aid in donning her pelisse, and when he turned her to face him, resting his hands lightly on her shoulders, she stood tensely before him.

She wanted to flee, to escape his overwhelming nearness, but he would not let her draw away. Instead he stood looking down at her, holding her captive with his penetrating gaze.

"Be assured, I don't intend to harm you, Vanessa," he vowed softly. "I am merely going to seduce you."

Vanessa felt herself flush. Harming her and seducing her would be one and the same, she had little doubt. Lord Sinclair was a boldly sensuous man, dangerous, fascinating.

He would prove her ruin, she feared.

She wondered if he would demand another kiss, or worse, but thankfully he released her. Without replying, she made her escape.

When he was alone, Damien returned to the window to watch thoughtfully. A moment later he saw Lady Wyndham emerge from the house and descend the front steps, her hood drawn around her face to protect her anonymity.

The driver handed her into the hackney, then climbed aboard and set the team in motion. Yet long after the carriage had faded from sight, Damien remained where he was, staring down pensively, his thoughts in a strange turmoil.

What the devil had he gotten himself into? He hadn't meant for events to unfold as they had. The last thing he needed just now was a mistress to complicate his life. Certainly not the determined, defensive elder sister of the man he'd sworn to destroy.

He had given the lady every chance to refuse his offer, expecting her to back down from his outrageous proposal. Yet he had to confess pleasure at the prospect of her fulfilling the wager. Intense pleasure.

Damien shook his head in bemusement. When was the last time he had felt such anticipation? The last time his pulse raced at the mere thought of having a woman in his arms, the way it did with Vanessa Wyndham?

"Forever," he murmured to himself.

It had been an eternity since anyone had made such an impression on him, if indeed ever. He had tasted the charms of Europe's most beautiful women, and no one had intrigued him quite the way Vanessa Wyndham did, with her stunning combination of defiance and vulnerability and beauty. It was remarkable, the hunger she roused in him so effortlessly.

Briefly he shut his eyes, remembering the taste of her, the delicious feel of her ripe breasts straining for his touch . . . and his own wild reaction. A simple embrace had inflamed him beyond reason. He'd nearly lost his head, his blood surging thick and hot. Even now the memory affected him.

Damien stiffened as heated images of her flickered before his mind's eye. He envisioned her naked in his bed, lush and wanton, arching against him as he explored the mysteries of her silken body. . . .

The sensual image set him on fire.

"Have a care, man," he muttered under his breath. Roughly he locked his jaw against the sudden, painful swelling in his loins.

But then his unexpected arousal had a likely explanation. It had been weeks since he'd enjoyed a woman—weeks spent at his country estate in Warwickshire keeping his injured sister company. He wasn't accustomed to abstinence. The exquisite Silver Swann had been the last warm body in his bed, in a long line of warm bodies, and he'd been forced to abandon her abruptly when he learned the news of his sister's crippling fall.

In apology, he'd instructed his secretary to send the actress an emerald necklace to match the bracelet he'd already given her, with a charming note implying that she should find herself another protector. He hadn't had the opportunity—or, frankly, the desire—to touch another woman until his lovely visitor this morning. . . .

His thoughts again claimed by Vanessa Wyndham, Damien abruptly turned away from the window and gave the bellpull a sharp tug to summon his secretary.

What the devil is so special about her? Why he should find the lady so provocative, so enticing, particularly considering her obvious dislike—perhaps even fear—of him was beyond rationalization.

But he wanted her. And he intended to have her.

His motives were not particularly noble, he admitted. His first base impulse had been to ruin Rutherford's sister the way his own had been ruined. Forcing Lady Wyndham to serve as his mistress would be a fitting—if incomplete—vengeance.

But that was before he'd kissed her, tasted her. . . .

Damien frowned, wondering why his conscience should

suddenly stab him. Was there really any need for him to feel contrition? At her pleading, he'd given up a fortune and the chance to destroy his sister's seducer. And despite her reluctance, Vanessa Wyndham had bargained herself like any courtesan, traded her body for the chance to save her family.

His concession was more than generous.

And while he was more than willing to seduce her, he had no intention of forcing her to share his bed. In the first place, the *appearance* of her ruin in her brother's eyes was far more important than her actual ruination. No matter how dissolute and reckless young Rutherford was, he wouldn't relish the thought of his sister in the role of mistress.

In the second, Damien reflected, he'd never had to force his attentions on any female. He felt certain he would manage to turn her aversion to enchantment, her reticence to willing surrender.

And that had suddenly become of prime importance to him.

He wanted her willing, wanted her pale, perfect body hot and wanton beneath him. He wanted to hear his name tremble on her lips. He wanted her. . . .

There would be difficulties, of course, in the unusual arrangement they'd agreed upon, with her living in his ancestral home alongside his young, innocent, invalid sister. Certainly he couldn't advertise that she was his mistress. In fact, his seduction of the lady would be more complex than any affair he had ever embarked upon. But every primal instinct told him the effort would be worthwhile.

"Indeed, a prize worth winning, my angel."

Damien's mouth curved in a half-smile. It would be a war of wills between them, he had no doubt. But he looked forward to the challenge of penetrating the lovely Vanessa's defensive armor.

He would find great pleasure in teaching her about satisfying a man's desires—and about satisfying her own.

Chapter Four

Lulled by the sway of the well-sprung traveling coach, Vanessa allowed herself to relax against the velvet squabs. Seven hours of enforced intimacy with Damien Sinclair had taken a toll on her nerves.

They had spoken little on the journey north from London. Upon joining him in the carriage this morning, she had sensed his need for silence and readily complied. Now, however, Vanessa turned her head to observe her traveling companion. He was staring out the window at the passing Warwickshire landscape, engaged in his own private thoughts.

It was a mistake to regard him too closely, she realized. His handsome, noble profile still had the power to make her heart flutter, reminding her once again that she was out of her element in dealing with him.

For the hundredth time, Vanessa wondered what madness had led her to strike a wanton's bargain with such a man. She had no illusions that he truly wanted her for his mistress. Far more likely, he wanted her as a pawn in his game of revenge.

She could understand his desire for vengeance, certainly. He wanted to strike back at the man who had seduced his sister, Vanessa knew, and she was a convenient tool. But she would make him regret forcing her to pay for her brother's sins, she promised. He would not find her the submissive puppet he thought her.

His mood had seemed to darken as they drew closer to his country estate. But they were nearing their destination now, and she still knew little about the situation to which she had committed herself.

For a moment her own gaze lingered on the enchanting pastoral scene outside the carriage. The rolling English countryside was a patchwork quilt of crop fields and emerald green meadows, embroidered with hedgerows and copses of woodland. In the distance, draft horses lumbered along narrow lanes, past peacefully grazing sheep and cattle.

Finally, however, she summoned the courage to speak.

"If I am to be a companion to your sister," Vanessa said quietly, "perhaps you should tell me something about her."

Damien stirred, as if suddenly recalling her presence, and shifted his gaze to regard her with storm-gray eyes. "What do you wish to know?"

"What is she like in character and manner? What precisely is the present condition of her health? Anything that will allow me to better deal with her."

His mouth curved with a hint of bitterness. "Her health? She is presently a cripple. She has no sensation in her lower limbs and will not make an attempt to leave her darkened room, or to use the invalid chair I had built for her. As for her character and manner . . ." His demeanor softened, as did his voice. "She was always the sweetest child in nature, and she grew into a lovely young lady, generous and unspoiled as one could wish." He shook his head sardonically. "How that was possible with the Sinclair lineage is beyond me. She must be a changeling."

Hearing the rough emotion in his voice, Vanessa felt an

odd constriction in her throat. Perhaps she'd been mistaken to believe Lord Sin deplored being burdened by his crippled sister. The gentleness in his tone suggested he cared very deeply about her welfare.

It was strange to think of this notorious lord caring deeply for anything but his own pleasure.

He bent his head, rubbing one temple with elegant fingers, as if to ease the pain. "I bear part of the blame for her current misery. I should have been more vigilant in protecting her."

He was silent for a moment. "I neglected her far too much, I realize that now. Our parents perished in a carriage accident when Olivia was ten years of age, and I took over the raising of her." Sinclair grimaced. "What the devil do I know about rearing innocent young girls? I saw that she received an excellent education befitting a lady of wealth and rank, but other than the occasional visit home, I rarely saw her. I spent most of my time in town."

"She is seventeen now?" Vanessa ventured gently.

"Eighteen, but she hasn't had her come-out. I refused to bring her to London for the Season and a presentation at Court. Perhaps I was overly protective, but I thought she was too young." He gave a soft, acrid laugh. "How I wish . . . But wishing is for fools, is it not?"

He took a slow, steady breath. "I never realized how much Olivia chafed at her restrictive life in the country. It made her vulnerable to the attentions of the first scoundrel who came along . . . men like your brother. She succumbed to his clandestine wooing like a pigeon ripe for plucking. She thought herself in love."

The harsh inflection he placed on the word *love* made Vanessa wince, but she could find no ready reply. Perhaps Damien Sinclair's bitterness was justified. She stifled the urge to express her sorrow yet again and instead asked, "What do the doctors say?"

"To pray for a miracle." Damien turned to gaze out the window. "I did discover a physician in Oxfordshire who offered reason to hope. His radical views are widely condemned, but he suggested that, given the nature of the accident, Olivia's spine may be only severely bruised, and that with aggressive treatment, she could recover at least partial use of her limbs in time. Perhaps it's only desperation driving me to put my faith in a quack, but I am willing to risk being taken for a fool if there's the slightest chance he could help her."

"Sometimes it is wiser to ignore the so-called experts and follow your instincts," Vanessa murmured.

When Damien's gaze returned to her, she could see pain in the depths of those smoke-silver eyes. "If it were left to me, I would have commissioned Dr. Underhill to begin treatments at once, but Olivia has refused to allow him to attend her."

"Why would she refuse? Does she dislike the man?"

"Their rapport isn't the issue. The trouble is that she sees no point in making the attempt to improve her condition. As devastating as the physical impairment has been, the blow to her spirits was nearly as destructive. Not only did her heart suffer, but in Olivia's eyes, her life is ruined—and perhaps it is."

"The aborted elopement?"

His mouth hardened. "Indeed. It left her reputation in tatters and destroyed her chances to marry well."

"She is still an heiress, is she not?"

"True, but the stain of scandal will always follow her and preclude her association in certain circles. I did my utmost to stifle the gossip. I put about the tale that Olivia had ridden to the coaching inn at Alcester to greet a visiting cousin, but met with a tragic accident there." Damien clenched his teeth, as if reminded of his fury. "As soon as I was able, I called on the two young bloods who made the wager with your brother and secured their word to keep silent about the affair. But the rumors persisted."

Vanessa nodded in sympathy but refrained from pointing out the obvious: A rakehell like Lord Sin attempting to quiet a scandal was like using oil to quench a fire. The methods he had probably chosen wouldn't be helpful, either. In all likelihood he had threatened the two gentlemen with bodily harm before seeking out Aubrey in order to destroy him financially.

No one in his right senses would dare to cross the vengeful Lord Sin, but that didn't mean he could silence the entire world.

"My worst mistake, however," Damien continued in a low voice, "was my failure to reckon with the prudishness and cruelty of her governess-companion. That witch of a woman only heightened Livy's sense of shame, making her feel tainted and oppressing her spirits even further. She was even encouraged to entertain thoughts of suicide." His eyes locked with Vanessa's. "Perhaps you can understand why I thought it crucial to find a replacement companion for my sister."

Hearing the rawness of his quiet words, Vanessa looked at him in dismay. "Yes," she replied in a whisper, regretting with all her heart the harm her reckless brother had caused poor young Olivia. "I understand. And I promise you, my lord, I will do everything in my power to help her."

It was a long moment before the intensity of his gaze relented. Slowly Damien nodded and then turned his head once more to stare out the carriage window.

Some quarter hour later Vanessa felt the carriage slow and turn off the main road onto an avenue lined by stately elms.

"We have arrived," her host informed her absently.

In the distance a glimmer of water captured Vanessa's attention. When the carriage rounded a curve, she caught her breath at the vista. Rosewood obviously was not only the family home of a wealthy nobleman; it was a place of stunning beauty.

A shining lake lay in the center of the park, which was dotted with groves of beech and chestnut, while crowning a slight rise, an imposing estate built of mellow golden ironstone stood in magnificent glory. Vanessa spied a red deer grazing near the water's edge before the carriage moved on and swung around the cobbled drive. The instant the conveyance came to a halt, several grooms and footmen leapt to assistance.

As Lord Sinclair helped Vanessa alight from the carriage, she was greeted by the sweet fragrance of roses that filled the soft, late-afternoon air.

"You must be fatigued from the long journey, Lady Wyndham," he said in a voice strong enough to carry to his servants. "I shall have your trunks taken to your room at once."

"Thank you, my lord. I would be glad to wash off my travel dust, but then perhaps you will introduce your sister. If it is not too late, we might even take tea together."

Damien's mouth curled in a frown. "If you can persuade Olivia to take tea, you will have accomplished more than I have. You'll find she doesn't eat enough to keep a sparrow alive."

He escorted her up the marble stairway and into the house, where they were met by a formal staff. Lord Sinclair spoke briefly to a tall, ruddy-cheeked steward, whom he then introduced as Bellows.

"Lady Wyndham," he added, "has graciously agreed to be our guest for a time and hopes to provide companionship to Miss Olivia."

Vanessa realized the conversation was for the benefit of his employees, but she was grateful he had couched her position in such genteel terms.

Bellows in turn presented the stately butler, Croft, and the portly housekeeper, Mrs. Nesbit, who curtsyed and beamed a good-natured smile. " 'Tis an honor to have you at Rosewood, my lady."

"We usually keep town hours when I'm at home," Damien informed her, "with dinner served at eight. Mrs. Nesbit will show you to the Chalice Chamber, and when you are ready, I will introduce you to my sister."

With a polite smile at Damien, Vanessa allowed Mrs. Nesbit to lead her upstairs. The housekeeper, it seemed, was the chatty sort, confiding in an affable tone that "young Miss Olivia, bless her soul, could do with a friend. If you can aid that dear child, we will all be forever indebted to you."

The bedchamber that awaited Vanessa was a bit opulent for her taste, with its gold and green brocades and damasks and walls hung in watered silk. But it was elegant enough for a duchess . . . or a cherished mistress.

The room was immense, with a separate sitting area in addition to the curtained bed. Arrayed before the large fireplace were a plush chaise lounge and a pair of Chippendale wing chairs. For refreshment, decanters of brandy and port rested on a side table, while on another table, between two tall windows, stood an ornate silver cup embellished with intricately carved roses.

"Is that why the room is called the Chalice Chamber?" she asked curiously, indicating the cup.

"The very reason. That fancy silver 'twas said to be a gift from Queen Elizabeth herself to the first Baron Sinclair."

While the housekeeper made a quick tour of the room to check that all was in order, Vanessa went to the window and looked down. Evidently the three-story manor was made up of a vast central wing with two side wings surrounding a garden courtyard. To her surprise and delight, she discovered that the courtyard was ablaze with roses, and that the terraced gardens seemed to stretch far into the distance.

"How beautiful," she murmured involuntarily.

"Indeed it is," Mrs. Nesbit seconded. "His lordship has a way with roses, that he does."

"His lordship? You can't mean the present Baron Sinclair."

"I do, my lady."

"*Damien* Sinclair?"

"None other." Mrs. Nesbit grinned. "These gardens were but a shadow of their present glory before he took an interest in them. You might be surprised to learn that botanists and scholars regularly come to study here, my lady, and famous artists as well. Most times in the summer you can't stroll down a path without tripping over a stranger sketching or painting."

"I confess, I am exceedingly surprised."

"Well, 'tis true. His lordship even has a strain or two named after him by some highbrowed horticulture society, not that he sought the honor. In any event, roses have been in the family since the Crusades."

Vanessa remembered seeing the roses on the Sinclair coat of arms displayed on the coach door.

"If you will permit me, my lady, I'll fetch warm water for you to wash with and light a fire to keep away the night chill. Would you like your tea served in the parlor or drawing room, or would you prefer a tray be brought here?"

"Here would be fine, but first I should like to meet Miss Olivia."

"Certainly, my lady. I'll take you to his lordship directly."

"Thank you, Mrs. Nesbit."

"Did an abigail accompany you, my lady?"

Vanessa shook her head. "No, I have no abigail with me." While a lady's maid would have lent her a measure of consequence and respectability, she could ill-afford personal servants all her own, nor did she want to take them away from her mother or sisters.

"If you wish," the housekeeper offered, "I shall send Miss Olivia's personal maid to help you dress for dinner."

"That would be most appreciated."

When she was alone, Vanessa turned back to the window to gaze down thoughtfully. Damien Sinclair was turning out to be a man of unexpected depth. And she wasn't sure whether to be pleased or wary.

When Vanessa had freshened up, the housekeeper escorted her to a bedchamber in the main wing. The door had been left open, but the curtains were drawn and the room was dim, just as she'd been warned it would be.

In the faint light, she could see Damien sitting beside the bed, silently contemplating the invalid lying there. When Vanessa rapped softly on the door panel, he rose with a murmured "Come in."

His features remained expressionless as she entered, as if he had clamped down on any show of emotion. His tone of voice, however, held a hint of anger. "Lady Wyndham, please allow me to present my sister, Olivia."

When her eyes adjusted to the dim light, Vanessa could make out the young woman on the bed. The Honorable Olivia Sinclair was more striking than beautiful, with the same ebony hair and elegantly chiseled features as her older brother. Yet she had none of the intensity or vitality or aura of tightly leashed power that Damien Sinclair had in such abundance. Olivia's complexion was pale, her expression wan and listless.

Her heart aching for the girl, Vanessa smiled gently and stretched out her hand. Asking "how do you do?" would have been totally inappropriate, so she said instead, "I am pleased to make your acquaintance."

Olivia made no effort to take the proffered hand. She merely turned her head away.

"Olivia . . ." Lord Sinclair said in a low, warning voice.

Vanessa shook her head briefly. Olivia's spirits not only had fallen into a decline, they seemed to be nonexistent. Yet haranguing her would serve no purpose.

"Might we have a few moments alone, my lord?"

His dark brows drew together as he glanced sharply at her, but he acquiesced. "If you wish."

Vanessa waited until he had gone before taking the chair beside the bed and addressing Olivia in a friendly tone. "I wished to speak to you without your brother present. He is a formidable figure, is he not?"

There was a long silence. "I suppose some people might think so." Her tone was flat, as if she could summon little interest in anything.

"But you do not?" Vanessa prodded gently, believing even a grudging response was better than none at all. When none was forthcoming, she added, "But then you have known him all your life, so you wouldn't find him intimidating—"

"Lady Wyndham," Olivia interrupted softly, turning her head to gaze at her, "I know my brother means well, but I have no need of a companion."

Vanessa smiled easily and settled back in her chair, refusing to be defeated. "Perhaps not. And in your circumstances, I might feel similarly. It cannot be pleasant to have a stranger foisted upon you. But you and I do not have to remain strangers. Indeed, I hope we might become friends. If you don't wish it, however, perhaps you might just allow me to attend you occasionally, to provide you with company."

"I don't wish to seem impolite, but I do not want any company."

"Even so, you might agree to bear *me* company. Since I am to be here in the country for several weeks at least, I imagine I will grow exceedingly lonely with no one to talk to. Would you mind very much if I visited you occasionally? You wouldn't have to speak to me, or even acknowledge my presence. And I could refrain from conversing with you. Then again, it might prove awkward with us each ignoring the other. We would resemble an old wedded couple who scarcely say a word to each other from dawn to dusk."

The image brought the faintest hint of amusement to the girl's lips, and Vanessa felt a small ray of hope that eventually she could get through to her.

"Of course," she added casually, "you might come to find my companionship agreeable. I could read to you, comb your hair, share confidences . . . the sort of things sisters do."

Olivia looked away, before saying sadly, almost wistfully, "I've never had a sister."

"I have two of them, both younger. Come to think of it, you remind me a little of Fanny. She has your coloring, although I cannot tell about your eyes. Are they gray like your brother's?"

There was a long pause. "Blue. My eyes are blue."

"I've always wanted to have blue eyes. Mine are dark, like a horse's. My brother always ribbed me unmercifully about them when we were children. He used to call me Old Ned, after an aging hack who had been turned out to pasture."

When Olivia remained silent, Vanessa leaned forward in her chair. "I brought you a present."

For the first time, Olivia showed a spark of interest. She cocked her head a degree. "A present? What is it?"

"Telling would spoil the pleasure, wouldn't it?"

"I suppose."

She held out the small package. "Would you care to open it, or shall I?"

"You do it."

Vanessa carefully untied the ribbon and removed the tissue paper. Inside was an exquisite gold-embossed volume bound in calfskin. It had cost her dearly, a sum Vanessa could ill-afford, yet she considered it a small price to pay if one counted what her family owed this young girl.

She handed the book to Olivia, who peered at the cover but couldn't seem to make out the title in the darkness.

"Should I light a lamp?"

"Yes . . . please."

Vanessa obliged, but although she kept the flame low, Olivia shielded her eyes as if in pain. A moment later, however, her vision seemed to adjust.

"Oh . . ." The word was a whisper spoken almost reverently.

The gift was a collection of sonnets by William Shakespeare, chosen because Aubrey had said Olivia liked poetry.

Vanessa felt a sharp twinge of guilt at the reminder. She was here under false pretenses, and yet her subterfuge was necessary. She couldn't reveal her connection to the man who had brought the girl low. Olivia would certainly never allow her close enough to help if she knew the truth.

"Thank you, Lady Wyndham."

"Do you think you could bring yourself to call me Vanessa?"

"Yes . . . Vanessa. Thank you."

"So you enjoy Shakespeare?"

"Very much. And the edition is beautiful. I shall cherish your gift."

"I would be happy to read to you sometime, if you would permit me."

For a long moment Olivia regarded her, searching her face with intelligence and a quiet wisdom. "You are very persistent, I think."

Vanessa smiled. "Quite. My mama says it is my greatest failing. But, like Old Ned, I have excessive reserves of endurance."

To her delight, the two of them shared an intimate moment of accord.

"Where did you find so lovely a volume?" Olivia asked softly.

"At Hatchard's bookshop in London. If you like, I shall take you there the next time you are in town."

"I doubt I will be going to London anytime in the future," the girl replied bitterly.

"No? Your brother told me he hoped to take you there next

year for your come-out." That wasn't quite true, but Vanessa had no doubt that if Olivia expressed even the slightest interest, Damien would give her a dozen come-outs.

Olivia raised eyes that were full of pain. "How can I have a Season," she asked, her voice low, desolate, "when I cannot walk, let alone dance?"

Her heart hurting, Vanessa reached out to take the girl's hand. "My dear, I cannot pretend to know how difficult this all must be for you, but I do know you needn't face it alone. You have people who care for you, who will help you through the worst of it, if you only let them."

"I suppose Damien told you . . . what happened."

"He told me that you met with a tragic accident which you in no way deserved."

"I thought . . . he was angry with me . . . for behaving so foolishly."

"No. If anything, he is angry at himself for not protecting you better. From what I've seen, your brother cherishes you. He would do anything in his power to help you get well."

"He doesn't cherish me, not really." Olivia's voice trembled. "He never paid me the slightest heed until my . . . accident. I've always been alone."

"I know he regrets that. And you aren't alone, Olivia. The servants obviously adore you, and I'm certain you have friends who are concerned for you."

A tear spilled down her pale cheek. "Some of my friends called at first, but I . . . turned them all away. I didn't wish them to see me like this."

"That is understandable," Vanessa said gently. "And were I in your place, I daresay I would have felt the same way. It would be easier simply to give up, to believe my life over, to lie on my couch and never have to face the world. It would be easier . . . but it would not be fair."

"Fair?"

"To your brother. I cannot believe you have any notion how much he blames himself for letting this tragedy befall you."

"He wasn't to blame," Olivia admitted in a low voice.

"You will never convince him of that, not as long as he can do nothing to help ease your misery. He is hurting for you, Olivia. Is that what you want?"

There was an obvious hesitation. "No . . ." she said reluctantly. "I don't want Damien to hurt for me."

"Then you might begin by agreeing to see the physician he has engaged for you. Even if you show little progress, you will at least have tried for his sake."

When Olivia turned her face away, Vanessa felt her heart sink.

"There," she murmured, "I believe I've said enough. I shan't badger you any longer, but will leave you to rest." She paused. "Would you like me to turn out the light before I go?"

"No . . ." Olivia said in a small voice. "Leave it on, please. I should like to read my sonnets."

Vanessa felt the constricted feeling in her chest ease a little. She had made a tiny measure of progress, at least. And she had given the girl something to think about besides her sorrow and shame. Yet it would be a long, difficult task to bring Olivia Sinclair to any semblance of her former health or spirit.

She changed for dinner several hours later with the assistance of a maid whom the housekeeper sent. With inordinate care, Vanessa chose a high-waisted gown of powder blue silk, more for its demureness than for its admittedly flattering lines. Unfamiliar with her new role of rake's mistress, she preferred to err on the side of modesty.

It was with renewed trepidation that she sought out the drawing room on the lower floor. Daylight was fading with the setting sun, and the moment was swiftly approaching when she would be required to fulfill the amorous duties she had agreed to.

She found her nemesis standing at one of the open French doors, staring out at the courtyard gardens. The soft golds and crimson of approaching twilight bathed the scene and entwined with the scent of roses to create a magical aura, yet Damien Sinclair did not seem to have passion on his mind. He stood still as a statue, his lean-muscled frame looking sleek and powerful in a tailored blue dinner jacket.

Drawn to him in spite of herself, Vanessa crossed the elegant room silently and came to stand beside him. He didn't immediately acknowledge her presence, and yet she was certain of his awareness. Her own senses had taken on a fresh alertness, heightened by misgivings about what the evening would bring.

When at last he spoke in a low voice, the question he chose surprised her a little. "Do you like roses, Vanessa?"

"Very much. Your gardens are spectacular." When he made no reply, she ventured her own comment. "I understand they are your own creation."

"Not creation. Resurrection. In my younger days I rescued them from oblivion and my noble sire's willful destruction."

Hearing the edge of cynicism in his tone, Vanessa glanced up at Damien's profile. The snowy white linen of his cravat seemed to accentuate the chiseled beauty of his face. Her pulse quickened, as it always did at his overwhelming nearness. And yet his mind was obviously not on her.

"So what is your assessment of my sister?" he asked with a casualness that seemed feigned.

She hesitated, not wanting to raise his hopes excessively. "I think you were correct. She is a deeply troubled young lady. Not only because of her physical infirmity, which is daunting enough in itself, but because she perceives little reason to hope for a better future. But I also believe it is too soon to despair."

His gaze remained hooded as he stared out at the golden-hued beds of roses. "Olivia used to love roaming these paths. Now she won't come near the gardens."

"You care for her very much." It wasn't a question.

"If I could bear her suffering in her place, I would. Gladly." The soft conviction in his voice left no room for doubt.

Vanessa looked away. She could not imagine this strong, vital man as an invalid. He was a man who would reach out and grasp fate and shape it to his own desires.

With a shake of his head, however, he seemed to shrug off his dour mood, while the grim line of his mouth relaxed. "But I am acting an uncongenial host. Forgive me."

He turned to regard her. His gaze swept over her slowly, lingering on the modest cut of her neckline. His smile, when it came, was soft, apologetic, ripe with unconscious sensuality.

Vanessa shivered at the quivering feeling of intimate warmth that overcame her.

"Allow me to escort you in to dinner, my lady."

When he offered his arm, she placed trembling fingers on his sleeve and allowed him to lead her to the smaller of two dining rooms. Even so, the mahogany table was immense. A pair of tall, silver candelabra graced the center, while one end was laid with twin settings of crystal and china.

With reluctance, Vanessa took her seat at his lordship's right, self-conscious about the intimacy of dining alone with him in such close proximity.

The Madeira wine proved delicious, the meal a treasure of culinary delights. The first two removes featured clear turtle soup with truffles, and a dish of smoked salmon with aspic, followed by a ragout of veal, roast venison, green peas, and cauliflower, and braised pigeons with mint sauce. Despite the long day, however, Vanessa found herself with little appetite.

The conversation remained desultory. While Lord Sinclair put himself out to be charming, narrating some interesting history of the house, Vanessa grew more and more quiet, responding in monosyllables and only picking at the food on her plate.

Her appetite had deserted her by the time the sweets were served, and her nerves were keenly on edge. She barely tasted the cheese brioche, the pineapple cream, or the almonds toasted with sugar and cinnamon.

"Are the dishes not to your taste, my lady?" Damien finally asked mildly. "Shall I reprimand the cook?"

Vanessa swallowed. "No . . . everything is delicious." Her voice held a thin, breathless note.

"Then why have you scarcely touched a bite?"

Instead of replying directly, she murmured, "Shall I leave you to your port now, my lord?"

"We needn't stand on ceremony with just the two of us."

When Damien motioned to the footman to refill her wineglass for the last time and then dismissed the servants, she felt her panic rise. No doubt he wished to discuss the matter of her carnal duties and preferred to do it discreetly.

Forcing herself to meet his gaze, she indicated her wine-glass, which had been filled to the brim. "Is it your strategy to ply me with wine, the better to render me susceptible to your advances?"

He studied her for a long moment. "When the time comes, angel, I will have no need of wine to render you susceptible, I assure you." He smiled, a tender, charming smile. "In truth, I want you fully in command of all your senses. The better to enjoy the moment."

An irrational surge of anger sparked through Vanessa. "Does my agitation amuse you, my lord? Does it please you to mock me?"

She flinched when he rose abruptly, but he merely went to the bellpull and rang for the butler. When Croft arrived almost instantaneously, Damien had settled in his chair once more.

"Be so kind as to send Mrs. Nesbit here, Croft."

"Certainly, my lord," the stately butler replied. "At once."

Vanessa waited in bewilderment, wondering why he would summon the housekeeper.

Mrs. Nesbit, when she arrived, looked just as puzzled. "You rang, my lord?"

"Do you have the key to the Chalice Chamber?"

"Key, my lord?"

"Yes, to Lady Wyndham's room. I presume you carry it on your ring?"

"Yes, my lord." She patted the giant ring hanging from her waist. "I carry the keys to all the rooms of the house."

"May I have it, please?"

The housekeeper searched her accumulation of keys for

a moment. When she found the one in question, she handed it to his lordship.

"Is this the only key to that room?"

"To my knowledge, my lord."

"Thank you, Mrs. Nesbit, that will be all."

When they were alone once more, Damien held out his hand to Vanessa, the key resting in his palm. "If it will make you feel safer, angel, you are welcome to keep this in your possession."

She searched his handsome face, looking for any hint of deception. She found none. He seemed entirely serious.

"I will repeat, Vanessa. You needn't fear my forcing myself on you," he said softly. "Despite my numerous faults, I would never ravish an unwilling woman. You are safe from me for now."

Vanessa swallowed. The silence stretched between them.

"Take it."

The key was still warm from his palm as she closed her fingers around the smooth metal. "Thank you," she murmured thickly.

"My pleasure."

The word was a husky whisper. She froze when Damien reached up to touch her. His hand stilled for an instant, before he caressed her cheek with a gentle finger.

The startling tenderness of the gesture held her immobile. This side of him, this sensitive, considerate side, contrasted so starkly with the heartless devil who had compelled her to become his mistress.

"I am just a man, no monster," he murmured. "In time you will come to accept that."

With a sigh then, Damien picked up his wineglass and leaned back in his chair. "Go to bed, angel."

"To bed?"

His mouth twisted faintly at the hint of alarm in her tone. "Alone, love. You are free to retire alone. I won't demand to share your bed. I'll wait until you invite me."

Vanessa rose on trembling legs. He meant to let her go. "Sleep well."

She made her escape before he could change his mind.

When she reached the Chalice Chamber, Vanessa shut the door behind her and leaned weakly against it. Damien had given her a reprieve. For tonight, at least, he didn't mean to force her to fulfill their brazen bargain.

The key in her hand seemed to burn a brand in her flesh.

After a moment's hesitation, she bolted the door and then placed the key on the dressing table. Then she turned to survey the elegant chamber, wondering what she should do.

The lamps had been lit and a fire burned cheerily in the grate, while the covers of the bed had been turned down invitingly. At the moment, however, she felt too restless to sleep or even to read.

The draperies had been closed against the night air, but she drew them wide, letting the moonlight stream into the room. For some time Vanessa stood at the window, watching the silent gardens below, letting the silver-white peace soothe her frayed nerves.

Finally, though, she turned away and put out the lamps.

In the semidarkness she removed her gown and donned a cambric nightdress, wondering wryly what Damien Sinclair would think of her modest attire. She supposed that when he did at last demand that she honor their bargain, he would require a filmy negligee or some such trifling costume.

The bed was soft and welcoming. The long journey and the tension of the evening had taken a greater toll than she realized, and before she knew it, Vanessa fell asleep.

She dreamed of him . . . of Lord Sin restlessly walking the night. Of Damien taking her in his arms, of his kissing her.

His kiss was tender and passionate, sweet and fiery all at once. It had the power to rob her of breath, to make her limbs melt like warm honey. . . .

When she came awake, the delicate scent of roses greeted her while her body throbbed with a strange heat.

She couldn't tell what had roused her from sleep. For a moment Vanessa lay there listening to the quiet crackle of the fire in the hearth and the slow beat of her own heart.

Moonlight poured through the open draperies, and in the luminous glow, she realized something lay on the pillow beside her.

Hesitantly she reached out to touch it. It was a rose, slender, fragile, soft as velvet.

Wondering if she were still dreaming, she lifted her gaze to stare across the room . . . directly into the silver-smoke eyes of Damien Sinclair.

Chapter Five

He was lounging before the fire in a brocade dressing robe of midnight blue. Still watching her, he raised a snifter to his lips.

"Would you care for a brandy, angel?"

He was no dream, she realized. His voice was soft and sensual as the moonlight, the expression on his handsome face just as beguiling.

Unsure whether to be alarmed, Vanessa fumbled for the silk wrapper draped across the foot of her bed. "What do you want, my lord?"

"Would you be surprised if I said companionship?" When she stared at him, he shrugged. "I find sleep eludes me at times, especially since my sister's accident. I prefer not to deal with my demons alone. Will you not join me here by the fire?"

Not wanting to remain in such a vulnerable position, she drew on the wrapper over her nightdress and rose from the bed. When she had buttoned the garment to her neck, she approached him cautiously, moving to stand near the fire.

"How did you get in here? You must have used a key."

"No, you possess the only key."

"Then how?"

"Would you believe me if I said a secret passageway? A former Baron Sinclair had it built during Cromwell's bloody reign to provide a swift means of escape. But my father made use of it to gain convenient access to his mistresses." Damien gestured toward a corner of the room closest to the windows. "A panel in the wall moves aside."

A surge of anger claimed Vanessa at his deception. "Why then did you make such a show of giving me the key to my bedchamber if you had entry all along?"

"Confess, did you not feel easier in your mind, believing yourself safe from me?"

"You said you wouldn't come here until I invited you."

"I said I wouldn't demand to share your bed—and I won't."

She could think of no immediate reply, knowing he was right, yet his rationale only rekindled her resentment.

His gaze remained soft. "I meant what I said, Vanessa. You have nothing to fear from me."

She stared at him, cursing her own foolhardiness. Damien Sinclair should have presented a menacing, sinister figure, wandering like a ghost in the night, intruding wherever he pleased, watching her sleep. But, strangely, she wasn't afraid of him. She was merely angry. First he had forced her into this untenable situation. Then he'd failed to honor his word in spirit, if not in letter.

"I do not fear you," she retorted, raising her chin.

"But you don't trust me." He smiled faintly. "Your eyes are eloquently expressive."

"Most certainly I don't trust you. I believe you've given me little reason to."

"I shall have to convince you otherwise."

She shifted uncomfortably on her bare feet, wondering if she had the right to demand he leave.

"Meanwhile . . ." His gaze surveyed her, lingering on the plaited braid of her hair. "Will you not join me?" he repeated. "I am not bent on seduction tonight, I promise you. All I am interested in coaxing from you is perhaps a little conversation." When still she hesitated, he took a different tack. "I came to thank you, actually."

"Thank me?"

"I visited Olivia after dinner. She has agreed to see Dr. Underhill."

Despite her anger, Vanessa was relieved to hear the news. "I am glad."

"What did you say to persuade her?"

"Nothing much. I played on her sense of familial duty, I suppose. I made her aware of your remorse at not being able to help her. Perhaps she decided to make an effort for your sake, if not her own."

Damien frowned. "I find that hard to credit. As you've no doubt deduced, we aren't on the best of terms."

"Olivia says she doesn't blame you for her misfortune."

"Perhaps not, but she blames me for neglecting her all these years. I've spent the past two months trying to improve our relationship, to little avail." Damien shook his head. "You were able to draw her out in less than a day. I was exceedingly surprised to discover her reading Shakespeare. That is the first time since her accident, I believe." He paused before adding reluctantly, "You have my gratitude."

His praise sounded somewhat grudging, as if he meant to withhold judgment about her and her methods.

"It is only a first step," Vanessa observed, her own tone just as grudging. "She still has a long, long way to go."

"A long way indeed," Damien murmured darkly, staring down at his brandy for a moment. "How did you know her taste in poetry?"

"My brother told me."

Damien's jaw hardened visibly, reminding Vanessa of her own deception regarding his sister. But he appeared determined to shrug off any somberness.

He gestured toward the chaise lounge. "Will you oblige me by joining me, Vanessa?"

Although extremely reluctant to be so near to him under such intimate circumstances, Vanessa clamped down on her resentment and capitulated. She chose the wing chair opposite him, however, recalling the last time she had found herself on a couch with the decadent Lord Sin. Trying to banish the memory of his erotic kisses and his even more erotic caressing of her breasts, she curled up in the chair and tucked her feet beneath her.

For the space of a dozen heartbeats, she waited for Lord Sinclair to say something, but he only sipped his brandy in silence while he stared into the flames.

Vanessa found herself watching him warily. The firelight played over his features, illuminating the stark beauty of his face, making her breath quicken.

She had been truthful about not fearing him, yet his presence here, in the moonlit darkness, still seemed a threat. The sensuality of the moment disturbed her greatly.

Even so, she had to remember the bargain she'd made. As much as she deplored his extortion, it was still better than the alternative—her family cast out of their home and living in penury. She had agreed to become his mistress. *She,* at least, would honor her word. She would provide him with conversation if he asked it of her.

"What shall we talk about?" she asked, the question more curt than welcoming.

He raised his gaze to her. "Why don't you tell me about yourself."

"What would you like to know?"

He shrugged. "Whatever you choose to tell me. I wonder, for instance, why we never became acquainted before this. You must have spent time in London."

"A fair amount. Until my father's passing two years ago, my family removed to town every spring."

"I don't recall meeting you, and I think I would have remembered."

She couldn't help but smile. "I doubt you paid any attention to schoolroom misses." Vanessa eyed him curiously. "I could not help but notice *you*. During my first Season, you attended several of the same functions I did. I remember one ball in particular where you caused quite a stir. Something about a certain lady pursuing you into your club on St. James Street. The scandal provided the ton entertainment for at least a week."

His mouth twisted in a wry grimace. "I would prefer you not remind me." He studied her. "You are no stranger to scandal yourself, I believe. I knew your husband, although not well. If memory serves, Sir Roger was embroiled in his fair share of scandal."

It was her turn to grimace. "I try not to dwell on it."

"Why did you wed him then, if you were so averse to his way of life?"

She looked away, gazing into the fire. "Why does any young lady wed? To oblige my family, of course. It was considered a highly advantageous match, and my father wished it. In truth, Papa was . . . in rather desperate financial straits. Roger was flush in the pockets, having just come into his inheritance."

"Still, I would have thought you would have some say in the matter."

Turning her head, Vanessa met his eyes directly. "You

have a sister for whom you're willing to go to great lengths. Is it so difficult to comprehend why I would wish to help my family?"

"Were there no choices other than Sir Roger?"

"He seemed the best. At the time, he hadn't embarked on his . . . wild career." She couldn't repress a sigh. "I would rather not discuss my late husband, if it is all the same to you. That was an unpleasant time in my life, and I have endeavored to put it behind me."

"Very well. I shall make a pact with you. You refrain from mentioning your brother in my hearing, and I will refrain from mentioning your late husband."

There was a short silence while Damien sipped his brandy, his eyes heavy-lidded but watchful. "So after your marriage ended, you returned home?"

"Yes. It was then that I discovered the . . . true state of my finances." Vanessa struggled with another painful memory; the shock of Roger's death had scarcely passed before a swarm of creditors descended upon her. She'd been dazed to learn that he had managed to squander his vast fortune on gaming and expensive mistresses. "It seemed foolish to try to maintain a household of my own. And by that time my father was gone and my family needed me with them."

"Your father suffered a riding accident, did he not?"

"Yes, he was thrown from a horse while hunting. How did you know?"

"After my sister's calamity, I made it a point to investigate her seducer. Your mother has not been incapacitated for long, I think."

"No. She took to her bed when my father died and never fully recovered from her period of mourning. Much of her suffering, I believe, is of the heart rather than physical in nature. She was very much in love with my father."

Damien's mouth curved cynically, but he let her observation pass and cast a casual glance around the chamber. "Are you comfortable here?"

"Yes . . . at least I was until a short while ago," she added wryly.

His eyebrows rose. "Until a certain midnight visitor dropped in on you unexpectedly?"

"Precisely."

"You don't mince words, do you?"

"Under these circumstances, there seems to be little point. I did warn you that I had no experience as a gentleman's mistress. I'm sorry to disappoint you, but I am not practiced in the arts of coyness and flirtation."

His smile was amused. "You haven't disappointed me, angel-eyes. On the contrary, I find candidness refreshing in a lady."

"Oh? And are you acquainted with many ladies? I own I'm surprised."

He chuckled. "I see I shall have to try to be a better host. In addition to giving you the opportunity to exercise your sharp wit on me, I will endeavor to find activities to entertain and occupy you. Do you like to read?"

Vanessa replied with all seriousness, "Very much."

"You are welcome to use my library whenever you please."

"Thank you. I shall take you up on your offer—whenever you are not availing yourself of it."

"And you ride, I presume?"

"Yes."

"Then you should choose a mount from my stables. Olivia's horses badly need exercise." He frowned. "One of her greatest pleasures was riding. She frequently was in the saddle from morning till night."

Sensing his darkening mood, Vanessa offered a consoling thought. "Perhaps in time she will be so again." When Damien made no reply, she made an effort to change the subject. "I am also surprised that you enjoy such mundane pleasures as reading and riding."

"I enjoy many pleasures, sweeting."

"So I understand. Your enjoyments are legion. The tales one hears of you are enough to set even the most jaded tongues wagging."

"What exactly have you heard?"

"That you founded the latest order of the Hellfire League, for instance."

"Cofounded. I and some half-dozen of my colleagues."

"Its reputation is rather unsavory. Rumor has it that you regularly indulge in orgies and perversions."

"You give us too much credit. We are a pale imitation of the Hellfire Club that was active during our grandfathers' time."

"But it is still a fraternity for depraved libertines, I imagine."

"Depraved libertines? Is that not a redundancy?"

"Not in your case, I expect, my lord."

He gave a mock wince. "I thought you agreed to call me Damien."

Vanessa ignored his personal remark. "Is it true the price of membership is ten thousand pounds?"

"Yes."

She started to demand why he had invited her brother to join, but she knew the answer to that; he was intent on bankrupting Aubrey. Besides, she had made a pact to refrain from mentioning her brother.

"I trust the price is worth it," she said instead. "Do you allow women to become members?"

His brow arched. "Not at the moment, but I imagine we could make an exception. Are you wrangling for an invitation?"

"Certainly not," she responded with amusement. "In the first place, I could not afford the subscription fee. And in the second, I have never much cared for the company of rakes."

"You've made me well aware of your opinion on that score. But have you never considered that perhaps I'm not as debauched as you think?"

"No," she answered truthfully.

"Sweeting, you still have a great deal to learn about me. I expect to enjoy teaching you."

She suspected that he was baiting her, but she answered in kind even so. "Perhaps you will, but you flatter yourself if you expect *me* to enjoy it. Not every woman is eager to fall under the spell of the wicked Lord Sin."

A silver gleam entered his eyes. "I am devastated."

"I doubt it. Were you devastated, you would not be so glib with your rejoinders."

The suggestion in his hedonist's smile made her pulse quicken. The smile reached his eyes, and Vanessa found herself captivated. It was a mistake to allow herself to be drawn into banter with him, no matter how much she might enjoy it. She was far too vulnerable to the sensual charm of this legendary rake.

To her surprise, he rose slowly to his feet. "You are too clever by half, vixen. I can see I will have my hands full, dealing with you."

She tensed as he moved toward her, but he merely stood gazing down at her. "I could continue trading barbs with you, but I should go and leave you to sleep. Unless you would consider inviting me to stay the night . . . ?" Her pointed silence gave him his answer. "Very well. It has been a pleasure, sweeting."

She was surprised that she could honestly agree.

"I hope you will permit me to return here occasionally when I am too restless to sleep and share your company for an hour or two."

"I suppose you mean to tell me I have a choice?"

"Most certainly. But you might find yourself enjoying the companionship. Rosewood can be a lonely place."

He spoke from experience, she suspected, hearing the oddly wistful note in his quiet voice.

She held her breath as he reached out to her, but he only touched her cheek in farewell, brushing his thumb lightly over her skin. Then he withdrew his hand and turned away.

Without speaking, he approached the side of the room. She watched as he pushed aside the panel and disappeared into the secret passageway like a silent phantom. The panel slid closed behind him with a soft click, leaving her alone in the moonlit chamber.

After a moment, Vanessa rose and went to inspect the panel. She could find no mechanism that allowed entry. Wondering at Damien Sinclair's sorcery, she turned and leaned back against the wall. There had been a dreamlike quality to his remarkable visit, and she had enjoyed every moment of it.

Bewildered, she shook her head. She had wanted to despise the profligate nobleman, but instead found herself intrigued by their game of wits. Her common sense had deserted her, along with the need to protect herself.

The growing intimacy between them was a worse threat. She didn't like feeling sympathy for him, yet she sensed in him a loneliness as great as her own.

When her eye caught the dark splash of red on the white

linen of her pillow, she remembered the rose he had brought her. Slowly Vanessa crossed the room to lift the velvet bloom to her nose, taking care to avoid the thorns.

More troubled than she cared to admit, she drank in the sweet scent. If only a few days ago someone had predicted she would willingly entertain the notorious Lord Sin in her bedchamber, or that she would walk away unscathed, she would never have believed it. He was still the heartless devil who had bargained for her soul. Thus far, however, he had made no demands on her. He hadn't touched her, if one discounted the gentle, spellbinding stroking of her cheek when he'd said good night.

Yet he was still incredibly dangerous. Quite apart from his sensual charm and heartbreaker handsomeness, Damien Sinclair possessed a potent quality that beckoned and lured, a compelling vitality that called to everything deeply feminine within her. Despite her hard-won experience with notorious rakes, she was so very vulnerable to him.

Heaven help her, she had only her wits with which to protect herself, a pitiful weapon indeed. He'd made no secret of his aim. He had vowed to seduce her—and to make her enjoy her seduction. And if she were not careful, he would succeed.

She slept well and dreamlessly and awakened later than usual, to bright sunshine flooding the chamber. With an unusual sense of anticipation, Vanessa rose and dressed and went downstairs to breakfast.

She was unsurprised to discover the sideboard groaning with hearty fare including broiled kidneys, ham, eggs, scones, and jam tarts. A footman stood ready to assist her, but there was no sign of Damien, much to her relief.

Barely was she seated when the butler, Croft, made an

appearance. When Vanessa casually asked where Lord Sinclair might be, she was told he had breakfasted early and was closeted with his steward.

"His lordship has placed his stables at your disposal, if you care to ride this morning, my lady," Croft informed her.

"Thank you, I might. I think I should visit his sister first to discover her wishes."

When she finished eating, Vanessa made her way back upstairs to Olivia's room. She found the girl lying in bed, still in her nightclothes, but at least the curtains were open a crack and the room wasn't in total darkness.

From the way Olivia's expression brightened, Vanessa concluded that her presence was welcome.

"I thought I might investigate your beautiful rose gardens this morning," she began cheerfully, "but I could use a guide. Since your brother is occupied with his steward, I hoped you might be willing to show them to me."

"You want me to show you the gardens?" Olivia asked warily.

"I'm told you are very fond of roses." Vanessa nodded toward the wheeled invalid chair standing in the corner. "We could have a footman carry you downstairs, and I think I could push your chair along the paths."

Olivia made a face. "I despise using that chair. I feel so helpless in it. But I suppose that is a childish sentiment."

"No indeed. But it can offer you a measure of freedom you couldn't have otherwise."

"I suppose so." The girl raised her chin gamely. "Very well. I will show you the gardens if you like."

"You will need a bonnet to protect your lovely complexion. The sun is quite bright, even for the first day of June."

"Is it June?" Olivia asked, startled. "I hadn't realized."

Her voice turned wistful. "I've been lying abed for so long, all the days run together."

She rang for her abigail, who, along with two other maids, helped her dress in a white Swiss muslin gown and red velvet spencer as well as a heavy shawl to ward off the last of the morning chill.

Her eagerness was heartbreaking. When the footman carried her out into the garden, Olivia blinked at the golden brightness. But the instant she was settled in her invalid chair, she raised her face to the warmth of the life-giving sunlight and gave a sigh of pleasure.

"I have missed coming here," she murmured as Vanessa moved behind her to guide the wheeled chair.

"There is no reason you cannot come every day, is there?"

Olivia's mouth curved in a wry half-smile, and when she glanced up, Vanessa caught the hint of amusement in her blue eyes. "You will not need a guide every day."

"No, but I will need a companion."

"You are indeed persistent, Lady Wyndham."

She smiled. "I did give you fair warning. And, please, call me Vanessa."

They wandered the paths slowly, admiring the flowers and discussing the variety of roses in the vast gardens. Olivia was quite knowledgeable about the subject, and could even quote details about individual bushes.

They were not alone. Gardeners moved among the beds with hoes and shovels and pruning shears, and several strangers dressed as scholars occupied the paths, pens and notebooks in hand. In a corner near the house, an artist had set up an easel and was thoughtfully painting in watercolor.

Vanessa took care to avoid the others and stopped frequently for Olivia to rest. There were benches scattered here and there, arranged artfully beneath ornamental shade trees, and several times she guided the girl's chair to get her out of the sun.

"I never realized," Vanessa said during one of those intervals, "how complex the breeding of roses could be."

"Indeed. Damien deserves credit for reestablishing the cultivation program. He made Rosewood famous for its collection. Even Napoleon has heard of us," Olivia added with pride. "Several years ago, when Empress Josephine acquired a sample of every living rose for her gardens, her nurserymen began the search here. The Prince Regent issued special passes for them to work here. And despite our naval blockade of France, the Admiralty ruled that if her plants were ever intercepted at sea, they should be forwarded to her at once."

Nearly an hour had passed when Olivia's head began to droop wearily, even though they hadn't seen half the acreage or gone near the conservatories.

"Would you like to return to the house?" Vanessa asked. "I don't want to tire you."

Olivia nodded, then gave a sigh of frustration. "How absurd that I cannot even sit in this horrid chair without becoming exhausted."

"Your brother tells me you've agreed to see the doctor. Perhaps he can suggest some ways to alleviate your weariness."

The girl grimaced. "I doubt it. But I decided the sooner I gave in to Damien, the sooner he would leave me in peace. You cannot believe how vexing he has become, always pressing me to stir myself from my bed, as if I weren't really a cripple. I wish he would just return to London."

"I'm certain he's only thinking of your welfare."

"No," the girl disagreed. "I am merely a burdensome duty to him, and he wants to be done with it as soon as possible."

When they turned back toward the house, they saw the tall, lithe figure of Lord Sinclair striding toward them.

"Speak of the devil," Olivia murmured with evident bitterness.

Upon reaching them, Damien came to a standstill and stood searching his sister's face intently.

"I seem to have shocked you speechless," she observed dryly.

"A pleasant shock, my dear." He bent to kiss her forehead. "It is good to see you up and about."

When he straightened, he met Vanessa's gaze for a moment. She could read the gratitude in his eyes before he returned his attention to his sister. "Dr. Underhill should arrive this afternoon, if you are up to seeing him."

"Very well, but there is no need for such haste. He will not be able to cure me today . . . if ever."

"I didn't want to risk your changing your mind. And the sooner he can advise us on a regimen for therapy, the sooner your healing can begin."

Damien took over pushing the chair, and he himself carried Olivia upstairs to her bedchamber, where he left her to rest. But the tension between them was obviously distressing to them both.

Observing their brittle interaction, Vanessa suspected it might be easier to find a cure for Olivia's health than to heal the rift between brother and sister.

"I don't believe her infirmity is necessarily permanent, my lord," the radical-minded Dr. Underhill announced as he exited Olivia's room several hours later.

Vanessa, who had been present for the examination, followed him into the hall to listen to his explanation to Lord Sinclair.

"I could find no evidence of fractures," the doctor continued, "but the bruising of the spine suggests severe trauma. I have seen this same sort of injury twice before. In both cases the patients recovered at least partial use of their limbs."

Damien kept his expression inscrutable, Vanessa noted, while his tone suggested carefully controlled emotion when he said, "So you think it possible she can walk again?"

"With therapeutic activity and enough determination, yes, it is possible."

Damien shut his eyes and expelled an uneven breath. He looked like a man who had been given a reprieve from death, Vanessa thought.

"What sort of therapeutic activity, Doctor?" he asked in a voice that was not quite steady.

"Gentle yet consistent physical exertion. The worst thing she can do is remain abed." He glanced at Vanessa. "Forgive my plain speaking, but too many ladies fancy themselves invalids. Their physicians prescribe endless bed rest, when what they truly need is fresh air and exercise to cure what ails them. They lie about till they are limp as sacks of meal, and then wonder why they haven't the energy God gave a fish."

Vanessa couldn't help but smile, which the doctor returned cheerfully.

"As I said, gentle physical exertion is crucial, but other activities may be highly beneficial. Heat, warm baths, massage—anything to stimulate the nerves and muscles and keep the rest of her form from weakening beyond repair until she heals."

"How long do you think healing will take?" Damien inquired.

"Perhaps in a few months she might begin to regain

sensation in her limbs. If so, then we will know we are on the right course."

"And if not?"

The doctor's craggy brows drew together. "Then I might have to admit failure. But a few months may not be adequate to judge. It could take a year, perhaps even two for the spine to recuperate fully. It would help her recovery if she had an attendant who could assist her with mild exercise and perform massage on her limbs."

"I know of a nurse-midwife who attends my mother sometimes," Vanessa broke in. "She is said to have healing hands."

"That would be ideal," the doctor proclaimed, nodding briskly with approval. "I should like to examine Miss Olivia again in three weeks, my lord, and there are some medications I would like to prescribe, if you will direct me to a pen and paper."

"Certainly. I would very much like to discuss this further with you, sir. But will you first give me a moment with my sister?"

"But of course, my lord."

Entering Olivia's room, Damien went to the bed where she was lying. From her position in the hallway, Vanessa saw him reach down and clasp the girl's hand.

"You heard?" he asked softly.

"Yes." Her pale face was shining with hope.

An ache rising to her throat, Vanessa prayed with all her heart that the unconventional doctor was right.

Chapter Six

Another rose lay on her pillow when she awakened. Slowly coming to consciousness, Vanessa reached out to touch the velvet petals with a fingertip. Last night's bloom had been bloodred. This one looked almost silver in the moonlight, with faint striations of what might be coral along the veins.

"That variety is called a Shropshire Beauty," said a familiar male voice from across the room.

Her heartbeat quickening, Vanessa raised her head and saw a pair of lazy-lidded gray eyes calmly watching her in the moonlit darkness.

He was lounging in the same wing chair, dressed casually in shirtsleeves and breeches, like any squire or yeoman farmer might. Yet with his inherent aristocratic grace, no one would have mistaken Damien Sinclair for anything but a nobleman. With his shirt open at the throat, the white cambric presented a severe contrast to his dark good looks and sun-warmed skin.

Despite her vow to keep her feelings for him under control, Vanessa felt a surge of pleasure. He had as much as promised her he would return for future late-night tête-à-têtes, and, mad as it might be, she was glad he had come.

It seemed almost natural to rise and put on a shawl and

slippers and join him in front of the hearth, where a pleasant fire burned.

Then again, perhaps she had made a mistake. Damien gave her a soft smile, ripe with the seductive charm that made strong women weak. To hide her response to that devastatingly sensual smile, she bent her head to the rose, inhaling the fragrant scent.

How far and fast she had fallen—behaving like a wanton at the first opportunity. How dangerous he was. How captivating. All he did was beckon to her and she came running like a hound to heel. But she could no more resist him than she could have repressed the need to breathe.

She tried to compensate for her brazenness by avoiding his gaze. "I inspected the entry panel to the passage," she murmured. "I could not manage to open it."

"I will show you how if you like."

"Where does it lead?"

He gave her a long look, until she finally raised her head. "To my bedchamber."

Meeting his silvered eyes, Vanessa felt her heart accelerate into a rapid rhythm. "It doesn't seem to have a lock."

"True. It doesn't. You may wedge an object in the junction to prevent it from sliding open. But you needn't look so worried. I won't press you to share my bed without your full cooperation."

"You are likely to have a long wait."

He smiled. "Anticipation merely makes the pleasure all the more sweet, angel."

She drew an unsteady breath. "Does everyone know about the passageway?"

"It's a secret, to my knowledge. I was a boy when I first discovered it. My illustrious father used to invite . . . certain female guests to stay here. The first time I found him, he was with a married lady."

"His mistress was married?"

His lip curled. "I fear I was disillusioned quite young."

"Did you aspire to be like your father?"

"God forbid." He took a long swallow of brandy and stared pensively into the flames. "Now *he* was a reprobate of the first order. You would not have cared for him. . . . Then again, you might. He had a way with women. He kept a string of mistresses—until he became so ensnared by one that he forswore all the rest, including my mother."

The dark edge to his tone suggested pain as well as censure, and Vanessa studied him curiously. "I confess you are not what I expected."

"How so?"

Vanessa pursed her lips thoughtfully. At his country home, Lord Sin seemed vastly different from his reputation. She'd seen little of his rakish ways here. On the contrary, she'd seen how he treated his sister, his protectiveness and gentleness toward her. He could not be all bad if he cared so deeply for someone. "You just seem different. Not as wild and wicked as I would have thought."

"I rarely indulge in orgies and perversions at home," he responded wryly. "And I draw the line at adultery."

"I am comforted to know that."

Her reply elicited a quick grin from him.

"Seriously," Vanessa remarked, "you do surprise me. Your interest in roses, for example. Horticulture is an unlikely pastime for a man of your stamp. Mrs. Nesbit tells me you rescued the gardens from near ruin."

"It was merely a diversion I dabbled with many years ago, in my youth. The roses rarely require my attention now. I have an excellent head nurseryman in charge, and the conservatories are practically self-sufficient."

"Your library seems as well tended as your gardens. I spent a few moments examining your collection this afternoon. I never expected to find such a wide selection of volumes—everything from novels to political discourses to technical treatises."

"My secretary deserves much of the credit. Last year he arranged and catalogued the lot. The library in my London house has space for only a modest collection, so I usually have the volumes shipped here. You met George Haskell in London, I believe."

"Yes."

"Poor George. He's a clever young man but intensely studious." Damien flashed a self-deprecating smile. "He would doubtless be happier in someone else's employ. In his opinion, I'm an abject failure."

"A failure?"

"Because I won't take my seat in the House of Lords. George writes excellent speeches that I have no intention of delivering."

"Why not?"

"I've never taken much of an interest in politics. Yet he won't give up hope that I will develop political aspirations someday."

Vanessa eyed Damien curiously. "The books I saw in your library seemed to have been well perused. Did your secretary read them all?"

"No, I am the culprit, I'm afraid. I tend to read a great deal here. There is little else to do."

"You actually read Wollstonecraft's *Vindication of the Rights of Women*?"

"Yes. Have you?"

"Yes." Her chin rose somewhat defiantly. Mary Wollstonecraft's publication arguing against the subjection of women by men was considered seditious among the noble class. "And I found myself in accord with a number of her convictions regarding marriage. Especially those refuting the divine rights of husbands."

"She made some interesting points about the social tyranny exercised by men," Damien agreed, "but I thought some of her opinions stretched credibility."

"Perhaps," Vanessa acknowledged.

His glance seemed to measure her. "I confess, you are not precisely what I expected either. You are far more innocent. I never would have guessed you had been married before."

"Why do you say so?"

"Because you're so skittish with men."

"Not all men."

"Just myself?"

She gave him an arch look. "I think you've given me good reason to be skittish, if that is what I am."

"Perhaps so. We will have to remedy that."

Vanessa shook her head mentally at the velvet promise in his tone. It was mystifying, how she could feel safe with him when he had as much as threatened her virtue.

An easy, contented silence settled between them. Some moments later Damien broke the quiet spell by asking, "Do you always plait your hair before sleeping?"

"Usually." She looked wary. "Why?"

"You have lovely hair. I want to see it loose and fanning across my pillow."

It was a deliberately provocative remark, which she determinedly ignored. Even in the moonlight, however,

Damien could make out the flush on her cheeks, and he was enchanted.

Catching her off guard was not easy. Breaking through her prickly defenses required a deft and delicate touch.

He'd spoken truthfully. She was indeed unexpected. He'd been mistaken about her experience, obviously, prejudiced by the scandals involving her late husband and the rumors about her afterward. Vanessa was really nothing like her rakehell of a husband or her cur of a brother.

Damien was willing to admit he might deliberately have misjudged her. Many of the highborn ladies of the ton were thoroughly selfish and self-centered, only out for themselves. Yet Vanessa seemed quite different.

Her success with his sister had surprised and gratified him. It remained to be seen if her kindness and warmth was truly real, but if her concern for Olivia wasn't genuine, she was giving an excellent performance.

Her intelligence was surprising as well. He had never expressly sought intellectual stimulation or clever conversation in his usual mistresses. One with a keen mind would be a novelty—a novelty he suspected he would enjoy. He found himself wanting to know Vanessa better, to explore her hidden depths.

Precisely because of his growing doubts about her, though, he'd found himself wrestling with an ironic dilemma: whether or not to hold her to their bargain and make her his mistress.

His seduction of her had begun as an irresistible challenge. Her mask of reserve and her cool disdain for men like him were as tempting as a thrown gauntlet. He'd been so positive he would easily conquer this beautiful, intriguing woman. Yet to his surprise, and perhaps perplexity, his goal had subtly changed as he'd come to know her over the past few days, while his own deepening interest had only burgeoned.

He was still set on winning their war of wills, of course, yet he wanted more than her grudging submission. He was determined to turn her cool contempt to burning hunger.

Perhaps it was best, Damien acknowledged, his eyes appraising her thoughtfully, to let events unfold in their natural course, to woo her until she lost her wariness of him.

It was tantalizing to contemplate her surrender. It would be a pleasure, showing her passion. Teaching her to desire and to express that desire . . . Yet a cardinal rule of seduction, Damien reminded himself, was not to overstay one's welcome. As much as he regretted terminating this intimate interlude, he'd been here long enough for one evening.

With reluctance, he rose to his feet and moved to stand before her. "I shall go now, sweeting, and permit you to rest. I hope you will invite me to return."

Her look of surprise was quickly masked as she lifted her shoulders in a delicate shrug. "I imagine you are free to come and go as you please, my lord. This is your house, after all. But I shall not await your arrival with bated breath."

He flashed a slow, wicked grin. "I look forward to the day when you give me an entirely different response."

Deliberately then, he reached out and brushed a finger lingeringly across her cheek, as much to fulfill his need for physical expression as to accustom her to his touch.

The spark that flared between them at even that light contact shocked her more than it did him. Her midnight eyes held a startlement in their luminous depths that pleased him immensely.

And with that small victory, Damien knew he would have to be content.

At least for now.

His plan for her seduction proceeded apace, with ample opportunities for intimacy. He spent some part of each day in her company, dining with her each evening and occasionally joining her afternoon visits in the gardens with his sister.

The nurse-midwife with the healing hands arrived from Kent shortly and took over Olivia's physical therapeutic activity, which left Vanessa with unexpected time to herself.

She began to ride almost daily, exploring the beautiful estate and the surrounding countryside, attended by a groom. Once or twice she made excursions into the village of Alcester to purchase some trifles and trinkets to entertain Olivia. The most enjoyable rides, however, were the rare occasions when Damien accompanied her.

She made free use of his library, which soon became her favorite refuge in the house. The room's decor was sumptuous—Aubusson carpets, rich wood paneling, and gilded, frescoed ceilings—but it was the treasure of leather-bound volumes lining the walls that drew her. Vanessa spent hours curled up on the window seat overlooking the rose gardens, lost in pleasure.

When she wrote letters home to her mother and sisters, she took care to mention Lord Sinclair sparingly, so as to maintain the pretense that she'd been hired to provide company for his sister. Only Aubrey knew the truth about her role as Lord Sin's mistress.

She had argued vehemently with her brother before she left, since Aubrey had balked upon realizing the lengths to which she would have to go in order to have his debts canceled. She hadn't spared his sensibilities, for she wanted him to clearly understand the burden he'd placed on her with his reckless exploits. In the end she prevailed, simply because they had no other recourse.

The family, however, believed she had become companion to the incapacitated Miss Sinclair for the income—a genteel enough position for an impoverished noblewoman.

Vanessa disliked having to deceive them, and disliked even more having to deceive her charge by concealing her own connection to Aubrey. She dreaded to think of Olivia's reaction should the truth ever come out. Yet despite the heavy press of guilt, she firmly believed she was doing far more good than harm. As wealthy as Olivia was, the lonely girl was starved for friendship, and she was touchingly grateful not to have to bear her trauma alone.

Attending her had proved a delight rather than the burden Vanessa had feared. And with the hope of possible recovery, even Olivia's chill relationship with Damien had begun a slight thawing.

Initially there was some discussion about escorting the invalid to Bath to take advantage of the hot mineral waters there, but aside from the journey by coach being too arduous to attempt in her fragile condition, Olivia didn't want her infirmity widely known. So instead, Damien proposed to build a special bath at Rosewood for his sister, and his mornings were occupied with the design and construction in the conservatory where his rare strains of roses were cultivated.

Much to her dismay, Vanessa discovered his absence almost as compelling as his presence, for she couldn't banish him from her thoughts, or from her dreams. His sensual magnetism haunted her waking or sleeping.

He was a far more complex man than she had first

imagined. It was only gradually, however, that she learned more about what had driven him to become the legendary Lord Sin.

One morning during her second week at Rosewood, Vanessa encountered him at the stables and with great pleasure accepted his invitation to ride. They enjoyed a brisk gallop but slowed to a more sedate pace as they returned through the park. When they came to a rise overlooking the lake, Vanessa drew a breath at the shimmering splendor.

"How beautiful," she murmured.

"Yes, I had forgotten." Damien sounded almost wistful as he halted his horse beside her.

"You don't spend much time here at Rosewood, I understand."

His mouth twisted in a grimace. "I try to avoid it as much as possible."

"Why?" she asked curiously. "If I had a home this beautiful, I doubt I would ever wish to leave."

"My childhood gave me an aversion to the place, I'm afraid. It holds too many unpleasant memories."

"What sort of memories?"

He didn't answer for a moment. Instead, he slowly dismounted and stood staring off into the distance.

"My parents' marriage was a battleground," he said finally in a low voice. "My father became so obsessed with his mistress that he sought to divorce my mother, and she hated him for it."

"Divorce? Isn't securing a decree difficult?"

"He had ample grounds under English law, since she was as faithless to him as he was to her. But her family was powerful and wealthy enough to prevent him dragging her through the courts." Damien shook his head, as if remembering. "She took a procession of lovers—primarily out of revenge, I suspect. But one day she found herself spurned by her beau in favor of a younger beauty, and their marriage turned even uglier . . . more bitter.

"Fortunately for me, I went away to university and was required to return here infrequently. By the time I graduated, I'd come into a substantial inheritance and was able to make my home in London, independent of my father. He lived in the London town house, while my mother retired here to the country. They refused even to share the same house."

Damien gave a humorless laugh. "It was something of an irony that they perished together in a carriage accident after a ball Prinny gave. It was the first time in years they had even attended the same function. I can't say I greatly mourned their passing, to be brutally honest."

He glanced over his shoulder at Vanessa. Sunbeams heightened the sharp clarity of his gray eyes, and she could see the pain the dark memories dredged up for him.

As if recalling himself, he shrugged and came around to help her dismount. When he set her down, she moved a few steps away, unnerved by even so casual a touch.

"That was when you assumed your sister's guardianship?" Vanessa asked, not wishing his revelations to end.

"Yes." Damien bent to pluck a blade of grass to chew. "I discharged my legal obligations adequately enough, but I never realized until these past few months how greatly I neglected Olivia. She had all the advantages a girl could ask for—wealth, rank, education. But she had to grow up alone. She resents me for that, I know. And I can't really blame her. I have no excuse for my neglect, other than my complete unsuitability for raising a young lady."

"Perhaps you should try to talk to her."

"And what would you have me say?"

"I don't believe she knows how much you care. You might tell her of your regrets, how unqualified you felt to be her guardian. She probably never considered you might actually be inept at something."

Damien smiled faintly. "And you expect her to forgive me?"

"I think she will, yes. My guess is that she wants you to be a real brother to her. You're her only family, but she's never really known you. She's felt intensely lonely . . . ignored by you, isolated from society by her straitlaced governess. Her loneliness is doubtless what allowed Olivia to be led astray—" Vanessa bit off the words "by my brother," and instead added, "And now she feels trapped by her chair. She needs you now more than ever, Damien, even if she doesn't see it at the moment."

He grimaced wryly. "She most certainly doesn't see it."

"Have you ever simply asked her what she wants?"

"What do you mean?"

"The other day she remarked about the unfairness of being female. Men can ride out into the world in search of adventure, but girls must remain at home, waiting to be courted. And you said yourself that her home was often like a battleground. You were able to escape, but Olivia wasn't."

His brow furrowed with skepticism, but Vanessa suspected he took her advice quite seriously.

He was still deep in thought a short while later when he helped her remount her horse, and he seemed not to notice that Vanessa flinched at his touch. She could only chastise herself for her lack of control.

Yet it was startling how effortlessly he affected her

senses and was not in the least sensible that she'd begun to crave his company.

She found herself eagerly anticipating his nightly visits and the roses he brought her, each a different hue and size, from tiny, delicate buds of yellow, to lush, ripe blooms of palest pink, to elegant blossoms of wine red.

Those midnight tête-à-têtes were ripe with sensual intimacy, even though he rarely physically touched her.

A few nights later they sat as usual before the fireplace, although Damien had lit a candle to augment the waning moonlight. He sipped brandy while Vanessa buried her nose in this evening's rose, which was pure ivory.

"At this rate," she murmured, "you won't have a single bloom left in your gardens."

"I doubt there is any danger of depleting my gardens just yet," Damien responded wryly, his half-smile lavish with the devastating charm she had come to expect from him.

No doubt that sinful smile had served only to heighten his reputation for wickedness, Vanessa surmised.

"How did you come to be known as Lord Sin?" she asked curiously.

His answer surprised her by being unexpectedly thoughtful. "I suppose I was following in my father's footsteps. I was a wild young blood, with no one to curb my excesses or set limits. And London held a treasure trove of forbidden delights for a green youth."

"And later, when you grew older? You were no longer a youth when you established the Hellfire League."

Damien shrugged. "A gentleman must have some diversions. When it was new, the League provided an excellent remedy for ennui."

"And now?"

"The novelty has long since worn off, I'm afraid."

Silence fell between them while they both became lost in thought. Vanessa suspected Damien suffered from much the same complaint as her brother—too much license and too little serious occupation. Her late husband, too, had turned to gaming and wenching to fill his time, especially in London, where the opportunities for vice and iniquity were so much greater.

"I don't much care for London," she remarked, changing the subject a little.

"No?"

"It holds . . . unpleasant memories for me. Most of my marriage was spent there. And I became a widow there." She shuddered, recalling that terrible time. "I remember that day so vividly. A friend of my husband's came to tell me Roger had been killed, and then his body was brought home. . . . The time afterward is a blur, though. Thankfully my brother was there to support me. He took care of the details of my husband's estate, dealt with the tradesmen and moneylenders—" With a start, Vanessa recollected what she was saying. "I'm sorry, I agreed not to talk about Aubrey."

"Surely your memories of London aren't all bad," Damien said, ignoring her slip.

"Not all. I might have enjoyed it under different circumstances."

"I wager I could have shown you a more pleasurable side of the city."

She smiled. "I doubt I'm licentious enough to qualify for entry into your realm."

He cocked his head, surveying her skeptically. "Have you never wanted to do anything wicked?"

"Perhaps, although my definition of wicked and yours are entirely different matters. There were any number of times when I was sorely tempted to flout society's conventions. I remember a certain ball when the Duchess of Salford made a particularly vindictive remark. . . . I nearly threw my cup of rack punch in her face."

"That is wicked indeed." He gave her that soft fallen-angel smile that could ensnare a woman's heart.

She flushed and averted her gaze, staring into the fire. "Why do I always tell you such personal things?"

"Because I tend not to be judgmental, perhaps?"

It was true, Vanessa realized. She never felt as if he was sitting in judgment of her.

"In any case," Damien added lightly, "turnabout is fair play. You've made me bare my soul often enough."

Yet it wasn't simply that the intimate atmosphere of their midnight exchanges lent itself to confession, Vanessa suspected. Lord Sinclair was deliberately trying to draw her out, to learn her secrets so that he might better lure her to his bed.

His strategy was succeeding, at least in part. She had lost her intense wariness of him. And yet she found it harder to maintain an air of composure when he was near. He could make her quiver with a glance, render her breathless with a simple touch.

Perhaps it was her dread of what was to come that so unnerved her. Damien had been exceedingly patient with her reticence, not demanding so much as a kiss from her. Vanessa felt certain, however, that the situation couldn't remain that way. Before long he would require her to become his mistress in truth.

One night during the beginning of her third week at Rosewood, the conversation turned even more personal—deeply, disquietingly so. Again they were sitting before the fire in the warm glow of candlelight. At first Vanessa remained undisturbed when she felt his heavy-lidded gaze lingering upon her. She'd grown accustomed to his lazy, searching perusals.

Yet she was not prepared for the question that broke the pleasurable silence between them.

"How long has it been for you?" he asked softly.

She could have pretended to misunderstand. Could have refused to answer such an intimate, intrusive query. But candidness had been a hallmark of their relationship from the first, and she had come to value it, despite how unsettling such honesty often could prove.

"Two years."

"So long?"

She had to look away from the intensity in his observant eyes. "You have misjudged me," she replied, a tremor in her voice. "I told you the truth. I am not experienced in carnal matters. I haven't had countless lovers. Only my husband."

"And you didn't enjoy that," he said, low and hushed.

"It . . . was not pleasant." She flushed, ashamed that Damien had managed to draw such an admission from her.

"Let me guess," he continued, keeping his voice quietly modulated. "He never took the time to arouse you. Instead he sought his own pleasure without considering yours. You lay beneath him, tense and unresponsive, expecting pain and dutifully receiving it."

The stark picture he painted struck too close to the truth. Vanessa bowed her head, reliving the dark memories. "It *was* my duty, but he . . . hurt me."

"You may trust me never to hurt you, Vanessa."

Slowly she raised her gaze to his, searching his face. Trust was not a word she would use with Damien Sinclair. But, startlingly, she did trust him. Why else would she have so readily revealed her secrets to him? She should have deplored his insistent probing and her own intimate confessions; but, in a bewildering way, she was almost relieved to have her private shame exposed.

His eyes captured hers and held them. "Carnal relations needn't be unpleasant for a woman. Indeed, they should not be."

"He thought me cold . . . unfeeling. Because I couldn't bear his touch."

A swift spark of anger flickered in the storm-silver eyes. "He was a damned fool."

She stared at Damien, wanting to believe the firm conviction in his pronouncement.

He kept his voice soft and even when he continued. "Vanessa, your dislike of physical intimacy stems from a cruel experience. While you might be lacking in education and experience, I doubt you are cold or unfeeling. I would wager my entire fortune that inside you is a warm, passionate woman yearning to break free."

Against her volition, her throat constricted with emotion. For so long she had lived with the shame and guilt of her inadequacies. If she had been a better wife to Roger, perhaps he would not have sought other women's beds. He might even have moderated his wild and reckless lifestyle and never met an ignominious end with a bullet through his heart on the dueling field.

The possibility was like balm to a raw wound, and Vanessa was absurdly grateful to Damien for suggesting a reason that she had never responded physically to her husband.

"You . . . think me passionate?"

He was watching her, his eyes half-closed yet so sensual, so compelling, he made her heart ache. "I'm sure of it. I could show you, if you would put your pleasure in my hands."

Her lips parted, but no sound emerged.

With unhurried deliberation then, he set down his glass and rose from his chair. "Shall I show you what it is like to feel wanted, desired?"

Moving slowly, Damien reached down and drew her to her feet. Immobile, she stared up at him, seeing the flames warming the depths of his eyes. His closeness stirred a pleasurable spark that flickered along the ends of her nerves.

"I do desire you, angel. More than you could possibly imagine."

"Damien . . ."

"Hush. Don't fear me. I will allow you to take the lead." He took her hand and pressed her palm to his cheek. "Just touch me."

He guided her hand, letting her fingers trace slowly over his features. With a breath of a sigh, Vanessa closed her eyes, exploring the planes and angles of his beautiful face, learning the masculine shape, the unique contours, the subtle flex of flesh and bone.

The sensation was new to her, and yet somehow heart familiar. In her dreams she had touched him like this, savoring the warmth of his skin, the faint rasp of stubble that shadowed his jaw, the flow of his breath when her fingers sketched the pliant curve of his mouth.

"What do you feel?"

What she felt was a stirring of heat deep within her, a softening, a melting. What she felt was wonder at the breathless enchantment he wrapped around her so effortlessly. What she felt was longing.

Her eyes opened slowly, and she stared up at him, dazed.

The silver eyes were tender and knowing. But he made no further move.

He knew his power over her, knew how dangerously sensual he was. And yet he was not prepared to take advantage of her, it seemed.

"No," he murmured, his voice dropping to the husk of a whisper. "You are not yet ready."

Without taking his eyes off her, he brought her fingers to his lips to kiss their pale tips slowly, lingeringly.

Then just as gently, he released her.

"I won't press you further tonight, sweeting. When you finally share my bed, it will seem as right to you as it does to me."

The velvet promise in his voice echoed in her mind long after he was gone. Remembering, Vanessa shuddered. She was still quivering from the enchanting fire he had aroused deep within her. Still trembling with the sweet, intimate feelings his tenderness had stirred.

She looked down, staring at her fingers. Impossibly, she could still feel the imprint of his burning kiss and the brand of his soft lips. But it was the inexplicable yearnings in her heart that frightened her more.

Chapter Seven

She had never thought her role at Rosewood would be an easy one, but neither had she expected her emotions to be so conflicted. In only a short time, both Sinclairs had managed to affect her beyond reason—Damien captivating her senses and enmeshing her in his sensual spell, and young Olivia tugging powerfully at her heart.

Her response to Damien bewildered and disturbed Vanessa most. She didn't at all like the tender feelings he aroused in her. It was foolish in the extreme to allow herself to become emotionally drawn to him. She had to remember that her seduction was a game to him, driven by revenge, and she was his prey.

She almost wished he would end the uncertainty. For whatever reason he had given her a stay of execution, holding off the fulfillment of their bargain. But Vanessa had nearly reached the point where the prospect of sharing his bed was not as distressing as the strain of waiting for the ax to fall. She could not contemplate the sexual act with anything but dread, nor could she, in the cold light of day, bring herself to believe Damien's supposition that she might be a passionate woman.

The sooner they consummated their brazen bargain, Vanessa reasoned, the sooner he would discover the truth about her, and the sooner he would end his tormenting pursuit. Once he saw what poor sport she was, he would tire of his game and of her, perhaps even send her packing.

Except for the threat hanging over her head, however, her life here was far more pleasurable than she had a right to hope for. It seemed especially strange not to have to constantly worry about making ends meet. For the past two years she'd spent a significant part of each day determining how best to stretch a farthing, but cost was no object to Damien when it came to his sister's recovery. He agreed readily when Vanessa suggested bringing in a dressmaker and milliner to raise Olivia's spirits.

Olivia refused to leave the estate for any reason, even to shop, but Vanessa believed it would be beneficial if the girl could be persuaded to take an interest in her appearance.

"But I have no need for new gowns," Olivia protested, showing renewed evidence of a stubborn streak. "I have nowhere to wear them, since I never plan on going out again."

"Perhaps not," Vanessa cajoled, "but my sister Fanny believes there is nothing like a new bonnet to make one feel pretty, and you could do with a shawl or two for our visits to the garden. Besides, you will need a bathing costume for the bath your brother is constructing for you in the conservatory."

When the milliner arrived with her wares, proffering bonnets trimmed with ribbons and bows and lace and ostrich feathers, Olivia did find two she particularly admired.

"I suppose the bonnets sold in London are more elegant than those found here in the country," she said to Vanessa rather wistfully when they were alone again.

"Not always, although prices *are* more exorbitant there."

"It must be wonderful to live in London."

"I don't much care for town, actually."

"No? But there is so much to do, so much to see. Lending libraries and bookshops and museums, plays and opera performances . . ."

"Those are advantages, indeed, but I was thinking of the social whirl."

"You mean balls and routs and supper parties?"

Vanessa nodded as she folded tissue paper around the lemon-colored bonnet Olivia had chosen. During the height of the Season, it was not unusual to receive a half-dozen invitations for a single evening. When she was Olivia's age, the prospect of a ball had held excitement. But as she grew older, she'd become less enthralled with the gilded cage of London society—the emptiness, the relentless pretense, the stinging, vengeful gossip. And once her husband had begun his downward spiral into decadence and scandal, the evenings had become almost unbearable. Vanessa recalled standing stiff-faced for hours, a smile pasted on her lips, enduring the stares and darkling glances of those people who once professed to be her friends. Yet she didn't want to encourage Olivia's solitary leanings.

"A ball can be highly pleasurable," she said lightly, "but after years of such affairs, they all seem to run together. Still, every young lady of means should experience a Season at least once. You should go and make up your own mind."

Olivia looked away. "I don't know that I ever will now." There was a long silence while her lower lip trembled. "My former companion, Mrs. Jenkins, said I deserved what happened to me. That I was fortunate to survive as a cripple."

"You deserved nothing of the kind!" Vanessa responded, speaking sharply to Olivia for the first time.

"I am not so certain. The fault *was* mine for being so foolish and wicked."

"It isn't foolish to fall in love. Your only mistake was in choosing the wrong man."

"A dreadful mistake," Olivia agreed in a whisper.

Putting down the bonnet, Vanessa moved to sit on the edge of the bed and take the girl's hand.

Olivia looked up, tears in her blue eyes. "What did Damien tell you about my folly?"

"He said that you were a victim of a cruel wager, that you were persuaded by a scoundrel to elope." She saw Olivia's chin quiver but felt it was better for her to talk about her traumatic experience, to try to deal with the painful feelings of loss and betrayal, rather than to bottle them inside.

"Olivia, you are not the first young woman to be deceived by a handsome stranger," Vanessa said gently.

"I was indeed deceived. I thought he wished to marry me. I wanted so badly to believe him when he said I was beautiful, when he said he loved me." Her shimmering gaze grew distant. "He was so charming, so gentle, with such laughing eyes. He made me feel . . . special. And he loved poetry. It was so romantic . . . or so I thought. Until that horrible night."

"What happened?" Vanessa prodded quietly. She had heard Aubrey's version of events, and Damien had told her the story he'd pieced together after the accident from bystanders and servants and Olivia's own reluctant confessions. But many of the details were still unclear.

"We had planned to travel to Gretna Green," the girl murmured, identifying the small village across the Scottish border where eloping couples could take advantage of the permissive marriage laws, which required only a witness to make the vows legal. "I was frightfully nervous but excited all the same. I walked the entire way to the coaching inn at Alcester, not wanting to raise any alarm by taking a mount from our stables.

"I knew something was wrong as soon as I arrived. Au... he didn't look happy to see me. He had booked a private room, and two of his friends were there—two gentlemen I had met at a local assembly some months before. They were dreadfully foxed. I wanted to leave, but Aubrey wouldn't come with me. He said he had changed his mind about the elopement. I remember his friends shouting with laughter, declaring that he'd fairly won the wager."

Her cheeks colored with shame. "It was a large sum, a thousand pounds, yet I didn't understand at first. I must have looked so stupid standing there with my bandboxes. Then his friends divulged that Aubrey had never intended to go through with the marriage, that it was all a lark. When one of them offered to take me under his protection, Aubrey got angry and demanded an apology, but I couldn't bear to hear any more. I turned and ran out the door.

"I think when I reached the stairway I must have slipped on a riser or tripped over my bandboxes. I remember trying to catch myself. . . . The next thing I knew, I was waking in my own room, unable to move. They said I had fallen down the stairs."

The tears spilled over. "I never heard from him again."

Vanessa felt tears fill her own eyes. She could have told the girl why Aubrey had apparently abandoned her after the tragic incident. Damien had seen to it that her seducer never set foot near his sister again. Yet Vanessa felt strongly that it was the wrong time to divulge her own connection to Aubrey. She was making progress with Olivia, coaxing her to give her life a chance, and another betrayal might very well put an end to their fledgling friendship.

Hearing the tale, though, Vanessa felt a fresh surge of anger. She was still horrified, still furious at her reckless, immature brother who had left this young girl a cripple, with her character in ruins. Olivia was like a delicate, untouched flower, sullied and trampled in the muck.

"So you see why," Olivia whispered, "I can never show my face again in polite society."

Vanessa squeezed the slender hand in sympathy. "I can see why you might think your world has ended, Olivia. But it hasn't. You will get through it, just as I did my marriage. I was not much older than you are now when I wed and was forced to deal with scandal."

Her own voice dropped to a murmur. "My husband . . . ran through his substantial fortune in less than a year and became mired in debt, yet that never stopped him from plunging into one reckless affair after another. I remember times I thought I would die of mortification. Even Roger's end proved ignominious. He was killed in a duel over another woman. An actress."

"How terrible for you."

Vanessa tried to smile, but she couldn't completely repress her bitterness. "I thought so at the time. But there was nothing for me to do but hold my head high. I learned to go on with my life, to ignore the tempests. Trust me, my dear, this scandal will pass. And the best way to deal with it is to meet it head-on. Cowering will avail you nothing."

Olivia searched her face. "Like I have been doing here in my room?"

She nodded gently. "It is understandable that you would be reluctant to face the world, to expose yourself to savage gossip and slights, but if you shut yourself off from everyone who cares for you, you are the one who suffers."

"Damien . . . says he cares for me."

"I'm certain he does."

"He told me he greatly regrets that he hasn't been much of a brother to me. He asked me to give him another chance."

"And will you?"

"Yes," the girl replied tremulously. She wiped her eyes. "I didn't really mean to take my resentment out on him. It's just that I have felt so trapped here."

"You needn't be."

"There are so many things I can no longer do. Until I fell, I was always quite self-sufficient, but now it takes at least two maids to help me dress, and a footman to carry me down the stairs. And I used to ride every single day, rain or shine."

"You can still ride in a carriage, can you not? And you can certainly visit your horses. The stable master tells me they miss you greatly."

Olivia bit her lip. "And I miss them. There are many things I have missed."

"What else besides riding?"

"My music. I was considered rather accomplished at playing the pianoforte, but . . . I cannot operate the pedals now."

"Not yet, but perhaps in time you can. And there is nothing wrong with your fingers, is there? You could keep in practice until the day comes when you can play. I know that if I do not play regularly, I get very rusty from disuse."

Olivia nodded slowly. "I suppose I can still sing, as well."

"Mrs. Nesbit tells me you have the voice of an angel."

"Well, not an angel . . ." she returned modestly even while flushing with pleasure.

"I should love to hear you sing."

This time when Vanessa squeezed her hand, Olivia squeezed back. "I am glad you have come," she said with quiet fervor.

Vanessa smiled. "So am I," she replied with complete honesty.

It was later that evening when Olivia made her first major effort to rejoin the world.

Vanessa and Damien were in the drawing room, preparing to go in to dinner, when the butler entered and cleared his throat.

"My lord, Miss Olivia has expressed a wish to join you and Lady Wyndham at table."

Behind him Olivia appeared in the doorway, seated in her invalid chair, guided by a strapping footman. Damien rose abruptly to his feet, a look of surprise and concern on his features.

"I am quite all right," Olivia reassured him quickly. "Vanessa tells me I should stop cowering under the covers. And since I must begin somewhere, I chose tonight. Oh dear, I fear I have shocked you again."

Damien shot an eloquent glance at Vanessa before returning his attention to his sister. The slow smile that claimed his handsome features rivaled the sun for brilliance.

"You may shock me whenever you like, sweetheart." He looked at the butler. "Croft, fetch a bottle of champagne, if you please. I believe this calls for a celebration."

If Damien was surprised to have his sister join them for dinner, he was more surprised by the familial warmth that pervaded the atmosphere. When his parents had been alive, meals at Rosewood were trials of endurance—cold and formal, with icy silences punctuated occasionally by barbs and recriminations. Nothing like the cordiality that enveloped the three of them at the table that evening.

The friendly intimacy continued when they adjourned together to the music room, where they made use of the exquisite pianoforte Damien had given his sister for her sixteenth birthday—a gift he now lamented having left to his secretary to deliver.

Vanessa played while Olivia sang, and Damien watched with fondness and growing pleasure.

He hadn't expected such remarkable progress with his sister. It seemed a stroke of genius now to have brought Vanessa here. Her breeding and education qualified her as a suitable companion, certainly, but he could have searched for years and not found anyone who could have made such an impact so quickly. In a few weeks she had persuaded Olivia to take a renewed interest in life, a task at which he had failed for months.

He was supremely grateful for her efforts, and for the warmth she had brought to his home. This evening was one of the most enjoyable times he could remember at Rosewood—and it was not yet over.

At his urging, Olivia retired early so she wouldn't become overly fatigued by her first venture into company. Damien himself carried her upstairs and then returned to the music room to find Vanessa seated on the settee, sipping her wine.

A rare tenderness filled him as he regarded her. She looked relaxed and content, her eyes soft, dreamy, her defenses lowered.

A warning voice whispered in his head that his judgment

was becoming sadly impaired and entangled in emotion, but Damien purposely ignored it, just as he pushed aside any twinges of conscience at what he was about to do. The time had finally come to attempt to penetrate her weakened armor.

Yet the possessive urges sweeping through him were more than simple carnal hunger, he knew. He felt a fierce need to hold Vanessa in his arms and teach her about desire, about passion. To unlock the unfulfilled secrets of her body and strip her of her shocking innocence. For all her familiarity with scandal, she was appallingly inexperienced in carnal matters.

How very wrong he'd been about her in that regard. It struck him, suddenly, the sacrifice she'd made for her family's sake. It had taken considerable courage for her to agree to become his mistress when she was so averse to physical intimacy. A courage he had to admire.

Her disdain of men and sex, Damien had no doubt, stemmed from her unsavory relationship with her former husband, and he very much wanted to remedy her woeful ignorance—for her own benefit as well as his own. He wanted to free her of her fear.

"I am more grateful than you know," he murmured, coming into the room, "for your kindness to my sister."

Vanessa looked up with a smile. "She is deserving of kindness and easy to love."

"You seem to enjoy her company."

"I do, very much."

"Then your stay here has not been so very onerous?"

She hesitated. "No, not at all."

He read the implication in her pause: not onerous *yet*. Not as long as their bargain remained unfulfilled.

"Will you accompany me to the gardens?" he asked. "There is something I would like to show you."

Her sudden wariness was reminiscent of her previous nervousness around him. "At this time of night?"

Damien kept his tone light. "Pray, don't look as if you expect me to assault you, sweeting. I have nothing so ominous in mind, I assure you. The bath for Olivia is almost finished. I thought you might care to see it, without all the workmen present."

Vanessa glanced at the window, whose curtains had been drawn against the darkness, and then down at her silk dinner gown. The square neckline and short, puffed sleeves would expose a wide expanse of flesh to the evening air.

"Perhaps I should fetch a wrap," she said uncertainly.

"I think you'll be comfortable enough without one. The conservatory is quite warm."

"Very well . . ."

His eyes smiled at her as he took her arm and escorted her through the doors into the garden. The night air was cool on her bare flesh. The moon was nearly full and quite brilliant, while the stars shone like diamonds on black velvet.

She must be mad to venture into a serene, moonlit garden with such a man, Vanessa reflected, and yet a reckless pleasure filled her, a keen sense of anticipation. Perhaps she had partaken of too much wine. . . .

"You are suddenly quiet," Damien observed into the silence.

"I am questioning the wisdom of being here with you."

"Would you rather inspect the conservatory on your own? I will leave you to go on alone, if you wish."

"No, I don't wish to go alone."

"Come now, sweeting, I won't have you afraid of me. If I haven't pressed myself on you in all my visits to your bedchamber where we enjoy absolute privacy, I'm unlikely to do so here where we might be spied upon."

"Even so, you will forgive me if I am wary of your hedonistic tendencies."

He shook his head slowly. "It saddens me that you have such a poor opinion of my character. And to think I've attempted to apply my most charming manner of address with you."

Vanessa bit back a smile, determined not to succumb to his sensual appeal, yet she had to admit she enjoyed their verbal sparring and the challenge of keeping pace with him in their game of wits. "I imagine I shall manage to resist your charm. You would do better to practice it on a more willing lady."

"Alas, there are no others available at present. I fear you will have to suffice."

"I doubt a single female would be able to satisfy a man of your vast appetites."

"I think you underrate yourself."

"And I think you *over*rate yourself."

He raised an eyebrow. "Is that a set-down? Come, darling, I might become insulted."

"Would it be possible to insult you sufficiently to make you give up your pursuit of me?"

The long, vaguely amused look he gave her made her heartbeat quicken. How could she allow herself to be so affected by the wicked charm in those arresting eyes?

Vanessa shivered with awareness. Whenever she was near him, she fought temptation. And there was so much of it.

"Here we are," he murmured after a moment as they came to the end of the terraced garden.

They had reached the conservatory. When Damien held the door open for her, Vanessa hesitated to enter the dark, cavernous hothouse.

"Wait a moment, and I shall light a lamp." He entered, and a moment later she heard the flare of a lucifer being struck.

"There . . . does that dispel your anxiety?"

She couldn't say that it did. If anything her anxiety increased, for the lamp's glow only highlighted the chiseled beauty of his face.

Her wariness increased more when she saw Damien latch the door behind them. He must have seen her response, for he said casually, "I prefer not to be disturbed, but if it will ease your mind I shall help you arm yourself."

He moved over to a shelf where gardening tools were kept. After searching a moment, he handed her a two-foot length of pipe.

"This will make a substantial weapon. You may beat me off with it if I make untoward advances."

His warm eyes touched by lazy sensuality, he smiled down at her, obviously not worried that he was in any immediate danger from her. Vanessa accepted the pipe with skepticism, suspecting that it, like the key to her bedchamber, was designed to engender a false sense of security.

He led her into the vast interior of the conservatory, along aisles of potted roses and exotic orchids, toward an array of lemon and lime and orange trees. The air was much warmer here, moist and fragrant with the scents of blossoms and damp earth.

Eventually they reached a pair of exquisite Chinese silk screens that had been erected for privacy. Beyond was a tiled pool, partially sunk into the ground, filled with gently swirling water.

"An existing boiler heats the water," Damien explained, "but new pipes had to be routed."

The pool was obviously designed for an invalid, Vanessa saw. The near end was equipped with a wide ledge approximately thigh high, while inside the pool a narrow ramp sloped downward, so that the patient could be eased into the water.

"So what think you, sweeting? Does it meet your expectations?"

She nodded honestly. "I find it quite impressive. Indeed, I am astonished."

"Astonished that I could be creative? I do possess a few modest talents. Depraved libertines are allowed them, you know."

"Your ability doesn't surprise me. Just that you would put your mind and talents to such good use. Most noblemen of means have a decided lack of interest in productive accomplishments."

He smiled gently. "Then I hope I may prove to be different from the noblemen of your acquaintance."

He showed her an oak cabinet that held towels and blankets and dressing gowns. Then he set the lamp on a bench.

"Would you care to test the water? It is warm and quite pleasant."

"Now?"

He gave her one of his soul-stopping smiles. "Now is an ideal time. And if you enjoy the waters, you will be in a better position to persuade my sister to make use of them."

She couldn't look away from his heated gaze. He was bold, shameless, compelling—and she was falling hopelessly under his spell.

Damien sat on the bench to remove his shoes and stockings and rolled up the hems of his evening breeches above the knee. When he stood, Vanessa's eyes widened.

"Never fear, I am not undressing entirely." His tone was light, enchantingly playful; his eyes beguiled.

Moving to the bath, he sat on the ledge and swung his legs around to immerse them in the pool, before sighing with pleasure. "Will you come and join me?"

When she hesitated, he lowered his voice to a husky murmur, as seductive as sin itself. "Take off your slippers and stockings, Vanessa. Dare to live dangerously. It is not so very wicked to go barefoot, after all."

Vanessa felt her willpower faltering, yet she remained immobile.

His voice dropped to a caress. "Indulge me, angel-eyes, if you won't indulge yourself."

When still she wouldn't respond to his persuasion, Damien shook his head sadly. "Do you know what your trouble is? You are too repressed. You refuse to let out the passionate woman inside you."

She winced as he struck a sensitive nerve. Roger had frequently accused her of being devoid of passion, and it hurt to have this man make a similar accusation, even in jest. It hurt more to know how Damien would react when he realized she was, in truth, cold and passionless. He wouldn't want her in his bed then.

Her chin lifted defiantly. She didn't *want* him to want her. And she had given him fair warning more than once that she would make a poor choice of mistress.

Although realizing she was allowing herself to be brazenly manipulated, she did as Damien asked, removing her shoes and stockings and joining him on the ledge. He had clearly known how she would react to his prodding, for she saw the satisfaction in his devilish eyes as she sat beside him. Feeling wicked all the same, she raised her skirts a few inches and let her bare feet dangle in the water, which was deliciously warm and soothing.

He slanted her an amused glance. "You really must learn to trust me."

"I would more readily trust a wolf."

In mock dismay, he clasped a hand to his breast. "Ah, fair witch, you wound my decadent soul."

"Perhaps you should ask Dr. Underhill to bandage it for you."

Damien laughed, a low, husky sound. "I cannot fathom why you are so skittish around me. I've never made any truly serious attempt on your virtue."

"No? You could have fooled me."

"I have kissed you but once, and that was before I knew you."

"I would not say that you know me now."

"Ah, but I do. I've learned a great deal about you in the past weeks. You are kind and generous. Spirited and clever—with a rapier wit I am hard-pressed to defend myself against. And you are afraid of men." His blithe tone had suddenly acquired a serious edge.

Vanessa bit her lip but remained silent. Why ever had she been foolish enough to divulge her secrets to him?

"You shouldn't allow one wretched experience to mark you for life, you know."

She looked down at her hands. She didn't want to fear men, to dread an intimate touch. She didn't want to be burdened by her past, by the dark memories of her marriage. But there was little hope of banishing her ugly memories.

Damien seemed to read her thoughts, for his voice

dropped to a mere murmur. "I intend to make it my chief aim to help you conquer your fear."

It made her angry to hear him suggest his pursuit of her was for her benefit. "Surely you don't expect me to believe your interest in me is altruistic? I am not *that* green, I trust."

"No. I admit, I hope to benefit as well. A beautiful woman sharing my bed is reward enough."

She could feel him studying her, and it prompted her to ask a question that had often preyed on her mind. "I . . . have wondered why you haven't required me to fulfill our agreement. Is it just to torment me, to draw out your revenge?"

"No. Of course not." He sounded surprised.

"Then why?"

"You aren't yet ready."

She gazed up at him, disbelieving his answer. "How do you know?"

"Experience. Masculine intuition. The most obvious sign is your aversion to being touched."

He raised a finger to her cheek to stroke gently. "Ah, progress. You didn't flinch from me this time. It leads me to hope that someday I'll hear you whispering words of sweet surrender." His expression was warm, gentle, as his thumb traced her lower lip. "I warn you, nothing short of your complete surrender will do."

His thumb dipped to brush the inner corner of her mouth in a blatantly sexual gesture. Vanessa's breath caught in her throat, while a spark of fresh anger kindled inside her. For weeks now Damien had played his nerve-shredding game of cat and mouse with her, and it had reached the point of cruelty.

"If you brought me here to seduce me," she muttered,

regarding him with a baleful glare, "I wish you would hurry up and be done with it."

He went still. "I brought you here to show you the bath," he replied levelly. "If I intended to seduce you—" He bent his head. "—I would move closer . . . like this."

His warm breath touched her cheek. Vanessa froze, waiting for the warm brush of his lips. Yet he didn't attempt to kiss her. Instead he drew a finger along the delicate line of her collarbone. "You really are utterly enchanting, you know."

The heat in his voice passed through her skin, making Vanessa shiver with a keen awareness. Damien Sinclair was a dangerous devil who possessed the power to bewitch her.

His hand wandered with tantalizing slowness, leaving a fiery trail after its passing, driving her anger away. Vanessa shut her eyes, fighting the relentless urges he stirred in her, wondering how she could resist this man whose raw virility gave him sensual power over any woman he wanted.

A moment later she felt him move. To her surprise he had slipped easily from the ledge into the pool. The level was not deep, reaching just above the knees, but the water swirled around his thighs, calling attention to the swelling at the groin of his breeches. He was boldly, unmistakably aroused, Vanessa realized.

When he noted the direction of her gaze, his mouth curved wryly. "As you see, your attractions fascinate me."

Disconcerted by his boldness, she glanced away, but he would have none of her modesty. With a languid finger beneath her chin, he made her lift her gaze.

She went still, riveted by his tender expression. His scrutiny brushed over her with an intimacy as physical as a stolen kiss.

"Will you not trust me, angel?"

She wet her lips, staring at him. She was certain he could see the thickly beating pulse in her throat.

"Let me kiss you. I promise I will stop whenever you wish."

Mutely, Vanessa gazed up at him, desperately trying to ignore the temptation of his beautiful mouth, yet it was impossible. She wanted his kiss, his touch. It was folly to think she could escape his spell.

His hand was moving on her throat. His slow finger strokes vibrated through her, thrumming softly at her senses. She felt her resistance weaken at the enticing wickedness of his expert caress. Yet it was his gaze that held her captive. Behind the soft seduction of those warm eyes was a promise of gentleness, of passion beyond anything she could imagine.

"Sweet siren, let me. . . ."

His dark lashes lowered. His head was bending, his beautiful mouth descending toward hers.

She sighed at the first taste of his mouth. His lips were warm and vibrant and oh so magical.

The last of her resistance fled as his palms framed her face. His tongue slid delicately into her mouth, meeting hers. At the hot sensation he aroused, she softened against him helplessly.

Responsively he deepened his kiss, smothering her with intimate tenderness and sensuality, drinking her in. It was a long, long moment before the kiss ended . . . but then it was only to move his lips hotly across her cheek to her ear. "You taste so sweet . . . like a rare wine."

His deep, velvet voice reached out to touch her, feeding the wild recklessness that was building inside her.

Vanessa swallowed in an effort to slow her jagged breathing, yet there was a heavy ache between her thighs, a melting, heated yearning deep inside her that she was powerless to deny.

He must have known the effect he had on her, for he drew back slightly. "Surrender feels right, doesn't it?" he whispered.

Yes, she wanted to say, but the words remained trapped in her throat.

He moved closer, bringing his body inch by inch against hers. His eyes held hers, hot and silvered, as he eased her legs open with his knee. Her breath shallowed. To her shock, Damien drew her into the water slowly, so that she rode his granite-hard thigh.

Her body remained taut and tense as his strong arm encircled her waist, pulling her in to the heat of him. Beneath her skirts, she could feel his rigid flesh pressing against her softness.

"Don't be afraid to let yourself feel, Vanessa. . . ."

His thigh moved against her feminine mound. A moan hovered in her throat at the erotic friction. He kept her held against his fully aroused body until bonelessly she let herself sway into him, giving in to the flare of pleasure, of desire.

Gently then, his hands swept lower to cradle the swell of her hips, and he began to rock her slowly, rhythmically, guiding her toward a dark, secret pleasure she had never in her life known before.

"Damien . . ."

"Hush . . . don't fight it." He began kissing her again, his tender, warm lips so incredibly beguiling.

A feverish sound escaped her throat. She was so hot. She felt weak, faint. The pleasured ache in her body was growing beyond her control. Her hips moved shamelessly, asking for something she couldn't identify, while his lips and tongue sweetly plundered her mouth, exploring deeply.

Powerless to stop the riotous sensations he aroused in her, Vanessa strained against him, her breasts pressing against the solid wall of his chest. She needed desperately to assuage the fierce hunger that was burgeoning inside her, to satisfy her frantic craving for him.

Her heart thrumming in a wild rhythm, she gripped his arms fiercely, her fingers biting into Damien's corded muscles as he urged her closer to the forbidding, throbbing pleasure he promised. She was writhing now, her passion at a fever pitch.

"That's it, love . . . yield to it. . . ."

The shattering, unexpected climax sent her reeling; surprise and panic captured her features as the tempest exploded in a firestorm of brilliantly colored sparks. Yet Damien only held her tighter as wave after wave of shuddering pleasure washed over her. She clung to him, shaking helplessly, surrendering to the wild assault on her senses.

With intense satisfaction Damien heard the soft cries of the irresistibly aroused woman in his arms. Each tremor burned through him with exquisite torture, reminding him of his months of celibacy, but he kept his own body rigid, fighting the painful throbbing of his erection as she crested in the sweet rage of need.

He could have taken Vanessa there and then, he reflected. She was hot . . . on fire for him. Her skin was feverish with erotic warmth, every flame-hot inch of her flesh ripe for the taking. And yet he hesitated—and he was not even sure why.

It baffled him that he should hold back now. It would be so simple to thrust himself between her soft thighs and ease his violent lust. . . . And yet he felt more than lust for her. He wanted to cherish her, to claim her . . . but not this way . . . not this place. This was somehow wrong. He wanted her first time with him to be more than just a hasty physical coupling she would later regret.

With a soft oath, Damien gathered her close, holding her limp, trembling body as he struggled for control. She was as exquisitely sensual and responsive as he'd known she would be, and it took every ounce of willpower he possessed to fight the wrenching desire he felt for her, the tender, carnal need.

A long moment later, he drew back to survey her flushed face. She gazed up at him, startled, bewildered, her beautiful, soft doe eyes questioning.

His tone was husky and soft, yet edged with a touch of irony. "If I had meant to seduce you, sweetheart, I would have aroused you precisely like that."

She stared up at him, her expression slightly dazed, bereft, and he cursed himself for a fool. She was trying to understand what had just happened to her, and he had made a jest of it, distancing himself from her when he should have soothed and consoled and praised.

His hard countenance softening, he smoothed an errant tendril from her cheek and fiercely reined in his hunger. "Forgive me, angel."

"Forgive you?" she asked, her voice a shaky whisper.

"For making light of what must have been a first for you."

"I never knew. . . ."

"Knew what? That lovemaking could be so wildly pleasurable? That you could feel such sweet fire?"

"Yes . . ."

He smiled. "There is far more to passion than what you

just experienced, if you will allow yourself to discover it. I would very much like to teach you, sweeting." He bent his head, letting his hot breath caress her cheek. "I want to be the one to show you the mysteries of pleasure, Vanessa. The one to reveal all the sweet secrets between a man and a woman . . ."

He stopped himself. Exhaling softly, he set her gently away from him. "Perhaps I should return you to the house before my last vestige of control disappears."

He helped her from the pool while Vanessa struggled with her own turmoil. She had virtually demanded that Damien seduce her, yet he had drawn back at the last moment.

Somehow that seemed more cruel than forcing himself on her would have been. Damien had left her unforgivably aroused, filled with an aching yearning, shaken by wonder and doubts and uncertainty.

Not speaking, she wrung out her dripping skirts and put on her stockings and slippers. It would be bad enough if she were seen with a wet gown in Lord Sin's company, let alone barefoot.

She refused to look at him when he took her hand and the lamp and led her through the conservatory. They met no one on the return journey, by virtue of the fact that he escorted her back through the secret passage. They entered the house by way of a storage room off the rose garden, through a small door half hidden by tools.

The air inside the passage was musty but dry, yet Vanessa felt stifled. The space was so narrow it barely accommodated Damien's shoulders, the ceiling so low he had to keep his head bent. When they had climbed a steep flight of wooden steps, Damien touched her elbow, requiring her to pause beside a sliding panel in the passage wall.

"Your bedchamber." With a gesture of his head, he indicated the passage behind him. "This runs along the outer wall of the sitting room next to yours, beneath the window seats, and continues on to my chambers."

Silently he opened the secret panel to her room, demonstrating how the catch worked by exerting the slightest pull.

When he turned to go, Vanessa felt a keen sense of regret. "You don't mean to stay?" she was startled into asking.

His mouth curved in a sweet, sad smile. "I don't trust myself." He pressed a finger to her lips. "I want you very, very much, angel. More than you can possibly imagine. But I am willing to wait until you want me as well. When you are ready, I will not have to come to you. You will come to me."

He left her then, taking the light with him. Almost unwillingly Vanessa entered her bedchamber and slid the panel door shut behind her.

In the darkness of her room, she wandered about, restless and unsettled, her thoughts on Damien Sinclair. Try as she might, she couldn't forget the sensation of his body against hers, or the enchanting taste of his kiss, or the fierce explosion of pleasure he had aroused in her.

For weeks she had fought against succumbing to his powerful masculinity, but tonight she had lost the battle. Shamefully, though, she felt no remorse.

Briefly Vanessa shut her eyes. The memory of Damien's embrace filled her with a sweet, aching longing that was totally foreign to her. He had taken her someplace she'd never been before, someplace brilliant and terrifying. She had become a stranger to herself, to the frenzy of desire that had overwhelmed her. Damien had given her a glimpse of paradise, shown her how desperately a woman could want a man. How desperately *she* could want.

Vanessa shook her head and shivered. How could he be so gentle yet cause such a tumult of violent emotions within her? Such passion and desire and fierce, fierce need? He was unlike any man she had ever known, a fantasy lover who could draw the very soul from a woman's body.

Trembling at the memory, Vanessa disrobed and put on her nightdress. Mechanically she hung up her damp gown and brushed out her hair. Then she lay down on the bed, though she knew sleep wouldn't come. The restless longing she felt would not go away.

For a long while she stared up at the canopy overhead, her breasts keenly sensitive, a hollow ache between her thighs. In the darkness, an unbidden image of Damien flowed into her mind. His sensual, chiseled features. His heated silver eyes, warm with tenderness. His beautiful, breathtaking mouth. His vibrant encircling arms that promised such rapture.

Her nerves raw with conflict, Vanessa rolled over and clutched the pillow to her body. The naked, frightening truth was that she wanted him. Wanted him to show her the mysteries of passion, as he'd promised.

She buried her face in the soft down, remembering his whispered words. *When you are ready, I will not have to come to you. You will come to me.*

Should she go to him?

Her heart took up a wild rhythm.

Slowly she sat up, her pulse beating in a slow painful cadence, while a knot of tension coiled in her stomach.

What would happen if she went to him?

She felt herself trembling. For an endless moment she fought a confused tangle of emotions: hope and fear, excitement and dismay, anticipation and disquiet.

What if she proved as cold and passionless as she feared? What if she did not?

In the end the decision was not really a conscious one.

As if in a dream, Vanessa slipped from her bed and lit a candle. Moving to the panel that hid the secret passageway, she found the catch and pressed.

Then, with her heart thudding in her chest, she took a deep breath and slid open the panel door.

Chapter Eight

She reached the end of the narrow passage and stopped, scarcely daring to breathe. The panel in the wall had a catch similar to her own, she saw.

Hesitating, Vanessa snuffed out the candle and stood alone in the darkness, her heartbeat painful and clamorous. At length, however, she gathered her courage and slid open the panel.

She had little trouble seeing, for the draperies had been left undrawn. The sweet summer night air drifted through an open window, while moonlight flooded the chamber with blue-white intensity.

The huge bed that dominated the room was occupied. The man on the bed lay absolutely still, cast in a glow of silver light and shadow.

She thought Damien might be sleeping. His hands were clasped behind his head, a pale linen sheet drawn up to his hips. But she was wrong. He was watching her. Her breath caught harshly.

In the hushed quiet of the room, their eyes locked.

"Did I wake you?" she asked, the question a shaky whisper of sound.

Slowly he rose up on his elbows. "No, I wasn't asleep. But I must be dreaming. Are you a dream, angel?"

The warmth of his voice touched a quickness in her that left her trembling. "No. No dream."

"Will you come here?" he prompted gently. "I dare not move for fear of frightening you away."

He understood her terrible vulnerability, Vanessa realized. She moved unsteadily to stand beside the bed. She could hear the sharp sound of her own breathing in the quiet of the room.

His nearness made her excruciatingly aware of his nakedness. The sheet covered the lower part of his muscular body but did nothing to disguise the tapering chest, the lean, hard waist, the flat belly or narrow hips. . . .

When she stood paralyzed, Damien took the candlestick from her slack fingers and set it on the bedside table. Then, grasping her hand, he drew her slowly down to sit beside him.

For a long moment he said nothing, wanting to give her time to be certain of the decision she had made. After tonight there would be no turning back.

Her midnight eyes were huge and questioning as he reached to lift a curling tress from her breast. His fingers rubbed lightly, feeling the rich, silken texture.

"Your hair is exquisite. I've dreamed of having it wrapped around me."

She made no response, mutely staring down at him.

His hand slid down her arm in a gentle caress. "Do I frighten you?" he murmured.

"I . . . I suppose . . . a little."

"You frighten me as well . . . with your beauty, your innocence."

He took her hand and placed it on his bare chest, letting her feel the strong beat of his heart. "Feel my heart, sweeting, how it quickens at your touch."

When she remained immobile, his velvet voice dropped to a mere whisper. "I won't press you, Vanessa. We will do whatever you wish, no more. You will set the pace between us. You have nothing to fear from me, I promise you."

Her eyes remained riveted on his face. Moonlight danced over his features, accenting the high cheekbones, the lean jaw, the strong column of his throat. He was telling her the truth, she knew; the dark intensity in his gleaming eyes told her so.

Her gaze dropped lower, to the sleekly muscled chest beneath her fingertips, then nervously flickered back up to meet his.

"I . . . don't . . . know what to do. Will you show me?"

An unconsciously tender smile turned one corner of his sensuous mouth. "I would be honored."

His fingers closed over hers. "Touch me, Vanessa," he urged softly.

Under his guidance, her hand moved over his body, caressing uncertainly at first, then with more eagerness. She could feel the hard muscles ripple beneath his skin, feel the heated strength of him, and it stirred a now familiar warmth within her.

She faltered, though, when her palm neared his groin. Sensing her discomfort, Damien unhurriedly drew aside the sheet that covered his loins, giving her a bold view of his arousal, pulsing and erect, between his sinewed thighs.

"I am just a man, cherie," he murmured. "Flesh and blood, just like you. Feel me, sweeting. Feel how powerfully you arouse me."

Inexorably his hand guided her to his throbbing erection, closing her fingers deliberately around him. Her breath spiraled away from her at the shocking feel of him; the huge, swollen length was rigid and rock hard, yet covered in smooth, heated velvet. Not so frightening after all, perhaps . . . Rather, it was strangely arousing.

"My flesh can be an instrument of pleasure, not just pain, Vanessa. And I swear to you, it will be for you."

He moved on then, encouraging her hand lower, brushing the warm sac beneath his thick shaft, then over his powerful horseman's thighs with their faint dusting of dark hair, lingering at his lean flank. . . . Then, surprisingly, he released her hand.

" 'Tis your turn alone, angel. You may do as you like with me. I am at your mercy."

It was a novel experience, having a powerful, virile man such as Lord Sin vulnerable and pliant beneath her touch. Somehow liberating. Intoxicating.

With a will of its own, her hand resumed its sinful exploration of his magnificent nude body, stroking, touching, lingering. He was beautiful, she thought, savoring the feel of his hard, warm flesh, the taut, smooth skin, the supple sinews. His masculine beauty inundated her senses, entrancing her.

"Yes . . . that's it, sweeting . . . touch me."

Holding her breath, she returned to his thick arousal and tentatively brushed the engorged length. It quivered at her touch.

Damien closed his eyes and let out a soft groan.

Immediately Vanessa drew back. "Did I hurt you?"

He gave a soft laugh. "Indeed, a pleasurable hurt. You can drive a man wild with such exquisite ministrations. Don't stop, I beg you."

She bit her lip, tinglingly aware of her newfound sense of feminine power, and yet she hesitated, her courage faltering.

Thankfully, Damien took the decision from her. Reaching

up with a languid finger, he brushed her breast, which was hidden by the cambric bodice of her nightdress. Vanessa drew a sharp breath as her nipple peaked tightly beneath the thin fabric.

"Your nightdress, angel," he queried softly, his voice dark velvet. "Must you leave it on?"

She went suddenly still. The thought of being naked with this man, of completely exposing her body to him, unnerved her, and yet, she knew he would not force her against her will. Again he was giving her a choice.

Shutting her eyes tightly for a moment, she lifted her hips off the bed and drew the garment over her head, then let it drop to the floor. She heard Damien's intake of breath, saw his intent gaze flare with pleasure.

Her cheeks flaming, she started to cover her naked bosom with her arms, but he held her hands away. "No . . . let me look at you."

Shame and wanton excitement flowed through her at the possessive intimacy of his heated gaze.

"Your breasts are exquisite, angel, high and lush, the nipples like delicate rosebuds. You shouldn't be ashamed to let me see them."

At his brazen scrutiny, she felt her nipples begin to ache, her breasts grow heavy.

"Come to me, sweeting," he commanded. Reaching out, he took her by the arms and drew her down to lie against him, her bare, aching breasts pressed to his chest. Vanessa went rigid at the intimate contact.

"Just lie here with me a moment," he cajoled. "I want to feel you in my arms."

Obeying, she lay still, her entire body vibrating with shock and desire at the hard, naked heat of him. His hands stroked her back and he held her lightly, as if waiting for her coiled-tight tension to fade.

Eventually it did; after a time she felt her rigid muscles soften, grow weak. Without haste Damien drew her even closer, to lie fully against him, his lithe, masculine form imprinting his maleness onto her. She could feel his arousal pulsing against her belly, his lips moving against her hair. A hypnotic languor stole over her, while a slow heat built inexorably between them.

"Do you want me to stop?" he asked, the question a husky whisper.

She drew a shaky breath. "No . . . don't stop."

His long fingers came back to lie alongside her jaw and slowly turned her face up to his. He meant to kiss her, she knew. She felt a delicious drifting of his warm breath across her parted lips, then the tender caress of his mouth as he coaxed hers open.

He kissed her very slowly, very carefully, a lingering, intimate knowing of her mouth. A vibrant shiver ran through her as his tongue delved inside, drinking deep. The last vestiges of her resistance dwindled at his in-flaming kiss.

After a moment his hot mouth slid lower. His lips moved against her throat, his hand lightly caressing her body. Her breathing sharpened painfully when he found the rising swell of her breast; where his fingers touched, her skin seemed to burn.

Sensations of longing and desire surged inside her as her breast nested in his hand. With infinite care, Damien shifted their positions, pressing her onto her back, and bent over her. She started to tense, but then his searing breath touched her nipple, and her own breath turned to warm liquid in her lungs.

His lips traced a halo of kisses edging the aureole, then the rosy center. Instantly, all the fires he had aroused within her earlier again kindled to life, white-hot and urgent. She felt the same brazen, primal need she'd known in the conservatory among the roses.

His tongue glided slowly over a soft crest, and a weak trembling began in her limbs, a feverish yearning. Again his tongue touched the swollen flesh, tasting her, sliding over the distended surface of her nipple, igniting her senses. When his mouth closed around the hard bud with exquisite pressure, Vanessa arched up, wanting his mouth.

He sucked gently, sipping at her, and his erotic attentions drew a moan from her throat. He continued to lave the hard, aching peak, while his questing hand moved downward over her body with deliberate slowness, his fingers caressing her bare skin with soft strokes.

Her body was melting, yet she was unprepared when his hand slid between her shivering thighs to claim the womanly softness of her. She went rigid, pressing her hands against his shoulders in protest.

Damien rose above her, gazing down into her eyes intently. "Trust me, Vanessa. Together we can find where the stars are born."

"I don't know if—"

"Hush, angel." His mouth dipped to touch hers. "Can you not recognize desire when you feel it?"

Slowly he parted her thighs again, his fingers tangling in the dark curls at the portal to her femininity. Her eyes squeezed shut, but she let him continue, not protesting when he began to stroke the soft female cleft, dewy with warmth. She gasped as he discovered the delicate bud hidden there.

Sensually, expertly, his thumb caressed her, sweeping

away all thoughts of denial, the languid, tantalizing rhythm arousing a wild, relentless pleasure in her. She felt hot, feverish, throbbing. Her thighs fell open as he parted the sensitive skin of her inner lips.

A tremor rippled through her when he slid a long finger into her quivering flesh, finding her slick and wet.

"See, your honey flows for me," he whispered with satisfaction, watching her flushed face.

Her head moved restlessly on the pillow as she surrendered to the magic of his wonderful, caressing hands.

The fingers were bolder now, exploring her with hot, slick strokes, learning the intimate secrets of her, lavishing sensuality on the melting folds of flesh, the slow thrusts a sweet, delicious torture.

Writhing now, Vanessa arched against his hand, seeking ease for the hot, pulsing ache between her thighs. She thought she might faint, but not from fear. Fear was no part of the tumultuous feelings surging through her.

"Are you ready for me, sweet angel?" he rasped. "I think yes. . . ."

A fierce disappointment assailed her when his magic suddenly ceased, but he was only anointing his huge shaft with the slick wetness that seeped from her body. Then he moved over her, settling in the cradle of her thighs.

She felt his weight, the pressure of his powerful thighs against her bare skin, the controlled probing of his hardness.

Shivering helplessly, Vanessa stared up at him, a deep primal fear combined with excitement coursing through her. Their eyes locked as he eased the silken head into her quivering flesh.

She stiffened and gasped as the fiery brand intruded into the delicate softness of her, her newly sensitized body thrumming with panic and desire. Unbidden, her fear rose, yet he glided in smoothly, as if her body had been made expressly for him, for this.

Her tension eased as his body wrapped around hers, warming her, calming her.

"The stars, angel. Will you come with me?"

Tears sprang to her eyes as she gazed up at him. He was holding her so gently and his eyes were so soft. . . .

"Yes . . ."

She kept very still, desperately wanting him to stay inside her, wanting the heat of his fullness deep within her.

His mouth found hers again, tenderly arousing. "I want to get closer," he whispered against her lips, even as he buried himself deeper. "So close I can't breathe without you being a part of me."

His raw, silky voice caressed her as he roused a throbbing need that swelled and grew. He was murmuring sensual, coaxing words against her lips as his body began to move against hers.

Vanessa shuddered. He was a dark fire, igniting her senses. He was raw torment and searing pleasure. The tremulous desperation intensified within her, making her writhe and arch her back.

Her legs wrapped around his as she struggled to get closer, as the dark waves of pleasure built relentlessly.

"Damien . . ." His name was like a prayer on her lips.

Her nails dug into the flesh of his back. The pleading moan that came to her throat became another cry that was taken from her by his kiss. No longer was she conscious of her surroundings, only of Damien, of his ebony hair and silver eyes, of his hard-driving body, his feverish mouth and possessive thrusts. He was her world, the center of the spiraling madness that held her in its turbulent grip.

The hungry plundering of his mouth followed the urgent motion of his hips, his hardness impaling her, while his rough, sensual voice urged her on, deep into a heated wildness.

"Yes, be on fire for me. . . ."

Dimly, she knew she was sobbing.

He was moving faster, deeper, filling her to bursting, his breathing thick and heavy. Brilliant flames leapt against the blackness of her mind, and she cried out, a high, keening pleasure sound. She felt as if she were dying in his arms.

In mindless abandon she began to convulse beneath him. Her body surrendered to him, overwhelmed by blind desire that shook her, wrenched her, devoured her.

His mouth captured her scream of passion as she shattered around him. Giving her no surcease, his hands closed over her buttocks, lifting them so he could thrust even more deeply inside her.

His face contorted with pleasure and pain, Damien exploded inside her.

She was still clinging to him long moments later when he lowered himself to her side, shaking with aftershocks. He held her limp and trembling body, cradling her in his arms, his breath harsh, ragged.

She was weeping, he realized with alarm. "Angel?"

Concern flooding him, he turned her face up to his to search her shimmering eyes. "Did I hurt you?"

Swallowing, she nodded her head. "Yes, a pleasurable hurt," she returned huskily, echoing his earlier reply.

When he saw her tremulous smile, his concern eased. Her tears were tears of joy, of wonder. She had tasted the warmth and passion he knew her capable of, and it had shocked her, that was all.

Tenderness assailed him as he held her lightly. He

wanted to kiss those tears away. "Your body is becoming awakened to desire for the first time."

To his surprise, she reached up and tentatively touched his lips with her fingertips. "I never realized stars could be so lovely."

A smiled filled his eyes. In her deplorable innocence, she hadn't known lovemaking could be so powerful, so soul-wrenching. Nor had he, in all honesty. The shattering intensity of his climax just now had startled him. As jaded as he was with pleasures of the flesh, passion with her had seemed somehow fresh and new.

And he knew that one taste of her would not be enough.

A chill night breeze wafted over his skin, cooling his heated flesh and hers. Feeling her shiver, he reached down to draw the covers up over them both, then gathered Vanessa closer. Her body weak and sated, she buried her face against his shoulder, an unconsciously sensual gesture.

Damien felt a fresh stirring of desire and a dangerous tenderness. As she lay languid in his arms, he toyed with a lock of her satiny hair, his thoughts a strange fusion of emotions.

His plan to satisfy a fleeting hunger for her had ripened into something far more compelling. What had started as a carnal seduction had become a tender wooing . . . a wooing he was determined to continue.

Her sexual awakening would be like nurturing a hot-house flower, but before she left him, he would make her blossom fully as a woman. His lips pressed against her burnished hair as he made the solemn vow.

Vanessa sighed at his gentle touch. She felt cherished, protected, as she drifted off to sleep in his arms. Her dreams were a tangle of erotic images and sensual yearning, images of Damien, his hard male body moving against her softness, setting her aflame, driving her ever higher and higher until she shattered. . . .

She woke to the feel of his vibrant heat against her. For a moment she lay there, savoring the sensation, reliving the enchantment of his lovemaking.

He had won; Damien had succeeded in persuading her to share his bed. But she couldn't regret his victory. She could only feel a sense of wonder at the ecstasy he had brought her. Only a profound relief that she wasn't the cold, unresponsive woman she'd always condemned herself for being. That, and a fierce gratitude for the man who had led her to that revelation. Damien had shown her a passionate side of herself she had never known existed.

After her wretched experiences in the marriage bed, perhaps it was inevitable she would succumb willingly to his practiced seduction. She had never been wooed so ardently by a man, or treated so tenderly.

But she hadn't expected that wild hunger in herself, that fierce, sweet fire. Oddly, she felt no shame at her wantonness. But perhaps that in itself was shameful.

Shutting her eyes, Vanessa tried to summon a proper sense of contrition, but it eluded her. All she could remember was the magic of his spell, the straining thrusts of his body, and her cries of ecstasy as he brought her to fulfillment.

Aching at the memory, she sat up, holding the sheet to her breasts. Almost at once she felt Damien's fingers brush her naked back. He must not have been asleep.

She shivered at his incredibly gentle touch. "I should go," she murmured uncertainly.

"Why?" he asked, his voice soft, beguiling. "We have the entire night ahead of us."

She turned to gaze down at him, his face heart-wrenchingly beautiful in the silver moonlight. He had promised to show her the mysteries of pleasure, and, heaven help her, she wanted him to. The woman in her, who had never known true passion, yearned for it now, with this man. And yet she was afraid. Afraid she would be opening herself to far greater hurt than the physical pain the carnal act of mating had once brought her.

He must have seen her hesitation, for he reached up and cupped her cheek with his palm, the gesture intimate and infinitely protective.

"Stay with me. . . ."

His hand caressed her cheek and moved downward to the slim column of her throat. Vanessa let her head fall back, cherishing the sensuality of his touch. His hand trailed lower, to rest possessively on the curve of her breast, and she felt her heart jump against his palm. How could he arouse such deep hunger in her so swiftly? she wondered. Such fierce, tender emotion?

She made no protest when his hands twined in her hair and he drew her down to lie beside him. Willingly she pressed against his body, against his shaft that was rigid and full. . . .

She gave a start and stared at him in puzzlement.

His eyebrows rose. "What's wrong, love? Have I frightened you again?"

"I suppose I was just . . . startled. Roger could never—" She broke off in embarrassment, evading his gaze.

"Could never what?"

"Become . . . aroused again. Once his desire was spent, he left me alone. I used to pray that he would . . . finish quickly."

His eyes soft, Damien pulled her into his embrace and

whispered a promise in her ear. "I intend to make you forget he ever existed," he vowed. "We'll banish all your ugly memories. From this night on, we start anew."

He heard her sigh. She lay trustingly, with her cheek pressed against his heart, her hair spilling like a curtain of silk over his skin. His hands swept her back lightly.

"Some men can last longer than others, become stimulated more quickly," he explained. "When a man desires a woman as much as I desire you, his arousal is never entirely sated."

"Do you . . . desire me?" The soft question was serious, holding no coyness.

His fingers were moving on her back, sending cascades of shivers through her. "Immensely," he answered with complete honesty. "What red-blooded man would not find you irresistible?"

His hands moving to clasp her upper arms, he made Vanessa lift her head to look at him. "From the moment I first saw you in that gaming hell, I wanted you."

She gazed solemnly back at him, her dark eyes reflecting moonlight. "I never would have suspected. I thought you wished me in Hades."

"That was before I tasted your sweet lips. . . ." He kissed her softly, and her lips trembled against his. "I could make love to you for hours, I have no doubt."

She hesitated. "Hours?" There was both wonder and skepticism in her tone.

His mouth curved in amusement. "I fear my reputation as a lover has been maligned unjustly."

Her own mouth fought to hold back a smile. "Unjustly? But then you are not a particularly objective observer, I suspect."

"You require proof, my lady?"

"Would you be greatly put out if I said I did?" she asked with a combination of boldness and shyness that was enchanting.

A melting tenderness infused his laughter. "Greatly, indeed. Very well, love, at your insistence, we shall put my stamina to the test."

She could not find the breath to answer, for he was kissing her now with the fevered softness of a lover.

A spark ignited and flared upward between them as his magical hands moved over her body, and he whispered against her lips, "Let me show you how many ways I can pleasure you, sweet siren. . . ."

Chapter Nine

It was a night of pure enchantment, and over too soon. In the dawn of early morning, he escorted her back through the secret passage to her own chamber.

Impossibly, the kiss Damien gave her upon leaving roused her as much as the first touch of his mouth had, even though Vanessa thought herself so sensually drained, she couldn't conceivably feel any more desire or pleasure.

She slept deeply, replete and exhausted, and woke far later than usual. For a moment she lay there, remembering the night. She could still feel Damien's warm, elegant hands on her flesh, his sleek, lithe body pleasuring her, his soft, murmured words of praise and satisfaction as he brought her to ecstasy again and again.

He had swept her away with his consuming passion, into a world of rapture, and, in so doing, had banished her feelings of dread, her memories of pain. More remarkably, his exquisite lovemaking had left her shaken with the realization of her own passion.

Properly she should feel shame for acting like such a wanton, yet she couldn't bring herself to wallow in self-reproach. She had dutifully endured a joyless marriage and the misery of carnal relations with her husband, never knowing what it meant to be fully a woman, to feel cherished, desired, wanted. Damien had given her a taste of real passion—perhaps the only one she might ever know—and she wouldn't disavow this fantasy, however fleeting.

She closed her eyes, savoring the memories of his worshiping caresses. His male scent still lingered on her skin, and she felt an absurd reluctance to wash it off. . . .

The thought of washing was an intrusion, although a pleasant one, for it reminded her of the plans for the day. This afternoon Damien intended to introduce Olivia to the bath he had built for her in the conservatory.

Rising with an elated feeling of anticipation, Vanessa rang for her own bath.

She saw no sign of Damien that morning, however, or later at luncheon, since reportedly he was overseeing the finishing touches on his creation. Then she became busy helping Olivia prepare for the momentous event, helping her into her new bathing costume. When finally he arrived at his sister's rooms, Vanessa still had no opportunity for a private word.

It was just as well, she reflected, that they weren't alone, for she could scarcely meet his gaze. She suddenly felt keenly shy, while her heart fluttered in her chest in a rhythm akin to panic. Then he looked at her and smiled, a soft, quiet smile with the warmth of morning sunshine, and her pulse rate soared. Other than that brief gesture, however, he acted as if nothing unusual had occurred between them.

But, of course, Vanessa reminded herself, he wouldn't wish to advertise their newfound intimacy with a public display of passion, most especially in front of his sister.

Damien himself accompanied Olivia into the conservatory, along with Vanessa and two maidservants. Olivia's expression showed genuine delight at the healing bath among the roses.

"Oh, Damien, thank you," she declared sincerely as he pushed her chair right up to the edge of the tiled pool. "You've gone to such trouble for me."

"It was no trouble. Why don't you try it and see if the design is adequate?"

He showed her how to access the bath, and with help she managed to shift herself onto the low ledge. Vanessa held the skirts of her bathing costume to one side so that she could turn and gently slide down the ramp.

With a sigh, Olivia settled into the warm, swirling water. "This is heavenly. I am in raptures."

Vanessa scarcely heard her praise, for as Damien straightened, his shoulder briefly brushed hers. She glanced up at him sharply, deeply affected by this casual contact. For a moment, as she met the silver smoke of his eyes, she was assailed by memories of what had taken place between them last night. Her whole being throbbed with awareness of him.

She was relieved when Olivia blithely demanded that he vacate the conservatory and leave her to her bath. "Vanessa will care for me, I'm certain. I will send for you if I need you."

Damien winced in mock offense. "I believe I have been dismissed." But his mouth was smiling as he bowed to both ladies and turned to go.

Vanessa followed him with her eyes. She wondered how their relationship would change now that she had spent the night in his bed. It would be no hardship being his mistress, she suspected, but rather a delight and an enchantment.

She still had no chance to be alone with him, however, until that evening after dinner, when Olivia retired for the night. Damien carried his sister upstairs and returned to the drawing room, where he found Vanessa barely able to hold her eyes open.

"Forgive me, angel. I kept you awake much too long last night."

She smiled sleepily up at him. "I don't remember objecting very strenuously."

He bent to kiss her forehead, the sort of chaste kiss he might give a sister. "Why don't you retire and get some sleep?"

She gazed at him uncertainly. "Will you . . ."

His eyebrows rose. "Will I what?"

"Come to my room tonight?"

His beguiling smile made her heart flutter. "I was waiting with bated breath for an invitation. If you are certain you desire my company."

"I do," she answered boldly.

"In that case . . ." He settled himself beside her on the brocade settee. "Forgive me for bringing up a delicate matter, but I think it wise, under the circumstances, to take certain precautions."

He withdrew a small scarlet silk bag from his jacket pocket. "Are you familiar with these?" he asked, letting her peer inside.

"They look like . . . sponges."

"They are. When soaked in vinegar or brandy and placed in a woman's love passage, they can prevent a man's seed from taking root, thus avoiding impregnation."

There were perhaps a dozen little squares of sea sponge, Vanessa saw, each with a thin string sewn onto one end.

"I should have thought of it before last night," Damien observed. "I will be happy to show you how to use them."

She could well imagine how they were used. The thought of Damien giving her such intimate instruction brought a flush of color to her cheeks, and forcibly reminded her of her role as Lord Sin's mistress, as well as his desire for vengeance.

He was right, however. The scandal of a pregnancy out of wedlock would be devastating to her family.

It was possible, of course, that she was barren. She had never conceived when she was wed to Roger. But precautions were indeed wise. Her subterfuge of an innocent relationship with Damien would prove impossible to maintain were he to get her with child.

Yet the unsettled issues between them didn't seem to matter later when Damien came to her bedchamber. She was waiting for him, curled up in a wing chair before the hearth, when the panel slid open with a whisper.

He wore a midnight blue dressing gown, which fell open as he stepped silently into the room. He was naked beneath, giving her a full frontal view of his nudity.

Nerves thrumming, she watched his lithe, graceful motion as he crossed the floor to her. His magnificent body was already aroused, his phallus huge and straining.

He took her breath away.

For a long moment their eyes held. In the candlelight his eyes were luminous, his gaze hot and burning with a passion he made no effort to disguise.

"I thought the day would never end," he murmured hoarsely.

"I know," she whispered as he bent to draw her to her feet.

He touched her face, his fingers long and smooth and delicious against her skin, making her shiver under his light caress. "I want you."

Vanessa trembled, thrilled to be wanted by this magnificent, sinfully beautiful man.

Silently, then, he worked loose the tiny buttons of her

night rail and pushed the garment down over her shoulders, letting it fall to the floor.

When his hand curved to the heavy ache of her breast, Vanessa shut her eyes, feeling a sweeping pleasure beneath the erotic gentleness of his touch. She quivered as he traced a finger between her breasts and downward to her narrow waist, then slowly back up again.

When his thumb brushed against the rigid peak of her nipple, a melting glow began deep inside her, along with a fierce, tender craving.

She needed no other urging. With a pleasured sigh, Vanessa lifted her arms to entwine them about his neck. Damien's hot, sensual mouth came down to meet hers, while the night rose up and wrapped them in all its vibrant, sweet magic. . . .

He visited her room nightly after that. Damien proved an exquisite tutor, exploring the sensual side of her nature and confronting her inhibitions. Vanessa felt as if she were living in an enchanted dream.

By tacit agreement they never spoke about their relationship, not wanting reality to intrude. She refused to contemplate the future, or dwell on the fact that by sharing her bed, Damien was only satisfying his desire for vengeance. She'd been compelled to accept his infamous bargain to ensure her family's survival after her brother had recklessly gambled away their very livelihood. Yet it grew harder each day to remember her purpose for being here.

The following week saw a change in Damien's relationship with his sister as well. While Olivia still retreated into bouts of moodiness periodically, she seemed genuinely determined to shrug off her anger and despair and to accept his offer of a closer friendship. Moreover, for the first time she expressed a desire to leave her bed, not only for her daily baths and regular visits to the gardens, but to venture out onto the vast estate grounds.

Since the weather had turned cool and rainy, it took some persuading on Olivia's part to convince Damien that the dampness wouldn't harm her. But occasionally when there was a break in the clouds, he took her on short drives in the country, wrapping her in warm blankets to prevent her from taking a chill.

She had an easier time convincing him to expand one of their excursions into a picnic.

"Vanessa says she enjoys picnics prodigiously," Olivia pressed one rainy afternoon as she and Damien played a game of chess in the drawing room. "Surely you would not wish to disappoint her."

"No indeed." His eyes met Vanessa's across the room. "I will always do my utmost to please so lovely a guest."

Vanessa felt herself blush, recalling precisely how he had endeavored to please her during the night.

She forced her attention back to her book, but as the afternoon progressed, she found herself watching the two of them, their dark heads bent over the chessboard. They were laughing and jesting so easily that she was almost envious.

She had never expected to see the decadent Lord Sin so carefree, so mellow, and more than once she had to drag her gaze away from his face.

Each time she looked at him, Vanessa was conscious of a fresh wave of disquietude. Impossibly, she was falling under Damien's spell with very little effort on his part. He was as multifaceted as a hundred-carat diamond. And his affectionate warmth for his sister was even more devastating than his sensual, irresistible charm toward herself.

* * *

Later that same night, Damien became aware of a similar disquietude. He and Vanessa were sitting before the hearth, engaged in one of their more serious conversations, and he observed with surprise that this was his longest visit to Rosewood since his youth. "Usually after the first day I find myself bored to tears and eager to leave."

"I've often thought boredom stems from a lack of occupation," Vanessa murmured in reply. "Perhaps if you had a worthwhile endeavor to fill your idle hours, you wouldn't be so restless."

"I suppose you mean to suggest a remedy for me?"

"Do you have any particular interests that would require you to put your mind and talents to good use? Anything that stirs or excites you?"

"Other than my usual decadent pleasures, you mean?" Damien frowned thoughtfully. "It is hardly a gentleman's occupation, but I'm quite good at making money."

Vanessa smiled. "That is a valuable talent indeed. Surely you could find an unexceptional diversion along those lines?"

"Perhaps. What about you, my lovely dragon? Do you harbor any interests you've kept secret?"

She shrugged lightly. "I would have liked to have had children, like most women. But that is highly unlikely now."

"Why so?"

"Because I don't intend to marry again. My sole concern now is for my sisters and how to provide for them. I vowed they would never be sold into marriage as I was. If they marry, it will be for love."

When the corner of Damien's mouth twisted sardonically, Vanessa arched an eyebrow. "I suppose you don't believe in love?"

"Oh, I believe in it. Particularly in its destructive powers. Love can too easily become obsession. My father was a prime example. My sister is another. Olivia fancied herself in love, and it nearly destroyed her life."

In the silence that followed his cynical observation, Damien averted his gaze and stared down at the brandy in his glass. He'd never known love, nor had he wanted to, not after the abominable example his father had set.

Yet, for the first time, Damien became conscious of the risk he was taking with Vanessa. It alarmed him, the tenderness he was beginning to feel for her.

He'd had mistresses who could arouse his passion before, but softer emotions such as admiration and friendship and affection never invaded his affairs.

This warm, intimate sharing with a woman was new. And addictive. He found himself craving Vanessa's company, devising excuses to be with her.

If their acquaintance continued this way, Damien realized, he could run a grave risk of emulating his father.

Damien had promised his sister a picnic on the first clear day, which had Olivia eagerly searching the skies the moment she arose each morning. The rain ended at last one Monday, leaving a pristine morning. Damien ordered an alfresco luncheon packed, and by noon, the three of them were seated in the landau, with only a coachman and one footman in attendance.

When they stopped on a hilltop, Vanessa found herself enchanted by the picturesque view of the emerald-green, undulating countryside. The low hills seemed to roll on forever, forming an endless quilt of fields and pastures embroidered by hedgerows and patches of woodland. Damien handed her down from the carriage and then lifted his sister in his arms, as any burly footman might.

He had forsworn his usual elegant, impeccable tailoring for this occasion in favor of leather breeches, top boots, and a plain waistcoat, and Vanessa thought he looked more like a country gentleman than a dissipated nobleman, as at ease in this domain as he would be at the gaming tables or the opera.

They settled Olivia in the shade of a chestnut tree with a half-dozen pillows, and then enjoyed a delicious repast of cold chicken, cheese, fresh fruit, and wine, while the servants kept a respectful distance.

By the time the last crumb had been devoured, the day had turned lazy and warm. Olivia lay back on her pillows with a sigh, watching the fleecy clouds float across the sky.

"This," she murmured, "is quite lovely. I wish every day could be this beautiful. Don't you, Vanessa?"

Vanessa couldn't help but meet Damien's eyes in a conspiratorial glance. Their efforts to cheer the girl, to banish her loneliness and melancholia, seemed to be having an effect at last.

"Oh, I don't know," Vanessa answered lightly. "If every day were just like this, then today would no longer be special. Which reminds me . . ." She asked Damien to pass her the painted tin box that had been packed with the lunch. "I took the liberty of having your cook make these," she said to his sister.

Olivia opened the tin and smiled to see the baked meringues in the shape of swans. "How did you know these are my favorite?"

"I seem to remember your mentioning it a time or two."

"I can recall at least a dozen," Damien interjected wryly.

Olivia took a delicate bite of a swan and shut her eyes, savoring the sweetness. "I never can get Cook to make them for me. She says she doesn't want to spoil me."

Vanessa smiled. "Everyone can do with a little spoiling now and then."

"You are so wise."

"I'm glad you think so. My sisters consider me an over-managing tyrant at times."

Olivia laughed, a happy, musical sound. "I'm sure you are not!"

"Well, their complaints do usually come after I've refused them a new gown they've set their hearts on."

"I should like to meet Fanny and Charlotte someday."

At the innocent comment, Vanessa stole another swift glance at Damien. His face had hardened momentarily, while his gray eyes had turned cold.

She had no doubt he was recalling the conflict between them. He wanted his sister to have nothing to do with any of Vanessa's relations. *She* was here only because she was his mistress, Vanessa remembered.

Of late she'd been too eager to deny that bald truth. In recent days Damien had treated her as much like a member of the family as a lover, showing her warmth and affection as well as passion—almost as if he were coming to care for her. Clearly she'd allowed herself to be seduced by wishful thinking.

"Someday perhaps you shall meet them," Vanessa prevaricated, hiding the sudden, sharp pang of regret she felt. "Now what shall we read?" she asked, determinedly changing the subject.

They had brought several of Olivia's poetry books, and after a brief discussion, Vanessa began to recite aloud from

Wordsworth and Coleridge's *Lyrical Ballads*, her voice quiet and low.

Damien sipped his wine and listened, fighting his own darkening mood. The reminder of her family members had banished the intimate, convivial atmosphere and made him recall the circumstances that had led to Vanessa's presence at Rosewood.

It was good for him to remember, though, for it forced him to contemplate the dilemma he now faced: what to do about his growing need for her. Disturbingly, Vanessa was beginning to affect his judgment.

He could not regret bringing her here. He was consummately grateful to see her patiently coaxing his sister out of her wounded shell. Olivia had changed in the few short weeks since Vanessa's arrival. Her spirits had slowly begun to rebound, due in large part to Vanessa's warmth and wit and infinite patience.

His sister was not the only one who had succumbed to her subtle influence, however. The household staff willingly looked to her guidance, as if she were lady of the manor, and she had charmed the groundskeepers and undergardners so that they vied to show her the latest blooms and to provide her with the most beautiful bouquets for her rooms.

She had charmed *him* as well—and intrigued him more than he'd thought possible. He'd never known a woman with her tantalizing combination of innocence and sophistication, of warmth and intelligence, of vulnerability and strength. Certainly he'd never known a beauty with so little notion of her own power.

She was the reason his time here had passed so rapidly. The challenge of pursuing Vanessa had prevented him from experiencing his usual restlessness.

It had not been an easy task, overcoming her vulnerability, but she was no longer cool and guarded in his presence. Instead, she responded to him with a passion that still startled him.

" 'In hours of weariness, sensations sweet, felt in the blood, and felt along the heart,' " her musical voice intoned softly.

Damien's brows drew together as he watched her. *The blood and the heart, indeed.* He'd gotten more than he had bargained for when he demanded she become his mistress to satisfy her brother's debt. He had intended for her to assuage his physical needs, of course, but he'd never expected her to arouse such fiery hunger in him . . . or such inexplicable feelings of tenderness.

Damien frowned darkly. No courtesan, however skilled or beautiful, had succeeded in holding his interest as long as Vanessa had, certainly not with such intensity. She was sensual enough to enflame his senses, yet spirited and clever enough to prove a match for him outside the bedroom. Remarkably, he wanted her more each time he was with her.

A dangerous sentiment, he warned himself. If he didn't take care, he could become ensnared by passion, just like his father before him.

It would be madness, Damien knew, to allow one woman to dominate his life, to become so important to him that he allowed his heart to rule his head. He had vowed he would never succumb to that fatal affliction— yet he feared that's what was happening with Vanessa.

He was becoming too deeply involved. His attraction for her had grown much too forceful for his peace of mind, while their closeness was getting out of hand.

His gaze traveled over her elegant figure as she read. The graceful curve of her neck beckoned him to draw her against him and sample a taste of her. . . .

Devil take it, man, get your lust under control. His jaw clenched. He badly needed to put some distance between them, Damien reflected. She was too great a temptation while she was so near.

He couldn't send her away, of course. Not when she was doing his sister so much good. He would have to be the one to leave, then. There was to be a gathering of his Hellfire colleagues at week's end in Berkshire. Clune was holding a house party for gentlemen only, the sort of raucous affair that often degenerated into wild orgies. Damien had already sent his regrets, yet, if he attended, it might help to take his mind off a certain temptress who was occupying his thoughts far more than was comfortable, or prudent.

At the same time he could look at some nearby property his man of business had recommended buying. And he could use the occasion to travel farther north, to investigate a factory he had won at the gaming tables this past winter. The press of business would provide a valid excuse to be gone for a time. . . .

He had no desire to spoil the idyllic summer's day, however, or depress his sister's rare happiness. He would wait until this evening to break the news to her. And to Vanessa as well.

Damien took a long swallow of his wine and forced himself to look away from her.

Meanwhile he would have to rein in his fierce craving before it threatened to become a full-fledged obsession.

* * *

Olivia seemed reluctant for the magical afternoon to end, but when she visibly began to tire, Damien insisted on taking her home.

"I promise there will be more picnics in the future," he assured her.

As he carried her into the house, she recalled leaving her favorite shawl in the conservatory when she'd visited the bath that morning. Vanessa volunteered to fetch it, and found the shawl draped over the bench beside the pool.

She had just turned to retrace her steps through the conservatory when a hushed voice called her name. She looked up in startlement.

A man blocked her path, attired in a slouch hat and frayed frock coat, with a short growth of beard darkening his jaw.

She had grown accustomed to seeing strangers at Rosewood, since scholars and scientists and botanists regularly came to study the roses in the summer. But none had ever approached her or followed her. This man could be anything from a university student to a ruffian.

Her wariness seemed to amuse him, for his mouth curved in a slow grin as he drew off his hat to reveal a familiar and beloved face. "What, Van, can you not give your only brother a greeting of welcome?"

"Aubrey? What on earth . . ."

He came forward and embraced her, then stepped back to eye her fondly. "I didn't mean to shock you, my dear."

She stared at him blankly. "Whatever possessed you to grow a beard? I would never have recognized you if you hadn't spoken."

His mobile mouth twisted wryly. "That is precisely the idea, love. Sinclair would probably shoot me if he knew I had breached his premises."

"Oh, my word . . ." Vanessa exclaimed, recalling the enmity between the two men. "Are you mad? He will see you—"

"With luck he will never know I'm here. My disguise was effective enough to fool you, wasn't it? I bought this coat from a student at Oxford for a guinea."

"Yes, but . . ." She lowered her voice and, with a quick glance around, drew him farther into the conservatory, behind the Chinese screen. "What are you doing here?"

"I came to see how you fared."

"I'm well enough."

Aubrey's brow furrowed as he studied her intently. "Sinclair hasn't mistreated you?"

Vanessa looked away from her brother's penetrating gaze. "No, not at all. You shouldn't be here," she added.

"I couldn't stay away," he replied obliquely. "What of Olivia? I have no right to ask, perhaps, but I need to know. I saw her being carried out of the carriage a moment ago, but she was laughing. She looked . . . She didn't seem to be suffering terribly." His tone sounded hopeful. "At least not as much as I feared."

Vanessa turned cool. "She hasn't regained the use of her limbs, if that is what you are asking. She is still a cripple, and her physical state is wholly uncertain . . . although emotionally she has begun to recover a small measure."

"I wish I could speak to her, just for a moment."

"That is out of the question, Aubrey. It would only upset her to see you."

"Does she hate me so very much, then?"

"What do you think?" Vanessa asked bluntly.

Aubrey winced, then looked away. "I want to tell her how deeply sorry I am."

"I'm sure that would salve your conscience, but I cannot see how it would benefit her."

"Will you at least take a letter to her for me? I cannot write to her. All my letters are returned."

Vanessa shook her head. "No, Aubrey, I can't. It would only remind her of how you ruined her life."

His gaze grew bleak. "I can't bear to think of what I've done."

"Well, you will simply have to live with it," Vanessa returned, giving him no quarter. "She has had to."

To her surprise, she saw tears start to shimmer in her brother's dark eyes. "Will you tell her of my regret?"

"I don't dare, Aubrey," Vanessa said more softly. "Olivia trusts me because she doesn't know of my connection to you. It was bad enough that I had to deceive her, but if I were to reveal the truth after all this time, she would certainly feel as if I had betrayed her."

"I wish . . . there were some way for me to make amends."

"I know, but the best way for you to make amends is to go home and not show yourself here again."

He clenched his teeth, and Vanessa recognized the stubborn set of his jaw. "I cannot leave just yet. There may be something I can do for her."

"Are you certain it isn't a cockfight or a boxing match that has drawn you here, and not your conscience?"

He glanced at her sadly. "I'm certain. I'm here out of concern for her . . . and for you." His hurt seemed genuine. Evidently he had convinced himself that his motives were selfless.

Vanessa sighed. "Perhaps so, Aubrey. But you will only make matters worse by staying."

Gazing into her eyes, he took her hands and gave them a

gentle squeeze. "Vanessa . . . I want you to know how much I appreciate the sacrifice you've made for me. You should never have had to pay such a price for my sins. But I promise you it won't be in vain." His expression was as solemn as Vanessa had ever seen it. "I owe you more than I can say. You made me take a hard look at my life, made me realize how low I had sunk. And I swear I mean to change, to turn my life around. To become a different man."

Vanessa searched her brother's face. If Aubrey sincerely felt a measure of guilt, of remorse, perhaps he was beginning to grow up at least a little.

"It isn't so bad, truly," she replied quietly. "There are times when I quite enjoy myself. And I believe I am doing Olivia some good."

"I . . . wondered. Your letters home are cheerful enough, but I know there's much you leave out, for the sake of our sisters."

The rest of the family still believed she was here as companion to Miss Sinclair rather than as Lord Sin's mistress. Only Aubrey knew her true role.

"How are Charlotte and Fanny?" Vanessa asked.

"Well enough. Everyone misses you, Mama especially. You will never credit it, but the girls have been making a sincere attempt to cut down on expenses. Fanny has purchased only a single bonnet the entire time you've been gone."

Vanessa felt herself smile. "Tell her I appreciate her efforts at economy."

"You'll have to tell her yourself, in a letter. I'm not returning home just yet. I've taken an attic room in the village. Penance for my sins, and all that," he added wryly at her shocked look.

"Aubrey, you can't stay. You can't hurt Olivia Sinclair

again . . ." she implored, but he held a finger to her lips to hush her.

"Please try to understand, Vanessa. The last thing I want to do is hurt her. I'll keep away from her for now, but I can't leave just yet. I can't ignore what I did to her. I've tried everything in my power to forget it, believe me, but it hasn't worked. I can't leave her. I just can't."

After her brother's unsettling visit, dinner was an unnerving event for Vanessa. As much as she wanted to believe Aubrey's sincerity, she feared he was here for his own selfish reasons, that he was thinking only of himself, trying to ease his conscience. Haunted by feelings of remorse and guilt, he had convinced himself that apologizing to Olivia would make his pain go away. He didn't seem to care that the girl would be shattered to have to face him again.

Vanessa also feared the consequences of having her connection to Aubrey become known. Olivia would, perhaps, hate her if the truth about her deception came out.

Damien, too, would likely be outraged to learn Aubrey was within a hundred miles of his cherished sister.

Uncertainly, Vanessa watched Damien during dinner. He seemed withdrawn, preoccupied, his eyes cool, with none of the sensual heat he'd shown her recently whenever he merely looked at her. Compared to the intimacy of the past week, his manner was almost frosty.

Vanessa wondered if she had done something to anger him. He could not have known about her brother's visit. . . . And yet, she sensed something was wrong between them.

It came as a surprise when, midway through the fish course, Damien casually mentioned his intention to travel at week's end to settle some business matters in the north.

But his further revelation that he planned to attend this weekend's gathering at the Earl of Clune's frankly startled Vanessa.

Her gaze flew to Damien's. Lord Clune was one of the infamous leaders of the Hellfire League, and his entertainments were notorious for their debauchery.

Damien appeared to ignore her searching look. "I should like to depart on Friday, Olivia, unless you have any objections to my leaving you alone here?"

"Not at all," she answered lightly. "I'm sure I will fare well enough without you, since I won't be alone. Vanessa will bear me excellent company."

"I have no reservations about leaving you in her capable hands," he replied, finally meeting Vanessa's gaze.

His expression remained inscrutable, yet his cool detachment was significant in itself.

With a sudden hollowness in the pit of her stomach, Vanessa stared at him. Numbly, she wondered if he was giving her fair warning that the intimacy between them was coming to an end. That what for her had been a rapturous interlude was concluding because he had more novel pleasures to seek out.

She was sure of it later that night when, for the first time since beginning their torrid affair, Damien didn't come to her room.

Her heart contracting painfully, she lay there in the dark, alone, aching for his touch and the ecstasy she had known in his arms, unfulfilled longing taut within her.

Chapter Ten

The hungering ache hadn't left her by morning, when Vanessa woke groggy and in low spirits. But at least in the cold light of day, a semblance of rational thought returned.

She had been deluding herself, she realized. The enchantment of the past week wasn't truly real. She was no different from Olivia in that regard: she'd fallen under the spell of a practiced rake like a veritable innocent. And now that Damien had attained his goal—her complete surrender—he had no further reason to pursue her.

It was absurd to feel abandoned at his withdrawal, Vanessa scolded herself as she dressed. He'd been perfectly frank with her from the first. She was to be his mistress to satisfy her brother's enormous gambling debt. Their entire relationship was based on vengeance. Truthfully, she should be pleased if Damien's desire for her was cooling.

She was glad, however, to learn that he had already breakfasted. Her spirits were raw enough without having to face him and risk revealing her hurt and confusion.

She rode longer than usual and managed to work off some of her agitation in the beautiful summer morning, but her mood suffered another blow when she returned to find two callers at Rosewood, for she was again reminded of her tenuous position in the Sinclair household.

Surprisingly, Olivia had received the callers in the morning parlor. Seated in her invalid chair, she looked grateful to see Vanessa and quickly made the introductions.

"Lady Wyndham, may I present our nearest neighbors, Lady Foxmoor and her daughter Miss Emily Pryce? Emily and I attended school together."

"How do you do?" Vanessa murmured politely as she seated herself on the chintz chair. She nearly winced at the pair of cold blue eyes surveying her so haughtily. Her ancient riding habit was decidedly shabby, but not so unfashionable as to justify such a hostile reception.

Lady Foxmoor's greeting was as frosty as her look. "Ah, yes, the companion. I had heard you were hired to attend Miss Sinclair." She might have said "lowly worm" for all the respect in her tone.

Vanessa gritted her teeth and let the snub pass. Her status in society had fallen dramatically, since a lady's companion was seen as little better than a paid servant.

The visitor, however, seemed determined to establish her superiority. "Your reputation precedes you, Lady Wyndham."

"Oh?" Vanessa replied, raising an eyebrow. "How so?"

"Your late husband made quite a name for himself among the fast set in London, I believe."

"But then one cannot trust every tale one hears," she returned coolly.

"You will find we are not as free here in the country."

Olivia, who seemed taken aback by the derogatory tone of conversation, interjected quickly, "They have come to issue a personal invitation to their ball, Vanessa."

Just as quickly, Lady Foxmoor declared, "I am certain Lady Wyndham would not wish to attend our simple country gathering. It will be nothing compared to the grander London occasions she is accustomed to."

Vanessa grasped at once that she wasn't welcome at the ball, yet it didn't trouble her to be excluded. Before she could reply, however, Olivia warmly came to her defense. "I assure you, Vanessa is not high in the instep at all."

"Evidently not," the lady said with a sniff, "if she has taken up the role of lady's companion. But I'm sure she would not wish to advertise how far she has come down in society."

"She has not come down at all!" Olivia objected heatedly. "Indeed, she is more a sister to me than a companion."

Determinedly hiding her anger, Vanessa replied sweetly to the snub. "You are mistaken, Lady Foxmoor. I believe I would find the prospect of a simple country gathering entertaining. I should be pleased to attend your ball."

The lady's mouth grew pinched with vexation at having been foiled. Looking extremely uncomfortable, Miss Pryce lowered her eyes and left it to her mother to carry the battle, while Olivia quietly fumed.

The two callers remained several more awkward minutes before finally taking their leave. The moment they were shown to the door by the butler, Olivia bristled.

"The nerve of her! Excluding you from her invitation because you are keeping me company. You are still a guest in this house."

"It doesn't matter," Vanessa soothed. "I have no desire to attend their ball. I only said I would out of annoyance."

"Even so, she had no right to disparage you or treat you like a servant."

"I appreciate you championing me, Olivia, but I don't intend to let her slights discomfit me, and neither should you. Besides, we've forgotten the entire point of their visit. They came here personally to invite you to their ball."

The girl shook her head, frowning. "I am amazed they did, considering the scandal of my near elopement. I thought my name would be anathema, especially since Emily and I have never been great friends."

"They must not be as shocked as you feared."

"Oh, I have no illusions that they've forgiven me my sins," came her tart reply. "It is my brother they are after. They hope Damien will escort me to their ball. Lady Foxmoor has been trying for years to nab him for one of her daughters. He is a prime catch, and Emily is her last hope."

Absurdly Vanessa felt a stab of jealousy at the thought of Damien wedding anyone. Yet the pale, wide-eyed Miss Pryce did not strike her as the type of female to attract a rake of Lord Sin's stamp.

"Lady Foxmoor must be green with envy, finding you here as a member of this household," Olivia observed. "No doubt she sees you as a rival for my brother's affection and can't bear the thought that you have unfair advantage."

For a moment Vanessa was at a loss to reply. If her true relationship with Damien were known, she would be shunned by his genteel neighbors as a wanton. While polite society might accept a widowed lady's discreet affair with a wealthy nobleman, Lord Sin was not just any nobleman.

"I assure you, I have never sought your brother's affections," she prevaricated.

"Perhaps not, but you have affected him all the same."

"What do you mean?"

"He's different somehow." Olivia contemplated Vanessa thoughtfully. "Certainly he's never spent this much time at Rosewood."

"He has remained here for your sake, Olivia."

"No. I thought so at first, but there's more to it. He used to *hate* being here, but he doesn't seem to mind it any longer. He's not as restless, and his temper no longer has so sharp an edge. I think it's because of you, Vanessa. He enjoys your company, certainly. You might not see it, because you don't know him well, but I've noticed how he looks at you. The light in his eyes is softer. . . ."

Hoping to steer the conversation to safer ground, Vanessa feigned a smile. "I believe you are deliberately trying to avoid discussing Lady Foxmoor's invitation."

Olivia gave a sheepish look. "Perhaps I am."

"I'm surprised you received them at all, if you don't desire the acquaintance."

The girl sighed. "In truth, I didn't wish to. But I decided I must make a start somewhere."

"Would you like to attend their ball, then? You could make just a brief appearance. If so, I would be happy to keep you company."

"No, I don't want to go. I realize I cannot hide forever from polite society, but I am not ready yet for so large a step."

Vanessa thought the matter closed, but Olivia was still angry enough about the visit to complain to her brother that evening at dinner.

At first Vanessa paid little attention to the conversation. She was too busy struggling to hide her feelings and pretending a casual nonchalance. Damien still had given her no reason for failing to come to her room last night. In fact, he had scarcely spoken two words to her this evening. Yet she refused to let him know how much his coolness toward her hurt.

A few moments passed, though, before Olivia's remarks sank in.

"It makes me so cross to have Vanessa treated so shabbily. Lady Foxmoor was deliberately *rude*. You should have heard her, Damien. She practically ordered Vanessa to keep away from her ball, simply because she is acting as my companion."

A muscle flexed in his jaw, but he remained silent.

"She was eager to have you attend, though. Twice she bade me tell you how pleased she would be to see you. I think you should escort Vanessa to her ball, just to spite her. That would make it crystal clear she is a guest here and no servant."

His expressive brows arched. "When is the ball to be held?"

"Wednesday week," Olivia answered. "You said you planned to return home by then."

Sipping his wine, he nodded. "I should have concluded my business, yes." He shot Vanessa an impassive look. "I would be honored if you would permit me to serve as your escort."

Olivia let out a cry of delight. "Oh, famous! That will tweak the old trout's nose! She won't dare snub Vanessa in your presence."

"There is no need to put yourself out on my account," Vanessa objected.

"But it is necessary to uphold the Sinclair honor," Damien said with a cool smile.

"Yes, indeed," Olivia agreed. "And Vanessa must have a new gown for the occasion. You must," she insisted when Vanessa started to protest. "Turnabout is fair play. If I could endure being fitted for all those gowns you thrust on me, you can suffer just one. I will even help you choose the fabric. I have excellent taste, you know. And you have been pressing me to visit the shops in the village."

Vanessa wanted to refuse the offer. She could not be comfortable having Damien buy her clothing, indebting her even more. But if accepting a new ball gown would serve to get Olivia out of the house, then she would go along, however reluctantly.

The next few days passed slowly for Vanessa. Damien did indeed seem intent on avoiding her, while she pretended an indifference she didn't feel and tried to come to terms with cold reality.

She *had* to remember her position. She was Damien's mistress, only that.

Despite the tenderness he'd shown her in recent weeks, he considered her simply a carnal object. It was foolish to regard his incredible sensuality as anything more than a man's physical indulgence. Almost any warm female body would have sufficed. Damien Sinclair was still a wicked rakehell, a libertine with vast sexual appetites, one whose sinful charm made strong women weak. She would not be the first one he had casually seduced and then forgotten.

What she had taken as a desire for camaraderie was merely a means to keep his restlessness at bay. She would miss the charming companionship of their late-night discussions, for she'd come to value what had seemed to her a burgeoning friendship. Yet she should never have harbored any higher expectations for their relationship, or allowed herself to become so vulnerable.

She had best get her foolish feelings for him under control, before she opened herself to even greater hurt.

On Thursday, the day before Damien was to leave on his trip, Vanessa and Olivia went shopping in the village. They left the footmen to wait with the carriage and entered the dressmaker's establishment alone. Olivia didn't want any servants hovering over her, calling undue attention to her disability.

Vanessa had to admit the girl had exquisite taste in clothing. In less than an hour, they were both satisfied, having agreed upon a bronzed lutestring gown with an overskirt of gold tissue for Vanessa to wear to the ball. The price was one-tenth what she would have paid in London at a fashionable modiste's.

Upon leaving the shop, Vanessa turned Olivia's invalid chair toward the village green where the carriage awaited, but then paused to arrange a blanket over her lap. She was bending over the chair when the girl suddenly gasped.

"What is it?" Vanessa asked in concern.

"That man . . ."

She followed Olivia's gaze to see a horseman in the distance, riding a bay hack toward them at a slow jog. Vanessa drew a sharp breath as she recognized the familiar form of her brother, Aubrey.

Olivia had made a similar recognition, evidently; the girl had blanched, turning as white as paper.

For the space of several heartbeats, Vanessa stood frozen, unable to think what to do. By the time she realized she ought to remove Olivia from his presence, Aubrey had drawn close enough to notice the invalid chair.

Giving a start, he drew his horse to an abrupt halt.

For a long moment, he and Olivia stared at each other, unspeaking.

Vanessa's grip tightened on the blanket. She didn't believe her brother had purposefully orchestrated the meeting, but she was furious at him all the same for letting himself be seen. She stared daggers at him, but he only had eyes for Olivia.

Both women flinched when he began to dismount.

"Vanessa, will you kindly take me home?" the girl asked hoarsely.

"Yes, of course."

"No, wait . . . please," Aubrey said. "Please, hear me out for one moment." Drawing off his tall beaver hat, he moved to stand before them, blocking the path of the wheeled chair. "Miss Sinclair . . . Olivia . . ."

"You have no right to address me, sir," she said through clenched teeth. She was visibly trembling.

"Perhaps not." Aubrey dropped to one knee, so that he was at eye level with her. "I understand if you can't bear the sight of me. I don't blame you."

Vanessa heard the remorse in his tone, saw it in his expression, and gritted her teeth. The damage was done; Aubrey had made himself known to Olivia. He might as well be allowed to deliver his apology.

"I realize," Aubrey said quietly, "I don't deserve your forgiveness, but I wanted you to know how sorry I am. How ashamed I am for what I did to you." He glanced down at the invalid chair that held her prisoner. "If I could take your place I would."

Her gaze remained anguished, but there was a hint of steel in her voice when she replied rigidly, "Your concern comes rather late, doesn't it? It has been months since I last was foolish enough to believe your tender professions."

His faint smile was bleak. "I tried to see you, to write, but your brother banned me from the premises and ordered all my letters returned."

"I wish I had been half as wise when you first began to woo me." Her mouth trembled. "How pleased you must have been when you won your wager so effortlessly."

Aubrey shook his head. "No, I was never pleased. My

pursuit of you began as a wager, true, but it turned into something more, without my even knowing it. You see . . . I fell in love."

Vanessa could remain silent no longer. "Aubrey, stop this!" she demanded, taking a furious step toward him.

Olivia turned even whiter if that were possible, while her voice dropped to a mere whisper. "How can you be so cruel? Haven't you done enough? Must you make me the object of your malicious sport once again?"

"This is no sport, I swear it on my life. I haven't been able to forget you, Olivia." Tears shimmered in his eyes. "I know I've ruined any chance for a future with you, but I couldn't go on letting you think I didn't care. At least believe me when I say I never meant to hurt you."

Olivia glanced wildly up at Vanessa. She looked desperate, as fragile as crystal. "Please," she pleaded, "take me to the carriage."

Slowly Aubrey rose from his kneeling position. "You may set your mind at ease, Miss Sinclair. I won't contaminate you with my presence any longer. I shall take myself out of your sight."

He turned and mounted his horse, then glanced sadly down at his sister. "Vanessa, please . . . take good care of her."

He kicked his horse into a canter, leaving the two women to stare after him. They were both shaking.

Vanessa recovered first. Haphazardly arranging the blanket on Olivia's lap, she began pushing the chair toward the carriage, her thoughts in turmoil. How could Aubrey have been so cruel? Should she have intervened sooner? Could she have somehow spared Olivia the pain of seeing the man who had devastated her life? What could she say to Olivia now?

Yet the girl was so wrapped up in her own thoughts that she was blind to her surroundings. It was long moments later, after they were both settled in the carriage and on their way home, that Olivia raised eyes full of pain.

"He wasn't a stranger to you." The declaration was more bewildered than accusatory.

"No," Vanessa replied quietly. "Aubrey is my brother."

Olivia drew a sharp breath. She looked crushed at the betrayal.

For a long moment she said nothing as she searched Vanessa's face. "Why did you never tell me?"

"I was afraid to. I feared you wouldn't accept me as your companion if you realized my connection to him."

"Does Damien know?"

"Yes. We . . . agreed from the first it would be better not to tell you." She regarded Olivia solemnly, her heart aching. "I never wanted to deceive you. If you wish me to leave Rosewood now, I will."

The girl didn't reply at once. "Why did you come here?"

Vanessa looked away. She preferred not to tell Olivia the sordid truth, to reveal Damien's threat to her family or their shocking liaison, to explain that she had been forced to become his mistress in order to save her mother and sisters from stark penury. Olivia was still too young, too innocent, to be exposed to such bald facts.

"Because I wanted to help you," she said finally; at least that was completely true. "I was horrified to learn what my brother had done, and I wanted to make amends."

"Then . . . all along you knew what happened?"

"Yes. Aubrey told me himself, weeks ago." Vanessa leaned forward. "If you can't bring yourself to forgive me for concealing the truth, I will understand."

It was Olivia's turn to look away. "I don't know," she

said, gazing blindly out the window. "I need time to think about all this."

For the remainder of the afternoon, Olivia shut herself in her room, while Vanessa despaired and wondered whether to pack her bags. When she received a summons to join Olivia just before dinnertime, she complied with uncertainty.

The girl was sitting in her chair, gazing out the window, her expression a little sad.

"I do understand why you hid the truth from me," Olivia said, looking up. "If I had known Lord Rutherford was your brother, I never would have spoken to you, let alone allowed you to become my friend."

"I am your friend, Olivia," Vanessa replied earnestly.

"I know. And I don't want you to go."

The relief Vanessa felt was overwhelming. Before she could respond, however, Olivia spoke again.

"Did he mean it, do you think?" she asked quietly.

"Mean what?"

"He said he fell in love with me. Can I believe him?"

Troubled, Vanessa hesitated. Aubrey's declaration of love had startled and shocked her, but while it seemed to have come honestly, from the heart, she found it hard to credit that her reckless, devil-may-care brother would truly have fallen in love. More likely he was acting out of guilt. Still she couldn't be entirely sure. . . .

"I don't know," Vanessa answered truthfully. "I'm certain Aubrey deeply regrets his actions, but I don't know if he is really in love. I don't think he would be so cruel as to fabricate such a lie—but then six months ago I never would have thought him heartless enough to make that despicable wager, either."

Olivia's mouth twisted bitterly. "Do you know the worst part? I want to believe he loves me. Am I ten kinds of fool?"

Vanessa didn't know how to answer, but she wasn't required to. Olivia's chin rose defiantly, and for a moment she was the imperious baron's daughter, instead of an innocent young girl betrayed by her lover.

"If he thinks he can fool me again," she said fiercely, "he is greatly mistaken."

Olivia was quiet that night at dinner, so quiet that her brother asked if she was feeling well.

The girl's eyes flickered to Vanessa. "I'm well enough, though perhaps I exerted myself a little too much shopping today."

"Would you rather I postpone my trip?" Damien asked seriously. "It isn't absolutely necessary that I leave tomorrow."

Olivia shook her head. "No, of course not. You needn't worry about me. Vanessa will be here to look after me."

Vanessa was grateful for her answer. Thankfully she'd made no mention of Aubrey to her brother. Vanessa shuddered to think what Damien might do if he learned of Aubrey's presence in the district.

She only hoped Aubrey would have the sense to go home now that he'd had the opportunity to unburden his conscience. He was tempting fate to remain.

At least Damien would be leaving in the morning, for the better part of a week. She would be vastly relieved, Vanessa acknowledged, by his absence. Perhaps then she would be able to conquer the yearning ache he aroused in her with merely his nearness. To forget the burning enchantment she had known in his arms. To crush her foolish emotions.

She retired early, but to her dismay, she remained awake, nerves on edge, unable to sleep. After Damien's avoidance of her these past few days, she didn't expect him to come to her room that night, although she had prepared for him as on every other night, making use of the sponges he'd provided. Infuriatingly she found herself torn by conflicting desires—half praying he wouldn't come, half hoping he would. She was determined to give him a cool reception if he did.

Her heart took up a rapid rhythm when she heard the whisper of the secret panel from across the room.

She lay unmoving, with her back to him, yet she was palpably aware of Damien's presence. Moments later she felt the mattress shift as he sat beside her, felt the sensual brush of his hand beneath the veil of her hair, against her nape.

"I came to say farewell," he murmured, somehow knowing she was feigning sleep.

Reluctantly, Vanessa turned over to gaze up at him. In the moonlit darkness she could just make out his hard, virile features. "I wondered what brought you after all these nights."

He must have heard the chill in her voice, yet he didn't reply directly, or give an explanation for why he had stayed away. "Did you miss me, sweeting?"

Vanessa drew back, stung by his blitheness. "I think you flatter yourself, my lord. I didn't miss you in the least."

He went still, his expression unreadable. "I gather you are piqued at my neglecting you of late."

"Hardly," she lied. "I was glad to be given a respite from your lust."

Damien's smile was ironic. "I suppose I owe you an explanation. I thought perhaps our . . . association was becoming too heated for my peace of mind."

She stared at him, as if wondering whether she could believe him.

His fingers found her lips and stroked languidly over the sensitive surface. "You are dangerous to my control, Vanessa. I find myself wanting you a dozen times a day."

"Fortunately you will soon be able to satisfy your carnal urges with someone more willing. Your Hellfire gathering should provide you ample opportunity for carousing and debauchery."

Hearing the accusation in her tone, Damien held her defiant gaze. He had no intention of revealing how terribly vulnerable he was to her.

Vanessa might be startled to know he had no desire to attend Clune's house party. He was forcing himself to leave Rosewood in an attempt to distance himself from her.

Yet he couldn't go away without being with her just once more, without touching her, holding her. It had shocked him to realize just how powerful his need for her was. He had fought it—fiercely—but he had lost the battle.

He regarded her silently for a long moment. "Do you wish me to leave you?"

"And if I said yes?"

"Then I would try to persuade you to change your mind."

Vanessa gazed up at him, mesmerized by the cool fire in his eyes, aware of an undeniable sexual tension between them. She was his mistress, bought and paid for. That had always been the ugly truth between them.

But it was not her obligation to Damien that made her heart sink with a feeling akin to despair. It was the knowledge of her own defenselessness. He had only to touch her and she melted.

Just as now. The subtle brush of his fingers on her flesh riveted her, made her tremble. His caress moved lower, down her throat, along the line of her collarbone, dipping beneath the bodice of her nightdress to follow the rising swell of her breast. Vanessa shivered.

"What must I do to mollify you, sweeting?" he murmured as he softly stroked her skin.

The tempo of her breathing quickened. She had meant to resist him, but it was futile to think of escaping Lord Sin. In truth, she didn't want to escape.

When his knuckles brushed her nipples beneath her nightdress, heat rose to inflame her. She could feel the feverish ache starting deep inside her.

He knew precisely what his skilled caresses did to her, devil take him. His gaze locked with hers as deliberately he drew down the covers and rested his hand on her hip, only inches from the center of her desire.

She began to throb there, a vibrant, urgent pulsating. He was using the pleasures of her own body against her.

"Shall I go or stay?" he asked.

She returned his gaze, unable to look away. "Stay," she whispered involuntarily.

She saw the fire that leapt in his eyes, saw the determination in his expression, even though he didn't move a muscle. He meant to turn her reluctance to welcome invitation, she knew.

With unwilling fascination she watched as he shrugged out of his dressing gown. He was fully aroused, and the magnificence of his nude body took her breath away. The muscles in his chest and torso rippled as he joined her on the bed.

His face was hard, his eyes burning with intensity as he bent over her. "I want you, Vanessa. Now." Raw desire darkened his husky voice. "I want your softness clenching and shivering around my hardness."

He lowered his head, his fingers threading through her hair. His mouth hovered above hers, its beautiful lines stark and sensual.

Vanessa fought back a moan as his lips began to caress hers. She could feel her will weakening, feel the uneven beat of her heart.

"Don't deny me, angel. Don't deny yourself. . . ." His whisper filled her mind and stirred a quickening deep within her. His touch felt so right. . . .

She didn't protest when he drew up the hem of her night-dress to her waist or when she felt his thick, velvet-smooth shaft pressing against her thigh. Her lips burned beneath his deep, penetrating kiss, while her body quivered at the promise of that hot, rigid flesh giving her pleasure.

He kept up his sensual assault, stealing her will from her, until she warmed and softened and surrendered to the dark magic he commanded. Unable to disguise how desperately she wanted him, Vanessa threaded her arms around his neck and whimpered, needing him to ease the inexplicable hunger.

Damien felt her fiery response to his kiss and moved over her, covering her luscious form with his hard one. For a moment he braced himself above her, steeling his body against his raging need.

"Tell me you don't want this," he demanded softly, giving her the choice. "Tell me you don't want me inside you."

She couldn't say such a thing. She did want him, far too much. She wanted him loving her, filling her. . . .

When she didn't reply, he pressed her thighs wide and fit himself to her, thrusting in hard and deep, finding her sleek and hot and welcoming.

He heard her breath catch in a startled gasp of pleasure as his powerful length filled her. Sheathed tightly inside her, he began to move, withdrawing and thrusting again, until Vanessa arched and cried out, helplessly caught in the web of her own desire.

Damien captured her soft, wild sounds with his mouth, sharing her desperation, her ravenous need. When she wrapped her legs around him and lifted herself to match his hard rhythm, he drove into her fiercely. Blinding desire overtook him. When moments later she shattered, rigid and lost, he followed, shuddering and spilling his seed deep within her in a burst of explosive ecstasy, his hoarse groans mingling with her cries as he convulsed against her.

For a long while afterward he lay there, breathing harshly, shock waves still pulsing, his face buried in the sweet fragrance of her hair. Finally, though, he eased his weight from her and rolled onto his back, his skin still sheened with sweat from their wild lovemaking.

Drawing her into the curve of his body, he stared up at the canopy overhead, cursing himself for letting his passion become so uncontrolled. Hell only knew, he had meant to stay away. He understood all too well the danger Vanessa Wyndham presented. He was perilously close to becoming obsessed with her. Yet he could no more have denied his desire than he could have stilled the beating of his heart.

His fingers toyed absently with a curl of her darkly burnished hair. Even after sating himself so fiercely, need for her still ran like flame-warmed brandy through his body.

What the devil was happening to him? He'd had countless women in his admittedly licentious past, but the desire to completely possess one was utterly new to him. He wanted Vanessa Wyndham more than he had ever wanted any woman, and he didn't know why.

The depth of his desire was new as well. The gut-wrenching, fiery, primitive need was not only in his loins, but in his entire being. When she was near, all he wanted was to lose himself in her, in the feel of her, the taste of her, to drown in the exquisite pleasure of making love to her. To become part of her.

Damien shut his eyes. He very much feared he was succumbing to the fatal affliction he'd always despised in other men.

Despite his best intentions, he was becoming caught in his own seduction.

Chapter Eleven

He was gone when she woke, leaving her with memories of dark passion, spent and rekindled again and again. His ardent desire renewing her inner struggle, Vanessa passed the following days desperately fighting the emotions Damien had unleashed in her.

She thought she would be glad for his absence, yet that was before she persuaded Olivia to accompany her to church the following Sunday morning. Without Damien's noble consequence to shield her, Vanessa was given a chill reception by the genteel society present.

Apparently she had made an enemy of Lady Foxmoor. The woman spent the entire service whispering behind her prayer book and casting superior glances in Vanessa's direction. Afterward only a handful of people troubled themselves to make her acquaintance. The rest pointedly ignored her.

She should have expected as much, Vanessa realized— for failing to offer proper deference and humility in her role as lady's companion, for elevating herself to the level of family member, and for daring even to hold a post in Baron Sinclair's household where she might work her wiles on him.

Accustomed to scandal from the days of her marriage,

Vanessa was more angry on Olivia's behalf than her own. The girl bore the snubs with trembling grace, hiding her distress well, but she fell into a morose mood as soon as she was seated in the carriage.

When Vanessa tried to draw her out, Olivia responded with despair. "I told you it was hopeless. My life is ruined! My reputation has suffered irreparably."

Realizing Olivia mistakenly thought the disapproval directed at herself, Vanessa started to explain that *she* was the one their highbrowed neighbors objected to, but the girl had worked herself into a fret and wasn't listening.

"If my brother were here, they would not have dared look down their arrogant noses at me—which is the height of hypocrisy, considering Damien's libertine propensities." Seeing Vanessa's troubled expression, Olivia added, "I am not a child, nor am I blind. I'm well aware of my brother's reputation as a rake. My father was even worse, much worse. Why is it," she demanded bitterly, "that society can forgive a man any number of peccadilloes, but if a female dares a single misstep, she is ruined for life? It isn't fair!"

Vanessa had often wondered the same thing. But there was no use arguing that in a man's world, a woman simply had to make the best of her lot—especially since Olivia was in no mood to be consoled, then or later.

That afternoon when Vanessa tried to persuade her to attend her bath, Olivia replied with petulance, "What is the use? Nothing we have tried has made the least difference to my condition. I shall never walk again."

"You can't be certain of that," Vanessa reminded her gently. "It is still far too early to tell if the damage to your spine is permanent. The doctor said it might be months before you could expect to regain any feeling in your limbs."

"He also said I might never recover. If so, then I can never marry, never have children."

"Perhaps bearing children would be difficult, but marriage would certainly not be out of the question."

"You think not?" the angry young woman retorted. "With my reputation so tarnished, I can never make an eligible match."

Vanessa shook her head. "In that you are mistaken. From what I gather, you are a considerable heiress. Reputation or no, a lady with wealth and rank will always have choices. You can still wed if you wish."

"What man would want to be tied to a cripple? Your brother would not." Her mouth trembled, then hardened. "It would serve him right if he were forced to suffer for his cruelty, as I have done. He got off lightly under the circumstances. My brother wanted to kill him, but I made Damien swear he wouldn't. Lord Rutherford is fortunate to have escaped with his life."

Vanessa agreed, but she refrained from divulging that Damien had still managed to exact a revenge. Though he hadn't killed Aubrey, he had ruined him financially at the gaming tables and put his family at risk of destitution.

"If I am to be ostracized for my folly," Olivia added fiercely, "it is only fitting that knave shares in my misery. At the very least, he should be required to bear me company as long as I remain a cripple." She nodded grimly as she evidently came to a decision. "Is your brother still in the district?"

"I really don't know," Vanessa replied, surprised and wary. "He told me he would remain until he found a way to speak to you, but after your encounter the other day, he might have returned home."

The girl's chin rose stubbornly. "If he is still here, I

should like you to find him and give him a message, Vanessa, inviting him to call on me here at Rosewood."

"Olivia . . ." Vanessa began earnestly. "You can't imagine Damien would countenance such a thing."

"Damien doesn't have to know. Lord Rutherford can come in disguise, and if you are there to act as chaperon, his presence will raise no alarm among the servants."

"Still . . . would it be wise? Revenge is never as satisfying as it is made out to be. Seeing Aubrey again will only prove a torment to you."

"Perhaps so, but if he is telling the truth, it will prove a greater torment to *him*. If he truly feels remorse as he claims, then he can wallow in his guilt. Seeing me in that hateful chair should remind him of the consequence of his heartlessness."

"Olivia . . ."

"Please, Vanessa, do not try to change my mind. If you won't summon him for me, then I shall drive into the village in search of him myself, and then the fat will really be in the fire!"

As the curtain rose, a chorus of appreciative masculine applause greeted the tableau upon the stage. Lounging in a chair amid the audience, Damien plucked at the ruffle of his sleeve to hide his boredom.

Clune had arranged an entertainment for the benefit of his guests, all male. On stage, three nubile beauties engaged in a writhing dance upon a huge bed, their naked bodies undulating, their limbs contorting in fanciful positions, while a half-dozen other lovelies posed in diaphanous costumes that left nothing to the imagination. Their lips and nipples and feminine clefts were rouged to make them

appear more luscious and inviting, but Damien remained
strangely unaroused.

Once such delights would have cured him, at least tem-
porarily, of his ennui. In years past he had enjoyed Clune's
house parties; indeed, he'd often led the revelry. Yet he had
attended this affair for one reason only. To escape Vanessa
Wyndham.

It was said the best way for a man to banish a particular
woman from his thoughts was to lose himself in the
pouting lips and welcoming thighs of another.

Damien narrowed his gaze, trying to banish the memory
of that last night with Vanessa . . . the dark luster of her eyes
as she took him to heaven and back.

What the devil was wrong with him?

Always before, whenever he felt dissatisfied with his
life, he had sought out some fresh diversion or excitement,
some new lover who could satisfy his sophisticated tastes.
His wild pursuit of sexual gratification in the glittering
ballrooms and bedrooms of Europe was calculated to provide relief from his restlessness.

He'd never had difficulty finding willing partners. He had
discovered that most women, be they noble or common,
married or sweetly virginal, were his for the taking. Sex was
a fine art to him. He never allowed his emotions to become
involved.

Except with Vanessa.

He tensed, still feeling the thrust of her soft hips against
his loins. Making love to her that last time had been
unique, shattering. Never before had he been so lost in a
woman. . . .

God's blood, his infatuation had gone on long enough.
But how the hell was he going to end it?

A shout of ribald male laughter brought him back to the

present, making him conscious of the lewd entertainment before him. The profound, familiar restlessness seized Damien, and his mouth turned down in distaste.

Perhaps he was as dissipated and jaded as Vanessa thought him. By choice he was a devoted pleasure seeker, not an unusual pastime for an idle, rich nobleman. Admittedly, he was a profligate man. But these prurient amusements were becoming less and less appealing.

His dissatisfaction must have shown on his face, for a moment later his host, Jeremy North, Lord Clune, sat down beside him.

"You don't appear to be enjoying the entertainment, my friend."

"On the contrary," Damien lied. "I'm fascinated by the slender redhead with the beauty mark on her thigh."

Clune's mouth curved in amusement. "You show excellent taste, as usual. She is imported from France—the daughter of an aristocrat fallen on hard times during their hideous revolution. Speaks only a few words of English, but her talents are amazing."

Damien feigned a smile. "High praise, coming from a man dedicated to debauchery."

"Indeed. What is this I hear about the new beauty you have in your keeping?" Clune asked.

"Beauty?"

"A widow, I'm given to understand. Rumor is that you've actually ensconced her at your own estate. A bold move, even for you. Do you mean to share her with your friends, or will you selfishly keep her all to yourself?"

Damien exhaled a slow breath, troubled by the mistaken conjecture that Vanessa was in the same category as his usual mistresses. Just as troubling was the shaft of fierce jealousy he felt at the thought of sharing Vanessa with other men. Jealousy was a foreign notion to him—or it had been, until her.

"I fear your assumption is off the mark, Clune," he said casually. "The lady is employed as my sister's chaperon, nothing more."

Clune looked somewhat skeptical but didn't challenge the lie. Instead he lifted a hand and beckoned to the red-haired dancer upon the stage.

Damien surveyed her as she floated down the stairs to stand before him. Her eyes were huge but glazed. No doubt she was drugged with an opiate to make her task of welcoming the wicked perversions of a dozen gentlemen more palatable.

Damien frowned, realizing she was younger than he had first assumed. "Have you sunk to robbing the cradle, Jeremy?" he queried with a raised eyebrow.

His friend shrugged. "She is eighteen, or so she says. I'm not taking unfair advantage, I assure you. She is being well paid for her efforts, enough to keep her in comfort for a year. And if I hadn't found her, someone else would have."

Eighteen was his own sister's age, Damien realized grimly as the girl settled on his lap with a dreamlike smile.

When she parted the diaphanous robe and lifted her peaked nipples to his mouth, his host politely rose. "I shall leave you to your pleasures then."

The beauty rubbed the taut buds teasingly against Damien's mouth. She tasted sweetly of wine, yet rather than becoming aroused, he had to steel himself against a strange and sudden aversion.

Instead of showing his distaste, though, or denouncing Clune for being a less than satisfactory host, Damien came to an abrupt decision and lifted the girl in his arms. Leaving the entertainment behind, he carried her upstairs to his bedchamber.

She was half-asleep even before he laid her on the bed, yet she roused herself to give him a confused look when he covered her near nakedness with a quilt and stepped back.

His Hellfire colleagues would be astounded to see him rejecting such beauty, but he had discovered new limits to his debauchery. He couldn't take advantage of this girl. Instead, when he left, he would send her to London and order his secretary to see what could be done to find her a different sort of employment.

"Go to sleep, sweetheart," Damien murmured, keenly aware of the irony of his action: Lord Sin made an unlikely savior of feminine virtue.

He turned away, realizing another unsavory truth. Before his sister's accident, he would never have been so concerned with the fate of a young girl.

The afternoon air smelled of summer roses but was fraught with tension. With grave misgivings Vanessa watched her brother's approach along the garden path. She felt like the veriest traitor. She had agreed to act as chaperon for Olivia, yet she wondered if she was making a grievous mistake.

From the bottom of her heart she wanted only what was best for the girl. But even revenge, however ugly its beginnings, might not be such a bad thing if it gave Olivia a purpose in life, if it made her keep fighting rather than giving up in despair.

Praying she wasn't in error, Vanessa held her breath as Aubrey came to a halt in front of the invalid. Olivia sat cool as marble in her chair, her blue eyes unreadable. Only Vanessa knew how much of her indifference was pretense.

The former lovers stared at each other for a long moment, before Aubrey went down on one knee and whispered Olivia's name.

Vanessa averted her gaze from the anguished emotion on his face, feeling suddenly superfluous in the rose-scented garden.

Aubrey came several more times that week, blending well into the garden landscape, like any scholar there to study the famous roses. Olivia showed no signs of relenting in her desire for retribution, though, and whatever conversation took place between them was mostly one-sided. She was the ice princess, Aubrey a meek supplicant for her favors. Yet he seemed to accept her coldness as fitting punishment, much like wearing a hair shirt—an uncharacteristic humbleness that shocked Vanessa more than a little.

On his second visit he brought a volume of poetry, which he read aloud. Only by the faraway look in her eyes did Olivia give any indication she was even listening.

Vanessa felt highly uncomfortable with the state of affairs, and with her role in arranging their clandestine visits. She shuddered to think how Damien would react. He would be furious, perhaps enough to call Aubrey out. And he would despise her, as well, for aiding in the deception.

She seriously debated whether to tell him, but that would mean betraying Olivia's confidence. Too, it would end any possibility Aubrey had of earning the girl's forgiveness. And when Damien did return to Rosewood at midweek, any semblance of rational thought fled the moment Vanessa saw him.

She was in the music room, attempting to learn a difficult

piece on the pianoforte, when he suddenly appeared in the doorway. Vanessa looked up, her gaze colliding with his.

Yearning sprang up in her instantly, and she had to struggle to maintain an appearance of composure.

"I thought you were my sister," Damien said calmly, giving no sign that he had missed her in the least during his nearly weeklong absence.

"Olivia is in her room reading, I believe," she replied, adapting his same coolness of manner.

"I trust everything is well with her?"

Vanessa hesitated, but then let the opportunity pass to divulge the truth about her brother's secret visits. It was better, she hoped, to let Olivia resolve her problems in her own way. "She's well enough."

"I'll go directly to see her." Damien started to turn away but then paused. "Shall we leave at nine following dinner, then?"

"Leave?"

"The Foxmoor ball is this evening, or had you forgotten?"

"No, but I'm not certain it would be wise for me to attend." Briefly Vanessa told him about the chill reception she'd received at church from his genteel neighbors.

A muscle hardened in his jaw. "All the more reason to go. It is never judicious to allow your actions to be dictated by others, most especially by a pack of prudish social wolves."

Vanessa looked down at the piano keys. "It is all well and good for a nobleman of wealth and consequence to flout convention, but a lady of limited means has fewer resources to help her weather censure."

"I would never have thought you craven, angel." When she glanced up, Damien smiled almost tauntingly. "You yourself told my sister not to cower under the covers. Is that not what you are doing?"

"Perhaps so," Vanessa replied, stiffening her spine.

Damien was right, she reflected when she was alone. She was as guilty as Olivia of hiding from society, and that certainly was not the example she wanted to set for the girl. She might not relish the prospect of being paraded on Damien's arm in front of his neighbors, yet she shouldn't allow herself to be intimidated.

And it would do her good to get about more. She had once enjoyed balls. She might even make a few acquaintances tonight, which would be a welcome change after the solitude of Rosewood. Damien had been right about that as well. She could understand now why he felt so restless here.

That evening Vanessa took more care than usual as she dressed for the ball with the help of Olivia's maids. Despite her diffidence, she began to take heart when she saw the finished result in the cheval glass.

Damien was alone when she joined him in the drawing room before dinner. He looked utterly magnificent in form-fitting black cutaway coat and white satin breeches. His thick raven hair was a startling contrast to the stark white of his linen cravat, while the gold threads in his white brocade waistcoat matched the gold of her gown.

His expression remained enigmatic, however, when his gray gaze swept over the bronzed and gold confection she wore.

At least Olivia's reaction, when she entered the drawing room just then, was far more approving. She gasped.

"Oh, Vanessa, you are beautiful! I knew the gold would be perfect for you. Is she not beautiful, Damien?"

"Exquisite," he said softly, the caressing word absurdly making her heart leap.

It was his only display of intimacy. Vanessa was obliged to Olivia for providing the bulk of the conversation at dinner. Damien seemed distant, showing her none of the intimate charm that in the past had so effortlessly delighted and enchanted her.

He told his sister about his recent journey, claiming to have been occupied by mundane business affairs, although he made no mention of the Hellfire League or the gathering he had planned to attend. But then, the sort of debauchery he had doubtless enjoyed at Lord Clune's was not a fit subject for a lady of Olivia's tender years.

He spoke little after he handed Vanessa into the carriage. They rode to the ball in silence, which only heightened her riveting awareness of him. It was all she could do to disguise her longing, yet she was determined to maintain the same cold civility he offered her.

It was wiser to distance herself from him, she knew, before she developed an unbearable dependence on him. She had to remember theirs was merely a business relationship, to be kept on a strictly carnal level.

When they arrived at their destination, there was a short wait as carriages lined up before the entrance, and a longer one before they were greeted in a receiving line by Sir Charles and Lady Foxmoor and their daughter Emily. Lady Foxmoor hid her enmity toward Vanessa and fairly gushed over Lord Sinclair, who bore her toadying with good grace.

The ball was evidently a success, for the drawing room was filled with animated guests and the harmonic strains of music. Vanessa felt tension forming in her stomach, but she was determined to take her own advice: the best way to foil the gossipmongers was to hold her head high and ignore their disapproval. She'd had abundant practice, certainly, during her marriage to her scandal-seeking husband.

From the beginning, however, Damien made it apparent that he didn't intend to leave her to the wolves. He stayed by her side for the initial half-hour, seeing that she was introduced to any number of people. And he insisted on leading her out for the first dance.

"You needn't put yourself out on my behalf," Vanessa murmured as he took her hand.

He smiled slowly into her eyes. "It is no hardship, dancing with the loveliest woman at the ball."

His pointed interest in her was for the benefit of the other guests, she suspected. Despite her position as a paid servant, they would not dare snub her if she enjoyed Baron Sinclair's support.

Her heart began to race as she stared up at Damien. He was sensual, vital, with a lethal charm that made him irresistible. Even if his attentiveness was a pretense, she couldn't deny its powerful effect.

His strategy yielded the intended result. Although the ladies generally maintained a cool distance, Vanessa was soon surrounded by a virtual army of gentlemen, both young and old, begging to be introduced and requesting to fill her dance card. Determined to enjoy the evening, she allowed herself to be swept away.

She lost sight of Damien after that. Some time later when she paused between sets for a glass of ratafia, she let her gaze surreptitiously search for him. When she spied him across the room, his eyes briefly, hotly connected with hers. Vanessa felt the familiar sensual thrill ripple through her. Then her partner claimed her attention, and she had to turn away with a feigned smile.

Not everyone at the ball was a stranger to her. She had a nodding acquaintance with several ladies from her years in London, and one in particular she knew well. Lettice Perine had made her come-out the same Season as Vanessa, had married within a few months of her, and was widowed the same year.

Vanessa was heartened halfway through the evening to see Lettice approach her with a friendly smile.

"Darling, it has been ages," Lettice exclaimed as they pressed cheeks in greeting. "I needn't ask how you are doing. It's obvious you are a great success. I couldn't get near you for the crowd."

Vanessa sidestepped the remark and surveyed her friend, who was blazing in diamonds. "You are looking very well, Lettice. But I never expected to find you in Warwickshire. Do you live nearby?"

"We are merely visiting. Robert has a daughter here."

"Robert?"

"My new husband. I married again, did you not hear?" With a nod of her head, she gestured toward a portly, elderly gentleman standing near the punch bowl, and smiled fondly. "I am plain Mrs. Bevers now. Robert is a cit who made his fortune in trade. He isn't the most exciting or passionate lover, I fear, but I couldn't ask for more congenial companionship. I am surprisingly happy, Vanessa. Robert is a dear, and he's very good to me, even if we do live on the fringes of society."

She held up her hand to show off her diamond rings and bracelet. "After Percy's death I discovered myself nearly destitute. You suffered the same fate, I understand, poor darling. But you have come up in the world, I see."

Vanessa raised a polite eyebrow.

"The gentlemen are all wild for you, I notice. No doubt

they think you exceptional to hold the interest of the infamous Lord Sin. What is your secret, darling?"

"I have no secret, Lettice. I am here as companion to Lord Sinclair's sister."

Lettice gave her an arch look. "Of course. Well, companion or no, half the ladies here are green with envy. That's why you are being given the cold shoulder. But I'll wager most of them would offer their eyeteeth to have such a magnificent man in their bed."

Vanessa felt herself stiffen at the casual assumption she was sharing Damien's bed, although she managed to hide her dismay behind a bland expression. When she remained at a loss for words, her friend's gaze strayed to the far end of the room, where Damien was surrounded by a group of fawning ladies.

"I don't blame you in the least for setting your cap at him, Vanessa. What woman could resist him—a renowned rake who is sinfully handsome, outrageously charming, and devilishly rich? But you chose the most challenging bachelor in England. He has eluded countless lures, you know."

Vanessa forced a wry smile. "So I hear."

"You would be wise not to become too enamored of him. Lady Varley made an utter fool of herself last year, pursuing Sinclair after he had ended their liaison." Lettice leaned forward and lowered her voice. "Take my advice, darling. When he tires of you, as he is sure to do, find yourself a wealthy patron with the wherewithal to keep you in jewels and gowns for life. Better yet, find an elderly gentleman and drive him besotted, then persuade him to wed you. If you are fortunate, he will make an amiable companion, one you might even come to love. If not, well, you will probably outlive him by many years."

"I am not interested in marrying again, I assure you," Vanessa replied with conviction, ignoring her friend's other advice.

She was sorry when Lettice shortly begged her leave and went to seek out another acquaintance. She had enjoyed seeing a familiar face among strangers, and she was pleased that her friend had found happiness in such unlikely circumstances.

Yet the conversation had disturbed her. If Lettice assumed she and Damien were lovers, no doubt others had, as well. It seemed obvious now that that was a better explanation for the cold reception she'd been given than her lowered status as a mere servant. Her attempt to hide their relationship behind the respectable post of companion had failed. Lord Sin was simply too notorious a figure to support so frail a pretense.

It also was becoming clear she wasn't likely to escape the relationship without being branded as a wanton.

Suddenly warm in the heat of the ballroom and needing a respite from the crowd, Vanessa slipped through the open French doors, out onto the terrace. The summer night air was cool on her flushed skin, the scene peaceful, with the moon a huge, brilliant disk bathing the landscape below. Yet even the beauty couldn't calm the turmoil of her thoughts.

Her reputation would perhaps be in tatters by the time her term as Damien's mistress ended. Even so, Vanessa thought defiantly, she would have made the same decision again. Being ostracized by society was not too high a price to pay for her sisters' sake.

But she still had the difficult question of their future to resolve. She bit her lip. Perhaps when her association with

Damien concluded at summer's end, she should indeed consider seeking an arrangement like the one Lettice suggested.

Such dreams as love were probably beyond her reach. And she would never remarry and put herself at the mercy of a philandering husband. Yet it might be possible to achieve a comfortable relationship of sorts, one based on companionship and mutual attachment.

Vanessa had only a few moments for contemplation before the scrape of footsteps behind her warned her that she was not alone. She turned to see a gentleman weaving toward her—the elder son of a local squire whose name she couldn't recall. He was more than a little foxed, it seemed. When he reached her side, he favored her with a leering grin and leaned heavily against the stone rail of the balcony.

"Ah, m'lady," he said, slurring his words. " 'Tis my good fortune to find you alone."

"I was about to return to the ballroom," Vanessa replied, not eager to encourage familiarity.

"Pray don't go." He placed a restraining hand on her arm. "Since Lord Sin has abandoned you, I will be delighted to take his place. What do you say that I prove how agreeable I can be?"

"I doubt you wish to hear what I would say, sir," she said acerbically.

When he flung a heavy arm over her shoulder, she was not alarmed as much as angered. But when he groped her breast beneath the satin décolletage, Vanessa recoiled.

He refused to let her go, even when she tried to twist out of his embrace. With a muttered oath, he tightened his hold on her arm, surprising a cry of pain from her.

Then suddenly Damien was there, yanking her assailant away and hauling him up short by the cravat.

"I suggest you offer the lady an apology at once, Henry," Damien ordered coldly, his grip tightening.

Giving a choking sound, the young man nodded. When Damien released him, he staggered back, clutching his throat and breathing harshly as he stammered out an apology.

"Now you may take yourself home. No, the stables are that way," Damien added, indicating the stone steps leading down from the terrace.

When Henry had stumbled away into the night, Damien turned to Vanessa, who stood rubbing her arm where her inebriated assailant's grasp had bruised it.

"Are you all right?"

She fixed her gaze on him, shock still flowing through her. Her late husband might have dragged her through any number of scandals, but until tonight no man had ever treated her so disrespectfully. Because of Damien, she was now vulnerable to any number of indignities.

Her resentment flared. He must have known when he made her his mistress that her reputation would not survive. Indeed, that no doubt had been his goal in the first place.

"All right? But, of course! I am quite accustomed to defending myself against physical assaults. I'm overjoyed to have been made a byword, a target for any drunken fool who chooses to accost me." If her accusation held any injustice, she was too angry to acknowledge it.

"Would you like to go now?" Damien asked quietly.

"Certainly I would, but I shall endure the rest of the evening. To leave now would be to admit defeat, and I am not craven."

Her chin lifting, Vanessa swept past him through the doors to the ballroom, ignoring the questioning glances of several guests who had gathered to watch the spectacle.

She spent the next hours pretending she was not at the center of a brewing scandal. By the time Damien ordered the carriage, however, she had regained at least a semblance of composure and managed to feign an attitude of cool disdain.

Neither of them spoke much on the journey home.

"I was wrong to insist you come here tonight with me," Damien said at last, breaking the brittle silence.

"It was a mistake," Vanessa agreed coolly. "My presence only lent credence to the notion that we are lovers."

"I'm sorry you were subjected to such boorish treatment."

"Are you? I would have thought you'd be pleased. Isn't this precisely the retribution you wanted? My ruination for your sister's?"

Damien hardened his jaw, feeling a sharp stab of guilt. He had cared nothing about Vanessa's reputation, at least in the beginning. But that was a long time ago. Now he could only regret the insults she would doubtless suffer because of him.

If he had any nobility, he would set Vanessa free of her obligation to him. But he couldn't bring himself to be so noble, not yet.

"The damage is not irreparable, at least," he observed.

"Is it not? And how do you recommend we repair it? I cannot see the situation changing for the rest of the summer, and then it can only grow worse. I'm under your protection now, but the instant I leave here, I will be known as one of your cast-off lovers."

"Not if you are the one to break off the relationship. In fact, it will lend you a certain cachet to have spurned me. When our association has ended, I shall put it about that I fell out of your favor."

Vanessa bit back a retort, knowing no one would believe

that unlikely version of events. "I suppose I should be grateful for that small consideration," she said finally, her tone more caustic than she intended.

His gray gaze held hers. "You are free to walk away now, if you choose."

"And my mother and sisters will suffer for it," Vanessa replied bitterly. "Thank you, my lord, but I shall fulfill the terms of our bargain to the letter."

Chapter Twelve

"Vanessa, I am on tenterhooks to discover what happened at the ball," Olivia demanded the following morning as her invalid chair was pushed into the bedchamber by a female servant.

Not yet fully awake, Vanessa repressed a sigh and rolled over. She winced at the bright light that flooded the room as the draperies were parted.

"I've brought you breakfast," Olivia added insistently as another maid settled a tray on a table. "I thought you might eat while you tell me about last night."

Realizing she would get no peace until she satisfied the girl's curiosity, Vanessa sat up in bed and settled back against the pillows. Despite the delicious aroma of warm scones, she had no appetite, but she accepted a cup of chocolate and stirred it while mentally debating how much to tell Olivia about last night's disaster.

She had stayed awake half the night, forcing herself to face the unpalatable truth. Her reputation was severely damaged by her association with Damien, possibly beyond repair—

"Vanessa, are you attending me?" Olivia asked.

She forced a smile, realizing that Olivia had dismissed the servants and was waiting eagerly for an account of the

216

ball. "I'm sorry, I was woolgathering. I had a very enjoyable evening last night."

Olivia looked troubled. "That is not what I hear. Servants' gossip says that Damien was involved in a fight over your honor."

Vanessa grimaced. "It wasn't as bad as all that. One of your local gentlemen became foxed and tried to kiss me. Your brother had to intervene. The few witnesses to the scene," she added wryly, "must have embellished the tale."

"Who was the gentleman?"

Vanessa hesitated, reluctant to spread the gossip further. But Olivia seemed determined to hear the intimate details. And she should be warned in case she ever found herself in a similar circumstance. "I believe his name was Henry Marsh."

"Henry? How dare he!" Olivia exclaimed indignantly. "I never have liked him above half. Oh, Vanessa, it must have been horrible for you."

"It was not pleasant," she agreed. "But I learned a valuable lesson. In future I shall take care to avoid being alone with a strange gentleman. In fact, I think it wise for me to avoid such gatherings altogether."

Olivia gave a distressed frown. "I feared something like this might happen, that you would become the subject of ugly rumormongering, simply because you are a guest here. It is all Damien's fault. The most virtuous woman alive would be suspect in his company. I know. With the wickedness of my family, I have always had to behave like a saint, always had to be above reproach. It isn't fair," she added somewhat bitterly.

Last night Vanessa had agreed with the sentiment. Now, however, she felt only resignation. She should despise Damien for forcing her into such a position, but she couldn't bring herself to hate him. If she were totally honest, she would admit even to being grateful to him for helping liberate her from her fears.

"There is a solution to the problem," Olivia said, putting a finger to her lips thoughtfully. "Damien could undo the damage he has wrought. He could offer you the protection of his name and wed you."

Vanessa had to smile at the absurdity of the idea.

"I am quite serious!" Olivia declared. "You must do your best to make Damien fall in love with you. Then he would be compelled to make you an honorable offer of marriage. It would be delightful, don't you think? We would be sisters."

Vanessa was pleased to see Olivia excited about something, even though her plan couldn't possibly work.

"Of course, it wouldn't be easy," Olivia mused aloud, echoing her thoughts. "Damien seems quite fond of you, but he has always vowed he will never fall in love. He says that he's seen love destroy too many people, including Mama and Papa. That is why he has remained so unattainable, even though he's been pursued by countless females."

Vanessa shook her head. The suggestion was almost laughable. Damien Sinclair was not the sort of man ever to fall in love. Most certainly he would not allow himself to succumb to the sister of a mortal enemy.

She kept her tone light, though, when she replied. "Everyone knows that libertines never fall in love. And in any event, I have no desire ever to marry again."

Olivia's face fell. "I suppose it was a wild notion. But I should dearly love to have you for a sister."

They spoke of more mundane matters for a time, but when Olivia left her so she might dress, Vanessa was struck by a sudden spell of melancholy. She closed her eyes, weary from lack of sleep and emotional strain. It was hopeless to think she might redeem her reputation. As mercenary as it was to contemplate, perhaps she *would* be wise to consider her friend Lettice's advice to find a wealthy protector. . . .

Vanessa's eyes opened. She was resigned to the loss of her good name, but it might be possible to turn her ruination to advantage.

Frowning, she sat up slowly and struggled to focus her thoughts. Being a mistress was far better than being a wife, she was certain, for at least it offered a measure of freedom and independence. A mistress wasn't considered legal property with fewer rights than a slave.

And not all fallen women faced a future of whoredom and shame. If rumor could be believed, there were Cyprians in London who commanded fortunes in their chosen professions, highfliers who had half the gentlemen of the ton at their feet.

At the moment, Vanessa acknowledged, she was ill-equipped to join their illustrious ranks. She lacked the necessary skills to enthrall any man—although she was far more experienced at lovemaking now than before meeting Damien. . . .

Damien. *Of course.*

Vanessa's lips tightened. She'd always been adamant about saving her penniless younger sisters from unhappy marriages like the one she was forced to make, and her liaison with England's most notorious lover could prove her best chance to secure their financial welfare. Who better than the wicked Lord Sin to advise her on how to attract the attentions of even the most elusive gentlemen?

Her chin lifted defiantly. If she took so brazen a step as to join the muslin company, it would be difficult to return

to her old life. As a demirep, she would have to avoid her
sisters altogether so she wouldn't drag them into any
scandal attached to her name. Even then, her notoriety
could reflect on them and diminish their chances for a dis-
tinguished marriage. But at least they wouldn't be forced
into wifehood against their will.

It would be an enormous step, and doubtless irrevocable. Yet she could never hope to support her family on
the meager salary a governess or lady's companion commanded, even if she could manage to find employment.
Virtue and respectability couldn't provide even the basic
necessities such as food and shelter. And the world already
called her wanton. . . .

Gathering her courage, Vanessa pushed aside the covers
and rose to dress. She intended to seek out Damien now,
before she lost her resolve. She had to speak to him regarding the grave matter of her education.

Damien bent over the neck of the straining chestnut
gelding, urging the horse to greater speed. He was coldly furious at himself—for any number of transgressions. For
misjudging the difficulties Vanessa faced in society as his
undeclared mistress. For underestimating how savage the
petty cruelties of the ton could be. For allowing that idiot
son of a squire to accost her. For feeling such guilt at her distress. For having so little control over his own passion . . .

Hoping rigorous exercise would temper his desire,
Damien had gone riding to work off his frustrations, racing
across fields and charging up grassy slopes, recklessly
jumping the hedges and streams in his path, the beat of
churning hooves pounding in his head.

Finally, though, he slowed to spare his horse. It was
criminal to take his frustrations out on a superb animal,

and physical exertion had little effect on the emotions or sexual tension surging through him.

Bringing his sweating mount down to an easy walk, he turned back toward Rosewood. Threatening storm clouds swelled on the horizon, echoing his dark mood.

After a week's absence he should have forgotten Vanessa. But his plan to banish her from his thoughts and mind hadn't worked. She wouldn't be forgotten, devil take her.

He'd returned home after his journey, determined to deny his obsession, but the instant he'd laid eyes on her in the music room, sitting there so cool and beautiful, his heart had leapt. He hadn't taken her in his arms as every primal instinct urged him to do, but instead pretended a callous detachment.

His pretense had nearly shattered when he saw her in that stunning golden gown, looking as magnificent as a queen, as enchanting as any male fantasy. His loins had caught fire, and it had taken every ounce of willpower he possessed to refrain from sweeping Vanessa off her feet and carrying her upstairs to his bed, where he could spend the night ravishing her to his heart's content, instead of attending a damned ball.

At dinner and for the rest of the evening, her cool, regal demeanor had mirrored his own attempt at remoteness. Damnation, he should have been pleased she was astute enough not to protest his withdrawal. The warmth that had once been so much a part of their relationship, the intimacy, the friendship, had ended, just as he'd wished. Yet, to his dismay, Damien had found himself missing the sweetness, the sharing, the softness of her smile. . . .

And then had come the drunken assault on Vanessa and his own unrecognizable responses: his killing rage at the perpetrator and his fierce remorse afterward, when he had yearned to hold her and comfort her, to soothe away her distress. The depth of his emotion had stunned him.

Damien muttered a savage oath under his breath. He did indeed seem to be following in his illustrious father's footsteps. He had vowed years ago he would never succumb to the blind desire that had nearly destroyed his father; he never wanted to care that deeply for any woman.

But Clune's house party hadn't provided an escape or satisfied his fierce need. His longing to possess Vanessa hadn't ended, even when he'd sought out other feminine companionship in an effort to forget her. The bald truth was, he hadn't wanted anyone else. He hadn't been able to lose himself in the pleasures of the flesh as usual. And his restlessness, his empty longing, remained.

Damien hardened his jaw. He very much feared there was only one woman who could ease the burning desire inside him.

There was no use denying his intense need for her, Damien acknowledged grimly. He would simply have to let his obsession run its course.

It came as something of a jolt when, moments later, he saw a rider in the distance who looked very much like the object of his all-consuming thoughts. Damien hoped he might be dreaming, but when the rider grew close, he realized he was indeed seeing Vanessa.

He pulled up abruptly and sat waiting for her, cursing the quickening of his heart. Even in a worn riding habit, she looked beautiful. Desire stung him with fresh insistence, and he had to discipline himself severely to maintain an appearance of indifference when she reached him.

"I hoped I might find you alone," she said, drawing her gray mount to a halt. "If you have a few moments to spare, I have something to ask you . . . a favor, if you will."

"I am at your service as always," Damien replied noncommittally.

A slight flush rising to her cheeks, Vanessa glanced around her with uncertainty. Surprisingly then, she dismounted and released the reins to let her mare graze. Just as oddly, she turned her back to him, staring at the distant landscape with its patchwork of fields and hedges and gentle woodlands. She seemed reluctant to meet his gaze.

Curiosity aroused, he waited.

"I have been thinking . . ." she began hesitantly. "About my situation. Regrettably, my association with you has brought me . . . an unwanted notoriety. However, it could yet prove to my benefit."

"What do you mean?" he asked when she faltered.

She took a deep breath and cast him a fleeting glance over her shoulder. "I would like you to teach me how to satisfy a man's desires."

Damien frowned. "I'm not certain I understand."

Slowly, at last, she turned to face him. Her chin lifted a degree in determination, but her gaze remained clear-eyed. "I would like to learn the skills a Cyprian should know. . . . Whatever secrets that would make me alluring to even the most jaded lover, so that after my term as your mistress is up, I can win a wealthy protector who won't be particular about my scarlet past."

Damien felt his breath suddenly falter. She couldn't be serious. Yet Vanessa was continuing in a low voice, all the more credible for its very calmness.

"I must be pragmatic, I've come to realize. A woman without any means of independence is at the mercy of fate. It is the way of the world, and I can't change that. But I can try to make the best of it. Joining the demimonde seems to be the most feasible way for me to support my sisters."

Almost absently she reached out to stroke the mare's shoulder. "There are nearly two months left of our bargain, time in which I can prepare myself for a new sort of life. I calculate that if I make myself desirable to men, then I can improve my chances of finding one who might not be so very disagreeable as a bed partner, perhaps even someone who will be to my liking. I would be grateful if you could assist me. Your expertise in the art of seduction is unparalleled, and I doubt I could hope for any better tutor."

Damien's mind had gone numb. She wanted him to teach her a whore's tricks, how best to use her body so that she could seduce some unsuspecting moneybags.

"In short," she added quietly, "I should like you to teach me to be wicked."

Her smile was strangely stoic and cut at his heart. Damien felt a mask descend over his face to hide his turmoil.

Was her request some sly ploy to play on his guilt? It was disappointing to think Vanessa Wyndham might be as mercenary as countless other members of her sex. Yet she'd implied that greed wasn't driving her so much as devotion to her sisters. Was her concern for their welfare really any different from his desire to protect his own sister?

Other genteel ladies in her position might have demanded marriage in reparation for his brazen treatment of her. Instead, she asked only that he teach her how to pleasure other men, to groom her for a role he had foisted upon her against her will. Could he do it?

By any rational standards, he should be relieved by her proposal. If he could find her a rich protector, he would no longer have to feel guilty about ruining her. He could treat her coolly, could view their relationship as nothing more than a business arrangement.

Logically, her suggestion provided a good solution to their dilemma. He could indulge in his passion for Vanessa without concern for her future. More critically, he could let his obsession fade naturally, as it inevitably would, given time.

So why then did he fear such a new arrangement would leave him too vulnerable? Why, for one frozen moment, had he experienced a jarring sensation curiously like panic? And why now did he feel this odd numbness in the vicinity of his heart?

Damien shook his head, quelling the fleeting sensations of shock and confusion warring within him.

"Very well, sweeting," he found himself saying, almost as if he were outside of himself, divorced from his feelings. "I believe I can manage to accommodate your wishes in the matter."

Her instruction began that same afternoon, for why wait, Damien asked in a curiously dispassionate voice.

Rain was falling outside in a steady drizzle when he entered her bedchamber by way of the secret passage. Vanessa sat stiffly awaiting him on the chaise lounge, still attired in her riding habit. It was the first time Damien had visited her in daylight, and the gloom made the atmosphere seem colder, less intimate.

She stared at him uncertainly as he approached her, more nervous now than at any time since she had made the momentous decision to give herself to him fully. He still wore riding breeches and boots and was in his shirtsleeves, having removed his coat and waistcoat and cravat. His raven hair seemed very dark against the white cambric of his shirt.

Then he smiled, a slow smile that banished the gloom and her nerves with it.

"This will never do, sweeting," he murmured in the warm masculine voice that never failed to bring her senses alive. "I can see that I have much to teach you. We should begin with how to receive your lover. You look as if you are facing an execution."

His gray eyes warm, he took her hand and pressed a delicate kiss on the pulse at her wrist, making her heart stumble. "First lesson: When your lover expresses a wish to visit you, you must give the impression that you are eagerly awaiting his arrival. To that end, you should be appropriately attired—something suitable for the boudoir that emphasizes your natural feminine allure. Shall I help you slip into something more comfortable?"

"I believe I can manage," Vanessa replied, finding her voice. She was determined to remain as dispassionate as Damien seemed to be. His talk of other lovers shouldn't distress her. She had asked him to further her sexual education, and he was merely complying.

When she rose and went to the armoire to fetch a wrapper, Damien settled in her place on the chaise lounge, where he could watch her.

"Keep in mind that you are offering the promise of pleasure," he added casually. "It helps to set the scene, much as for a stage play. At night, a low fire, perhaps candles, a snifter of your lover's favorite cognac . . . small touches that express your welcome."

"And during the day?" she asked as she located a wrapper of pale cream satin.

His smile was soft and beguiling as sin, reminding her once again of how vulnerable she was to his effortless charm. "Daylight requires a bit more imagination, but the same rules apply. Your goal should be to make your lover feel as if he is the only man in the world you want. The only one who can stir your senses and make your pulse race."

Just as you make me feel, Vanessa thought silently. She stepped behind the screen to change out of her riding habit.

"Take now, for instance," Damien said. "Instead of hiding yourself away, you could make a display of undressing for me. Remove each item of clothing slowly, so that my gaze lingers on your charms. Turn the simple act of disrobing into a sensual game with the express purpose of arousing me."

She turned to look at him over the edge of the screen. "You consider this a game?"

Damien gave an elegant shrug of his shoulders. "All lovemaking is a game. One you want to learn how to win if you mean to command a wealthy clientele."

Vanessa winced at the reminder, wondering if she could ever treat such intimate relations as coldly as Damien did. She finished undressing and donned the satin wrapper. Then lifting her chin, she came out from behind the screen and went to him.

He surveyed her thoughtfully. "If you mean to make a name for yourself as a courtesan, you will have to shed some of your reserve, angel."

Rising, he took her hand and led her to stand before the floor-length cheval glass, where she could see her reflection in the mirror. Behind her, Damien reached up to pull the pins from her hair, stroking the thick, burnished mass till it fell in shining waves over her shoulders. His arms came around her then to unfasten the frogs of her wrapper, and he parted the fabric, exposing the full length of her naked body to both their views.

His practiced rake's glance moved over her reflection, warm and assessing. "You have an exquisite body, lush and slender and made for pleasure. You should not think to hide it."

His eyes seemed to brand her where they touched. Vanessa shivered when he ran a finger down her arm in a slow, unhurried caress, a deliberate attack on her senses.

"No, sweeting, don't shut your eyes. Look at yourself."

Brushing aside the silken strands of her hair, he bared the tempting nape and planted a soft kiss on her flesh. Then, easing the wrapper from her shoulders, he let it fall to the floor. "See how beautiful you are." His voice stroked her, just as his hands were doing.

He trailed his fingers over the warm satin of her back. Then he moved his hands slowly around to the front of her body, briefly grazing her belly, the sleek curves of her hips and thighs, then rising again to cup her full, lush breasts.

The nipples hardened and tightened in instant response, while Vanessa caught her breath in a sensual gasp.

"You have the body of a temptress," Damien murmured. Finding her ear, he touched it with his tongue. "For this luscious form a man might forget his very name."

A soft sigh escaped her lips as he pressed close against her back, his rich, luxurious warmth curling around her.

"No, watch yourself. Watch."

She obeyed, her eyes dark with passion as his warm, naked fingers caressed her breasts, lifting and defining their shape, stroking the tight buds of her jutting nipples with his thumbs. Arousal seared through her hot and thick as she watched her own seduction.

When his lips lowered again to kiss her nape, Vanessa

arched her neck, the slow overpowering of her senses making her weak. The heat of his caresses flared through her as his teeth nibbled at her sensitive skin.

"I want to touch you all over," he whispered huskily. "To kiss every delectable inch of you and make it mine."

His searing lips sent tremors of delight through her. She leaned back fully against him, melting against his warmth as he teased her thrusting nipples, pulling and rubbing the taut peaks till they ached with pleasure. It was acutely arousing, incredibly erotic.

Through a haze of desire Vanessa watched his exquisite ministrations. Before meeting Damien, she hadn't considered herself wicked, but she no longer recognized the flushed, trembling woman in the mirror. She no longer knew herself.

She repressed a moan as one of his hands moved lower, wandering with deliberate slowness over her stomach to the soft dark curls that covered her mons. His gaze locked with hers in the mirror as his fingers delved into the warm, damp softness between her thighs, stroking her moist flesh.

When she whimpered, he smiled in approval. "Consider this your next lesson, sweeting. A wanton response inflames a man. Let me see how much you enjoy my touch."

Slowly he parted her swollen sex lips and thrust two fingers inside her. Vanessa gave a soft cry of delight at the sensual shafts of fire that arrowed through her melting loins.

"Yes, that's it. . . . Let yourself go. . . ."

Almost shaking with need, she surrendered to pleasure, her straining breasts rising and falling with her ragged breaths. . . .

The explosive orgasm caught her by surprise. She convulsed in a climax all the more powerful because of Damien's determination to draw the last drop of rapture from her with his stroking fingers. The relentless intensity of it left her shuddering, while her flesh continued to pulse sweetly with aftershocks.

When she sagged weakly back against him, Damien took advantage of her lassitude. Catching her shoulders, he guided her the short distance to the wall, and with her back still to him, made her bend forward, her hands pressed against the hard surface. Behind her he unbuttoned the straining placket of his breeches.

She was shocked when she felt the hard, smooth flesh of his erection brush against her buttocks, but she was more shocked by the wild excitement that flared through her when she realized his intent. She wanted this, wanted him to take her this way, from behind.

She tensed, but Damien's voice came soft and hoarse in her ear. "Easy, sweet."

In mute helplessness Vanessa braced herself against the wall.

With unhurried grace he parted her thighs and gripped his iron-hard shaft, then eased its silken head into the sleek, hot passage of her womanhood.

"Open to me," he ordered.

She moaned with pleasure as he thrust deep into her quivering flesh, twisting restlessly as he began to move inside her.

In response he captured her writhing hips, holding her still to prevent escape. Yet she had no desire to escape. With hypnotic motion his loins caressed hers, slow and sure, sheathing, drawing away, until it became sweet, ecstatic torture.

Throbbing with heat, burning with the need to feel him driving deep into her, Vanessa thrust wildly back against him, impaling herself on his magnificent hardness. With each rocking jolt, her ragged breaths came faster. Her breasts heaved as he sweetly ravished her, forcing her upward with each powerful surge, plunging his full, great length inside her.

She was a mass of frenzied sensation . . . flame-hot with desire. . . . Then, suddenly, in the hammering wildness, the spasms broke over her, intense waves of pleasure that engulfed her entire body and caught Damien in their wake. She heard his low groans, felt him shake with the strength of his own fulfillment as her cries echoed through the room.

The explosive passion left her dazed and exhausted. Moments later he withdrew from her, leaving Vanessa leaning weakly against the wall, missing his warmth.

"A credible effort, sweeting," he said calmly, his voice holding only an edge of hoarseness as he rebuttoned his breeches. "With a little more practice, you should be quite proficient."

The cool observation brought cruel memory rushing back.

Vanessa shivered, her heart aching with a sensation akin to despair. Damien had done precisely as she had asked, showing her how to use her body to fulfill his insatiable carnal need. And in so doing, he had shattered any illusion of intimacy between them. His passion had been nothing more than an exercise for him, the discharging of a duty.

Vanessa felt the chill wrap around her nakedness.

She had never felt so sated, so replete, in all her life.

Or so cold.

Chapter Thirteen

It was a painful lesson, but one Vanessa was determined to learn: emotions had no place in her relationship with the wicked Lord Sin. He had agreed to teach her how to win a wealthy protector, and she had to be content with that if she had any hope of quelling the desperate yearnings he aroused in her so effortlessly.

He proved a superb tutor. During her time at Rosewood she had experienced nights of exquisite passion, filled with sensual delight, but now there were afternoons and mornings as well. When his sister was occupied with massages or baths, Damien gave Vanessa lessons in desire.

He educated her on the finer points of how to be a proper mistress. How to warm a brandy and offer it to her lover. How best to use perfumed scents on secret places on her body. How to lounge in disheveled majesty at her dressing table as she made her toilet.

More notably, he schooled her in the sexual arts—of dalliance, of seduction, of inflaming a man's senses and satisfying his carnal lusts.

"Lovemaking is an art, and you are the artist," Damien observed seriously, initiating his instruction.

"I thought you said it was a game."

He flashed a smile. "Don't be impertinent. Now pay close attention. . . ."

He taught her how to arouse desire in a man, how to break him into a thousand tiny pieces.

"Your body conveys a sexual language all its own. The way you move, the way you respond to a caress, can make a man feel like a king or the lowest of beggars. When you touch a man, give the impression that you enjoy it. Let your eyes soften, give a shiver, a whisper of pleasure. And when he touches you, you must seem eager, even hungry. . . ."

His expertise always startled her; his practiced, prolonged methods of arousal left her gasping. He was a master magician who ignited the flames of her darkest desires.

Vanessa spent the days that followed wavering between fantasy and awareness. When Damien looked at her with his heated silver eyes, when she experienced the scorching intensity of his passion, she could almost believe his desire for her was real. Yet she knew better than to indulge in foolish dreams.

One of his chief aims was to make her comfortable with the male body. To that end, he frequently required her to undress him slowly, focusing on the sensuality of the exercise. Then he would lie back on the chaise lounge, inviting her to touch and explore him.

The first time his sheer brazenness shocked Vanessa a little, but enthralled her as well. Entirely nude, he reclined on the chaise like some pagan god. Vanessa drew a sharp breath at the magnificent splendor of his form, all rippling male desire, his enormous arousal erect and throbbing.

His smile was burning and lazy as he regarded her from under long, dark lashes. Still holding her gaze, he reached down to take his swollen cock in his hand. The gesture was bold and sexual and altogether tantalizing.

"Do I meet with your approval, sweeting?"

"Yes," she whispered, her mouth dry with excitement.

"Come here and show me."

Delight tingled through her every nerve as she moved to sit beside him.

Damien waited, giving her no help.

With fascination, she smoothed her hands up his torso, caressing the hard-muscled chest, exploring the sculpted perfection of his body, so lithe and sleek and graceful. Then she let her hands move lower to the sinewed thighs. Then, finally, to his full erection, long and hard and ready.

She felt a surge of lust flow through her at the feel of him, remembering the exquisite pleasure he had brought her. Her fingers brushed the engorged crest, circling the smooth, swollen head, stroking the velvet-sheathed hardness. Then she let her touch glide downward to lightly grasp the enormous shaft, marveling at the thick, surging length, so strong and pulsing with life.

Damien's gaze turned to smoke while his breathing sharpened. "Feel how your touch makes me tremble."

He made her tremble as well. Vanessa quivered, need for him pulsing between her thighs.

"I can't wait," she whispered, her voice both a plea and an imperative.

"Then don't," he replied, his smile wicked with sensuality.

She was still fully clothed, but she raised the skirts of her morning gown and moved to sit astride him. Balancing herself on her knees, she slowly impaled herself, giving a whimper of pleasure as her yielding flesh absorbed him.

He aided her then by raising his hips a tantalizing degree.

Vanessa gasped.

"How deep do you want me inside you?" he asked provocatively as he thrust upward another inch.

"Deeper . . . please . . ."

Damien obliged, and it was more than she could bear. The inflammatory pleasure spread through her body, instant and all-consuming, and she began to move helplessly, grinding her sex against him.

When she pleaded with him for release, he finally took pity on her and caught her gyrating hips, holding her still and matching each silken thrust to her breathless rhythm. Vanessa answered with all the vigor in her trembling body.

She came almost at once. With a low groan, she fell forward on top of him, shoving her face against his warm shoulder to bury her burgeoning scream.

When eventually she recovered her dazed senses, she found herself draped over him languorously, while he was still huge and hard inside her.

Damien's amused voice sounded in her ear. "Your eagerness is highly flattering, sweeting, but I see our next lesson should be on the art of control."

Those sessions left her breathless and trembling, and made her task of protecting herself all the more difficult. To her dismay, Vanessa felt herself falling further under Damien's sinfully erotic spell. He was like a potent drug, obsessing her senses and addicting her to his touch. She found herself struggling desperately against her newly awakened desires and the enticing wickedness of his caresses.

Far more dangerous, though, were the powerful emotions he aroused in her. She feared the tenderness most. There were times during the quiet, intimate moments after carnal lust had been spent when it was hard for her to remember that their relationship was strictly professional. Yet she knew that if she hoped to shield her heart, she would have to dissociate herself from any and all feelings for him.

He spoke to her about practical matters as well as sexual ones—things she would need to know if she were to spend her future gracing the beds of rakes. He described what would be expected of her outside the bedroom, in the glittering salons and fashionable ballrooms of London. He advised her on the considerations she could expect in the way of jewelry and clothing, carriages and horses, houses and furnishings. He emphasized the importance of pretending an avid interest in her male companions, smiling at inane conversations, flirting with fops enamored with their own self-consequence, hanging on their every word, no matter how boring a spirited, intelligent woman might find them. He told her how to capitalize on the natural talents she possessed.

"Beauty is an asset, certainly, but that alone doesn't always make a woman desirable."

"If not beauty, then what?"

"Any combination of qualities can be arousing—a keen wit, a facile charm, a certain liveliness, a stylish flair, a subtle sensuality. Demeanor can be a greater temptation than even physical attributes. Even a plain Jane can prove irresistible if she has other merits in her favor."

Vanessa studied Damien curiously. "Have you ever found any woman irresistible?"

His mouth curved in a cynical smile. "A few. For a time. I make it a point never to allow my interest to be held for long."

Vanessa fell silent, remembering the reason Damien had given her for keeping away from her bed. *Our association was becoming too heated for my peace of mind. . . .*

That was why Damien had ended his pursuit of her, she

realized. Why he had withdrawn emotionally from her when it seemed their intimacy was growing too intense. He was determined to hold himself apart from her and never allow his emotions to become involved.

She felt her own heart constrict with regret for the loss, yet she couldn't allow herself the luxury of sorrow.

At those times particularly—during his dispassionate lectures where they cold-bloodedly plotted to ensnare an unsuspecting protector for her—Vanessa wondered if she could carry out her plan.

She didn't like to think of having to give her body to any other man. Indeed, the only man she could see in the intimate role of protector was Damien.

Yet her assessment was still rational. After having known the patronage of the notorious Lord Sin, she should be able to make an excellent liaison elsewhere, and her sisters would be safe from penury.

If there were moments when she felt a wave of despair at the course she had chosen, she grimly pushed it aside. There were many names for the role she was attempting to learn—high flier, bird of paradise, Cyprian, courtesan . . . but the bald, unvarnished truth was, she was learning how to be a whore. An expensive, elegant whore, admittedly. But still a whore. Yet she could not afford squeamishness or sentimentality.

She would not be the first woman to earn her livelihood between the sheets. There were any number of successful courtesans who had learned to live by their wits and beauty alone. Besides, the role of mistress was far preferable to that of wife. A wife was infinitely more vulnerable to a man's tyranny. Upon marriage a woman lost control of her fortune, her children, even her body.

And in many respects the life of a courtesan would actually be liberating. She would no longer have to feel trapped by society's rigid dictates and hypocritical judgments.

And so she forced herself to learn well the lessons Damien so expertly taught.

His second goal was to make her comfortable with her own body.

"You are an apt pupil, sweeting, but you still have much to learn about lovemaking. We have scarcely begun to explore the depths of your passion. . . ."

To that end, he introduced her to the delights of scented oils and body massage. For the lesson he spread several sheets over the chaise lounge to protect the brocade, then instructed her to undress. When Vanessa suggested he be the one to lie naked on the chaise lounge instead of her, Damien shook his head.

"No, lie back and enjoy your lesson. You should experience the pleasures of manual stimulation for yourself so you understand how best to arouse your lover."

He smoothed oil all over her body, starting from behind . . . her neck, her spine, her buttocks, her thighs. . . . His hands moved slowly, massaging gently, rhythmically, the heat and slow languid motion unbelievably sensual. Then he made her turn onto her back so that he could anoint her breasts and nipples.

Vanessa was trembling even before his magical hands moved to her legs. Spreading his palms, he stroked upward along her thighs to the feminine juncture, where he paused.

Damien gazed down at her with eyes that seemed to scorch her with searing heat. "If, by some misfortune, you have a lover who cannot arouse you, leaving you too dry for penetration, then you can use this method."

His oil-slick fingers slid inside her, his thumbs brushing

the exposed bud of her sex. With a shudder of pleasure, Vanessa closed her eyes and arched against him, letting him sweep her away to a world of bliss.

Oil was not the only stimulant he used. He also taught her the merits of roses in lovemaking.

Several afternoons later, Damien made her undress for him, so that she wore nothing but her corset and gartered stockings. Vanessa blushed when she glanced at the erotic image of herself in the mirror. The garment was nothing more than a tight-laced frame for her bare breasts, one that emphasized the thrusting ripeness of her jutting nipples and left the mound at the vee of her thighs completely exposed.

"Remind me," Damien said, surveying her thoughtfully, "to take you shopping for an appropriate wardrobe when we go to London. That corset doesn't do your exquisite body justice, as well as being much too plain for your intended effect."

She turned to eye him quizzically. "Are we going to London?"

His gaze suddenly became hooded. "It is the most obvious place to begin your search for a protector. We'll have to proceed discreetly, of course, as long as you are my sister's companion. But learning to negotiate the London demimonde is essential to your education. And there are some dangers you should know about if you mean to dwell on the fringes of the underworld."

"And who better to teach me about the dangers of wickedness than the notorious Lord Sin?" Vanessa asked archly.

"Exactly. Now come here."

He was sitting in one of the two wing chairs, holding a

long-stemmed crimson rose. Still flushing, Vanessa went to stand before him.

His devouring gaze ranged the length of her, over her breasts gleaming pale and bare ... her thighs with the crown of dark curls covering the cleft of her femininity. Offering her a beguiling smile then, he lifted the rose and teased her nipples with it, arousing her till she shuddered. Moving lower then, he drew the velvet petals slowly over the lips of her sex.

Vanessa drew a sharp breath at the delicate sensation.

Damien plucked a crimson petal and held it out to her. "Now your turn."

"My turn?"

"To touch yourself."

The color in Vanessa's cheeks rose higher, but Damien seemed to dismiss her embarrassment.

"Your lover may not be considerate enough to see to your needs. You should learn to achieve your own relief in the event you have a man who cannot satisfy you."

Obeying with reluctance, she took the soft petal and brushed it over the secret place between her thighs. Abruptly Vanessa felt a wild tingle of excitement surge through her blood.

"This," she whispered, gazing down at him, "is so decadent."

"Not yet," Damien murmured. "But it will be, I promise you. Now continue. Pretend those are my fingers caressing you, arousing you to pleasure."

Her gaze locking with Damien's, she did as he bid, exploring a world of forbidden mystery. Heat flared inside her as she stroked herself with the rose petal, gliding over the taut bud that was growing slick with her own juices.

Damien's eyes darkened as he watched. "Your nipples

are hard, sweeting. Does that mean you're becoming aroused?"

"Yes . . . but it isn't the same as when you . . ."

He smiled. "I'm flattered. Perhaps you're ready for the next lesson after all."

Drawing her hand away, he leaned forward and pressed a kiss on the intimate dewy center of her. Vanessa went rigid with surprise.

"Have I ever told you how much I like the scent of roses?" Damien murmured huskily.

His eyes gleaming like liquid silver, he stood and undressed her completely. Then, leading her to the bed, he pressed her down upon the sheets and arranged her position to his liking: her hair forming a torrent of tousled silk over her bare breasts, a pillow beneath her hips, her naked thighs spread for his sensual appreciation.

He held her gaze as he stood back to undress. "It's time you discovered just how pleasurable decadence can be."

She waited in rapt and aching anguish for him to come to her, aware of the most potent sense of anticipation she'd ever felt.

Naked and aroused, he joined her on the bed and knelt between her thighs. The heat of his gaze set her blood on fire. Yet he didn't enter her. Instead he bent to her breasts that were begging to be touched.

His tongue circled a dusky crest, now pebbled and eager. Vanessa whimpered with pure joy at knowing his caress again.

"I mean to show you," he whispered against her skin, "just how to use your mouth to drive a man wild. . . ."

He flicked his tongue over her nipples one by one, swirling over the aureoles, setting her nerves awake with each caress. Then his lips and teeth joined the assault, sending pleasure shafting deep within her loins.

Vanessa gave a low moan. Her sensitive nipples ached now, hard and pointed and tender to the point of pain. His mouth moved lower then, over the rest of her body. His flaming tongue struck sparks along her flesh, laving exquisitely each curve and swell and hollow, making her tremble with sensations so vibrant they hurt.

Between caresses Damien spoke to her, each low, sensuous word stroked her as his wicked tongue was doing.

"I want to kiss you, sweeting, all over your beautiful body. I want to explore every inch of your hot skin and make it mine. I want to hear you moan raw sounds of pleasure that will drive me mad. . . ."

The wanton images so vivid, so potent, stirred errant quivers of wanting in her midsection, between her thighs.

"I want you drowning in need, my name trembling on your lips. . . ."

His breath whispering against her skin, he kissed the soft satin of her stomach, leaving her trembling, driving her to madness with his deliberate slowness.

As if he could sense her need, his hand moved downward, slipping between her legs. She moaned as her softness flowed around his fingers' erotic stroking, and moaned again as his wet tongue trailed against the shivering surface of her inner thigh. She wanted this, hungered for his possession.

He moved still lower. "I want to love you with my mouth. . . ."

She saw his nostrils flare as he breathed in her spicy woman's scent. Then he kissed her, a tantalizing brush of sensual lips against her dewy warmth.

Gasping, Vanessa tried to twist away in shocked protest,

but he reached up to catch her hands, his grasp like velvet manacles on her wrists. Desire burned in his eyes as he bent to her again.

She moaned as his tongue traced the outer rim of her soaking cleft. Then he settled his mouth against her intimately, sucking and nibbling and softly biting, plunging her into a sea of raw sensation.

His mouth brought her the most riveting kind of pleasure she had ever known. Heat and dizziness swept over Vanessa. From a distance she heard his husky voice filling her mind with erotic words of how much he wanted her, desired her. His teeth nipped gently at the swollen, aching folds of her flesh, preparing her for his taking, until she was shameless in her craving for release.

"Damien . . ." she pleaded as she thrashed beneath his caresses.

He ravished her sweetly with his tongue, determined to find the deepest, most forbidden reserves of ecstasy. Finally she could no longer bear the tender torment. She came hot and wet and slippery against his mouth, shaking with sweet spasms. Even then he gave her no surcease. Moving upward swiftly, Damien covered her with the textured heat of his chest and plunged deep.

One rhythmic stroke was enough to spark a fresh tumult of excitement within her. When she arched upward eagerly, he drove hungrily between her thighs, groaning as her feverish, ready heat enveloped him.

She gave a responding cry as she felt the splendor begin anew. She was shaking with the fire of his possession, shattering. . . . With her tremors, Damien lost control of his savage need. As bliss ripped through her in white-hot waves, he joined her fierce ecstasy, uttering a feral growl as he plunged to a blind, furious release.

Long after he had collapsed on her, long after her trembling had ceased, she lay languid in his arms, pulsing with pleasure, lost in dreams. Contentment washed over Damien as he held her close. His fingers lightly stroked her fevered skin that was rapidly cooling, while he marveled absently at how perfectly she fit.

His satisfaction was short-lived. Shifting his weight, he felt the sting of the nail cuts she'd left on his back. Damien smiled grimly, remembering her raw cries of ecstasy. He had pleasured Vanessa, fulfilled her, and taken her to paradise with him—and become lost in paradise himself.

How wrong he had been. He'd thought that having her again and again would eventually satisfy his fierce craving for her. Had hoped to make his obsession run its course. But his plan was an utter failure. Far from ending, his desire was only burgeoning, his hunger more potent than anything he had ever known. He felt an ungovernable need to possess her endlessly, to brand her as his own, to make her as obsessed as he was becoming.

Damien swore silently. He would have to take Vanessa to London without delay. The sooner he found her another protector, the sooner he could be free of her.

With practiced detachment he clamped down on the sharp surge of disquiet that twisted inside him. He'd had dozens of paramours, ended dozens of liaisons before Vanessa. This time should be no different.

Willfully, Damien ignored the thought of how he would feel when she gave herself to someone besides himself. She would pass to another lover with his blessing, someone who would appreciate her intelligence, her rare spirit, and leave him free to regain control of his soul.

Chapter Fourteen

It was settled. They planned to leave for London the following Monday. Damien claimed to have business in town that required his personal attention. When he proposed that Vanessa accompany him to engage in some shopping, Olivia strongly supported the idea, saying that her companion's entire wardrobe badly needed replenishing.

Vanessa didn't like to think of leaving the girl alone at Rosewood, but Olivia maintained she wasn't yet ready to make the tiring journey, or prepared to leave the protective cocoon of her home. She confided as well that she would actually enjoy the solitude and the chance to assert her independence from her brother.

And so Vanessa reluctantly packed her bags, consoling herself with the knowledge that, in any event, she would be permanently relinquishing her role as companion at summer's end. Moreover, London was not so very far away, and they would be gone for only a handful of days. The trip would be a good test to see how Olivia managed on her own.

Vanessa intended to warn her brother to suspend his secret visits while they were absent, but she hadn't seen Aubrey in more than a week. She assumed he was keeping his distance to prevent being discovered by Lord Sin. Or perhaps he was tiring at last of his crisis of conscience.

The afternoon before their departure, she was alone in the garden, reading beneath a shade tree, when she spied Aubrey strolling toward her. Concerned that he might be seen by one of the gardeners, Vanessa glanced around. But thankfully they were alone.

"Where have you been this past week?" she asked as he settled on the bench beside her. "I was beginning to wonder if you had given up and gone home."

He gave her an arch look. "Certainly not. I've been too occupied to break free even for a moment. I've found a position of employment."

Vanessa stared. "You must be jesting."

Aubrey winced but flashed a grin. "It is a sad state of affairs when my own dear sister won't believe me. But it's true. I've taken a real job with the rich cit who bought Brantly Hall—a Mr. Jonah Goodwine. He's to be awarded a baronetcy soon, and he aspires to the gentry. I'm to teach him how to be a gentleman."

Vanessa shook her head. She couldn't have been more astonished if Aubrey claimed to have proof he'd flown to the moon and back.

"I am acting as Goodwine's private secretary," Aubrey explained, "but, fortunately, the role is more one of social adviser, since I'm not of a scholarly bent. Goodwine thinks it's a great coup to have a viscount in his employ. What, Van?" he teased. "Have I startled you speechless?"

"You have indeed," she replied finally, with bewilderment. "Whatever possessed you to take such a step?"

Her brother's laughing eyes grew serious. "The hope that gainful employment will prove to be the making of me. You've always said I should find something worthwhile to occupy me and keep me out of trouble. Perhaps this is my chance. It's long past time I grew up and fulfilled my responsibilities, instead of expecting you always to bail me out. And, financially, the position is extremely rewarding. I'm to be given an exorbitant salary, and in time I should be able to pay off my creditors."

He looked down at his hands, while his voice lowered. "It was unforgivable of me, putting you in such an untenable position—having to share Sinclair's bed in order to save us. I know I can never repay you for what you've done for me, Van, but I intend to do everything in my power to prove worthy of your sacrifice."

Vanessa felt an ache rise to her throat. Her scapegrace brother seemed entirely serious about turning his life around. Certainly his efforts thus far were laudable. . . . Now if he could just maintain his course.

She kept her tone light when she answered. "I believe there might be hope for you yet."

He nodded soberly. "I mean to try to regain Olivia's good opinion, if I can. I may have destroyed any possibility of winning her regard, but I wish to remain close to her. Brantly Hall is but ten miles from here, so I may still visit upon occasion—at least in secret. As long as Sinclair never finds out. And as long as Olivia consents to see me."

His admission made Vanessa recall the issue his startling news had driven out of her head. "Aubrey, that reminds me: I'm traveling to London tomorrow with Sinclair."

Aubrey frowned. "Is that not a trifle . . . indiscreet? It is one thing for you to live here at his estate where you're companion to his sister, but to be living with him in town. . . ."

"I don't intend to stay with him, but in our own house. We should be away for a few days, but I think it best if you kept away from Olivia during that time."

"Why?"

She met her brother's brown eyes directly. "I haven't prevented your visits because they seemed to have a positive effect on Olivia. But you've been strictly chaperoned the entire time. It wouldn't be wise for you to be alone with her. I don't want you hurting her any more than you already have."

She saw the pain in his eyes. "You still don't trust me, do you? I love her, Vanessa. I would cut out my heart before I hurt her again."

Vanessa hesitated. Until now, she had been highly skeptical of her brother's professions of love, but perhaps his heart truly was engaged. If so, then did she have a right to prevent a connection that might lead to Olivia's happiness? Aubrey's suit might progress better without her interference after all. . . .

"What does Olivia want?" he interrupted in low voice.

"I don't know. I haven't spoken with her about you lately."

"Then ask her. If she wants me to keep away, I will." Aubrey rose to his feet. "I know it must be hard for you to credit, after all I've put you through, but I truly have reformed."

Vanessa sat there long after he was gone, deeply conflicted by what her brother had said.

It was possible that true love could reform a man, and apparently that was what had happened to her brother. Driven by love for Olivia, he had taken stock of his life, found it profoundly wanting, and vowed to change.

And if her wastrel brother could undergo such a stark transformation, could someone like Damien Sinclair do the same?

Damien was a jaded libertine, perhaps, but not nearly as

wanton and decadent as she'd originally thought. He wasn't totally wicked. No one who saw his deep regard for his sister could believe him beyond redemption.

Still, he could be so much more, do so much more with his life. With his wealth and position, he could accomplish a vast deal of good. But he would need a reason to change. She held little hope that the unattainable Lord Sin would ever lose his heart to her, or any other woman. He would never allow it. Unless . . .

At the thought of Damien falling in love, yearning sprang up in Vanessa, so sudden and sharp it frightened her. Relentlessly, though, she forced the treacherous feeling aside. She couldn't afford nonsensical romantic dreams.

No, the best she could hope for was a swift end to their relationship. It was time she went to London, time she attempted to fix the attentions of a wealthy admirer.

Only then could she move on with her life. Only then could she try to forget she had ever known the magical enchantment of the wicked Lord Sin.

The journey to London was pleasant enough, if Vanessa overlooked Damien's growing remoteness as the drive wore on. He gave her little time to rest upon arriving. When he conveyed her directly to the Rutherford town house, she made do with the skeleton staff to bathe and change her attire.

An hour later he escorted her to a play at the Drury Lane Theatre, and then to the Green Room afterward, so that she could observe how the actresses made assignations with young bucks vying for their favors. Afterward he returned her home with scarcely a word.

The next night they made the rounds of the gaming hells, where high-stakes gambling was de rigueur.

"It would be wise of you," Damien advised, "to learn the rules of various games of chance. If your patron holds a fondness for cards, you might spend many of your evenings in establishments such as this."

Vanessa felt her heart twist in her chest, not due so much to the future Damien envisioned for her, as to his evident indifference. His gaze seemed flat and cold, his tenderness nonexistent. She found it difficult to hide her despair, yet she forced herself to keep up the bright pretense of enjoying their outings.

The following evening they attended a masquerade ball, where she could watch the flirtations of not-quite-respectable ladies and their chosen victims—to see how a straw damsel in search of a protector flashed her fine feathers so as to make the best possible arrangement.

The object of these excursions, Damien maintained, was to show her the life she would lead as a member of the demimonde. It was an elegant shadow world of passion and pleasure, a debauched realm in which he moved with as much ease as he did the glittering, golden arena of the ton. It seemed a mirror image of polite society; here gentlemen remained faithful to their mistresses, and wives were held in relatively low esteem.

To make her aware of the dangers inherent in her new profession, Damien also gave her a glimpse of Covent Garden, the notorious site of the lucrative flesh trade of the lower orders. Vanessa saw procuresses who looked as innocent as nuns and common streetware whose lives were often short and violent.

She counted herself fortunate that while she had chosen to sell herself to the highest bidder, it *was* her choice, under conditions of luxury and independence.

She was fortunate, as well, to have Damien as her tutor.

If he disapproved of her choice, he gave no indication of it. If there were times when she caught a glimpse of some other darker emotion in his eyes—a hint of bleakness, of anger—she decided she must have imagined it.

Her days were as fully occupied as her nights. To add to her feathered plumes, Damien took her to a discreet modiste patronized by demireps, where Vanessa was fitted for attire specifically designed for the boudoir, as well as evening gowns that were more risqué than those she was accustomed to wearing. One of the articles he ordered for her particularly disturbed her because of its intimacy—a pair of white doeskin garters exquisitely embroidered with gold roses.

When she protested his exorbitant expenditures, however, Damien shrugged in his charming, graceful way and said, "Consider it remuneration for your excellent care of my sister."

Uncomfortable about becoming even more indebted to him, Vanessa kept a careful account of his gifts, hoping to reimburse him someday. The jewelry he gave her, however, was far more lavish than she could ever repay.

On the evening he escorted her to the pleasure gardens at Vauxhall, Damien presented her with an exquisite emerald necklace and bracelet set to match one of the new gowns he had bought for her, and wouldn't hear of a refusal.

Vanessa managed to don the bracelet herself, but when she fumbled with the clasp of the necklace, Damien came to her aid. She found herself trembling as his cool fingers fastened the jewels around her throat. It was the most intimate contact she'd had with him since arriving in London. Each night he had left her at her doorstep alone, and had made no move even to touch her, let alone share her bed.

Bleakly, she told herself to be grateful he had ended

their physical intimacy. It was far better for them both to put a wide distance between them. Yet she missed his sensual warmth, missed the charming, caring lover she had once known—with an intensity that left her aching.

"You ought not have been so extravagant," she murmured in a futile attempt to distract her thoughts.

"It is no more than I would have done for any mistress," he replied coolly.

Flinching, Vanessa turned to face him. He was breathtakingly handsome, impossibly elegant, in a tailored blue coat and cream brocade waistcoat. And as cold as a statue.

It devastated her to be reminded how little she meant to him, that she was only one in a long line of women. She didn't want his gifts of jewelry. She wanted his friendship, his tenderness, his . . . love. *Sweet mercy . . .*

She stood frozen as he slid her emerald satin evening cloak over her bare shoulders. When he offered his arm, she took it in a daze and allowed him to escort her to the waiting carriage. Settling back against the squabs, Vanessa remained silent as she struggled with her desperate thoughts.

She had realized the terrible truth in a paralyzing instant. Against all dictates of wisdom or sense, against the stronger instincts of self-preservation, she had fallen in love with Damien.

All these weeks she had lied to herself, denying how much he fascinated her, bewitched her, ensnared her. His keen wit, his captivating charm, his affection for his sister, his consideration for her fears . . . there was so much to love about him. She had lost her heart to the tender lover who had so deftly taught her a woman's passions and set her free of her fears.

Horrified, she stared blindly out the carriage window.

As usual he seemed sensitive to her mood. "You are

quiet tonight," Damien observed, studying her in the dimness of the carriage. "Are you feeling unwell?"

Vanessa forced the semblance of a smile. "Well enough. Just a touch of the headache."

Shaking herself, she summoned the strength to pretend her world had not just shattered.

She would never allow Damien to know how thoroughly he had fragmented her heart. She didn't want his pity or, worse, his scorn. When it came time to part, she vowed fiercely, she would never behave so foolishly as his other former mistresses. When they said good-bye, it would be over.

Vanessa had visited Vauxhall Gardens in the past, though not since before her husband's death. The lavish gardens were as famous for the summer entertainment as for the graveled, tree-lined walkways illuminated by festoons of colored lanterns in crimson and gold. This particular evening, the music concert boasted a sizable orchestra, with vocal performers in two acts interspersed by a magical extravaganza of a cascading waterfall and a brilliant fireworks display.

Vanessa would have found great pleasure in the music had her emotions not been in such agony. Under the circumstances she was glad for the din, for she was spared the necessity of conversing with Damien as they strolled along the grounds.

At intermission he escorted her to a supper box adorned with paintings by Francis Hayman, where they dined on paper-thin slices of ham, sparrow-sized chickens, and pigeon pie, followed by strawberries and cherries and flavored ices.

Trying to conceal her desperation, Vanessa drank more of the potent Vauxhall punch than was wise. Perhaps that was why she felt light-headed when a party of gentlemen passed by their box, accompanied by two females who, from the scandalous cut of their gowns, did not appear to be ladies.

The gentlemen looked as if they had greatly enjoyed the punch, for they were weaving and laughing uproariously at some private joke. As a group they came to a halt when they spied Damien.

"Sin, do come and join us!" one slurred voice called out. "We mean to see what pleasure the Dark Walk can offer."

Unlike the other unexceptional pleasure walks, the Dark Walk had gained a reputation for infamy. Its shadowed alcoves and romantic hideaways had been designed for lovers but were often used for nefarious purposes, and more than one young damsel's good name had been ruined there.

"And bring your *lady*," another voice said, sniggering.

From the ribald laughter that followed this suggestion, they considered her of the same ilk as their own female companions. But perhaps that was only to be expected, Vanessa acknowledged grimly, when she was being escorted by a rake like Damien.

Disturbed by the bold way she was being eyed, she was glad when Damien didn't introduce her. Instead, with a dismissive wave of his hand, he declined the invitation and sent his dissolute friends on their way.

They were not the last unsettling visitors to the box, however. Moments later a couple strolled by. Vanessa recognized the gentleman as Lord Houghton, a friend of her late husband. The woman on his arm was a stranger—ravishingly beautiful, with silver-blond hair and a full-breasted figure draped in white satin. Sporting a tasteful hint of paint on her face, she looked the essence of an expensive Cyprian.

Lord Houghton acknowledged Vanessa and Damien with a brief bow and might have moved on but for the woman's musical voice issuing a mild protest. "Charles, do stop and make me known to your friends."

He flushed slightly and bowed again. "Lady Wyndham, Lord Sinclair, allow me to present Mrs. Swann, a most superior actress."

Vanessa felt herself blanch at the name. Suddenly numb, she scarcely heard the actress's reply.

"Lord Sin and I have met," Mrs. Swann purred. "I am currently performing at the Haymarket, my lord, and should love to have you in the audience."

Damien inclined his head in recognition and responded with casual politeness. "I should be pleased to attend a performance if time permits, but I'm in London for only a few days."

Turning to Vanessa, Mrs. Swann raised a delicate eyebrow. "I was acquainted with your husband as well."

"I believe you were," Vanessa choked out the reply. Roger had met his ignominious end dueling over this beautiful actress.

The Silver Swann seemed not in the least abashed by her notoriety. A sly smile curving her red lips, she lifted her hand to her throat to finger an emerald necklace similar to the one Vanessa herself wore. "Sin has excellent taste in jewelry, does he not?"

Vanessa was jolted from her frozen stupor as she realized the implication: the emeralds had been a gift from Damien. "He does indeed," she said, outraged and bitterly wounded at the same time.

Lord Houghton looked embarrassed that his companion would be so ill-bred as to flaunt her jewelry. Hastily taking his leave, he swept the actress away.

Alone with Damien once more, Vanessa took a long swallow of her punch. When she felt the weight of his gaze, she cast him a bleak, acrimonious glance.

His eyes had grown hooded, while the liquor she'd drunk had loosened her tongue.

"She was one of your former paramours, I gather?"

"For a brief time, yes." He met her gaze evenly. "I've never tried to conceal the fact that I've had liaisons in the past."

Or will in the future, Vanessa acknowledged bitterly. Damien had never lied to her about his affairs. Yet his honesty didn't make it any easier to accept that he'd been intimate with the very actress who had inspired her husband's foolish death. Or to stem the painful jealousy that surged through her. Or to quell the insistent clutch of despair and longing at the thought of Damien with any other woman.

How foolish she was to hope he might change.

Almost wild with misery, Vanessa averted her gaze and brought the glass of punch to her lips.

By the time the second musical act was over, she had consumed enough of the potent brew to somewhat numb her devastation. Her head was swimming and she felt dangerously despondent, but she managed not to cling too heavily to Damien's arm when they walked down to the riverbank to watch the spectacular fireworks, even though the alcohol sang in her blood like the brilliant rockets bursting overhead.

As the crowd dispersed to return to their boxes, they encountered the group of inebriated young bucks they'd seen earlier, this time no longer accompanied by the two females. All five gentlemen looked three sheets to the wind.

"Come with us, Sin," one called out. "We mean to tour the fleshpots of London, starting at Tavistock's."

"I'm afraid I must decline," Damien replied with obvious anger. "You may have noticed I have a lady with me."

"Zounds, bring her along. The more the merrier." Raising his quizzing glass, he squinted and ogled Vanessa's bosom.

She clenched her jaw in absolute torment, but maintained a fierce dignity as Damien swiftly drew her away from his friends.

Feeling grimly reckless and destructive, she feigned a smile as she glanced up at Damien. "I should indeed like to see a brothel. It might be highly . . . educational."

"I don't think so," he replied, stiffening.

"Why not?" she asked coldly. "You said you would show me the dangers of the wicked underworld. What could be more wicked than a brothel?"

"Indeed, but they're generally for the lower class of demimondaine. A discriminating Cyprian would not allow herself to be seen there."

Vanessa came to a halt, making Damien stop also. "But I've heard of ladies attending such places in disguise. They wear half-masks to conceal their identity."

"You wouldn't care for the form of entertainment to be found there, sweeting, I assure you."

"I think I should be allowed to judge that for myself. Besides, what do you care for my feelings?"

Anger gleamed darkly in his gray eyes as he stared at her.

When Damien still hesitated, Vanessa added with a chill smile, "I imagine those fine friends of yours could be persuaded to escort me, if you refuse."

Chapter Fifteen

As he escorted Vanessa up the steps of the most elegant sin club in London, Damien seethed with anger. He was loath to bring her here, to expose her to the decadence in which he himself was so well-versed.

His mood had become bleak and dangerous as the evening progressed. Seeing her ogled and demeaned by his drunken acquaintances was even more repugnant than her being taunted by one of his former paramours about her jewels.

He'd chosen emeralds for Vanessa to complement her dark beauty, to set off the burnished fire of her hair. He couldn't even remember what trinkets he'd settled on Elise Swann so many months ago. Indeed, his secretary had chosen the Swann's gifts, and any similarity was purely coincidence. Perhaps he should have simply told Vanessa that, no matter how ill-bred such an explanation would have been. He should at least have offered an apology.

Both incidents had left an acid taste in his mouth ... oddly like shame. Damien's jaw hardened as he recognized the uncommon sentiment.

Until tonight he would have termed their visit to London a marginal success. In the past few days he had managed to withdraw from their relationship, at least physically.

He'd kept their opportunities for intimacy to an absolute minimum, resorting to cold formalities and denying himself all but the most unavoidable contact with Vanessa. It had proven harder to dampen his fever for her, to maintain even a small measure of control over his unquenchable desire, to crush his alarming feelings of tenderness.

He dared not allow any tender emotions between them. Midnight trysts and quiet conversations had no place in their current relationship. If he found himself regretting the loss, or yearning for the friendship they had once shared, if he felt the hollow echoes of his past in this current sojourn to London—loneliness and emptiness—it was a price he was willing to pay to be rid of his obsession.

Vanessa's education was proceeding apace, and soon he would be able to wash his hands of her without his conscience flaying him. Or so he desperately hoped. . . .

"Will we find your dissipated friends here?" she coolly interrupted his dark thoughts.

He gave a sardonic smile. "I trust not. Tavistock Court, where they were headed, specializes in flagellation. I doubt you have any desire to be flailed with rods or nettles to stimulate sexual arousal."

"No," Vanessa said with a delicate shudder.

"Madame Fouchet's salon is known more for its stylized diversions than perversions."

"There is a difference?" Vanessa asked archly, a facetious question Damien didn't deign to answer.

Cursing her stubbornness, he rapped sharply on the door. Vanessa had insisted on coming here, even threatening to find another escort if he refused. But she would discover, Damien reflected darkly, a vast difference between the pleasurable carnal games she enjoyed with him in private and the sordid kind of public debauchery to be found at Fouchet's. Shocked enough perhaps to keep away from such iniquitous dens in the future. If so, then it would be worth bringing her here, despite his grave misgivings.

They were admitted to an antechamber without question by a majordomo and greeted personally by Madame Fouchet, a Frenchwoman who seemed delighted by Lord Sin's patronage of her establishment. If she was curious about Vanessa's presence, she hid it well.

"And what pleasure may I offer you this evening, my lord?"

Damien favored her with a charming smile that hid his savage mood. "This lady has never attended a house such as yours, Madame. We would like to observe for a time, if we may."

"But, of course," Madame replied, as if his request was nothing unusual in a sporting house that catered primarily to aristocratic young bloods. "And will you be requiring a private room? Perhaps some companionship?" Her glance darted to Vanessa. "I would be pleased to offer a young man or two to entertain madame."

Damien's jaw tightened. "I believe we will choose our pleasure later. Meanwhile a measure of discretion would be advised. You have a mask for the lady?"

"But, of course."

She produced a demi-mask with ease, suggesting that protecting one's identity was an entirely common request. When she asked his lordship if he wished her to conduct a tour of the premises, Damien declined, saying he would see to the matter himself.

"As you wish, my lord. If you require anything at all, you need only ask." Madame withdrew then, leaving her noble clients to their own devices.

Without speaking, Damien led Vanessa across the antechamber to an alcove. Pulling aside a velvet curtain on the wall, he exposed a glass viewing window, beyond which was an elegant salon with gilt furnishings. A half-dozen young beauties dressed in translucent gowns sat or reclined artfully in various sensual poses that displayed their charms to advantage.

"This is where clients select their partners and their particular entertainment for the evening," Damien explained without inflection. "The hour is late. Those are the performers who have not yet been chosen."

"Is that all they wear?" Vanessa asked in a weak voice.

Damien feigned a smile. "No. They usually change into appropriate costumes for the entertainment. Madame Fouchet excels at satisfying fantasies, and costumes are part of the fantasy. For gentlemen with a preference for young virgins, there are schoolgirls and dairymaids, who, of course, miraculously regain their virginity overnight. For more forbidden fruit, one may chose a governess or nun. If you aspire to the nobility, you can have a duchess or even a queen. Or if your tastes run to the exotic, you can order slave girls or an entire harem, although the expense for a harem is far greater."

He paused, gauging her reaction. "There may very well be a harem in progress tonight. Would you care to see what delightful entertainment awaits, sweeting?"

Vanessa nodded hesitantly. The destructive recklessness that had driven her here still stirred her blood, yet, frankly, she was glad she was not quite sober.

Damien led her through a door to a long hallway, explaining as he went. "The rooms on this floor are used for group affairs. For more privacy there are a number of bedchambers above."

He paused at another alcove, this one boasting a much

smaller viewing window than the main salon. He hesitated for a moment before moving aside with obvious reluctance. Vanessa could smell the scent of incense as she stepped up to the window.

The exotic scene was of an Eastern palace, with swaths of filmy draperies and whisping smoke. Several nude men reclined on silken cushions like pashas, wearing nothing but turbans. One of them sported a rampant erection as he avidly watched a nude dancing girl whose swaying body glistened with oil and decorative bangles. The other clients were being fed grapes and sweetmeats while their limbs and genitals were stroked with oil.

Vanessa drew back, her face flaming with shock and embarrassment. Whatever had made her think she could go through with this? But she couldn't back down now, not after forcing Damien to bring her here.

He raised an eyebrow but refrained from comment. Leading her to the next alcove, he glanced through the window, then stepped back so she could look.

"The shipwreck is a popular entertainment here. The clients dress up as pirates and take captive a ship of female passengers."

The scene was a ship motif lit by flaming torches, Vanessa saw. Several naked women were tied to masts. A man was taking his pleasure with one of them, his face flushed with exertion as his buttocks pumped fiercely between her white thighs.

In another corner three men lay with another bound female, jointly fondling her breasts and mons and thrusting a large ivory phallus between her legs while she writhed in apparent ecstasy.

"Ravishment is a popular fantasy," Damien observed in a grim voice. "Here a man can have his wicked way without

consequence. And adventurous ladies can pay for the pleasure of being one of the captives."

Vanessa closed her eyes, feeling revulsion and arousal
at the same time.

"You should probably learn the techniques of bondage,"
Damien added coolly. "Your lover might well enjoy such
pleasures."

She winced, reminded of the future in store for her.
When he led her to the final alcove, Vanessa steeled herself
for what she might find.

"This one is merely a ballroom scene," he commented.
"Doubtless it began as a masquerade, but the ball guests
would not long be content merely to dance and eat."

The chamber, she saw, was brighter than the previous
ones, with light from several chandeliers reflected by walls
of gilded mirrors. Costumes and masculine garments lay
strewn haphazardly about the floor, while on a dais where
the musicians might normally play was a writhing sea of
naked bodies. The guests appeared to change partners
frequently and without discrimination. Vanessa drew back
from the viewing window even more quickly this time, her
face paling.

Watching her response, Damien was aware of a vast
sense of relief. At least he hadn't corrupted her so thoroughly that she could view an orgy with equanimity. Even
through her mask her shock was apparent.

"Have you seen enough?" Damien asked, his tone
challenging.

She nodded but retorted in an arch tone, "I never realized there were so many degrees of debauchery to be
found."

He managed a cynical smile. "Sweeting, you haven't
begun to see debauchery. In London there are hundreds of

houses like this. On this street alone you can find any manner of sexual perversions . . . torture, men enjoying men or even beasts. . . ."

"And *you* are the prince of debauchery," she observed.

Damien felt his anger swell again. "Actually my taste is fairly simple. I find I don't need much more than a willing woman to arouse me adequately . . . as you well know. Now," he said, taking her arm, "if you are quite finished, perhaps you will allow me to convey you home."

"But there is more, is there not?" Vanessa said defiantly, pulling free of his grasp. "Didn't you say there are private bedchambers abovestairs? Surely I shouldn't let this edifying opportunity go to waste. Or have *you* suddenly turned craven?"

His smile this time was icy. "Very well, angel, if you insist. . . . Wait here a moment, and I will make arrangements with Madame Fouchet."

He left her alone in the alcove, but Vanessa declined to watch the orgy. Although she would have much preferred to end her visit altogether, she refused to allow Damien to dictate to her any longer. In any case, the debauchery abovestairs couldn't possibly be as shocking as the scandalous scenes she had already witnessed. And it was far better to know what to expect in the event she ever found herself in another pleasure house like this.

A few moments later, Damien returned with a key. "A room has been prepared for us."

Leading her to the far end of the hall, he escorted her upstairs to another hall and then to one of several bedchambers. Ushering Vanessa inside, Damien shut the door softly behind them.

She glanced curiously around her. The dimly lit room was tastefully opulent, decorated in crimson and black with touches of purple. The large bed that dominated the center of the floor boasted black satin sheets, with a pair of silk sashes tied to each of the four posts. An odd assortment of paraphernalia lay unobtrusively on a side table—smooth ivory and tortoiseshell phalluses, glass balls, riding crops, bottles of oil, and several other wicked-looking items whose use Vanessa could only imagine.

Behind her, Damien leaned back against the door. "Do you want Madame Fouchet to find some strapping young bucks to service you? Doubtless she will have a footman or two who would enjoy performing such a special duty."

The cool question was insulting, and Vanessa, spurred on by the punch she had drunk, rashly replied in the same taunting tone. "What would you say if I did?"

She saw his jaw harden. "I would say that you might find being fucked by strangers an interesting experience."

"I might indeed," she retorted, refusing to let him see how his crudity wounded her.

His own expression showed absolutely no emotion, but there was a glittering flash of anger in his silver eyes that warned her of the danger in teasing a wolf.

Wisely relenting, Vanessa glanced at the outer wall beside him. "Are there spy windows for this room?"

"I'm certain there are. But I've been assured of privacy tonight."

"I believe I will pass on the footmen."

"Good." Damien pushed away from the door. "I don't feel like sharing you just now."

Crossing to her, he took her by the shoulders and bent his head. He kissed her, but there was no tenderness in his caress, only heat and hardness.

Defiantly, she returned his rough kiss, more inflamed than alarmed by the dark tension pulsing between them.

She could be the sort of woman he seemed to want tonight. What did it matter if he ground her heart to dust? Without it, she could make her way in his callous, dissolute world without looking back.

Their tongues warred, then mated, igniting a fever in her. It was as if Damien was bent on domination, yet Vanessa was determined he wouldn't win this battle of wills between them.

His lips were hungry, ruthless, as his hands worked the clasps of her gown. The low-cut bodice fell away easily, liberating her breasts to his mouth's ravishment. He bent over her, sucking her straining nipples until he forced a low moan from her throat. Her heart was hammering by the time he broke off.

His eyes would not free her from their intensity as he undressed her, starting with her mask and ending with her stockings. When she was fully naked, he led her to the bed and pressed her down on the cool satin sheets.

As she lay back, she was startled to realize that a gilt mirror was affixed to the ceiling overhead. She could see herself and all of her body's secrets, her pale skin a starkly erotic contrast to the black satin.

"So you can watch yourself being pleasured," Damien explained in a low voice.

She lay there willingly until he reached for a silk sash and began to tie her wrist to the bedpost. Vanessa tensed, gazing up at him warily.

"Surely you don't mean to turn shy now?" he dared her. "You insisted on experiencing a brothel. This is your chance."

She raised her chin at his taunt. Damien had become a stranger tonight, ruthless and more than a little dangerous, but she didn't believe he would ever actually hurt her. And she had become a stranger to herself.

"I only trust you will make the experience enjoyable," she retorted, throwing the challenge back at him.

He smiled coolly though his eyes smoldered. "I promise to do my utmost."

He completed his task of tying her arms overhead, but left her legs free, to her relief. She watched him as he went to the table and returned with an ivory phallus to sit beside her on the bed.

His scorching gaze swept over her nude body, touching her intimately. "This is my fantasy, angel, having you at my mercy."

"Hasn't that been the situation all along?" she replied tersely.

Her rejoinder was ignored. She felt the cool caress of the ivory on her skin as slowly he brushed it against her inner thigh.

Vanessa shivered as a rippling thrill of alarm and arousal ran through her. She could understand why some women enjoyed this fantasy—a powerful, sexual male, fully clothed and dominant, holding her captive, while she was naked and vulnerable to his every whim. The mound at the apex of her thighs was pulsing sweetly in anticipation of his attentions.

But Damien didn't immediately gratify her desire. For a moment all he did was stroke her lightly with the smooth ivory.

Vanessa moved restlessly on the black satin, her thighs instinctively stretching wider, hungry for his caress. He seemed intent, however, merely on sexual torment. Without haste he brushed her feminine cleft with the ivory tip, circling the outer rim, careful not to touch the delicate bud of her sex itself.

"Damien," she murmured in a pleading voice.

"Patience, sweet. I want you to be fully ready."

She *was* ready. In the mirror she could see the ripe lips pouting beneath her moist pubic curls, shining with her own juices, sleek with readiness.

For several moments longer he toyed with her, sliding the ivory crest over her warm, slippery cleft, anointing it with the honeyed liquid that seeped from her body. His free hand moved to her tingling, hardened nipples, playing lightly.

She was throbbing with need when at last he relented.

"You'll like the feel of this. . . ." He slid the ivory tip slowly into her pulsing depths.

Vanessa let out a gratified sigh—a sigh that became a breathless moan as he began to work the ivory shaft in a languid rhythm within her, withdrawing it almost to the end, then carefully thrusting the cool, thick length inside her again.

"Is this not highly arousing, sweet, being forced to experience pleasure?"

It *was* highly arousing. Wildness raced through her blood as he pleasured her. When he thrust deeper, into the shuddering reaches of her body, Vanessa writhed, her arms straining at her bonds, her inner muscles clutching tightly on the ivory shaft. His pace quickened as his hand stroked and squeezed at her throbbing breasts. She was burning with feverish need, a heartbeat away from delicious orgasm. . . .

And there Damien halted.

Her eyes opened in bewilderment to find him regarding her. The half-smile on his lips was slightly mocking.

"I would rather you wait for me, angel."

He left the phallus in place, between her thighs, as he rose from the bed. Vanessa wanted to curse him. He had abandoned her on the brink of ecstasy, trembling with the frustration of unfulfilled desire, humiliated and helpless. The erotic image in the mirror showed a nude woman on the threshold of climax, her skin flushed, her nipples peaked, her white thighs glistening with her own wetness.

She bit back a moan of thwarted longing. Damien comprehended full well what he was doing to her, leaving her in such acute need.

His gaze remained locked with hers as he stood over her to undress. The golden lamplight gilded the hard planes and muscles of his body and his darkly engorged erection. When the quivering tip arched against his belly, Vanessa trembled at the enormous pulsing size of him. Her inner flesh clutched helplessly at the thick ivory between her legs. She could almost feel Damien inside her; she wanted him inside her. Desperately.

He came to her magnificently naked, magnificently aroused. Joining her on the satin sheets, he eased the ivory shaft from between her thighs.

"Would you prefer the real thing, my sweet?" he murmured huskily, covering her body with his own. "Would you?"

"Yes," she rasped, impatient with his delay. She knew he could see how swollen she was, how sleek and ready. She felt the pulsing crest of his manhood probe for entrance, and she moaned, wildly eager to receive him.

His gaze plunged deeper into hers as her pliant flesh stretched at his slow thrust. His faint smile and glittering eyes were as triumphant and possessive as his body. He sank hilt-deep, and she knew she was lost. Her body clenched as wave after wave of shuddering tremors rippled over her, and she gave in to burgeoning ecstasy.

Damien managed only slightly more control. He'd spoken the truth earlier. With Vanessa he didn't need games or sexual instruments to feel desire. He never had. With her he felt a brilliant, heated glory of wanting. She was a fever in his blood, a yearning in his soul.

He'd told himself he wanted to be free of her, free of his insanity for this beautiful woman, but that was a lie. He wanted to brand her as his possession, to mark her as his own. His strongest urge was the primitive need to bind her to him now, this moment.

He took her with hammering wildness, surging upward, each plunging stroke merciless, uncurbed. He would make her remember him, remember the hurtling sense of pleasure, the fierce rapture, so that she could never lie beneath any man without thinking of him, only him. . . .

Her legs locked around him, drawing him even deeper. His breath came in harsh, rapid gasps as he plunged over and over again, but she arched and shuddered and matched his every stroke. When she cried out in another climax, he felt her joy and gritted his teeth, letting the madness take him. His body contracted as savage, unrestrained bliss exploded within him, and with one final thrust, he collapsed upon her, shaking.

For a long time afterward they lay unmoving, spent in the aftermath of passion, his chest crushing her breasts, their skin sheened with moisture.

Damien's thudding heartbeat was beginning to slow when he heard a muffled sound that might have been a sob. Startled, he raised his head. Vanessa's eyes were shut, but tears glistened on her flushed face.

His heart contracted. "Did I hurt you?"

For a moment she didn't reply. Damien eased his weight off her, feeling as much bewilderment as alarm. His love-making this time had been fierce, yet no more violent than in the past.

"Vanessa?"

He could see her swallow as she made a visible effort to stem the flow of tears. She couldn't wipe her eyes because of her bound arms.

"Did I hurt you?" he demanded, reaching to untie the silken scarf at her wrist.

Her eyes opened, while her chin lifted as if with determination.

"Not at all," she replied tonelessly, but the hurt in her luminous eyes belied her words.

Chapter Sixteen

Vanessa stared blindly out the window of Damien's traveling carriage as they sped steadily north from London, the wet, gray day mirroring her spirits.

She had lied last night. Damien had indeed hurt her. Not physically, of course. On the contrary, he'd given her body pleasure as great as any she'd known.

It was her heart he had shattered without even being aware of it. His cold, casual experiment in carnal gratification at Madame Fouchet's had reminded Vanessa of how foolish she was to dream about impossibilities. She wanted his love, while he wanted only her body.

Strangely Damien hadn't appeared to enjoy the visit to the brothel any more than she had. Instead, he'd seemed dangerously angry when he escorted her home last night, whether at her or himself she couldn't tell. His brusque announcement had startled her.

"I should like to return to Rosewood tomorrow."

"Tomorrow? So soon?"

"It is a few days early, I realize, but I should think you've seen enough of the demimonde by now. And I doubt there is much more I can teach you."

Truthfully Vanessa had seen enough of the depraved side of London to last her a lifetime. Far from being disappointed, she was actually relieved to be leaving. Damien's decadent world of luxury and license held little appeal for her, especially since the man she had fallen for so hopelessly seemed to have vanished. During their entire time in town she'd seen no evidence of the tender lover and friend she'd initially glimpsed at Rosewood. There was only the wicked rakehell known as Lord Sin.

A sadness swept over her, so intense it made her ache. Had she only imagined the intimate, caring part of him that he kept hidden from much of the world?

Beside her on the carriage seat, Damien was absorbed by his own brooding thoughts as his conscience soundly flayed him.

It had been a mistake to expose Vanessa to Fouchet's brothel last night. He'd seen her shock and disillusionment reflected in the dark luster of her eyes. Disillusionment with *him*.

Damien winced inwardly. Vanessa must have known the sort of life he led; certainly he'd never attempted to hide it from her. But the reality clearly was more unsettling than she'd expected, the entertainment far more salacious. If she'd thought him debauched and dissolute before, she now had irrefutable proof.

Her tears had cut at his heart. Almost as tormenting was her lack of candor when she'd refused to tell him why she was crying. Perhaps it was absurd, but he wanted honesty between them.

Had Vanessa perhaps been comparing him to her late husband? Had his wicked sexual games reminded her too closely of her pain and shame at Sir Roger's hands? Or had the comparison started earlier in the evening, upon seeing the Swann at Vauxhall? If memory served, Sir Roger's

last scandal was the result of a duel over an actress. . . .
Good God, Elise Swann.

Damien swore profanely under his breath as he remembered Vanessa's stricken expression at the encounter in the
pleasure gardens last night. How could he have failed to
see the reason for it?

He'd thought her wounded look due to simple jealousy.
Given the troubled history of her marriage, she would un-
derstandably be upset to have his own former relationship
with another woman brandished in her face. But her distress clearly went far deeper. Her husband had been killed
over the same actress he himself had enjoyed and show-
ered with emeralds. It had devastated her to have her most
terrible humiliation flaunted in her face—and he was to
blame.

Then he'd compounded her misery by taking her to a
brothel and treating her like any sophisticated harlot—
even though a sophisticated harlot was precisely what she
was determined to become, and what he had set out to
make of her.

Fiend seize it, he couldn't go through this charade any
longer. He couldn't pretend indifference while Vanessa
strove to win a place in his wicked realm. She didn't be-
long in his world, any more than his own sister did. There
were doubtless other less destructive ways for her to ob-
tain the financial independence she so determinedly sought.
He would have to end this gut-wrenching scheme of theirs
if his conscience was to have any peace at all.

Damien turned to stare out the carriage window, through
the gloomy mist. He despised himself just now.

His careful tutoring had been designed to forearm
Vanessa against the sort of libertine she would doubtless
encounter in her new role. Rakes of his own ilk. But if he

had any pretensions to nobility, he reflected darkly, he would protect her from *himself*.

The drizzle had subsided by the time they arrived at Rosewood. Damien escorted Vanessa into the house, where they were greeted by an unsmiling Croft.

When Damien asked where his sister could be found, the butler's frown deepened. "I believe Miss Olivia is in the garden, my lord. She is entertaining a gentleman caller."

Vanessa froze in the act of surrendering her pelisse. Her first thought was of her brother. With her heart suddenly quickening, she followed Damien through the French doors of the drawing room, out into the garden.

Olivia was not immediately visible, but a few moments later, they spied her in the distance, seated in her invalid chair beneath a linden tree. A man sat on the bench before her, holding both her hands in his.

Recognizing Aubrey, Vanessa blanched.

"Damien, wait . . ." she urged breathlessly, fearing what he would do. He merely quickened his step, long, angry strides that carried him rapidly toward his sister.

Hearing footsteps, the couple looked up guiltily as he approached. Both of them went still.

Vanessa knew the exact instant Damien identified the caller, for he came to an abrupt halt. She could see the wave of cold rage overtake him; every line of his body went rigid.

Far from fleeing in fear, though, Aubrey rose slowly to his feet. "My lord," he murmured, standing his ground.

Vanessa couldn't help but admire her brother's bravery. She felt the blistering force of Damien's wrath as she came to a halt beside him.

Silence followed, as potent as the aftershock of a lightning bolt.

It was Olivia who spoke first. "Damien . . . I did not expect you—"

"What the devil are you doing here?" Damien demanded of Aubrey. "I thought I gave you fair warning to keep away from my sister."

"I invited him to call," Olivia said hastily.

Damien turned to stare at her, as if she had lost her mind.

"I had a question to pose to Miss Sinclair," Aubrey said in a quiet voice.

His attention snapping back to the intruder, Damien clenched his hands into fists. "I suggest you take yourself off my estate before I forcibly remove you."

Vanessa caught his arm anxiously, remembering how violently Damien had dealt with the young man who'd tried to kiss her at the recent ball. His anger at Aubrey was a hundred times greater, and unlike the squire's son then, Aubrey showed no indication of backing down.

"I love your sister and hope to wed her," he declared in that same quiet tone. "She claims to love me in return."

Olivia held out an imploring hand. "It's true, Damien, I do. Please, don't be angry."

"Olivia, keep out of this!" he demanded, keeping his eyes fixed upon his foe. "I'll have a footman take you back to the house at once."

She stiffened. In one instant her girlish shyness was finally transformed into a woman's strength. "You cannot send me to my room as if I were a child."

"I assure you," Aubrey interjected in a conciliatory tone, "no one feels more remorse than I for what I did to her—"

"And I have forgiven him, Damien."

"Olivia, I won't brook your interference!"

Vanessa winced at his harsh tone, while Olivia raised her chin with defiance. "And I won't brook yours! This is my future you are dismissing so callously."

Concerned, Vanessa clutched at Damien's sleeve. "Please, couldn't we discuss this in a calmer moment?"

He ignored her plea and glared at his sister. "It is indeed your future. And I won't allow you to ruin it completely."

"What does it matter to you? You don't care about me, you never have."

When Olivia bit her trembling lower lip, Damien made a visible effort to control his raw fury. "Olivia, this man destroyed your life. You've said so yourself."

"I thought perhaps he had, but I was mistaken. Last week I felt a pain in my foot, Damien. I didn't tell you for fear I might have imagined it. But it happened again yesterday. Do you realize what that means? If your doctor is right, if my limbs do recover sensation, then I may regain full use of them in time."

He stared at her for a long moment, no doubt feeling the same startled gladness Vanessa was feeling at the possibility of his sister's recovery.

But then Aubrey grasped one of her hands, and Damien stiffened with renewed fury. "Vanessa, take my sister into the house."

It was an order she could not obey. "Damien, please, I think you should hear them out."

The searing gaze he turned to her almost made her flinch; his eyes had hardened to silver shards. "You actually condone this? But, of course, you would. He's your brother."

"That isn't why—"

"I suppose you knew about their clandestine meetings?" he demanded.

"She isn't to blame," Olivia said quickly. "I made her agree to chaperon me."

Vanessa returned his fierce gaze with unyielding resolve. "Olivia is mature enough to know her own mind, Damien. And it was obvious they still had strong feelings for each other. I thought they deserved the chance to work out their differences. Aubrey sincerely loves her. You ought not dismiss his proposal out of hand."

"You cannot be serious. He's a wastrel, a womanizer, a cad—"

"It's true," Aubrey agreed solemnly. "I once was all those things. I haven't led an admirable life, but I've vowed to change."

Damien's blighting glance returned to Aubrey, who made another effort at appeasement.

"Before meeting your sister, I never questioned my profligate tendencies. I never had reason to. I can understand, my lord, why you wouldn't want me wed to your sister—"

"How perceptive of you," Damien returned savagely, dripping sarcasm. "But I see what you're about. You're pursuing her fortune to save your own skin. Why else would you want to wed a cripple?"

Olivia flinched as if from a blow, anguish flashing across her face.

Damien gave a start, evidently realizing he'd been unforgivably harsh, yet he was clearly too enraged to render any apology. Vanessa felt her own heart wrench. He seemed capable of hurting everyone who loved him.

"You're wrong, my lord," Aubrey replied grimly, his

own anger finally showing. "I would love her even if she never walks again."

"I don't believe it. You're nothing but a fortune hunter, damn you. But perhaps you aren't aware that I could cut her off without a farthing."

"I'm fully aware of it. But it wouldn't matter if she were destitute. I will support her to the best of my ability, perhaps not in luxury, but I swear she will never want for anything."

"Your best isn't nearly good enough."

"I know," Aubrey said humbly, glancing at Olivia. "I can never hope to be worthy of her. But I mean to try."

Damien's expression was as cold as Vanessa had ever seen it. "I think you forget I control everything you own. Your gaming debts give me that power."

"I haven't forgotten." His tone was quiet.

"Then don't forget this," Damien gritted out. "I'll see you in hell before I permit you to wed my sister."

Olivia struck the arm of her chair as tears filled her eyes. "I *love* him, Damien. I truly do."

Her brother shook his head fiercely. "Livy, he has duped you all over again, rekindled your foolish infatuation—"

"No . . . he has *not*. I know my own heart, Damien. This is not infatuation. I've had ample time to consider it. I've done nothing else for months. It's true that I once wanted to make him pay for what he did, but I've learned to forgive him. As you will, if you give him a chance."

"I will do no such thing." His jaw hardened as he glanced at Aubrey. "I suggest you leave before I'm persuaded to put a bullet through you."

Alarmed, Vanessa gripped his arm more tightly. "I beg you, don't hurt him. . . ." Damien shook her off.

"I don't want your sister's wealth, Lord Sinclair," Aubrey insisted. "And I know I must earn the right to love her. But I will, I swear it."

"Meanwhile you hide behind her skirts as you hid behind your own sister's, leaving her to deal with your gaming debts."

Anger suffusing his expression, Aubrey took a step forward, his fist clenched. When Olivia gave a cry of fear, though, he stopped abruptly and glanced down at her. A look passed between them, one of tenderness, of resolve.

"For your sake, my love," he murmured, "I will go . . . for now."

He would not give up the battle, Vanessa knew. Aubrey might withdraw for the moment, but he would return to fight another day. She shuddered to think what would happen then.

Vanessa watched as he retrieved his hat from the bench and bowed to the company. With a lingering look at Olivia, he turned away.

When he was gone, Olivia gave a sob of outrage and turned on her brother. "You have no right to send him away!" she accused.

Ignoring her tears, Damien summoned a footman who was stationed discreetly a short distance along the garden path. "Convey your mistress to the house."

Olivia glared at him. "If you drive Aubrey away, I will hate you forever."

Damien's mouth tightened, but he made no reply. In a moment Olivia was wheeled from the garden, leaving him alone with Vanessa.

The silence that remained was fraught with tension. Vanessa faced Damien defiantly, her emotions torn between anger at his heartlessness, guilt at betraying his trust, and the desperate wish to make him see reason. She had feared this confrontation would come from the moment her brother had shown his face at Rosewood.

"I presume you mean to tell me," Damien began in a low, tight voice, "why you allowed Rutherford to prey on my sister again."

Vanessa took a deep breath. At least he meant to give her the opportunity to explain. "Aubrey was never alone with her until this past week when we went to London," she said firmly. "I made certain of that."

"Yet you conspired with them behind my back, encouraged their secret meetings."

"It was not a conspiracy. I simply afforded them the opportunity to discover how serious their feelings were for each other."

"*Damnation,* as Olivia's companion you were responsible for her welfare!" The controlled savagery of Damien's tone told her how close his temper was to shattering.

"I understand quite well my responsibilities toward Olivia," Vanessa returned evenly. "And I did what I thought was best for her."

"For her? You expect me to believe you weren't scheming to improve your brother's fortunes?"

Vanessa stared into Damien's blistering gray eyes. "I was not *scheming*, I assure you. Aubrey's wishes scarcely entered into my thinking. Olivia's happiness is what concerns me. She was clearly miserable without him. And she will be even more so if you refuse your consent for their marriage."

When he didn't reply, Vanessa added with quiet intensity, "Olivia is capable of making this decision for herself, Damien, and she should have that right, just as my own sisters should have the right to choose whom they wed."

A muscle knotting in his jaw, Damien strode over to the linden tree. His hand rose, clenched, as if he might strike the trunk with his fist. "Your brother is nothing more than a fortune hunter, a wastrel. He ruined Olivia's life. I refuse to entrust my sister to such a scoundrel."

"Perhaps Aubrey *was* all you say, but he's changed greatly, for the better. He is truly ashamed of what he did, both for crippling Olivia and for tarnishing her reputation. He's determined to reform . . . to make amends. He's honestly offered her the protection of his name in marriage, and I think you would be gravely mistaken not to consider his suit."

When Damien refused to respond, Vanessa continued her argument. "It would actually be a good match for them both. If not for his terrible transgression against her, Aubrey would make her an eligible enough connection. His rank exceeds your own. He is educated and intelligent. And while he may have lost the remainder of his inheritance to you, he's not without the hope of gainful employment. He has actually found work in the district as a social secretary to one of your neighbors. That is what finally convinced me of his sincerity. I've never seen him as single-minded and determined as he is now. I believe he's truly fallen in love." Vanessa paused. "What really matters, though, is that Olivia loves him."

Damien made a scoffing sound deep in his throat. "What does a green girl her age know about love?"

"Undoubtedly more than you do."

His head swinging around, he fixed her with a dark glare.

"Olivia claims to know her heart, Damien. If he is her choice, what right do you have to stand in her way?"

Anger flashed in his eyes like silver fire. "As her

brother, I not only have the right, I have a duty to protect her from unscrupulous rogues like your brother."

"You *would* be protecting her by allowing this match. Consider it. She will be a viscountess if she marries Aubrey. Unwed, she will always have the stigma of her recent scandal to live down."

"So you would have her wed her debaucher?"

"What, pray, is the alternative? Perhaps she *could* find a more eligible suitor than my brother, but would her heart be engaged? There is nothing worse than being trapped in a loveless marriage—believe me, I know. She could choose not to wed at all, to remain a spinster, but that is a lonely life for a woman, without husband or children. Olivia has been alone more than enough, in my opinion." Vanessa eyed him coolly. "Of course, she could seek companionship outside of marriage. But I doubt you would wish your sister to take the course I've elected, to become some wealthy gentleman's mistress."

His glance collided with hers, and Vanessa could see she had struck a nerve.

"The circumstances are quite different," he said tightly.

"Indeed they are. As an heiress, Olivia has choices I never had. *If* you will allow her to make them."

"You seem intent on making me out to be the villain in this piece."

"No, I'm merely intent on persuading you to keep an open mind."

His lip curled. "Two months ago Rutherford was a gamester and a reprobate. How can you be certain this miraculous transformation of his will last?"

"I cannot. I only know that Aubrey is a good man at heart. And I believe he would do his utmost never to hurt Olivia again."

Damien set his jaw. "That is a risk I am not willing to take."

Vanessa stamped her foot in frustration and despair, while her voice rose in anger. "Doesn't your condemnation of him strike you as the least bit hypocritical? How can you possibly be an adequate judge of anyone's character, a man of your lurid past and wicked reputation?"

When she received no reply, a hard smile touched her own lips. "Tell me, Lord Sin, how is my brother any more depraved or dissolute than you are? You might not wish or deserve the chance to prove you can love and be loved, but there *are* men who truly want redemption."

She waited, but he remained silent. Finally her shoulders slumped. "If you will please excuse me, I intend to go comfort Olivia. I expect she could use a sympathetic shoulder just now."

With that she turned on her heels and walked away.

Eyes fiercely narrowed at her back, Damien leaned against the tree trunk. He still wanted to hit something. Yet Vanessa's earnestness had given him pause.

It wasn't surprising to hear her plead her brother's case so passionately. He'd expected nothing less, although, strangely enough, he believed her claim that she hadn't conspired with Rutherford to prey again on Olivia.

The parting shot Vanessa had made about his own character, however, had cut too close to the bone. *How can you possibly be an adequate judge of anyone's character, a man of your lurid past and wicked reputation?*

Damien gazed out over the vast gardens, scarcely aware of the fragrant scent of roses surrounding him. What had she said about him that wasn't true?

If he looked at himself through her eyes, what would he see? A jaded nobleman driven by an unquenchable restlessness, engaged in the reckless pursuit of pleasure and indulgence. He'd always done his damnedest to live up to his name of Lord Sin, filling his world with sophisticated games and sensual depravity. To Vanessa, her brother would seem a veritable innocent in comparison.

Even so, his own conduct had no bearing in this instance. The only one whose character was at issue was Rutherford, whether he was worthy of Olivia's hand in marriage.

And the answer was an emphatic *no*.

Damien clenched his jaw as he renewed his resolve. Despite Vanessa's staunch defense of her brother, he wasn't about to turn over his cherished innocent sister to such a man. Olivia would simply have to learn to get over her infatuation.

It could be done; he had proven that with Vanessa. Even the deepest bonds could be torn apart with fierce perseverance.

Chapter Seventeen

Rosewood was like an armed camp, the anger in the house palpable. Even the servants felt it. The dissension between the lord and his sister, Vanessa learned from the housekeeper, was reminiscent of the previous baron's strife with his wife.

Vanessa did her best to ease the tension, but with Olivia locking herself in her room, and Damien disappearing on horseback for long periods at a time, she was at a loss to mend matters. Especially when she had unequivocally taken sides.

She did manage to question Olivia about her true feelings for Aubrey, which only made the girl bristle.

"I only want to be certain you are sure of your heart," Vanessa said soothingly.

"I no longer want to punish him by tying him to a cripple, if that's what concerns you," Olivia retorted. "I once felt that way, I know, but I was hurt and angry then. And there is a greater likelihood now that my infirmity isn't permanent." Olivia hesitated. "Are you saying you think my wedding your brother would be a mistake?"

"No, not at all. I just believe that remaining single is preferable to an ill-advised marriage." Vanessa gave a rueful smile. "Perhaps I'm not the best person to advise you in matters of the heart, considering how unsuccessful my own marriage was. But while I am no expert, I would think that if you truly loved him—"

"I do! I have always loved him. And he loves me."

"Still, there are practical matters to consider. Our family, though well connected, has never been rich. Aubrey is often only a short jump ahead of his creditors. You've never had to endure financial difficulties, Olivia. If your brother does withhold your fortune because you defy his wishes, you may find it a rude shock. It won't be easy to give up all this." She gestured around the bedchamber.

"I don't care," Olivia said adamantly. "I've had *this* all my life, and I won't miss it. I know better than most that wealth cannot buy happiness, or love, or a warm family, or a real home. Aubrey has told me about Fanny and Charlotte, and I want to have sisters like them, like you. I want to be part of your family. I want to be Aubrey's wife, Vanessa."

"Well, then," Vanessa said with complete sincerity, "you shall."

Satisfied the girl truly was in love, Vanessa refrained from voicing her other concerns. Damien could prevent the marriage simply by putting a bullet through Aubrey.

Even if he refrained from physical violence, he still possessed a powerful financial leverage. Olivia didn't know the whole story about Aubrey's utter indebtedness to her brother, Vanessa reflected, or about the bargain Damien had made with herself to redeem those debts in exchange for her becoming his mistress. The Rutherford estates might still be forfeit. If Damien wished, he could renege on his bargain and carry out his planned vengeance, claiming all of Aubrey's possessions, including his family seat. Then Olivia would have no home at all.

Vanessa pressed her lips together as she tried to convince herself that her worry was groundless. Damien might be a wicked rake, but she didn't believe he was dishonorable. As long as she performed satisfactorily as his mistress, then he was obliged to uphold their agreement.

It was almost a relief to learn Damien expected a party of friends the following evening, and that Cook had been given orders to prepare a sumptuous dinner. Perhaps, Vanessa hoped, the company might help to alleviate the dark mood. And if Damien was occupied with entertaining, he would have less opportunity to do her brother bodily harm.

Rising early the next morning, she found Damien at the breakfast table before he rode out for the day. When she questioned him about the identity of his guests, he responded with evident reluctance.

"They are fellow members of the Hellfire League. Regrettably, I couldn't avoid the obligation. They're on their way to a hunting box near here and mean to stop overnight. It's just as well that Olivia is indisposed."

He meant, Vanessa supposed, that he didn't want his rakish friends near his innocent young sister.

"Do you wish me to attend dinner?" she asked.

"Only if you care to."

"Is there a reason I shouldn't?"

He raised a sardonic eyebrow. "I doubt you will find my dissolute friends to your taste."

She responded in the same cool tone. "Possibly, but this could be an opportunity to test my progress under your excellent tutelage. And the acquaintance might prove beneficial to my new career. Your friends are precisely the sort of patrons I need to attract, are they not?"

Damien stared at her a long moment. Then he shrugged. "You must do as you wish. After dinner we will likely break out the cards, and we always play for high stakes. As you say, the experience could prove useful."

Despite his feigned indifference, Damien intensely rued his friends' intended visit. Ordinarily he greatly enjoyed the entertainment and camaraderie his Hellfire companions offered. In years past he'd been ripe for any diversion, no matter how outrageous or wild. Perhaps his idea of diversion had changed, but the amusements that had once held his interest now seemed shallow and tasteless.

His change of heart was due partly to a newfound sense of responsibility, which had emerged after Olivia's accident. Naturally he didn't want his young sister exposed to the likes of Lord Clune or the other rakehells who made up the association. Yet it was Vanessa, rather than Olivia, he felt the greater need to protect. Clune had already made several probing remarks regarding Vanessa's availability. Introducing her to a gathering of libertines would only make her fair game for their propositions and advances.

Damien clenched his teeth. He had agreed to teach Vanessa how to attract a rich patron, but he was damned if he would support her scheme any longer.

His dark mood hadn't improved by that afternoon when his friends arrived. Clune was in high spirits, however, laughing over a practical joke he'd played on Lord Lambton, who owned the hunting box that was their eventual destination.

"Lambton will be detained, I'm afraid," Clune told Damien. "It seems he woke up naked in Hyde Park this morning after an evening of carousing. Somehow he was mysteriously transported there during the night, bed and all. Regrettably he caught a chill walking home with only a bedsheet to cover him. But I intend to act as host in his place."

Of the eleven gentleman who accompanied Clune, all were well known to Damien except for one newcomer, an American cousin of the Earl of Wycliff. Nicholas Sabine reportedly ran a shipping empire in Virginia and was visiting England to finalize several lucrative trade agreements. Because of his noble familial connections, he'd been extended an invitation to join the Hellfire League.

"It's generous of you to allow a stranger to impose on your hospitality, Lord Sinclair," Sabine said when they were introduced.

"It is no imposition," Damien returned easily. "And you can't be considered a stranger if Jeremy vouches for you."

"I do indeed vouch for him," Clune drawled. "The chap's a good enough sort, even if he *is* a Yank and in trade. His latest shipment of Jamaican rum is prime stock, I assure you."

Sabine took no offense at the good-natured laughter that followed and, in fact, seemed to fit in well with the company. Tall, athletic, and fair-haired, he had the look of an adventurer, with the bronzed complexion of a seafarer and a dark-eyed gaze that suggested a keen intelligence.

He kept the lazy fire in those dark eyes banked throughout the early evening when the gentlemen gathered in the drawing room before dinner. But then the talk turned to the impressment of American sailors by the British Navy. From his pithy comments, it was clear the subject had struck a nerve in their American guest.

Damien was about to shift the discussion to less dangerous waters the very moment Vanessa chose to join them.

The conversation came to an abrupt halt as the gentlemen rose eagerly to their feet.

She wore a gown of ice-blue lutestring that Damien had purchased for her on their recent visit to London, one that showed her superb figure to advantage and accented her dark beauty. When he introduced Lady Wyndham around, he was acutely aware of the male glances of admiration and speculation she received.

Clune's covetous looks in particular roused his ire, and it was all Damien could do to keep his expression impassive and his fists at his side.

The tension inside him remained high when they went into dinner. From the far end of the table he watched as Vanessa charmed the company. Apparently she was acquainted with several of the gentlemen from the days of her marriage, and she seemed to have no difficulty upholding her end of a lively conversation.

She showed a remarked interest in what the American Nicholas Sabine had to say—whether it was America or Sabine himself she found fascinating, Damien couldn't tell. He recognized his own jealousy, however, and did his best to keep it under control.

Unfortunately his best proved sorely lacking. Each time Vanessa's musical laughter drifted down to his end of the table, Damien felt his teeth clench. And each time she favored one of his guests with a soft, sensual smile, he cursed.

Bloody hell and damnation, that alluring smile was a feminine weapon *he* had taught her, and she was wielding it with deadly accuracy.

With effort Damien clamped down on the overwhelming urge to spirit her away, out of sight of his lustful friends, but the irony of the situation didn't escape him. In grooming

Vanessa to be the perfect mistress, he had succeeded beyond even his wildest expectations, and his success made him furious.

At the conclusion of dinner, when Lady Wyndham left the gentlemen to their port, they subtly quizzed Damien about her. Yet, contrarily, he refused to satisfy their curiosity about her situation, only repeating that she was acting as his sister's companion. His guests didn't linger long but joined her shortly in the drawing room. When Clune pressed for cards, the company made up two tables, one of piquet and one of whist.

Vanessa declined invitations to both games. "I fear the play will be too deep for me," she demurred with a smile. "But I should be honored to watch."

She observed the gaming for a while and retired at midnight, despite numerous pleas for her to stay. Damien was glad to see her leave. It had proved difficult with her present, his concentration divided between keeping an eye on her and playing the hands he was dealt.

While the hour grew later, the excellent wine and brandy flowed freely as the gamesters' luck dried up. One by one, then, the players folded and went to bed, until at last Damien and Clune were the only ones remaining.

It was nearly three A.M., he noted with a glance at the ormolu clock on the mantel. After a few more moments of desultory conversation, Damien realized that Clune had a purpose for remaining behind, and that it concerned Vanessa.

"You were not very forthcoming about your sister's companion, my friend, which merely served to pique the interest of every last one of us. I can only assume that was your intent—to make us all green with envy."

"You assume incorrectly," Damien replied, pouring another two fingers of brandy for his guest.

"I can understand your fascination with Lady Wyndham. That combination of beauty and wit is rare. She is dazzling. But it is hardly fair of you not to give us a sporting chance, Sin. Perhaps you wouldn't be averse to a small wager."

"A wager? What did you have in mind?"

"My team of matched grays against the chance to woo Lady Wyndham."

Damien's jaw hardened. "She is not my possession."

"Perhaps not, but you have prior claim to her. I know better than to poach on your fancy piece without your express permission."

A shaft of anger arrowed through Damien. "She is a *lady*, Clune, despite present circumstances."

"Forgive me, your *lady*, then. I am prepared to raise the stakes, even though I know you'll drive a hard bargain. Just name your terms."

"You don't seem to comprehend," Damien said softly. "She is not for sale."

"Every woman is for sale," his noble guest replied cynically. "The only question is how high her price."

When Damien made no reply, Clune continued. "Her talents must be remarkable if you're so set on keeping her for yourself. What has it been, over two months? That must be a record for you. But I should think a man of your exacting tastes will eventually tire even of her."

Damien stared down at the remaining brandy in his glass, seeing Vanessa's beautiful eyes in the golden depths. He had begun to doubt he would ever tire of her.

His silence made the earl impatient. "Do I at least have your permission to pursue her once you end the connection?"

"No."

"No?" Clune raised an eyebrow. "It is not like you to be possessive, Sin. Women are only transient diversions for you, a momentary pleasure. You've always been dead set against becoming enamored of your mistresses."

Damien felt his mouth twist in self-mockery. "So I have."

His friend studied him for a long moment, before letting out a low whistle. "Never tell me the elusive Lord Sin is finally *smitten*."

Damien drained the brandy in his glass, feeling the fire burn his throat. "I won't tell you, then. You cannot have Lady Wyndham because she is my sister's companion."

A grin of wicked amusement spread across Clune's thin lips. "It seems to me there is more to this tale than you're letting on. Are you certain you haven't fallen for her and you simply refuse to admit it?"

Damien met his probing gaze levelly, but his sharp-eyed friend seemed to see straight through him.

Clune gave a chuckle of astonishment. "What a prime jest, the hardest heart among us the first to admit defeat."

"Aren't you leaping to conclusions?"

"Am I?" He grinned engagingly, with cheerful malice. "Deny it all you like, but I'll not credit it." Shaking his head then, he rose to his feet. "You'd best have a care, man, or you might find even a confirmed bachelor like yourself caught in the parson's noose."

He left Damien to his own thoughts, which were suddenly whirling in chaos. *Parson's noose. Marriage?*

Until this moment he had never considered the possibility of marriage to Vanessa. Yet, frankly, it was a practical solution to the dilemma she presented. . . .

It even offered advantages, chief of which was that she

could remain at Rosewood as companion to his sister. The marriage need only be a formality, which would leave them both free to pursue their own lives.

His eyes shut briefly as he digested the enormity of what he was contemplating. *Wedlock.* It was better than the alternatives.

He was not about to give her up to the likes of Clune—or any other man, for that matter. The thought of her pleasuring someone else was intolerable. So was the prospect of her earning her living with her body.

Damien flinched. How could he have ever countenanced such a travesty? No, not merely countenanced. Actively encouraged.

The memory of Vanessa's low voice in the garden flailed him. *As an heiress, Olivia has choices I never had.* He'd constricted her choices even further by forcing her to become his mistress. And then he'd made certain she developed the sensual skills to attract a wealthy patron so that he could be rid of her and his obsession.

Damien stared blindly down at his glass. Only recently had he begun to admit the depths of the disgrace he'd brought upon her. Shame was a rare experience for him, but he felt it now like a knife inside him. Shame and remorse. He had gravely wronged Vanessa. He'd brought her down to his level, sullied what was left of her good name. . . .

Wedding her would be the surest way to repair her tarnished reputation. To protect her from libertines like Clune.

It would also, Damien reflected grimly, provide a fitting punishment for himself. For it would bind him to his obsession for all time.

*   *   *

He waited until his guests had left the following morning before going in search of Vanessa. He found her in the library, reading. She was curled up on the window seat, her legs tucked beneath her—a position she had adopted so often during their late-night trysts.

A sharp stab of regret twisted inside him, along with a deep sadness. In the past Vanessa would have looked up and smiled. How he missed her smile. Now there was only bitter anger between them.

It was the anger he regretted most. That and losing her friendship. The sweetness was gone; he had deliberately driven it away.

From the doorway Damien watched another moment, his gaze tracing her lovely profile, the delicate curve of her cheek. A strange mix of desire and tenderness filled him, edged sharply by nervousness. . . .

He clenched his jaw at the irony. His Hellfire colleagues would laugh uproariously to see the wicked Lord Sin with trembling knees. But this situation was completely alien to him. In his long and licentious career, he had put propositions to numerous women, but never had he contemplated any step this serious.

As if sensing his presence, Vanessa looked up from her book. "Did you want me for something?"

Yes, he thought. *I want you, more than I've ever wanted any woman.*

Slowly Damien entered the room. Halting a short distance from her, he cleared his throat. "I have a proposal to put to you."

"Yes?"

His cravat felt too tight. He walked over to the mantel and gazed down at the empty hearth. "A proposal . . . literally. I would like to make you a formal offer of marriage."

The silence that followed was total.

When he realized she didn't mean to answer, Damien glanced over his shoulder. Vanessa had gone pale.

"Why?" she finally murmured.

This was not the reaction he'd expected or hoped for. She looked stunned . . . and wary.

"Why?" he repeated absently.

"Why would you offer me marriage when your planned revenge is proceeding so smoothly?"

Because it isn't proceeding smoothly at all. "Because it is a logical solution to your current difficulty. You desire a wealthy patron, and I am wealthy enough to fill the position."

Her eyes were as dark as a moonlit ocean, but far more troubled. "I married for wealth once, and it proved a disaster."

"I hardly think the situation is comparable."

"No, I suppose not." Distractedly she set down her book. "I understand the financial advantages our marriage would provide me, but that doesn't explain why *you* would wish to wed."

"Call it a crisis of conscience."

"I'm not sure what you mean."

"I was wrong to insist you become my mistress. This is a way for me to make amends."

"You mean to withdraw from our agreement? To claim the family estates my brother lost to you?"

"No, that is *not* what I mean," Damien returned with an edge of impatience. His heart twisted at the knowledge she could think him capable of being that underhanded. More-over, he had earned her distrust. "You've fulfilled our bar-gain more than adequately."

"Then why do you feel you must make amends?"

"I've come to realize how untenable the situation is that

I've put you in. Truthfully, it disturbs me to think I initiated your foray into prostitution. In reparation I'm prepared to offer you the protection of my name and fortune."

She studied him for a long moment. "You are proposing to me because of guilt? I won't fetter you to me out of guilt, Damien."

His mouth curved in a humorless smile. "Guilt is as good a reason to wed as any."

Her dark eyes remained steady. "For me, it isn't." She took a deep breath. "In circumstances such as these, my lord, I believe the proper etiquette is to express gratitude. So I will. I am honored and flattered by your generous offer, but I must politely decline."

Damien was glad he was so skilled at shielding his expressions, for it allowed him to conceal the turmoil he felt. "Am I allowed an explanation for your refusal?"

"A marriage between us would never work."

"I try not to be more than normally obtuse, but I fail to understand why it wouldn't."

"You don't love me," she said simply.

"Love?" His frown was cynical. "What does love have to say to the matter?"

"I've vowed never to endure another loveless marriage."

His features softened a measure. "I would never treat you as your boor of a husband treated you."

"Perhaps you wouldn't consciously intend to. But you may not be able to help yourself. You would never be happy having to honor your marriage vows, and I would be miserable with anything less."

He stared at her. "You are asking for fidelity."

"I suppose I am."

When he didn't reply, Vanessa gazed at him sadly. Damien was a born rake, a restless soul who had no use for love. He wanted her body for the moment. Yet once his desire for her faded, he would doubtless revert to form and cause her the same misery her late husband had. She couldn't bear loving Damien so desperately and enduring his betrayal.

"We are not at all compatible," she added quietly. "The life you lead . . . isn't the sort of life I would ever willingly choose again. I've had enough of scandal and debauchery."

"If you embark on a career as a Cyprian, you will likely find both."

"Perhaps. But at least it will be on my own terms. As your wife I would have few rights. Legally I would be little more than your possession. Becoming a Cyprian is still preferable to enduring a wretched marriage."

"And you're certain ours would be wretched?"

"For me, it would be." She saw a muscle flex in his jaw, and she spread her hands in a gesture of conciliation. "We have nothing in common, Damien."

"I would say we have a great deal in common." He moved toward her purposefully. "Passion, for one."

Taking her hands, he drew her to her feet and pulled her close against his body. The brief kiss he gave her to demonstrate his point was shattering and left her breathless with longing.

"You cannot claim," Damien asserted, his voice low with determination, "that we are physically incompatible. Your body would refute you."

Vanessa bit her lip, knowing he was aware of her flushed skin, her rapid heartbeat, her nipples peaked with desire.

"You arouse my body, I can't deny that. But marriage should mean something more than the gratification of physical desire. It should mean love and caring and commitment. Building a home and family. You don't want a family, any more than you want a wife. I would want children some day, Damien. You clearly don't."

He stiffened. "I doubt I am capable of being much of a father—look at my record with my sister. But I admit I have a duty to carry on the title. I would have no objection to producing an heir at some future point."

"I would never bring a child into your world," she replied, her voice low, bleak.

For the first time Damien showed a hint of anger. "Perhaps I should have chosen a more romantic setting. You might have found my proposal more amenable had I plied you with roses and moonlight."

"Roses and moonlight could not induce me to marry you." When his jaw clenched, Vanessa shook her head. "Come now, you don't truly want to wed me. I mean nothing to you."

His eyes darkened, something subtle and dangerous moving in the gray depths. "I could seriously debate that point." He captured her hand and pressed her palm against his groin, letting her feel his hardness. "Is this the mark of a man's indifference?"

Vanessa lifted her chin at his attempt to intimidate her. "It is the mark of a man with oversized sexual appetites—and I have no doubt there are countless women eager to satisfy them."

"There seem to be any number of men eager to satisfy yours," Damien retorted as she withdrew from his embrace. "Clune offered to wager me for your sexual services, were you aware?"

"And did you?"

"No."

"I confess myself astonished. A gamester like yourself is always primed for a wager."

He gave her a stony stare, his eyes hot and bright as molten silver. "I won't countenance your giving your body to the likes of Clune."

Vanessa returned his gaze defiantly, until another thought dawned on her. "You cannot possibly be jealous of your friend? Is that what this proposal is about? He's offended your sense of ownership?"

For the first time she saw vulnerability in Damien's shuttered face. Vanessa inhaled a steadying breath. "You may rest assured, I have no desire to have Lord Clune for a lover or protector. Or any of your other friends, for that matter. And most certainly you may ease your conscience. You are not responsible for my actions, or my welfare. There is no need for you to feel the least guilty."

"It isn't that simple," Damien returned through gritted teeth.

"No?" Vanessa paused, her own ire softening. "If my refusal angers you, it's only because you've always been accustomed to having your own way. But some day you will count yourself fortunate to have escaped my clutches."

For the second time in several days, she turned and walked away from him, this time leaving him alone in the quiet chamber.

With a curse, Damien flung himself into a chair. He was indeed jealous, but jealousy wasn't the only primal emotion he felt for Vanessa.

Damn her, why did he feel this fever, this desperate hunger only with her?

Damien swore again. He had meant only to seduce her, not cherish and desire her. The devil of it was, he was the one who had been seduced. She had crept beneath his defenses, even as he'd tried to shatter hers. He wanted her until he ached with it.

But wanting her, it seemed, was not enough. For her . . . or for himself.

Chapter Eighteen

Vanessa stood at the window of her bedchamber, staring blindly down at the rose gardens. Had she made a terrible mistake, refusing Damien's offer of marriage?

In the three days since his startling proposal, she'd asked herself that question a hundred times, going over and over every nuance of their conversation, every subtlety of emotion in his expression and tone of voice.

She hadn't found what she'd longed to see. Not even a hint of love. And without love, a marriage between them would be doomed.

Damien would never be content to settle down with one woman, to give up his life as a rakehell. Love alone might have the power to change him, but he didn't love her. That was the harsh, bitter truth.

Vanessa let out a deep sigh. Summer was almost at an end. Her term as his mistress was almost over. Then she would be free to go and take her own wounded heart with her. Free to start rebuilding her life. Free to begin the struggle of trying to forget Damien . . .

A rapid knock on her bedchamber door interrupted her melancholy thoughts. At her bidding, a footman entered, bearing a silver salver.

"Beg pardon, milady, but a carriage has come with this message for you from Lord Clune."

Vanessa wondered why Clune would be writing to her, unless it involved Damien. Damien had driven to his friends' hunting box early this morning for some dove shooting. . . .

Curiously Vanessa broke the seal and read:

Lady Wyndham—Do not be alarmed, but I fear Sinclair has met with a minor accident. The doctor has been sent for, but Sin is calling for you. My carriage is at your disposal. I pray you will come shortly.

Panic seized her as she pictured Damien lying wounded, his lifeblood seeping from his body. Her hand went to her throat where her heart had lodged. She couldn't bear the thought of his death. She *couldn't*.

"I must go to him," she breathed hoarsely.

She had the presence of mind at least to fetch a pelisse and to tell the footman she was going to join Lord Sinclair, before running down the stairs and out the front door to the waiting carriage.

They set a rapid pace, without stopping to change horses. Even so Vanessa deplored the delay. She couldn't control her dread or the dark images assaulting her. She kept remembering her final view of her husband when they'd brought his body home the morning of the duel. The fatal bullet wound in his chest, the blood . . . Clune's message said Damien's accident was minor, but she couldn't rest easy until she assured herself that he wasn't dying.

It was nearly an hour before the carriage turned off the country lane onto a gravel drive flanked by thick woods. Finally they halted before a large manor house. Vanessa scarcely noted the secluded setting as she climbed down from the carriage without assistance.

She nearly ran up the steps to the front entrance, and was supremely grateful when the door swung open to reveal Lord Clune himself.

"Damien, how is he?" she demanded breathlessly.

The smile Clune gave her was reassuring as he drew her into the house. "Well enough, my lady. He is upstairs resting comfortably."

"May I see him?"

"But, of course."

He led her through the elegant foyer, up a wide flight of steps to a long hallway. They passed numerous rooms, to which Vanessa paid no mind. At the end of the hall, Clune opened a door and stood aside to let her enter.

Anxiously, she took three steps and came to an abrupt halt. The large bed that dominated the room was empty. Damien was nowhere to be seen.

"Where is he?" she asked in confusion.

"He is still out with the hunting party, I would imagine."

When she turned to give Clune a questioning look, his smile was apologetic. "I must beg your indulgence, Lady Wyndham. I hope you won't object to being my guest for a short while."

"I . . . don't understand."

"I plan to play a prank on my good friend Damien, and your presence is necessary."

"A prank? Then . . . he hasn't been wounded?"

"No, not at all. I'm afraid that was merely a ruse to bring you here."

Relief flooded Vanessa, followed swiftly by anger and alarm. "I trust you mean to tell me why you require my presence?"

Clune flashed another smile, one full of disarming charm. "You needn't fear me, I assure you. You won't come to the least harm. I intend this to be a good-natured jest."

When she made to leave the room, however, he remained in the doorway, blocking her path.

"You mean to keep me here against my will?"

Clune shrugged. "Only for a short while. Damien should be returning any moment now."

"He won't be happy to find me here."

"I don't doubt it," the earl agreed easily. "But the opportunity is too priceless to resist. Sin is long overdue for a public humbling." Clune surveyed her for a moment. "I suppose it is asking too much for you to play along with me?"

"It is indeed," Vanessa replied, furious at his insensibility.

"You are angry," he commented almost sadly.

"Surely that doesn't surprise you. First you frighten me half to death by lying, allowing me to believe Sinclair wounded, perhaps mortally. Now you tell me I must remain as your prisoner."

"I'm afraid so. But it is only in fun."

"I don't find your idea of fun humorous in the least, my lord." She took a deep breath. "If you allow me to return home, I will say nothing of this to anyone, least of all Damien."

"Alas, that would destroy my well-laid plan."

"Just precisely what *is* your plan?"

"To compel Sin to show his hand. More precisely, to test the depth of his attachment to you."

"His attachment?"

"All these years he's vowed he would never give his heart. As recently as this week he denied being smitten. But I believe that the mighty Lord Sin has fallen, and I mean to prove it. I intend to make him admit his feelings for you before the Hellfire League."

"You are either a fool, or you are mad!"

Clune brandished that sensual smile again. "Perhaps a bit of both. But I should think you of all people would be keenly interested in the outcome. Don't you wish to know if you've managed to capture his heart?"

"No! Certainly not in this manner."

"I know of no other way to bring him to the sticking point. And, truly, I am acting for his own sake. If Sin is deceiving himself, he is better off realizing it. I have a simple scenario in mind that should shock him into revealing his true feelings."

Vanessa eyed Clune warily. "So I am to be the bait in your trap?"

"Precisely. At gatherings such as these, the entertainment is usually of a carnal nature. I will simply intimate to Sin that you are to be the prime attraction for the evening and see how he reacts. I doubt that he will be able to conceal his jealousy."

"He is apt to be more enraged by your trick than jealous."

Clune gave her a tolerant smile. "Sin and I have been friends forever. The worst he will do is plant me a facer, but I'm willing to risk it."

She'd heard enough boxing cant from her brother to understand his meaning, but she wondered if Damien would be content with only throwing a punch.

"Naturally I have no intention of actually putting you on display," Clune added, "but merely giving the suggestion of it. I'm afraid, however, that I must lock you in here for a short while to prevent your attempting escape."

She stared at him.

"I hope you will make yourself comfortable, my lady. I will send a maid up with some tea—or wine, if you prefer."

"How generous of you," Vanessa said, her tone scathing.

Without replying, he withdrew and closed the door softly behind him. Vanessa flinched when she heard the key turn in the lock.

Still somewhat dazed by her abrupt change in circumstances, she moved across the room to the window, only to discover it locked also. Even if she broke the glass, it was rather a long jump to the gravel below. She was likely to break an ankle, or worse.

Vanessa took a steadying breath to calm her nerves. It wasn't as if she were truly captive. The footman at Rosewood knew where she had gone.

Even so, she hadn't divulged a word about Damien's alleged accident for fear of alarming the entire household. They would think she was with him and wouldn't worry if she didn't return home before this evening. . . .

She turned away to pace the room. She would *not* allow herself to panic. Damien wasn't hurt, that was the important thing. She could bear the embarrassment of Clune's outrageous prank if she had to. And it looked as if she might have no choice but to go along.

Her anger swelling anew, Vanessa grimaced in disgust. She was getting a taste of the disreputable life she had chosen, and, frankly, it repulsed her. Even so . . .

She didn't know whether Clune was acting for his own amusement or out of spite, but in either event, she might be wiser to play his game. If Damien saw her outrage, it would only fuel his own. If this farce, however, could avoid being turned into a public spectacle, perhaps then she could manage to salvage some shred of reputation.

* * *

The hunting party returned in a jovial mood and settled in the gun room with glasses of ale all around, exchanging tall tales of past shooting exploits under the benign surveillance of the stags' heads mounted on the walls.

Damien was silent, his thoughts miles away rather than with his Hellfire colleagues. He'd found it nearly impossible to keep up the pretense of enjoyment. The endless pursuit of pleasure had palled entirely—

A burst of laughter interrupted his seditious reflections. Awareness returning, Damien realized that Clune was scrutinizing him thoughtfully.

"Is something on your mind?" Damien asked.

"Indeed there is. I've arranged a surprise for you." The earl flashed a secretive smile that Damien didn't much care for, and then turned to their American guest. "Sabine, you haven't had the pleasure of experiencing our initiation ritual into the Hellfire League. You have a real treat in store."

Several voices seconded the observation as glasses were raised.

"Oh?" Sabine murmured noncommittally. "What might that be?"

"You have to satisfy a court of maidens," Lord Thornhill replied.

"A court?"

"A dozen beauties plus a queen."

" 'Tis little more than an orgy," someone else remarked amicably.

"You have it wrong," Pendergast disagreed. "It's a test of how long you can stay aroused without spending."

"You must prove," Clune explained, "that you possess the stamina to service the entire court before dawn. They then pass judgment on your performance and score how well you bring them to pleasure."

"We've all been through it," Thornhill commented, "with varying degrees of success."

Cheatham laughed. "Devil a bit. The year Penny was inducted he nearly expired, the queen drained him so dry."

"By Jove, so did I. I've never fucked so hard in my life."

Ribald laughter was followed by several admiring remarks about Sin holding the record for most accolades of any court. Damien modestly acknowledged their praise by lifting his glass.

"If your cock passes inspection," Penny added, "you become a full-fledged *member* in the Hellfire League—pun intended."

Nicholas Sabine smiled wryly at the strained humor.

Another lewd joke or two ensued before Clune regained control of the conversation. "Since Lambton couldn't be here, and I am acting as host, I've begun arrangements for an induction ceremony later in the week. I'm pleased to report, gentlemen, that I've found the perfect queen to reign over the proceedings. But I should like Sin's approval before I make the final decision." He glanced at Damien. "Will you accompany me upstairs to inspect my choice?"

"You have her here?" someone asked.

Clune nodded. "Yes. And you will be hard-pressed to imagine a lovelier queen. But as Sin is the noted expert, his blessing is warranted."

"By all means show him this beauty you promised us," Cheatham said.

A chorus of male voices indicated agreement with the suggestion.

Something in Clune's tone made Damien suddenly

wary, but he reluctantly acceded to the plan. Rising, he accompanied the earl up the stairs and along the hall.

Clune rapped gently on the door and unlocked it. Then, with a grin at Damien like a cream-fed cat, he swung open the door.

A woman stood at the window, her back to them, yet her silhouette was heart familiar. When she turned slowly to face him, Damien went rigid.

Vanessa returned his gaze levelly, her lustrous midnight eyes cool and unwavering.

His gaze shot to Clune, who maintained an owl-eyed look of innocence. "What the devil is the meaning of this? What is she doing here?"

"She will make a perfect queen, don't you think?" Clune queried in a silken tone.

Damien clenched his fists at the thought of Vanessa being the prime attraction of an orgiastic ritual. "You intend her to rule the ceremony?" His eyes narrowed with disbelief. "And you agreed?" he demanded of Vanessa.

Clune replied for her. "She hasn't yet consented to be our queen, though I tried to persuade her." He cast Damien a probing glance. "Truthfully, Sin, I brought her here merely to see your reaction."

"My reaction?" Staring at him, Damien recalled the locked door and Clune's speculative glances earlier. Vanessa wasn't here willingly then. A quiet, poisonous rage surged through him.

"You bastard . . ." Lunging unexpectedly, he grabbed Clune's cravat and pushed him from the room, forcing him against the hall's far wall with a resounding thud. "Is this reactive enough for you?"

The earl gave a triumphant laugh, despite his friend's

ferocity. "Quite. I never expected you to permit anyone to touch her."

"By the blazes," Damien gritted out through clenched teeth.

Clune bared his own teeth in a taunting grin. "I thought you claimed indifference, Sin. If you aren't besotted, then why does the prospect of her becoming our queen upset you so?"

Tight-lipped with fury, Damien increased the vise of his hand. "She is under my protection, damn you!"

Clune had difficulty speaking with the grip on his throat. "You . . . are still . . . deluding yourself, my friend."

Damien's fist tightened further in the silk. When Clune made a choking sound, Vanessa protested behind him, "Damien, stop . . . you're hurting him!"

Just then almost a dozen Hellfire League members appeared at the far end of the hall, apparently alerted by the commotion.

"What the devil is going on?" Thornhill exclaimed.

"Damien, stop . . . please. . . ." Vanessa implored anxiously, but he refused to loosen his grip.

When Clune's strained face turned crimson from lack of air, several gentlemen voiced protests of concern and alarm. Finally one of them physically intervened.

Nicholas Sabine stepped forward to put a restraining hand on Damien's arm. "You don't wish to kill him, do you?"

"Don't I?" Damien retorted savagely.

Releasing his hold, though, he made a visible effort at controlling his violent urges and stepped back, his blazing gaze fixed on Clune. "You will give me satisfaction. The choice of weapons is yours."

He heard Vanessa gasp at his challenge. "Damien, you cannot—"

"I advise you to name your seconds," he told Clune tersely, the hushed vehemence of his tone deadly serious. "I trust Thornhill and Matthews will act as mine."

Ignoring the astonished gazes of his colleagues then, Damien took Vanessa by the arm and ushered her along the hall, away from the spectacle.

Chapter Nineteen

The curricle ride home was fraught with tension. Vanessa felt herself shiver in fear, while beside her Damien seethed with fury.

"You can't possibly mean to challenge Clune to a duel," she said finally as he guided the pair of chestnuts onto the road to Rosewood. "Surely you will call it off."

A wintry smile touched his lips. "I have no intention of calling it off."

"Damien, it was a prank, nothing more. Harmless enough—"

"Harmless?" His jaw clenched. "Clune compromised you before a gathering of the premiere rakes in England. That is hardly harmless, to my mind."

"My identity might have remained secret if not for your outburst. Whatever possessed you to such violence? Had you behaved rationally, your friends would never have been aware of my presence."

"Clune would not have been satisfied with a rational response from me. He deliberately orchestrated my outburst. But he overstepped the line, holding you prisoner."

She took a deep breath, trying to control her own anger. "What he did was ungentlemanly, even despicable, I'll agree, but it is over now. And a duel would only publicize my humiliation and compromise me further. Please, can you not simply forget the incident?"

Damien slanted her a fierce glance. "It's too serious to forget. I would be fostering the notion that he can dishonor a lady under my protection with impunity. I won't sanction his scurrilous behavior."

"*You* won't sanction?" Her own glance was scathing. "What gives you the right to sit in judgment of others? To play God with people's lives? First Aubrey, and now Clune—"

"Enough! I don't intend to discuss it further."

Vanessa pressed her lips together to stifle an angry retort. She would have been furious, if not for her feelings of dread.

She endured Damien's simmering silence for the entire journey home. But the moment he drew up before the manor, Vanessa stepped down from the curricle.

Without speaking another word, she marched up to her bedchamber and changed into a traveling dress. With the help of two maids, Vanessa packed her trunks and ordered them taken to Damien's carriage. It was late afternoon, but she intended to try to catch the stage at the coaching inn in Alcester. If she could make London tonight, she would reach her own home in Kent by tomorrow.

She gave one last glance around the bedchamber where she had known such pleasure and heartache, then shut the door quietly behind her. She went downstairs again without stopping by Olivia's room. She couldn't bring herself to say farewell just now, not when she was so emotional. But she would write the moment she arrived home.

She found Damien in his study, sitting at his desk, inspecting a set of dueling pistols that, according to the name engraved on the case, were the exquisite work of Manton. Vanessa paled.

For a moment she studied his perfect profile, her heart aching with fear and love. "You really mean to go through with this?" she asked finally.

"Yes," Damien replied without looking up.

"You could die, don't you realize that?"

"I don't expect to die. I'm considered a crack shot."

"And that makes it all right? You could kill Clune. Doesn't that mean anything to you? Taking another man's life?"

He raised his head to stare fixedly at her. "Honor won't permit me to back down."

"This is not about honor! This is two spoiled, reckless schoolboys fighting over a prize." Vanessa swallowed the fierce ache in her throat. "I won't stay to watch. I can't bear the thought of your killing another man—or worse, being hurt or killed yourself. I am leaving."

His gaze took in her traveling cloak. "Where will you go?"

"Home, to my family. I mean to take the stage."

"What about our bargain?"

She stared into eyes as gray as a storm. "My term as your mistress is nearly up. If my leaving means that I forfeit our wager, then so be it."

His expression remained impassive.

Vanessa bit her lip to contain her frustration. "You wanted to know why I refused your proposal," she said finally. "This is why." She gestured angrily at the dueling pistols. "I could never be certain if you would return home to me alive or dead. I still have nightmares about Roger's death. About his life and the scandals he caused. I won't go through that again."

She might have been talking to a stone statue for all the emotion Damien showed.

The fury that filled her vibrated in her voice. "Do you know what is so incomprehensible? Why you insist on wasting your life, living this meaningless existence. Your Hellfire League is bent on self-gratification and carnal indulgence, but has your profligacy ever brought you any real joy?"

Damien simply looked at her and smiled a slow, cynical smile. "And if I were to swear off debauchery? Would I then meet your standards of eligibility? Would I become worthy of being your husband?"

There was a terrible sense of raw tension vibrating in the air around him.

"You want a bloody saint," Damien said grimly when she made no reply.

She stared into his eyes, but she could read nothing of his feelings for her; he had locked his heart away.

"No, I don't want a saint. I want a man who loves me. Only me. I want a husband who will hold his marriage vows sacred, who won't betray me with other women. Someone I can trust not to plunge himself into the next scandal—or be killed in a senseless duel!"

For the first time he showed a response. His jaw clenched. "I am nothing like your late husband."

"No? There is little difference between you that I can see."

Their locked gazes warred. Vanessa could hear the sharp sound of her own breathing in the intense quiet of the room.

Her throat constricted when she realized she was getting nowhere. "Damien . . ." Her voice softened to a plea. "You could do so much with your talents, your wealth. I've seen your devotion to your sister, and at times even your indulgent friendship toward me. You have a vast potential to live a life of significance and meaning, and you insist on throwing it away in empty pursuits."

His smile was oddly, chillingly sweet. "You had better leave then, before I shatter any more of your illusions."

"Yes," she agreed, her voice low, desolate.

"Take my traveling carriage. It's safer than the stage."

She nodded, her throat burning. She turned to go, but when she reached the door, she faltered.

"How could I have deluded myself so?" she asked bleakly. "Fool that I am, I thought I loved you. I was wrong. You aren't the kind of man I could ever love."

She could feel his shocked stillness in the hush that followed.

"Vanessa . . ."

She heard Damien rise, heard his footsteps behind her. She tensed as his strong arms reached out to draw her back against him.

He murmured her name again hoarsely. "Vanessa, stay."

She could feel the seductive power of his plea, his warmth, shaking her resolve, shredding her will.

She drew a shattered breath. "I can't," she whispered. "I can't bear it."

Gently she freed herself from his embrace and fled.

Standing in the darkness of the secret passageway, Damien pushed open the panel to Vanessa's bedchamber. The room was empty—as empty as the hollow ache inside him. She was gone.

As if sleepwalking, he moved over to the window to gaze down at the gardens. Her scent remained to haunt him, while her parting words were branded upon his memory with a sharpness and clarity that was painful. *Fool that I am, I thought I loved you.*

Her admission of love had struck him like a physical

blow, as had the look in her luminous eyes—despair, fear, disillusionment. Disillusionment with him.

A terrifying sense of loss gripped him. Only now, in her absence, did he understand the enormity of what he'd done.

You aren't the kind of man I could ever love. . . .

No, he was the kind of man who ruined innocent women for revenge, a selfish bastard who sought empty, meaningless pleasures of the flesh without thought for anyone or anything but his own gratification.

Vanessa was right. His endless pursuits of debauchery had never brought him joy. He had prowled restlessly from woman to woman because none of them had been able to satisfy his hunger. His emptiness. No one until Vanessa. She filled the empty places inside him. Filled his heart. With love.

He loved her.

The realization staggered him anew. He had never known love. He'd lived a licentious existence too long to recognize that enigmatic emotion easily. He'd called it desire and fought it fiercely. Yet his obsession had burgeoned into something far more profound than desire.

I love her.

There was such sweetness in those simple words, Damien thought. A sweetness he hadn't known existed. Yet they couldn't heal the bleakness of his soul.

He had driven her away. And it was too late to make amends.

Moments ago the arrangements had been concluded. The duel was set for tomorrow at dawn.

Dawn's rosy fingers curled over the eastern horizon, illuminating the small party of gentlemen in the misty clearing: the two principals, their seconds, and a solemn-faced physician.

They stood somberly as Lord Thornhill reviewed the rules that had been agreed upon. The duelists would walk off twenty paces, then turn and fire.

"My lords, do you accept these terms?" Thornhill asked quietly.

Clune's mouth twisted with grim humor as he contemplated his foe. "Yes, yes, let's get this unpleasant business over with. Penny, you are to inherit my team of grays should I not survive."

His face set like flint, Damien made no acknowledgment of the misplaced levity.

The two men moved to the center of the clearing and stood back to back, while the other participants took up positions at the perimeter. The silence in the clearing was total, vibrating with raw tension.

In the hush Damien was surprised to hear Clune's low murmur.

"For what it's worth, I'm sorry to have impugned your lady. I regret causing her reputation any further damage."

Damien tightened his jaw grimly. "We both have regrets. You don't bear all the blame."

"My lords, you may begin," Thornhill called out. "One . . ."

Damien took a steadying breath and began to walk.

Slowly they paced off the distance: ten, fifteen, nineteen steps. . . . Damien's hand curled around the smooth handle of the pistol.

"Twenty . . ."

Both men turned and took aim.

Damien saw Clune's finger tighten on the trigger, but the image in his mind's eye was stronger: Vanessa's beautiful face as she pleaded with him not to kill another man.

Vanessa . . .

His hand jerked upward the instant that he fired. In the same fleeting moment, he heard the explosion from his opponent's pistol, felt the ball burn through his flesh like a shaft of fire. . . .

The blow of the gunshot felled him. Damien lay motionless on the ground, struggling for breath against the surprising pain. Through his daze came shouts from the sidelines. The next thing he knew, Clune was bending over him.

"Bloody hell, man, do you have a death wish? Why the devil did you delope?"

Damien frowned. In some twisted way perhaps he did have a death wish. At the last second he'd raised the muzzle of his weapon skyward and fired in the air, leaving himself vulnerable to a bullet. But he couldn't go through with killing Clune. For Vanessa's sake, he'd had to stop. He couldn't add murder to the crimes he had already committed in her eyes. He couldn't put her through that pain.

"Keep still, Sin, you're wounded."

He felt his jacket being ripped open and winced as Clune probed his left shoulder

"My lord, if I may examine him."

Vaguely Damien was aware of someone else kneeling beside him. The doctor perhaps . . .

"Looks as if the ball is lodged there. I shall have to dig it out."

"Is it serious?"

"Quite, but not fatal, I think."

Damien closed his eyes, savoring the pain. He should be grateful Clune hadn't killed him, perhaps, but a fatal wound would have been fitting punishment for his sins.

His recuperation was slow and painful. Damien was laid up for four days at his friend Lambton's hunting box before the doctor even declared him well enough to move.

When he returned home to Rosewood, Olivia refused to speak to him once she'd satisfied herself that he wasn't in danger of dying. She was furious with him, and not only for risking his life in a duel. She wouldn't forgive him for driving Vanessa away.

Nor could he forgive himself.

Lying in bed day after day, Damien had had ample time to confront his wickedness. He had nearly destroyed the woman he loved—sullying her innocence and dragging her down to his debauched level. He'd done far worse to her than Clune ever had. He had prepared her for whoredom; that was the ugly truth.

He wondered how many years would pass before he could face the memory without being sick at heart from it. Even when he'd offered to make her his wife, he'd shown her none of the respect or consideration she deserved. Instead, he acted as if he were conferring an honor, never saying a word about how much she had come to mean to him.

It was little wonder she had refused him.

You aren't the kind of man I could ever love.

Damien shut his eyes, blocking out the cheerful morning sunlight. He could take no pride in the life he had chosen, or the man he had become.

Bloodlines often bred true. He had inherited an ingrained tendency toward vice and dissipation, and never questioned those proclivities. He'd placed no limits on his wildness and thrill seeking, ignoring the warning signs, even when he'd begun to feel ravaged by the excesses in his life.

Damien murmured a low oath. It seemed he had degenerated into as thorough a libertine as his detested father. The thought left him filled with self-loathing.

Perhaps it wasn't too late to change, though. Perhaps he could still redeem himself in Vanessa's eyes.

He took the first step when Clune came to visit his sickroom seven days after the duel.

"I would like," Clune began in a contrite voice, "to offer my apologies once again—and to thank you for not putting a period to my existence. It was unforgivable of me to have compromised Lady Wyndham as I did, and I am truly sorry."

Damien's mouth curled in the grimace of a smile. "And I'm thankful your aim wasn't an inch further to the left."

"It was still closer than I intended."

"You never were a proficient marksman."

Assured of a genial welcome, Clune settled into a chair beside the bed.

Damien contemplated his guest with curious sadness. He and Clune had been friends for a long, long while, sharing wicked pursuits together since their university days. But the time had come to part ways. He wouldn't miss that jaded, shallow life, although he would miss his friend.

"The hunting party is over, I take it?" Damien asked.

"Indeed. Your brush with death put quite a damper on things. Most of us are off for London. I wanted to speak to you alone, but you'll be getting more visitors shortly."

"Good. It will allow me to say farewell."

Clune raised a quizzical eyebrow.

"I intend to resign my membership in the Hellfire League."

"Sin . . . surely you are overreacting. You needn't give up your friends over this unfortunate episode."

"I don't mean to end my friendships, but my days of playing the rakehell are over."

The earl frowned. "It's because of her, isn't it? Lady Wyndham. I was right. You *are* smitten."

"Yes, you were right."

Clune shook his head. "I confess not much astonishes me these days, but you've managed to floor me. You vowed you would never be trapped into love. What the devil happened?"

"I met Vanessa," Damien said simply.

"Love will not guarantee you happiness. Quite the contrary, in fact."

"I'm aware of that."

"You will be opening yourself up to all manner of misery."

"Perhaps."

"Well," Clune commented, still marveling, "better you than I, my friend. Love can turn a man into a fool."

"The worst sort of fool," Damien agreed pleasantly. "Otherwise I would never have challenged you to pistols at dawn."

Clune studied him a long moment, amusement and pity warring in his expression. "This humility is not like you, Sin."

"I know." He was not ashamed to admit he'd fallen. He'd lost his heart beyond all pride or reason. "But I'll thank you to cease calling me 'Sin.' I'm doing my best to divest myself of that appellation."

"As you wish," Clune said skeptically. "When may I offer felicitations?"

Damien frowned. "That I can't say. She refused my offer of marriage."

"She *refused*?"

"She didn't wish to wed a man of my ilk."

"Ah. Thus the resignation from the League. You'd best beware, my friend, or she will turn you into a milksop."

His gaze grew distant. "She may turn me into anything she wishes, if she will only forgive me."

His sister was more skeptical about his desire to reform. As soon as he regained enough strength, he summoned Olivia to his rooms. She obeyed reluctantly, her jaw locked in a stubborn set as she was wheeled in by an attendant footman.

"I have nothing to say to you," she began even before the servant was dismissed.

Grimacing in pain, Damien sat up in bed. His left arm was immobilized in a sling to prevent movement and protect his injured shoulder, but the flesh wound was still quite raw.

He waited until they were alone before taking the wind out of her sails. "I am withdrawing my objection to your wedding Rutherford."

Olivia stared. "Is this some sort of cruel trick?"

"No," Damien replied. "I still question his sincerity, but I'm willing to give him the chance to prove himself. I want you to be happy, Livy. If Rutherford can make you so, then I won't stand in his way."

Hope flickered across her face. "You really mean it?"

"I really mean it."

Joy dawned in her smile and in her sparkling eyes. "Oh, Damien . . . you don't know how happy that makes me."

"I have some idea," he said mildly.

"I must tell Aubrey—" She stopped suddenly and gave her brother a questioning glance. "*May* I tell him? You won't shoot him if he calls here at Rosewood?"

His mouth curved wryly. "No, Livy," he said with the teasing charm that once characterized their relationship. "I promise to be on my best behavior. I'm through dueling."

Her blue eyes grew serious. "I'm so glad you've given

up your revenge, Damien. Vanessa was right; vengeance is never as sweet as it is cut out to be. I thought that was what I wanted with Aubrey, to punish him for his cruelty, but what I really wanted was for him to love me."

Damien allowed himself a bleak smile. "You are wiser than your tender years, puss," he observed quietly.

He called out to the footman in the hall and winced at a sudden, painful twinge in his shoulder. "Now go and celebrate your victory with your betrothed."

The servant responded at once. Before she could be wheeled out of the room, though, Olivia said over her shoulder, "I've received a letter from Vanessa. It seems she arrived home safely."

"Oh?" Damien tried to keep his tone casual.

"She wanted to explain why she left so abruptly."

"And what did she say?"

"That you and she had strong differences of opinion, but that she would always be my friend."

Damien felt his chest tighten. "You are fortunate then," he said softly.

He felt her gaze search his face, before she said tentatively, "Damien, I do miss Vanessa terribly. Would you mind if I begged her to return?"

He gave his sister a quiet look. She was no expert at subtlety; her expression nearly radiated earnest manipulation.

"She won't return," he answered. "But thank you."

Her sad smile wrenched his heart.

When Olivia was gone, he lay back, thinking bleakly about what she'd said about the sweetness of vengeance. To his sorrow he'd discovered how bitter its taste could be.

It was ironic, perhaps. He'd been fiercely set on revenge, but Vanessa had had her own revenge by making him love her. Against his will he had been caught up in a dance as old as time.

Love. He had lain awake nights wanting it, hungering for it, never naming it. Irresistible desire had grown into undeniable love.

The poets were right, Damien reflected. The power of love could shake even a world-weary rake to his jaded core.

His longing was a fever that never left him. Vanessa always held the greater part of his conscious moments. She was the last thought he took to bed and the first thought he awakened to. She filled his dreams. His heart. In Vanessa he had met his match. Only she could ease the restlessness, the emptiness inside him. . . .

He would never be content with anyone but her. Never be free of her. He didn't want to be free.

Damien squeezed his eyes shut. Dear God, was he too late? Was there any possible way to win her love after what he'd done to her?

He was willing to change, to try to become a better man. How he should change was the question. The example his cold, selfish parents had sent him was no model. Ignored as a child, he'd been raised in unbridled self-indulgence and scandal. As an adult, he'd had too little purpose in life, too little meaning.

But he could try to reform. He could prove to her that all rakes weren't alike, that even the most hardened libertines could be redeemed by love.

His heart contracted with desperate hope. Perhaps it wasn't too late to win her, to earn the love he so terribly needed from her.

He had nearly been her ruin, but he prayed she would be his salvation.

Chapter Twenty

Vanessa sat in the morning room with her mother and sisters, paying little attention to their desultory conversation as the younger ladies worked their tambour frames. She felt nothing but a frightening, deathlike dullness.

She had returned home to Rutherford Hall over a week ago, and shortly afterward received the letter from Aubrey that she could now recite by heart.

> *My dearest sister,*
>
> *I'm certain you would not wish to learn the outcome of Sinclair's duel from a stranger, so I will take it upon myself to report. Pray, do not be overly alarmed, but he was wounded rather seriously in the shoulder and surgery performed to remove the bullet. His opponent, Lord Clune, remained unscathed. It seems that Sinclair deloped, to the shock of his many friends.*
>
> *I understand he is expected to recover fully, but as I am not allowed communication with that household, I must rely on hearsay to fathom events about the latest scandal. My own situation remains unchanged, regrettably.*
>
> *Faithfully yours,*
> *Aubrey*

Vanessa closed her eyes, trying to shut out the unsettling image of Damien lying wounded. She'd endured nightmares over it, even after receiving Aubrey's second note saying that Sinclair was indeed convalescing better than anticipated.

She couldn't recover so easily from her own hidden wounds. Her love for Damien was a pain she couldn't seem to conquer. Leaving him was the hardest step she had ever taken.

She would never again look at a rose without thinking of him, without her heart aching from a haunting sense of loss—

"The post has come," her sister Charlotte said, interrupting her misery.

A maidservant entered the morning room a moment later and curtsied before Vanessa. "A letter for you, milady."

"Thank you."

Her heart twisted when she saw the Sinclair frank, but she recognized Olivia's hand. With trepidation Vanessa broke the seal. The message was hastily written, with ink blotches and exclamation points and crossed lines that were difficult to decipher.

> *Dear, dear Vanessa,*
> *You will never credit it! Damien has relented! He has given his permission for us to wed!! He says he only wants my happiness, and oh, I am the happiest of creatures!!! I will now be able to call you sister. Perhaps you can guess at my state of agitation and exhilaration. I can scarcely hold the pen, my hand is shaking so. It was you, my dearest Vanessa, who brought about my brother's remarkable change of mind, I have no doubt. Damien has always put great store in whatever you say.*

The details are still to be settled upon—where and when the wedding will be held, and where we are to reside—but I hope it will be before winter, and that I might be welcome at Rutherford Hall. Will your mother be put out by becoming the Dowager Viscountess, do you think? I cannot wait!! I cannot begin to express my joy at the prospect of becoming Aubrey's wife!! I must thank you, dearest Vanessa, for helping to bring it all about—

"What is it, Vanessa?" Charlotte asked with a perceptiveness that was lacking in their younger sister or mother. "Not bad news, I hope."

Still a little stunned, Vanessa looked up. She had never expected Damien to relent, certainly not so quickly. . . . "No . . . not bad, indeed it is excellent news. Aubrey is to marry Olivia Sinclair."

"Oh, famous!" Fanny exclaimed.

Their mother, Grace, sat up from her reclining position on the couch. "Aubrey to be married? I was not aware he even knew the girl. Why was I not told he was courting her?"

"I'm certain he didn't wish to worry you, Mama," Charlotte answered soothingly, "or raise our hopes unnecessarily. But it would be a most splendid match for him. You remember Miss Sinclair. Vanessa told us all about her in her letters. . . ."

Vanessa was grateful to her sister for taking responsibility for the conversation and putting their mother's mind at ease. At the moment, she could not have managed it.

It was some time before she could escape her family for the privacy of her own bedchamber, and even then her emotions were in a state of turmoil. She couldn't help but feel Olivia's joy. Nor could she help but wonder what had caused Damien's radical about-face. Had she truly been instrumental in persuading him to allow the marriage? Had he actually taken any of her admonitions to heart?

No, it was foolish to read too much into his singular actions. Fiercely Vanessa steeled herself against the surge of hope welling inside her. Simply because Damien had relented over the issue of his sister's marriage to Aubrey didn't mean anything had changed between *them*. He didn't love her; that was the bitter truth.

Leaving him had been her only course. Even a life without him was preferable to the anguish she would have endured had she agreed to a loveless union.

Her throat constricted as despair returned to deaden her heart.

For the next several weeks Vanessa managed to go through the motions of living, but she showed so little enthusiasm, even her mother wondered if she was coming down with an ailment.

In the interval she had regular reports from Olivia regarding plans for the wedding. The banns had been read for the first time in church. The ceremony would take place in Alcester in early November. Meanwhile, in September Damien planned to take her to London to choose wedding clothes. And Olivia was ecstatically happy.

It was Aubrey's next letter that startled and astonished Vanessa as much as Olivia's first missive had.

> *My dearest sister, you will never credit what Sinclair has done. You will not be surprised, of course, that he restored the vowels I lost to him at cards. Relinquishing his claim to our family estates was only fitting, since you earned them fairly with your services to his sister.*

And naturally he would not wish Olivia to live as a pauper.

But he has gone far beyond the dictates of a brother-in-law's duties. He asked for an accounting of my outstanding gambling debts and tradesmen's bills and paid them in total. I intend to reimburse every penny out of my secretary's salary, but I don't see how I can repay his further generosity. Incredibly, he has dowered our sisters! And with no small sum, either.

You cannot know how greatly that relieves my mind, to have Charlotte and Fanny well provided for. As I'm certain it relieves yours. Imagine, Vanessa, with ten thousand pounds each they can now marry whomever they choose.

I take back every ill word I ever spoke about Lord Sinclair. He has given me a second chance to prove myself, and I vow to do my utmost to live up to his expectations.

Frankly, his behavior is a marvel I cannot explain. Not even by a word did he threaten me regarding Olivia's welfare this time (although he would doubtless put a bullet through me if I harmed another single hair on her head). Pride makes me reluctant to accept his charity, but I feel I cannot refuse for our sisters' sake, and for Olivia's as well. I love her so much, Vanessa. . . .

Vanessa could only stare at the letter in wonder and amazement. Ten thousand pounds each for her sisters? Aubrey's debts wiped clean? Whatever was Damien thinking? He had settled her brother's gambling debts and provided for her family's financial security—and eased the burden that had weighed so heavily on her shoulders ever since her father's passing.

Once more the fledgling spark of hope kindled in Vanessa's heart, but this time it was harder to repress.

In the following days there was more happy news coming from Warwickshire. Olivia had begun to make breakthrough progress in her recovery, regaining a great deal of sensation in her lower limbs. And while she could not yet walk, the doctor believed that with continued treatments of therapeutic massages and baths, she might be able to stand on her own two feet for her wedding.

> *Each day I grow a little stronger, and I may accept your invitation to visit sooner than you think. If I suffer no ill effects from the journey to London next week, Aubrey has promised to bring me to Rutherford Hall the following month, so that I may meet your mother and sisters before the wedding. I cannot wait, dearest Vanessa . . .*

By all reports the shopping excursion to London was a grand success. Olivia's letters were almost effervescent in their joy. The Little Season had begun, and with Aubrey escorting her to an occasional ball or evening party, she was finding her introduction to society far more agreeable than anticipated, possibly, she admitted, because she was very much in love with the most wonderful man in the world.

Each time Olivia made mention of her brother, though, Vanessa felt her heart wrench. She could not fathom the change that apparently had come over Damien. He no longer even seemed the same man she knew, an aimless rakehell whose only goal in life was the search for pleasure. Olivia's last letter from London held the biggest surprise of all.

Aubrey accompanied me the past few mornings to Oxford Street and the bazaar at Exeter Change, for Damien was occupied much of the time—you will never believe where. Whitehall, of all places! He's accepted a post advising the Chancellor of the Exchequer on governmental financial affairs, which, considering Damien's Midas touch, should prove extremely advantageous to the national Treasury.

Moreover, he plans to assume his seat in the House of Lords when Parliament convenes in January. He and Mr. Haskell (his secretary) have spent several evenings debating and discussing potential speeches. It is all politics, which I find a bit confusing (and rather dull, I confess), but there are several issues that arouse Damien's interest. In fact, he intends to stay in London when Aubrey and I return to Warwickshire tomorrow. Damien says he is a natural Whig, which Aubrey tells me is the party of reformists and rabble-rousers. But since Aubrey is a Tory, then, as his wife, I will be a Tory as well.

His wife. Those are quite the most beautiful words in the English language! You must faithfully promise to attend the wedding as my bridesmaid, Vanessa. . . .

Vanessa viewed that last request with trepidation. She had mixed feelings about returning to Rosewood. On the one hand, she couldn't imagine missing her only brother's wedding. On the other, she wasn't certain she could bear to see Damien again, to endure his nearness and be reminded so painfully of what she could never have.

Two days later she received another letter that puzzled more than surprised her. It was from George Haskell, Damien's private secretary.

Dear Madam:

I am writing you on behalf of Baron Sinclair to re-
quest an interview with you a fortnight hence. Lord Sin-
clair's solicitor, Mr. Naysmith, will travel to Kent the
first week in October and will call upon you at your
convenience. If you find this acceptable, would you be
so kind as to designate a particular date and time?

Your obedient servant,
George Haskell.

She couldn't imagine why Damien would send his solicitor to see her, but she responded politely to Mr.
Haskell's letter, agreeing to ten o'clock on October third
for an appointment.

When the day came, Vanessa made certain her sisters
were out riding and her mother was resting comfortably in
her rooms. Then she settled with a book in the study,
where she planned to receive Mr. Naysmith.

The solicitor was prompt to the minute, and courteous
almost to a fault. As soon as he was seated, he quickly
came to the point of his visit.

"I wish to make you aware of certain arrangements I
have executed on your behalf, Lady Wyndham. Lord Sinclair has deeded a substantial fortune to you, along with a
large manor house in Kent, close to London. The house is
situated on a prime piece of property and is fully staffed,
with a park that is quite agreeable."

Vanessa stared at him, wondering if Damien had dared
charge his solicitor with setting her up permanently as his
mistress. "I . . . am afraid I don't understand," she managed to say evenly, despite her welling ire.

"His lordship thought you might wish to have your own
household once your brother's bride becomes mistress of

his estates, but that you might prefer to be near your family. Thus the location in Kent. As I mentioned, it is in close proximity to London as well. The stables are not yet stocked, but he was of the opinion you would prefer to choose your own mounts and carriage horses—"

"Mr. Naysmith," Vanessa interrupted with impatience, "I have not yet considered where I wish to live once Miss Sinclair becomes mistress here, but that is hardly any of Lord Sinclair's concern. And it certainly fails to explain the reason for his . . . generosity."

The solicitor nodded solemnly. "To put the matter delicately, my lady, he wished you to be financially independent so that you might be free to choose your own future—particularly whether or not to wed again."

Vanessa's shocked silence lasted a full minute.

When she made no reply, the solicitor explained in more detail. "The legal arrangements are slightly unusual, but not unheard of. Without dwelling overly much on the particulars, let me assure you that the sum in question is tied up so that any future husband of yours cannot control it, as is standard under English law. The majority of the principal, some two hundred thousand pounds, will remain in trust for any heirs—children—you might have, with a substantial quarterly interest paid directly to you. In short, my lady, you are a wealthy woman."

Withdrawing a sheaf of papers from his case, he handed it to a stunned Vanessa. "I anticipated that you might wish some time to digest this news and perhaps read these documents, my lady, and so I planned to remain in the district at least until the morrow. I shall be happy to return at a later time to discuss the arrangements further, if you like."

"No . . ." Vanessa said absently. Under normal circumstances, any self-respecting woman would be insulted by such a blatant offer of money. But she was certain Damien hadn't meant to insult her. Quite the contrary. "Thank you, but I don't believe that will be necessary. Your explanations have been thorough enough."

She did wish for privacy, however, and was glad when the solicitor shortly took his leave. She needed time to reflect on the bewildering turn of events.

If she understood correctly, she was now independently wealthy, completely free to make her own decisions about her future. Her fate was entirely hers to decide, unlike when Damien had obliged her to become his mistress, or when she had married a reckless rogue to satisfy her father's debts.

Independence was Damien's gift to her.

What did he mean by such generosity? Did he truly expect nothing in return? Did he know how much his gesture meant to her? Of course he did. He knew how vital independence was to her.

Absurdly Vanessa felt tears burn her eyes. She had to see him, to discover why he had given her such a precious gift. Was it due to guilt? Or because of some deeper, more profound reason, something closer to the heart?

Her sisters chose that moment to walk into the study, although she hadn't even heard them come home.

When Fanny saw her, the girl stopped her chatter in midstream. "What has happened, Vanessa? Did that solicitor bring bad news?"

"No . . ."

"Then why ever are you crying?"

Swiftly Vanessa wiped away her tears. "I don't know exactly. I suppose it's because I am happy." She stood up, clutching the sheaf of papers. "I must go to London at once."

"Now? But Cook promised a chilled custard pudding for luncheon."

Vanessa forced a smile. "You may have my portion, Fanny. I don't believe I could eat a bite."

Once again Vanessa found herself ascending the front steps of Lord Sin's London mansion, completely disregarding the impropriety of calling alone at a gentleman's residence. Yet after all that had happened between them, a touch more scandalous conduct would hardly register on the scales.

She wondered if she would find Damien at home. It was nearly six o'clock, too early for him to have gone out for the evening. If he had not yet returned, she was resolved to wait for him forever, if necessary.

She was greeted by the same stately majordomo as before and informed that, yes, his lordship was indeed in. Her heart beating erratically, she stepped inside and was unexpectedly surrounded by the fragrant scent of roses. Vanessa stared in puzzlement, certain the large pots of white and crimson blooms ornamenting the entryway hadn't been there on her first visit. Had Damien sent for them from his conservatories at Rosewood? She'd thought he wouldn't want to be reminded of his life there.

Assailed by bittersweet memories, she followed the servant to a salon, whose lamps had been lit against the deepening autumn twilight. The beautiful room boasted a gilded ceiling and a cheerily burning fire. Gratefully Vanessa moved to stand before the hearth, holding out her chilled hands to the flames. She wasn't surprised to find herself trembling—a condition that only grew worse as the interminable moments drew out.

She sensed his presence before he spoke her name.

"Vanessa . . ." The low murmur made her heart leap.

She turned around slowly, scarcely daring to breathe. Damien stood just inside the room, watching her, completely still, as if he, too, feared risking a breath.

Her heart jolting in her chest, she drank in the sight of his beautiful face. It was their first meeting since the duel, and although she searched, she could see little outward indication of his injury—except that he looked thinner and a shade paler, and perhaps he held his left arm a bit stiffly. His eyes, however, were wary, intense.

"Why?" she said simply.

He gave a shrug of his elegant shoulders. "I wanted to give you the choices you said you never had."

A frown darkened her brow. "The freedom to wed anyone I choose, your solicitor said. You realize I could choose someone other than yourself? You are willing for me to wed elsewhere?"

"Yes." His voice was the husk of a whisper. "If that is what you truly want." His mouth twisted in a joyless smile. "Of course, I would far rather it be me."

"And in return for your generosity . . . what do you want from me, Damien?"

His troubled gaze was as gray as an ocean and just as fathomless. "Salvation. Merely that." Again that painful, fleeting smile. "I know it is a great deal to ask."

He moved farther into the room, halting a few steps from her. "I have countless regrets about my life, Vanessa, and the greatest by far is my treatment of you. But I profoundly believe I've learned from my mistakes. A man can reform, given sufficient reason. Your brother taught me that. I've never before had a reason to change, until you."

Vanessa felt her throat constrict. "Aubrey said much the same thing about Olivia."

"He and I have more in common than I like to admit."

A long tormenting moment of irresolution passed.

"I've vowed to try, Vanessa. You couldn't love the man I was, so I intend to become a different man, someone worthy of you."

"You have always been worthy, Damien."

His shadowed gaze was skeptical. "No. The things I've done, the empty life I've led . . . I'm determined to change all that."

"But why, Damien?" she whispered.

"Because I love you."

When she stood transfixed, Damien took a step closer, gazing down at her. Vanessa didn't pull away.

With a jagged breath, he drew her into his embrace. He winced at the strain on his healing wound, but ignored the pain and her resultant murmur of dismay and wrapped his arms about her. He wanted to hold her, simply hold her, until the emptiness waned.

He felt the faint tremors of her body as she pressed against him. "Do you know that I dream of you at night?"

"That doesn't mean," her reply came muffled against his good shoulder, "that you love me. How can you be certain it is truly love?"

"I feel joy just being with you. I feel pleasure at the sound of your voice. Even the smallest moments have meaning when you're there to share them with me. Is that not love?" When she remained silent, he went on in a hushed voice. "I never knew joy until you, Vanessa. I never knew what true pleasure was." He could feel the trembling doubt and hope pulse through her body. "I do love you . . . so much I hurt."

Vanessa stood mutely in his embrace. She wanted to believe him so badly that the depth of her longing terrified her. She heard Damien's voice against her ear, low and pleading.

"I spent far too long trying to escape the truth. I tried desperately to deny what I felt for you. You frightened me. I feared I would lose my soul to an obsession. I did lose it, but I found something far more precious. . . ."

He drew back, tilting her face up to his. She was crying, he realized. His heart wrenching, he reached up to rest his hand against her tearstained cheek, gazing into her eyes, her beautiful, soft, doe eyes.

"I do love you," Damien whispered. "You are everything I've ever wanted in a woman."

She caught her breath, pinned by the raw emotion in his eyes. Her heart aching, she touched her fingertips to his lips. "Damien, you don't have to offer marriage. I will continue to be your mistress if you wish."

"No, sweeting, that wouldn't be enough. If you come to me, it will be as my wife. I want to marry you, Vanessa. I want to spend the rest of my life proving my love for you. Will you give me that chance?"

She searched the lean, high-cheekboned beauty of his features. The naked vulnerability she saw there struck her like a physical blow. "Damien . . ."

When she hesitated, wanting to ease his hurt, he shut his eyes in desperation. "Vanessa, don't torment me. If you don't want me . . . if you can't bring yourself to love me, then tell me so."

"I do want you," she whispered. "I love you, Damien. I love the man you are. I always will."

Focusing on her, he stared into her eyes as if in a mirror, seeing reflected there all his own turbulent emotions . . . wonder, fear, love. His heart seemed to stop beating.

"Then . . . if I renewed my declarations, could I dare hope for a different answer?"

She smiled at him, her eyes misty. "Yes."

That lovely smile trapped his breath in his chest. Hope flaring inside him, Damien swallowed thickly. "I discovered a proposal in a volume of Olivia's poetry, which I memorized in the event I ever had the incredible fortune to ask you again." He kept his gaze riveted on her face, his voice low. "Will you have me, though I come to you corrupt? My armor tarnished with sin and decadence?"

Vanessa couldn't contain another trembling smile. She had no choice but to have Damien. He owned her heart.

She was his, body and soul.

"Yes, I will have you," she said softly. "Gladly."

He framed her face with infinite gentleness, dazed with love and desire. "And you will marry me and be my love?"

"Yes."

"Vanessa . . ." He said the word as a husky breath as he bent down to her.

His mouth claiming hers, he kissed her with all the new, brilliant tenderness in his soul. His hands moved blindly in her hair as desire spilled through him.

He didn't deserve her, a woman so rare as this. She had become his heartbeat, his breath.

And he would spend the rest of his life proving it to her.

Epilogue

Rosewood, November 1810

Damien paused at the door to his bedchamber and gazed down at his bride of eleven hours.

"At last," he murmured huskily, raising her hand and pressing his lips into her palm. "I thought we would never be alone."

Vanessa gave him a dreamy smile. "You were the one who insisted on a large wedding."

"I wanted the world to know of my good fortune."

He had procured a special license to marry without the banns so they could hold a double wedding with his sister and her brother. The church was filled to overflowing, since half the peerage of England had turned out to watch the notorious Lord Sin meet his fate.

After a sumptuous feast at Rosewood, Olivia and Aubrey had departed for Kent, along with Vanessa's mother and sisters. The last of the guests had finally driven away moments ago, leaving the baron and new baroness alone on their wedding night.

"Wasn't it wonderful that Olivia could stand upright for the ceremony?" Vanessa remarked as Damien opened the door for her. "She made a beautiful bride, don't you think?"

He gave her a smile so brilliant it shamed the sun. "I scarcely noticed. I had eyes only for my own bride."

Her heart too full of joy, Vanessa entered the bedchamber, which had been prepared for the night. Several lamps burned welcomingly, while a fire blazed in the grate to ward off the autumn chill. The huge vase of crimson roses that graced a side table scented the air, and the bedcovers on the four-poster bed were turned down invitingly.

Vanessa shivered with anticipation of the night to come. Remarkably Damien had insisted they remain chaste until they could consummate their vows. Thus the past weeks had been fraught with sensual tension and the frustration of being able to touch but not satisfy. But he was her husband now, and the moment at last had arrived when they would solemnize the commitment of their hearts.

When Damien closed the door gently, shutting them inside their bridal bower, Vanessa met his gaze. The heated promise she read in the silver depths of his eyes sent excitement flaring deep within her.

As he moved around the room, extinguishing all but one of the lamps, Vanessa crossed to the window whose draperies had been left open, as the lord preferred. For a moment she stood gazing down at the moonlit gardens. She still could scarcely believe her own good fortune. Damien loved her, and each day that passed only affirmed his devotion.

She felt his warmth at her back as his arms wrapped around her.

"Happy?"

"Deliriously. I never imagined it was possible to be so happy."

His whisper brushed close against her ear. "You're certain you won't regret having to live in London a good part of the year? I could give up my new post at the Treasury."

"Quite certain. I could be content to live anywhere as long as I have you."

"You will have me, sweeting, for a long, long while. Will forever do?"

Vanessa smiled, dazzled by the warmth in his voice. Damien was determined to prove the adage that reformed rakes made the best husbands, and thus far he was succeeding admirably. "Forever will do nicely, I think."

His lips grazed her temple as his hand slid lower to caress her abdomen. "We should find something to keep you from being lonely while I'm occupied with mundane governmental affairs."

"You don't find them mundane in the least," she replied with amusement. "I know very well that you relish your new challenge, spinning gold from dross for the good of the country."

"Quite so. But perhaps you need a new challenge as well, now that you've succeeded in taming a wicked rake. Would a child or two fit the bill, I wonder?"

Her heart welling at the thought, Vanessa turned to gaze up at Damien. Moonlight poured through the window, highlighting the sculpted contours of his face. "Having your child is the only thing that could make me happier than I am at this moment."

"Then we must give it our sincerest efforts, my angel."

She searched his face. "Damien, are you certain you want the encumbrance of a family?"

"Absolutely certain. I've been alone and lonely far too long. It's high time I gave up my wild ways and settled down."

The slow smile Vanessa gave him was provocative. "Then we needn't use the sponges any longer?"

His gaze burned deeply into hers as his thumb stroked her jaw. "No. No sponges."

He reached beyond her to draw the draperies shut, enclosing them in intimacy. Slowly he bent down to her. His mouth moving upon hers, he kissed her so softly, so deeply, that a silky fire flowed into her, smoldering and spreading. Vanessa sighed with pleasure and pressed closer, murmuring his name.

"Patience, wife," Damien admonished in a husky whisper. "We have forever—and I intend to enjoy every single moment."

They undressed each other slowly, pausing frequently to taste and explore. Vanessa's eyes darkened when she saw the scar in Damien's shoulder where the bullet had lodged, but he captured her mouth and drove away all her dark thoughts of the past. They had only a glorious future ahead of them, a future that began at this moment.

Having been deprived of each other for so long, the deliberate delay was a delicious form of torture, yet they drew out the sensual mating dance to its fullest. Their lips met often as they indulged in the utterly consuming need to touch and be touched. When finally they were both nude, Vanessa marveled again at the elegant, virile grace of her husband's body, while his eyes swept every tempting curve of hers.

Their gazes held as he removed the pins from her hair, beginning with the exquisite diamond roses he had given her as a wedding present. With reverence he spread the shining mass around her bare shoulders. Joyously, then, Damien swept her up in his arms and carried her to the bed.

As he lowered her to the silken sheets, he kissed her again

hungrily, smothering her low moan between their pleasured mouths. The rhythm of his heartbeat turbulently echoed her own as he followed Vanessa down to lie beside her.

Desire was a desperate need inside him, yet Damien forced himself to go slowly. He wanted to savor the moment when he made her his wife.

Shifting his weight, he raised himself on one elbow to search her beloved face. He wanted to see the desire and love in her eyes, and he found what he was seeking. Liquid radiance shone in the dark depths.

Tenderness ran through him, still startling in its wonder. "You intoxicate me," he murmured.

His fingers sculpted the lovely planes of her face, treasuring the velvety texture. His caressing hand moved lower then, as he bent his head to taste her. He felt her delicate shudder as his lips found her throat.

He tongued her sensitive flesh, pulse point by pulse point, while his hand roamed lightly over her bare skin.

"Everything about you entices me, excites me. . . ." he murmured, touching, fondling. "I love your breasts. . . . The sensuous curve of your spine . . . The silken hollow between your thighs."

Heat throbbed through Vanessa, strong and insistent, reverberating with each sensual caress.

"I love your grace and courage. . . ."

She moaned softly as his fingers lightly stroked the lips of her sex.

"I love your pleasure sounds. . . ."

She pleaded with him. "Damien . . . please."

"There's no hurry, love."

His own voice, though, was hoarse and indistinct, with an urgency that betrayed his need and longing. Even so, he fought the burning ache in his loins. Crushing the urge to ravish her, Damien settled himself gently in the cradle of her femininity.

Vanessa gave a breathless sigh of contentment as his muscled thighs spread hers wide. A tremor quivered through her body when he thrust slowly, filling her with his magnificent hardness.

Already intensely aroused, she wrapped her legs around him to draw him deeper, but Damien wouldn't hasten the moment. Plunging to the hilt one tantalizing inch at a time, he penetrated her silken heat and then withdrew just as deliberately, maintaining a measured, maddeningly gentle possession, even when she was hot and feverishly restless beneath him.

"Damien . . ." She pleaded with him again, but still he wouldn't relent, wouldn't give her ease.

Disregarding her soft, keening moans, he tortured her with exquisitely slow thrusts, his own desperate hunger restrained as he whispered erotic love words in her ear, telling her how much he wanted her, what it was like to lose himself inside her . . . how much he loved her.

Love. It was an unyielding, hungry joy that filled him to brimming. A violent flame that seared his heart. His love burgeoned inside him, diminishing his careful control.

He drove into her more forcefully, his longing tumultuous and raw. Trembling now, Damien surrendered to the wrenching, powerful need, yet Vanessa met and matched his fierce hunger, frantically arching against him.

They came together in an explosion of fiery need, of possession and surrender. Her whimper of pleasure became a sob of joy as shattering ecstasy rocked her body. Seized by the same stunning splendor, Damien poured himself endlessly into her in a melding of flesh and spirit.

He gave her his soul, and she took it willingly.

In the heated aftermath, they lay close, still shaking from the force of their mating. When the fury of heartbeats settled into a less violent rhythm, they remained entwined, their skin damp.

Weakly, Damien nuzzled his face in Vanessa's hair. The bliss that had convulsed his senses was as powerful as anything he'd ever felt, but the fierce emotion that flowed through him was stronger still.

It was an act of love, done in love. He had never experienced it before.

Love. How had managed to live without it? Without her? Vanessa was his life now. He hadn't known how empty he was until she had filled his heart. Hadn't known what rapture was until he became a part of her.

With her, he felt complete, whole, fulfilled in a way he never imagined possible. She had brought laughter and warmth into his home, joy to his life, a life that had been so cold and barren. He had tutored her in the arts of love-making, but she had taught him to love. And now, with their joining in marriage, the fervent passion that had always marked their lovemaking was only intensified.

Yet, with all his expertise at lovers' games, with all his sophisticated, practiced charm, Damien still found it hard to express how deeply he felt.

"I never realized," he murmured, drawing back on the pillow so that he could see her face, "how much greater the pleasure could be when a man makes love to the woman he loves."

Her half-lidded eyes opened dreamily. "Nor did I. Is it possible to die of pleasure?"

"I profoundly hope not." His mouth twisted with amusement, but then his expression sobered. "Do you have any notion how much I love you?" For all the softness in his tone, he was fiercely intent.

"I'm beginning to fathom it."

Damien placed her palm on his chest so she could feel the powerful beat of his heart. "This belongs to you, Vanessa. For always."

Her gaze soft with love, she reached up to brush his lips with her fingers. "As mine belongs to you."

"Say it," he demanded quietly, never tiring of the words.

"I love you, Damien."

His eyes took on a smoky tenderness that made her heart melt. "I'll make you happy, I swear it."

She smiled and moved her mouth closer to his. "You already have."

Read on for a sneak peek at

The Passion by Nicole Jordan

At first glimpse he seemed infinitely dangerous, even barbaric. And yet something in his eyes called to me. . . .

British West Indies, February 1813

The scene was pagan: the half-nude man bound in chains, his sinewed torso bronzed by the Caribbean sun. Silhouetted against the ship's tall masts, he stood defiant, unbowed.

For a brief instant Lady Aurora Demming felt her heart falter as she stared up at the frigate's railing.

He might have been a statue carved by a master sculptor, all rippling muscle and lithe strength . . . except that he was a flesh-and-blood male and very much alive. Sunlight warmed the hard planes and sinews of his body, gilded the dark gold of his hair.

That tawny shade of gold was familiar. At first glance Aurora had flinched with the memory of another face forever lost to her. But this brazen, nearly naked man was a stranger, possessing a raw masculinity quite unlike her late betrothed.

He was stripped down to his breeches, but though he wore the chains of a prisoner, he remained unbroken, his gaze fierce and remote as he stared out over the quay. Even from a distance, his eyes seemed to glitter dangerously, giving the impression of simmering anger tenuously controlled.

As if he felt her gaze, his focus slowly shifted and locked on her, riveting her in place. The bustle and noise of the waterfront faded away. For a fleeting moment, time ceased and only the two of them existed.

The intensity of his stare held her motionless, yet Aurora felt herself tremble, her heart suddenly drumming in a painful, almost wild rhythm.

"Aurora?"

She gave a start as her cousin Percy recalled her to her surroundings. She stood on the harbor quayside of Basseterre, St. Kitts, before the shipping office, the warm Caribbean sun beating down upon her. The pungent smells of fish and tar permeated the salt air along with the raucous cries of seagulls. Beyond the busy quay stretched brilliant blue-green waters, while in the distance rose the lush, mountainous island of Nevis.

Her cousin followed the direction of her gaze, to the prisoner on the naval frigate. "What has you so fascinated?"

"That man . . ." she murmured. "For a moment he reminded me of Geoffrey."

Percy squinted across the quay. "How can you possibly tell at this distance?" He frowned. "The hair color is similar, perhaps, but any other resemblance must be superficial. I couldn't imagine the late Earl of March as a convict, could you?"

"I don't suppose so."

Yet she couldn't tear her eyes away from the prisoner. Nor could he from her, it seemed. He still watched her as he stood at the head of the gangway, prepared to disembark. His hands manacled, he was guarded by two armed, burly seamen of the British navy, but he took no notice of his captors until one jerked viciously on the chain that bound his wrists.

Pain or fury made his fists clench, but he offered no other sign of struggle as he was herded at musket point down the gangway.

Once more Aurora heard her name called, this time more firmly.

Her cousin touched her arm, his look full of sympathy. "Geoffrey is gone, Aurora. It will do you no good to dwell on your loss. And your grief can only prove detrimental to your upcoming marriage. I'm certain your future husband will not appreciate your mourning another man. For your own sake, you must learn to quell your feelings."

She had not been thinking of her loss, she was ashamed to admit, or the unwanted marriage her father was forcing upon her, but she nodded for her cousin's benefit. She had no business showing an interest in a barely dressed stranger. A criminal, no less. One who evidently had committed some heinous crime to warrant such savage punishment.

With a small shudder, Aurora forced her attention away. The primitive display was no sight for a lady, much less a duke's daughter. She had rarely seen so much naked male flesh at one time. Certainly she'd never been *shaken* by a man, as she had moments ago when he caught her eye.

Chastising herself, she turned to allow her cousin to hand her into the open carriage. She'd come to the docks with Percy to confirm her passage to England. Because of the conflict with America and the danger of piracy, there were few ships leaving the West Indies. The next passenger vessel was scheduled to depart the island of St. Kitts three days hence and was only waiting for a military escort.

She dreaded returning home and had delayed as long as she dared, months longer than originally planned, using the excuse that travel was dangerous while a war raged. But her father was adamant that she present herself at once to prepare for her wedding to the nobleman he'd chosen for her. In his last letter he'd threatened to come and fetch her himself if she failed to honor the agreement he had made on her behalf.

Aurora had one foot on the carriage step when a disturbance across the quay made her pause. The prisoner had reached the end of the gangway and was being harangued to climb into a waiting wagon, obviously a difficult task because of his chains.

When he moved too slowly, he was given a savage shove that sent him stumbling almost to his knees. Saving himself by clutching the wagon's rear gate, he drew himself up and turned to eye his guard with a contemptuous stare.

His cool insolence seemed to infuriate his tormentors, for he received a musket butt to the ribs, which doubled him over in pain.

Aurora's cry of protest at the vicious attack lodged in her throat when the prisoner swung his chains at the guard. It was a futile gesture of defiance, for he was bound too tightly to cause any real damage, but apparently his rebellion was the excuse his guards wanted.

Both seamen set upon him with the stocks of their muskets, driving him to the cobblestone with cries of "scurvy dog!" and "bastard sea scum!"

Aurora recoiled in horror at seeing someone treated so viciously, without mercy. "For pity's sake . . ." she murmured hoarsely. "Make them stop, Percy!"

"It is a naval matter," her cousin replied in a grim tone,

speaking in his role as lieutenant governor of St. Kitts. "I have no justification for interfering."

"Dear God, they'll beat him to death. . . ." Without waiting for a reply, she picked up her skirts and ran toward the commotion.

"Aurora!" She heard Percy curse under his breath, but she never slowed her steps nor paused to consider the danger or the madness of intervening in the violent dispute.

She had no weapon at hand and no clear plan beyond attempting a rescue, but when she reached the guards, she swung her reticule at the nearest assailant and managed to hit the side of his face.

"What the 'ell . . .?"

When the startled seaman flinched at the unexpected attack, Aurora left off her flailing and pushed her way between the fallen prisoner and his assailants. Hiding her own fear, she sank to her knees, half covering the nearly unconscious man with her own body to shield him from being struck again.

The guard swore a vulgar oath.

Coldly furious, Aurora lifted her chin and stared up at him, silently daring him to strike her.

"Ma'am, ye've no business 'ere," he declared angrily. "This man is a vicious pirate."

"You, sir, may address me as *my lady*," she replied, her normally serene voice almost fierce as she called upon the power of her rank. "My father is the Duke of Eversley and claims the prince regent and the lord high admiral among his close acquaintances." She could see the sailor assessing her and her attire; her fashionable silk bonnet and walking dress were the gray of half-mourning, with only a touch of lilac trim on the lapels of the spencer to relieve the severity.

"And this gentleman," she added as Percy hurriedly

reached her side, "is my cousin Sir Percy Osborne, who happens to be lieutenant governor of Nevis and St. Kitts. I would think twice before challenging him."

Percy's jaw tightened at her declaration, and he murmured in disapproval, "Aurora, this is quite unseemly. You're causing a spectacle."

"It would be more unseemly to stand by while these cowards murder an unarmed man."

Ignoring the guard's glare, she glanced down at the injured prisoner. His eyes were closed, but he seemed to be conscious, for his jaw was clenched in pain. He still looked half-savage—his bronzed, bare skin glistening with sweat and blood, a growth of dark stubble shadowing his jaw.

His head seemed to have suffered the worst damage. Not only was his temple bleeding profusely, but his sunstreaked hair, a much darker gold than her own, was matted black with dried blood, evidently from an earlier injury.

Aurora tensed as her gaze dropped lower, yet even so, she felt her heartbeat quicken. The raw masculinity that had unnerved her at a distance was even more obvious this close, the sinewy hardness of his body unmistakable. His chest and shoulders rippled with muscle, while the canvas breeches hugged his powerful thighs.

He opened his eyes and fixed them on her. His gaze was dark, the rich hue of coffee flecked with amber. His intent stare gave her the same jolting sensation she'd felt earlier: the feeling of being totally alone with him, along with a keen awareness of her femininity.

Nearly as strange were the tender feelings of protectiveness his injuries engendered. Gently Aurora reached up to wipe the smear of blood from his forehead.

Chains jangling, he grasped her wrist. "Don't," he muttered hoarsely. "Stay out of this. . . . You'll be hurt."

Her skin burned where his fingers touched, but she tried to ignore the sensation, just as she disregarded his entreaty. At the moment she was less interested in protecting herself than in saving his life. "You don't expect me to watch your murder, do you?"

The pained smile he gave her was fleeting as he released her wrist and struggled to push himself up on his elbows. For a moment his eyes shut dizzily.

"You need a doctor," Aurora said in alarm.

"No . . . I have a hard head."

"Obviously not hard enough."

She had forgotten they weren't alone, until her cousin leaned over her shoulder and gave an exclamation of dismay. "Good God . . . Sabine!"

"You know him?" Aurora asked.

"Indeed, I do. He owns half the merchant ships in the Caribbean. He's an American. . . . Nick, what the devil are you doing here?"

He grimaced in pain. "An unfortunate encounter with the British navy, I fear."

Aurora realized his speech was much softer and flatter than her own clipped sounds, as her cousin turned to the guards and demanded an explanation.

"What is the meaning of this? Why is this man in chains?"

The guards were spared having to reply when their commanding officer joined them. Aurora remembered having met Captain Richard Gerrod at some polite government function a few weeks before.

"I can answer that, Sir Percy," Gerrod said coolly. "He is bound in chains because he is a prisoner of war, condemned to be hanged for piracy and murder."

"Murder, Captain? That is frankly absurd," Percy rejoined. "I know this man. You must have mistaken his identity."

"I assure you I have not. He was reckless and arrogant enough to visit a woman on Montserrat in the midst of a war, where he was recognized by one of my crew. He most certainly *is* the notorious pirate Captain Saber. Not only has he commandeered at least two British merchantmen since the war began, but he sank the HMS *Barton* just last month."

"It was my understanding," said Percy, "that the *Barton*'s crew was saved from drowning by that same pirate and deposited on the nearest isle."

"Even so, he has committed acts of war against the Crown. And he is indeed guilty of murder. He killed one of my men while resisting capture."

Percy turned to the fallen man. "Is this true, Sabine? You're a pirate?"

His half-smile held cold anger. "In America we use the term *privateer*, and we've never yielded the right to protect our own ships. The *Barton* was attacking one of my merchantmen, and I intervened. As for commandeering your vessels, I considered it a fair exchange for the loss of two of my own."

Aurora wasn't as horrified as perhaps she should have been at the accusation of piracy. With their two countries at war, Britain considered any armed American ship guilty. And Sabine should indeed have a right to defend his own ships.

She knew her cousin would agree. Though such political beliefs were disloyal, Percy considered the war a mistake and Britain primarily at fault for instigating it.

"Pirate or not . . ." Percy said to the captain, obviously

troubled, "there will be ramifications for taking this man prisoner. Are you aware Mr. Sabine has any number of connections to the Crown? Including several island governors as well as the commander of the Caribbean fleet?"

The captain scowled. "His connections are the only thing that stopped me from hanging him out of hand. But I doubt that will save him. When Admiral Foley learns of his crimes, I have little doubt the order will be given to execute him." Grimly, Captain Gerrod looked down at Aurora. "My lady, you would do best to keep away. He is a dangerous man."

"Oh, indeed," she said scornfully, rising to face the captain from her full height. "So dangerous your crew must beat him senseless, even with him trussed up like a Christmas goose. I quite fear for my life."

Gerrod's lips tightened in anger, but Percy quickly intervened.

"What do you intend to do with him, Captain?"

"He'll be turned over to the garrison commander and imprisoned in the fortress until he can be executed."

Aurora felt her heart clench at the thought of this vital man losing his life. "Percy . . ." she implored, gazing at him.

"I'll thank you, Sir Percy," Gerrod said darkly, "not to interfere with the performance of my duty. Get to your feet, pirate."

Sabine's lip curled, his simmering hatred of the captain evident in the blistering heat of his dark eyes. But his fury remained tightly controlled as he struggled to his knees.

Aurora helped him stand, lending support when he swayed, and felt her pulse quicken as his hard body momentarily leaned against her. Even bruised and bloodied, the overwhelming maleness of him affected her.

Her cousin must have been reminded of the impropriety,

for Percy gently grasped her arm and drew her away. "Come, my dear."

Obviously stiff with pain, Sabine moved toward the wagon. Aurora flinched when she saw the bloody lacerations marring his broad shoulders and muscular back, and again when one of the burly guards grasped his arm and urged him into the wagon.

Helpless, Aurora bit her lip to keep from crying out in protest.

Captain Gerrod gave her a stern glance as both guards climbed in after the prisoner, but he addressed her cousin. "I hadn't planned on escorting the prisoner to the fortress— I should be preparing my frigate to sail for the American coast to join the naval blockade. But I see I must, to ensure my orders are carried out to the letter."

"I intend to visit the fortress myself," Aurora threatened rashly, fearing what they would do to their prisoner once they were alone. "If you dare beat him further, I promise you will regret it."

She felt her cousin's fingers tighten on her arm in warning and barely refrained from shaking off his grasp.

The captain gave a stiff, angry bow, and then climbed into the front passenger seat and ordered the elderly black driver to drive on. Aurora and Percy watched as the pair of draft horses drew the wagon away.

"You will *not* involve yourself further, Aurora," Percy muttered under his breath.

Stubbornly she freed her arm from his tight grip. "You don't condone such vicious treatment, I'm sure of it. If Mr. Sabine were an English prisoner in American hands, you would expect him to be dealt with humanely."

"Of course I would."

"What will happen to him?" she asked, her voice suddenly hoarse.

Percy didn't respond at once, which confirmed her worst fears.

"Surely there will be a trial," Aurora protested. "They wouldn't hang someone of his consequence at once, would they?"

"It may not come to hanging," her cousin answered grimly. "The admiral might very well show leniency."

"And if not? Can you intervene?"

"I have the authority to overrule an admiral's commands, but doing so would perhaps mean the end of my political career. My views on the war are frowned upon as it is. And setting free a condemned prisoner would likely be considered treason. Piracy and murder are grave charges, my dear."

Aurora gazed back at Percy bleakly. "You must at least send a doctor to see to his injuries."

"Of course. I'll speak to the garrison commander myself and see that Sabine receives proper medical care."

She stared into his blue eyes that were so much like her own and could read the concern there—as well as the comment he didn't voice.

What did it matter if Nicholas Sabine's wounds were treated if he shortly was to hang?

Percy's wife was alarmed by the bloody condition of Aurora's gown but less appalled by the reason than might be expected.

"I don't know that I would have had the courage to intervene," Jane said thoughtfully when she'd heard the tale, "but I am glad you did."

The two women were alone in Aurora's bedchamber.

After Percy had escorted her to his plantation home and then left to fulfill his promise regarding the prisoner's medical treatment, Aurora's maid had helped her change her gown and then taken it away for cleaning. Lady Osborne remained to get a more detailed, private accounting of the morning's events.

"Mr. Sabine has prominent family in England," Jane said, responding to Aurora's expressed fears about his fate. "The Earl of Wycliff is his second cousin. Besides possessing enormous wealth, Wycliff has always commanded a great deal of power in government circles. He could very well intercede on his cousin's behalf."

"They may hang him long before news of his imprisonment reaches England," Aurora replied darkly.

"Aurora, you haven't developed a *tendre* for Sabine, have you?"

She felt herself flush. "How could I? I met the man only this morning and just for a moment. We were not even formally introduced."

"Good. Because frankly he isn't at all a proper sort of gentleman, despite his connections. Indeed, I suspect he is rather dangerous."

"Dangerous?"

"To our sex, I mean. He's an adventurer and something of a rake—and an American, besides. Common gossip says he was the black sheep of his family who spent his adulthood traveling alien lands and engaging in any manner of wild exploits. Only after his father died did he become in the least respectable—and only because he inherited a fortune and took over the family business interests."

"You haven't accused him of being much worse than half the wild young bucks in England."

"He is indisputably worse, I assure you. Otherwise he

would never have been accorded membership in the notorious Hellfire League, despite being sponsored by his cousin, Lord Wycliff."

The Hellfire League, Aurora knew, was an exclusive club of the premier rakes in England, dedicated to pleasure and debauchery. If Sabine was a member of that licentious association, he was indeed wicked.

"And you cannot dismiss the fact," Jane added pointedly, "that he is a condemned pirate, with blood on his hands."

Aurora looked down at her own hands. One of her dearest friends, Jane was both attentive and shrewd enough to evaluate a situation objectively—attributes that made her an ideal politician's wife. Percy quite rightly adored her, a sentiment that was wholly reciprocated.

"Aurora," Jane said, "is it possible you've become absorbed with this man to escape your own concerns? Perhaps you are trying to ignore your own plight by involving yourself with a stranger's fate."

Aurora laced her fingers tightly together. Quite possibly her sympathy for Sabine was greater because of her own difficult situation. She could identify with him; she knew what it was like to be powerless to control her own future, to have her life become not her own. He was at the mercy of his captors, while she was soon to be ensnared in a supremely distasteful marriage.

Jane must have read the truth in her expression, for she said gently, "You have more important worries than a pirate's fortunes. You would do far better to forget this incident entirely." She rose to her feet with a soft swish of silk skirts. "Come down to luncheon when you are ready. You'll feel better when you've eaten, I daresay."

Aurora, however, did not feel better, nor did she have

any appetite. She merely toyed with her food as she anxiously awaited word from her cousin.

When the message did finally come from his offices in Basseterre, Percy's note said little other than to reassure her that he'd spoken to the garrison commander, who promised to have the fortress physician examine the prisoner's injuries.

Aurora shared the note with Jane and pretended to dismiss any further thought of the matter. A short while later she excused herself, claiming she needed to contemplate her packing for her return to England. But she made absolutely no headway. Instead she found herself staring down at the floor, remembering a pair of dark eyes gazing at her intently and the trembling way they had made her feel—

For mercy's sake, stop thinking of him, Aurora scolded herself.

Logically she agreed with Jane. It was far wiser to put the notorious pirate out of her mind. She would be leaving St. Kitts in a matter of days. And she had her own serious troubles to deal with—namely, marriage to a domineering nobleman some twenty years her senior. A man she not only didn't love but actively disliked for his imperious, overbearing manner and his strict, almost Puritanical adherence to convention.

For a moment Aurora felt the same jolt of panic the thought of her marriage always engendered. Once they were wed, she would be a virtual prisoner to decorum, indeed would be fortunate to be permitted even an original thought of her own. But as she'd done for months, she forced her disquiet away.

Abandoning the notion of planning for her journey, she picked up a book of poetry. But when she tried to read, she was unable to focus on the page. Instead she saw the bloodstained features of Nicholas Sabine as he lay helpless at her feet, half-naked and in chains. When she tried to push him out of her mind, she failed miserably.

She didn't have to close her eyes to picture him lying in a prison cell, wounded and in pain, perhaps even near death. Would he even have a blanket to cover his near nakedness? Despite the warmth of the Caribbean sun, it was still winter. The brisk ocean breezes blowing off the Atlantic side of the island could make the nights quite chilly. And Brimstone Hill Fortress, where he had been taken, was perched high on a cliff, exposed to the elements.

Even more alarming, a condemned prisoner could disappear forever in the vast, sprawling warren of dark chambers and narrow passageways of the fortress. Its massive citadel was defended by seven-foot-thick walls of black volcanic stone that had taken decades to construct.

She'd once attended a military reception at Brimstone Hill with Percy and Jane and found even the officers' quarters unwelcoming. She shuddered to think what the prisoners' accommodations were like.

It was no consolation to remind herself that she'd done all she could for him. No use arguing with herself and demanding that she be sensible. All she could think of was Nicholas Sabine.

Perhaps if she paid him a brief visit, just to make certain he was being cared for, she would be able to ease her mind enough to forget him. . . .

Feeling her anxiety lessen for the first time since the disturbing incident on the quay, Aurora quietly set down her book. Her heart took up an erratic rhythm at the prospect of seeing him again, yet she quelled the forbidden feelings as she went to the bellpull to ring for her maid.

She would be defying propriety with a vengeance, perhaps even risking scandal to visit a condemned pirate in prison, yet this could well be one of the last acts of independence she would ever make.

He was dreaming again. Of her. The savage throbbing in his head eased as she bent over him. The tender brush of her fingers on his feverish brow was gentle and soothing, but her touch roused a worse throbbing in his loins.

She was the essence of every male fantasy: angel, Valkyrie, goddess, sea siren. She was golden temptation and primal torment. He wanted to draw her down to him and drink of her lips. Yet she held back, just out of reach—

"You there!"

He awoke with a start, memory and pain flooding him with brutal intensity. Woozily, Nicholas lifted a hand to his aching head and felt the bandage there. He was lying on a bare cot, no longer bound by chains. The musket butt prodding his sore ribs, however, was regrettably familiar, as was the burly guard hovering over him.

"You there, bestir yourself!"

His blurred vision steadied. He'd been taken prisoner, he remembered, and brought to the fortress on St. Kitts, where he would probably hang for piracy and murder. At first he'd paced his cell like a wounded animal, his frantic thoughts on his half sister and the debacle he'd made of his promise to protect her. But exhaustion and pain had finally forced him to lie down. He'd fallen into a tortured slumber, only to begin dreaming of the golden-haired beauty who had defended him so valiantly on the quay.

What the devil was he doing? Nicholas swore at himself. Lusting after a strange woman, no matter how beautiful or courageous, was completely mad under the circumstances.

Instead he should be focusing on his sister and ward, trying to think of a way to ensure her safety once he was dead. . . .

"I said bestir yerself! There's a lady to see you."

Nicholas slowly raised himself up on his elbows. Beyond the guard, the cell door was partway open. . . . His gaze shifted, and his heartbeat seemed to stop.

She stood there just inside the dim chamber, tall, slender, regal as a princess. Even with the hood of her black cloak casting her exquisite features in shadows, he knew her. Yet unlike the avenging angel he remembered from the quay, she appeared hesitant, uncertain. Wary.

"I'll leave the door ajar, milady. If 'e gives you a hint of trouble, you just call out."

"Thank you."

Her voice was low and melodious, but she said nothing else, even when the guard had left the cell.

Wondering if his vision was an illusion, Nicholas sat up. The watery beam of sunlight filtering through the tiny barred window highlighted dust motes dancing around her dark skirts but did little to illuminate her features.

Then she pushed back the hood of her cloak, uncovering her bright hair coiled in a smooth chignon, and giving Nicholas a jolt of sexual awareness. Her uncommon beauty seemed to light up the dark stone cell.

She was quite real, the living fantasy of his dreams . . . unless he had died and this was his version of heaven. Followers of the Muslim faith believed a blessed man would be surrounded by beautiful maidens upon reaching Paradise. The pain from his injuries, however, made Nicholas suspect he was still in temporal form.

She was gazing at him in surprise, studying his face.

Then, as if she realized she was staring, she flushed a little and shifted her gaze to the bandage that wrapped his head.

"I see they at least summoned a doctor. I was afraid they wouldn't. No, please don't get up on my account," she added when he tried to rise. "You are in no condition to stand on formality."

"What . . ." His voice came out too hoarsely, so he cleared his throat and began again. "Why are you here?"

"I wanted to make certain you were all right."

Nicholas frowned, trying to sort out the confusion in his aching head. Perhaps the blows had indeed rattled his brain.

No lady would risk her reputation to enter the bowels of a prison on behalf of a stranger. And she was every inch a lady, he knew—blue-blooded to the core. In fact, hadn't she claimed to be a duke's daughter when she'd dressed down that seaman this morning?

Nicholas stared at her, wondering if he'd missed some vital clue to the enigma she presented. Then a sudden thought struck him.

Was it possible she was here to deceive him? Was that bastard Gerrod up to some sort of trickery, using her to ferret out information?

Nick's eyes narrowed in suspicion. His ship was still at large in the Caribbean, for he'd gone alone to Montserrat to fetch his sister, aboard a Dutch fishing ketch, not wanting to risk the lives of his crew on his own personal mission. But Captain Gerrod was fiercely set on determining the American schooner's whereabouts.

It could greatly advance the captain's naval career to capture an enemy ship—a likely reason, Nick suspected, why he'd been spared immediate hanging. That and the fact that Gerrod hadn't wanted to make any political missteps by offending his prisoner's illustrious connections.

Grimly Nicholas contemplated his beautiful, unexpected visitor. Was she somehow in league with Gerrod? Her compassion had seemed entirely genuine this morning and so had her animosity toward the captain. But perhaps she'd somehow been persuaded to work with Gerrod against him.

Had she been sent here to torment him? To tempt a condemned man as if holding out the promise of water to a man dying of thirst in a desert? The stark possibility that such beauty and kindness could be a ruse stabbed Nicholas with anger.

His jaw tightened. He would do well to remember their nations were at war. As an Englishwoman, she was his enemy, and he had to be on his guard.

She seemed uncomfortable with the way he was watching her, and when he deliberately dropped his gaze lower to linger on her breasts, he thought he saw her flush in the dim light.

"I don't believe we were properly introduced, madam," he began.

"No. There wasn't time. I am Aurora Demming."

An appropriate name, he thought irrelevantly. Aurora was Latin for dawn. "*Lady* Aurora. I remember. You made mention of it on the quay."

"I wasn't certain how conscious you were of your surroundings."

At the reminder of the assault, Nicholas raised his hand to feel his bandage. "You find me at a disadvantage, I fear."

An awkward silence stretched between them.

"I brought some items you might need," she said finally. When she took a tentative step toward him, he focused on the bundle she held in her arms. She seemed oddly nervous as she set her offering down on the cot and glanced around the dim, spartan cell. "I should have brought candles. I didn't think of it. But here is a blanket . . . some food."

Her gaze met his briefly and then slid away. "I also borrowed a shirt and jacket from Percy's overseer. You seemed larger than my cousin. . . ."

It was his state of undress that was tying her tongue, Nicholas realized. If she was like other gently bred ladies of her station, she would hardly be accustomed to visiting a half-nude man or estimating the size of his physique.

"How did you get past the guards?" he asked cautiously.

She seemed grateful for the change in subject. "I prevailed upon the garrison commander, Mr. Sabine." Her smile was fleeting. "Actually I resorted to a slight deception. I implied that my cousin Percy sent me."

"And did he?"

"Not exactly."

"I thought Gerrod would have forbidden me any visitors."

"Captain Gerrod has no authority over the fortress garrison, nor is he much liked here on the island."

"Then he didn't send you to question me?"

A look of puzzlement drew her fine brows together. "No. Why would you think so?"

Nicholas shrugged. If she was dissembling, he would be much surprised. But if she had an ulterior purpose for coming here, he couldn't fathom what it was. Did she want something from him?

When he reached for the bundle she had brought him, she retreated a step, as if fearing his proximity. He withdrew the shirt and carefully pulled it on, wincing at his aching muscles.

"Forgive me, my lady," he mused aloud, "but I fail to understand your reason for championing me, a stranger, and a condemned prisoner, at that."

"I didn't care to see a man murdered before my eyes. It seemed the captain was far too eager to find an excuse to kill you. At the very least his men would have beaten you senseless."

"That still is no reason for you to play Lady Bountiful, bent upon kindness and good deeds."

The cynicism in his tone made her chin lift a degree. "I wasn't satisfied that you would be cared for."

"And you wish to make my final days more comfortable? Why?"

Why indeed? Aurora wondered. It was impossible to explain the affinity she felt for him. Even harder to deny. He was a privateer at the very least, a man with blood on his hands.

And now that he was no longer defenseless, his effect on her was even more pronounced. He'd been given a chance to wash off the blood, and even with the stubble on his jaw, his handsomeness was astonishing.

She could well see why her cousin's wife called him dangerous with the ladies. He had the sinful allure of a fallen angel, with hair the color of dark amber and a face whose planes and angles were beautifully sculpted. The brazen sight of his bronzed shoulders and hard-muscled arms, too, had stirred an odd fluttering in her stomach.

Yet his face could have been carved in stone now, and the cold insolence of his stare took her aback. He seemed highly mistrustful of her motives—which was not so surprising, since she wasn't certain of them herself.

"I expect I came because you remind me of someone who was very dear to me," Aurora replied rather lamely.

When he raised a skeptical eyebrow, she averted her gaze from the expanse of sun-warmed flesh on his bare chest where his shirt remained open.

She stood stiffly as she felt his eyes moving down her body, touching her breasts in insolent perusal. He seemed to be assessing the gown beneath her cloak, a severely cut day dress of charcoal-gray bombazine.

"You wear half-mourning," he observed. "Are you widowed?"

"No. My betrothed was lost at sea some eight months ago."

"I don't recall seeing you on St. Kitts before."

"I arrived last summer. My cousin and his wife were visiting family in England shortly after the tragedy occurred. They thought a change of scene might help me to forget my grief and so invited me to return with them to the Caribbean. We set sail before word reached England about America's declaration of war. Had I known, I never would have come. And in fact, I will be returning in a few days."

Aurora was aware her voice had dropped, and knew he must have heard the bleak note of reluctance she couldn't hide. The last thing she wanted was to return to England and face the fate that awaited her there.

Nicholas Sabine was still studying her, as if trying to determine her veracity. "You don't seem particularly eager to go home, my lady. I should think you would be impatient after all this time away."

Her smile was pained. "I suppose my lack of enthusiasm stems from the marriage my father has arranged for me."

"Ah," he said knowingly. "A cold-blooded contract. The

British upper class are so very fond of selling their daughters into marriage."

Aurora stiffened at his presumption. She had not meant to share personal confidences with Mr. Sabine, nor did she care for the intimacy of this conversation. "I am not being *sold*, I assure you. It is more a matter of social expedience. And my father wishes to see me well settled."

"But you are not exactly willing, either?"

"His would not be my choice for a husband, no," she admitted quietly.

"I wonder that you haven't considered rebelling. You don't strike me as the meek type. On the quay this morning you were a veritable tigress."

"Those circumstances were hardly usual," Aurora said, flushing. "I am not in the habit of challenging convention."

"No? And yet you are here. It was rather unwise to risk your reputation like this, you must admit. Where I come from, ladies don't visit convicts in prison."

"They don't in England, either," Aurora replied, forcing a wry smile. "I am entirely aware of the impropriety . . . and normally I am quite sensible. But my maid accompanied me, at least. She is waiting outside . . . along with the guard."

The pointed reminder of the guard seemed to have no effect on Mr. Sabine. He buttoned his shirt slowly, regarding her from under long, dark lashes.

When he stood, she took a wary step back. She was tall enough that he didn't dwarf her with his broad-shouldered, long-limbed body, but this close his masculinity was almost overwhelming, his nearness threatening.

"You aren't afraid of me?" he asked, his silken tone sending shivers down her spine.

Aurora fought for control of her rioting senses as she

stood her ground. "You don't seem the sort of man who would hurt a woman."

"I could take you hostage; had you thought of that?"

Her eyes widened. "No, I hadn't. Percy says you are a gentleman," she added uncertainly.

His smile flickered as he closed the distance between them. "Someone should have taught you not to be so trusting."

Reaching out, he captured her wrist in a light grasp. His fingers seemed to burn her skin, yet she was determined not to show how unsettled she was by his touch.

"Someone should have taught you better manners," she retorted coolly, adopting her most regal air. When he didn't release her, she stared him down. "I did not necessarily expect gratitude, Mr. Sabine, but neither did I expect to be manhandled in this fashion."

The hardness in his dark eyes abated a degree as he let go her hand. Several heartbeats later he lowered that taunting gaze. "Pardon me. I do seem to have misplaced my manners."

Absently she rubbed her wrist where his touch had branded her. "I understand you have had a difficult time. And you are an American, after all."

His smile was mocking. "Ah, yes, a heathen Colonial."

"You must admit you are very . . . direct."

"And you must realize condemned men are given to desperate acts."

Her expression sobered as she remembered he was to be hanged. "Percy means to exert his influence on your behalf, but he might very well lose his post were he to demand your release. He is already suspect for sympathizing with the American cause. He believes the war is absurd, and that we British are more at fault than you Americans are."

Nicholas stared down at her beautiful upturned face. If she was innocent of duplicity, he had greatly wronged her. He felt a savage anger toward many of her countrymen, but he should never have taken his fury and resentment out on her.

"Forgive me," he said grudgingly. "I am indeed in your debt. If I can ever repay the favor . . ." He let the comment slide, knowing he was unlikely now to be in a position to repay her kindness.

A sudden sadness filled her eyes. "I wish there were more I could do."

"You've done enough already."

She bit her lip. "I suppose I should be going."

Nicholas found himself staring at her mouth. "Yes."

"Is there something else you need?"

He flashed a wry smile that held grim amusement. "Aside from a key to my cell door and a fast ship to make my getaway? A bottle of rum wouldn't go amiss."

"I . . . shall try."

"No, don't. I was entirely in jest."

He reached up to brush her cheek lightly with the back of his knuckles. Her lips parted, and he heard her soft intake of breath. Nicholas felt his loins stir.

"You shouldn't be here," he said quietly. "For your own good, you should stay away."

She nodded and took a step back, her blue eyes misting. As if unable to speak, she turned without another word and fled the gloomy cell.

With a clang the door swung closed behind her, no doubt drawn shut by the prison guard. Nicholas bit back a curse at the grim reminder of his imprisonment.

For a moment he stood there, breathing in the faint scent of lilacs she'd left behind and wanting to hit something. He wished to hell she hadn't come. Whether intentionally or not, she had set his blood on fire.

Amazing, considering the sort of woman she was—blue-blooded, proper, straitlaced. The exact opposite of the women he was usually drawn to. Yet if he were free, he might very well have pursued her.

If he were free . . .

His jaw clenching, Nicholas glanced up at the high, barred window of his cell. Damnation, he had to get out of here—or at the very least, find a solution to his crisis.

Turning, he began to pace the narrow confines of his cell, his thoughts once again caught up in turmoil. What would happen to his sister once he was dead? He'd sworn a solemn oath to his father to see to her welfare, but because of his blundering miscalculation, he'd been taken prisoner and rendered powerless to help her.

His pacing became more agitated . . . until suddenly he came to an abrupt halt. Nicholas stared unseeing, a wild notion invading the back of his mind.

He had never feared death, although he'd always taken immense pleasure in living his life to the fullest. If he was hanged, his chief regret would be his failure to honor his promise. There might still be a way, however, for him to discharge his responsibilities, albeit from beyond the grave.

Lady Aurora Demming.

Could she be prevailed upon to help him once more?

He started to rake a hand through his hair but stopped when he encountered the bandage—a bandage that had been her doing. He'd been mistaken about her, obviously. She wasn't in league with Gerrod, or anyone else for that matter; she was indeed an angel of mercy.

Angel and siren, Nicholas thought, remembering her eyes that were the color of sapphires. She was also younger than her regal, aristocratic manner suggested, perhaps barely twenty. Yet despite her recklessness in first coming to his rescue and then visiting him in prison, she was no doubt well bred and virtuous . . . and high-ranking enough to command respect, if not awe, among the beau monde. As a duke's daughter, she would have entry into the loftiest echelons of British society.

He had no desire to drag her into his concerns, but if it meant protecting his sister, he would use the devil himself.

Recklessly Nicholas flung himself on the cot, ignoring the protest of his aching muscles. His thoughts spun furiously as he stared up at the grimy ceiling overhead.

The lady could be the answer he was seeking. He could use her to help his ward, take advantage of her prominent standing in English society. . . .

His mouth curled in a grim semblance of a smile. He must still be reeling from the blows to his head if he were entertaining such fantasies. It was highly doubtful a duke's daughter would be receptive to a mad proposal admittedly conceived in desperation.

And yet he had to convince her. If there was the slightest possibility of fulfilling his promise, he had to seize it.

by Gaelen Foley

THE PIRATE PRINCE

Taken captive by a fearsome and infuriating pirate captain
come to plunder her island home of Ascension,
the beautiful Allegra Monteverdi struggles to deny her
growing passion for her intriguing captor. Lazar di Fiore is
a rogue with no honor and has nothing in common with
the man of her dreams—the honorable and courageous
crown prince of Ascension, who is presumed murdered
with the rest of the royal family by treacherous enemies of
the throne.

PRINCESS

Darius Santiago is the king's most trusted man, a master
spy and assassin. He is handsome, charming, and ruthless,
and he has one weakness—the stunning Princess Serafina.
Serafina has worshiped Darius from afar her whole life,
knowing that deep in the reaches of her soul, she belongs
to him. Unable to suppress their desire any longer, they are
swept into a daring dance of passion until a deadly enemy
threatens to destroy their love.

PRINCE CHARMING

Destiny casts its hand when Ascension's most elusive high-
wayman, the Masked Rider, chooses the wrong coach to
rob. For inside is Rafael, the prince of the kingdom. The
failed raid leaves the Masked Rider wounded and facing a
hangman's noose. Then Rafe realizes his captive is Lady
Daniela Chiaramonte, a defiant beauty who torments him,
awakening his senses and his heart as no woman has
before.

Published by The Ballantine Publishing Group.
Available at bookstores everywhere.